Vintage Contemporaries

Also by Dan Kois

How to Be a Family

The World Only Spins Forward (with Isaac Butler)

Facing Future

Vintage Contemporaries

A Novel

Dan Kois

HARPER

An Imprint of HarperCollins*Publishers*

VINTAGE CONTEMPORARIES. Copyright © 2023 by Dan Kois. All rights reserved. Printed in the United States of America. No part of this book may be used or reproduced in any manner whatsoever without written permission except in the case of brief quotations embodied in critical articles and reviews. For information, address HarperCollins Publishers, 195 Broadway, New York, NY 10007.

HarperCollins books may be purchased for educational, business, or sales promotional use. For information, please email the Special Markets Department at SPsales@harpercollins.com.

FIRST EDITION

Designed by Bonni Leon-Berman

Library of Congress Cataloging-in-Publication Data has been applied for.

ISBN 978-0-06-316241-9

22 23 24 25 26 LBC 5 4 3 2 1

Life never worked out so well! Love
never had it so good!

—front cover copy, *Happy All the Time* by Laurie Colwin,
Pocket Books paperback

1991

Joy in the Face

*Y*ou are not the kind of girl who would be at a place like this at this time of night, Emily thought. Louis somehow heard her little chuckle of recognition over the noise in the club, turned to her, and said, "What."

In answer, she pointed at the girl with the shaved head, who despite her thoroughly modern look was dancing like a character in the beach-blanket movies Emily's mom used to watch. The girl twisted; she shagged. She drew men toward her—a stockbroker type in a tie, a tall guy in a fedora—and then dismissed them with a turn of the shoulder. Emily loved watching her.

Emily Thiel was standing by the wall in a nightclub she didn't like, nursing a drink she couldn't afford. She was a nervous young woman of twenty-two. She liked to think of herself as sensible, but knew that others saw her as prissy. They always had. She wore jeans everywhere, even to this dance club, where women wore skintight vinyl pants or they wore miniskirts, but they sure didn't wear jeans. She was trying to be a good friend to Louis, who had been lonely since they moved to New York and had asked her to come out with him tonight.

The club was on the first floor of an elegant, run-down building on Thirtieth Street and had been famous, in an earlier incarnation, for being the place where Madonna danced in a movie. That was how they knew what name to look up in the Yellow Pages. She knew its heat was waning because when they got there the doorman had let them right in.

Louis danced in place next to her. He was wearing his favorite shirt, the one with the blousy sleeves that a boy had complimented him on once in college. The music just kept on thumping away, the beat seemingly never-ending, which she understood must be the sign of a good DJ but which to her seemed to eliminate what she loved the most about listening to music. There was no melody to grab hold of, just an imperative to dance.

"Dance!" Louis shouted. He held out a hand. "New York won't eat you," he said, and she wasn't so sure, but she finished her drink and followed him out.

On the dance floor the music turned, somehow, to a New Order song she liked, and she threw herself into it. The girl with the shaved head was to her right, and Emily felt happy that while she wasn't *with* her by any means, she was included in the broader circle of the girl's attention. Once they made eye contact and the girl smiled. She tried to copy her, not her exact steps but the way she seemed to move with purpose. Even when she had gone out with her college boyfriend, Paul, Emily had always felt stuck inside herself while dancing—she had tried to encourage him to take her to movies, but he thought since she liked music she wanted to go to shows. She did, but she didn't want to dance. But this girl in the club seemed to know how to dance *with* people, directing her energy toward others and receiving energy in return, speaking to them with her arms and hips and responding to the ways their bodies replied.

For just a moment she had that with Louis—they twirled around each other in a way that surprised them both into laughter. But then the song segued into something a little darker and more cruel-sounding, and Louis started dancing with a man he'd pointed out to Emily earlier, so she made her way back over to the wall.

As she watched Louis and the man get closer and closer to each other, she relived the twirl with exhilaration. Her sister had told her a story about the surf lesson she'd taken on her honeymoon. Anne-Marie had spent half an hour fruitlessly paddling and was wondering what was even the point, but then she caught a wave and rode it for what seemed like forever. The feeling was so unexpectedly wonderful that she signed up for a second session the next day. That's how Emily felt about that moment on the dance floor. It made the whole night worthwhile.

Neither she nor Louis had real jobs yet—they were both temping—so theoretically they could stay out until dawn and just skip a day, but by one in the morning they were both exhausted. "You wanna do one more cigarette and then go?" Louis asked her. They stood at the edge of the ballroom, as far from the speakers as they could get.

"Hey, look at this," Louis said, and pulled a napkin out of his pocket. He opened it just enough for Emily to see the phone number scribbled on it and then slipped it into his coat.

"Oh, wow," Emily said. "I'm proud of you."

"I'm proud of me, too. Did you dance with anyone you liked?"

"Only you."

"Stop."

"Can I bum one?" It was the bald girl, and as soon as she spoke Emily recognized her. Emily pulled out a cigarette, handed it to the girl, lit it for her. "Thanks," she said. "I'd stay and talk, but I've got a guy to seduce." And indeed she immediately walked toward a group of young men and took one of them by the arm. He followed her a few steps, casting nervous laughter back at his friends. Emily was reminded of the scenes in nature documentaries in which a lion culls the weakest wildebeest from a herd.

"Do we know her?" Louis said.

"We worked with her last month," Emily said. "In a mortgage office."

"Did she have hair then?"

"Yeah."

"You're always watching," he said.

Outside, he thanked her for coming with him and asked if she wanted to try again the next week. "I don't know," she said. They walked east together, sharing the unspoken knowledge that they couldn't afford a cab. The air smelled of snow. During that second surfing lesson, her sister had told her, she'd never caught a single wave, and the hot guy who was teaching her shrugged and said, "That's the way it goes sometimes," and she decided that as glorious as that ride had been, it was not worth the effort to keep trying. Emily suspected she felt exactly the same way about dancing in clubs.

"What's your man's name? Who you got the number from?"

"Austin, I think."

"You *think*?"

"It was loud in there!"

"Look, call Austin I Think," she said. "Go dancing with *him*. But if you need me to come with you again, of course I will."

Emily and Louis had arrived in New York in the fall, after spending the summer working together in the dingy library of the small college they'd just graduated from in Connecticut. They rented a ground-floor apartment on Seventh Street that cost $850 a month and featured, when the subletter first showed it to them, an enormous mushroom growing out of the floor under the futon. "Yeah, my cousin was staying here a long time, so we had the futon as a bed?" the guy had explained. "So I guess that floor there was, like, in the shade."

"Of course," Emily and Louis had said, nodding in unison. It was in the shade, the tile was pulling apart at the seams, so it made perfect sense that an enormous fungal growth had colonized the apartment.

Anne-Marie, who was studying for her Wisconsin real estate license, had told her to make sure they signed a sublet agreement. She had one in her bag, photocopied from a tenants' guide in the library, tucked into a Redweld folder Louis stole from a temp job. But as they'd stood around the grimy, windowless living room, Emily simply could not imagine asking the guy to sign it. She could anticipate the sweet, baffled look he would give if she smoothed the document out on the scratched kitchen table, and she didn't want him to feel bad, so she'd stuck out her hand instead.

"We'll take it," she said.

In lieu of a handshake, Louis, a germaphobe, nodded with authority. "Why are you subletting, if you don't mind me asking?"

"Oh, I'm moving in with my girlfriend?" the guy said, suddenly bashful.

"Oh, congratulations!" said Emily.

"It's just, I'm saving so much on rent," he said. "We've been dating for, like, a month."

Louis very visibly didn't say anything. Emily could not not say something. "Well that's not very long!" she said, in a way that she'd imagined would be lighthearted but that came out appalled.

The guy shrugged. "We both really love money," he said. Emily would remember this for a long time and, even years later, would often say, after complaining about her boss making her work evenings and weekends, "Well, I do love money."

Louis's parents drove up from North Carolina to help them move in. They spoke with an accent Emily remembered from freshman year, when she and Louis had briefly dated, before Louis diligently shed the accent, along with all other accoutrements of his high school life, like heterosexuality. Louis's boxes mostly contained clothes; Emily's mostly contained books. It didn't take that long to carry everything in, and Louis's parents had been shocked by the neighborhood the entire time, which had helped make Emily feel they were doing the right thing.

Now they arrived at their dark building on their dark street. On the advice of a girl at another temp job who told her she'd averted not one but two attempted muggings, Emily had taken to carrying her keychain in her fist, the keys themselves sticking out between her fingers in order to impart maximum damage upon anyone who might accost her. She unlocked the door and turned on the light and a mouse bolted from the living room into the kitchen.

"I'm too tired to scream," Louis said. They collapsed on their futon, installed on the now-mushroom-free floor. They had somehow lost the remote control to their television, so Louis got up, turned it on, and sat back down. It was on the public access channel. A clearly insane woman ran around a set filled with drunk people, wearing a black crocheted bikini. Then the woman was suddenly nude, and then there were other naked women, and then the men on the show were naked, their dicks bouncing around like . . . well, like dicks. They just looked like dicks.

"Is this real?" Louis asked.

"I think we're asleep," Emily said.

Eventually they did fall asleep, Emily with her head on Louis's lap, Louis stroking her hair. When they woke up, the TV was a test pattern.

— • —

"So you don't have any money."

"I *do* have money."

"Then why do you *need* money."

"I just can't *get* to my money."

Emily heard Anne-Marie laugh over the phone. Every second that the conversation went on, Emily felt a ticking in her head as the long-distance bill grew. She should have called collect. She liked to give fake names sometimes: "Caller state your name," the operator would say, and Emily would shout, "Ronnie! Bobby! Ricky and Mike!" It made her sister laugh and annoyed her husband when he picked up.

"But so why can't you get to it?" Anne-Marie asked.

"The bank machines here only have, like, twenties. Like they only disburse money in units of twenty dollars."

"Well how much are you trying to get out?"

"I have nineteen dollars in my account."

"Jesus, Emily. What have you been spending your money on?"

"Nothing! New York is expensive, that's all. I start my job Monday."

She'd been hired as an assistant at a literary agency, hooked up by a writing professor she hadn't even thought had liked her.

"Are you on drugs?"

"No!" In truth, Emily was offered drugs every day, but she was far too frightened ever to say yes. One dealer at the fence surrounding Tompkins Square Park had turned it into a little routine he performed every morning as she walked down Seventh on her way to the subway. "Oh, here come the good girl!" he'd call at her approach. "Hey, good girl, you stay away from me. I don't sell to no good girls!"

In a way, she thought of the dealer as her friend.

"Are you literally spending all your money on books?" Anne-Marie asked.

Emily looked around her room. There were books on her bedside table and books scattered on one side of her bed and books stacked atop the windowsill, obscuring what little sunlight made it through the grime and the bars. There were books on her top closet shelf and books on the floor of her closet and books atop the plastic wheelie bin she used as a dresser. There were books in stacks on the floor, deckle edges flush to the wall, spines out. Also, there were books on bookshelves. She had made the shelves from boards she'd scrounged from her building's unspeakable basement hallway and cinder blocks she'd taken, one per day, from outside the community garden between B and C, hauling each, wheezing, to her home.

The books on the shelves were alphabetized by author.

"Not literally, no."

And though Anne-Marie had, on three previous occasions, mailed her a check, this time—even though her husband's family was rich as anything, even though they lived in that beautiful house in Mequon—she did not offer. "Ask Mom and Dad," she said.

Rather than do that Emily grabbed her keys, stuffed a paperback in her purse, and careened into the living room. Louis was on the futon watching television. "I'm going for a walk," she announced.

"It's pretty late," he cautioned.

"Can I borrow five dollars?"

"Nooooooo."

Outside it was almost completely silent. Nine o'clock on an early spring night and it might as well be Wisconsin, she thought. No cabs came down Seventh, not that she took cabs anyway, so she clip-clopped down the sidewalk from streetlight to streetlight. It made her feel better that Anne-Marie would be horrified to know she was out in her neighborhood at this hour. She imagined with grim satisfaction the look on Anne-Marie's face when she got the phone call telling her that her sister, her only sister, her poor, beloved little sister, had been murdered and stuffed into trash bags.

She held off her nervousness all the way to Avenue B trying to work out how many trash bags the murderer would need. In the end she settled on four; she wasn't exactly small, but she thought a murderer *could* fit her entire torso in one bag, if he was determined. On Avenue B the cabs swept south toward the bridges, and she felt a little less acutely how foolish this entire piqued journey was. Shit happened in New York. A guy had boiled his roommate and served her as soup to the homeless in Tompkins Square Park. Her mom had mailed her a newspaper clipping about his trial.

At Veselka's she settled into a booth and gratefully accepted a mug of coffee that she was pretty sure she couldn't afford. She dug in her purse, which had a lot of surprising pockets and sometimes yielded treasures. This time, though, she found only a quarter—not even enough for the coffee. Well, she was here, and she had the coffee, and if she was going to get yelled at by a waiter she might as well get warm before it happened.

She leaned against the paneled wall, which gave ever so slightly behind her back, and propped her shoes on the bench. At one of the other booths, a couple with matching buzz cuts was locked in a quiet, intense debate.

She had a quarter because that was the change she'd gotten from the guy with the table on St. Marks when she bought the book she was reading now. She had bought it based entirely on the striking cover, which featured a white rabbit on a beach with a snow-covered palm tree in the distance. She liked the idea of a book filled with incongruities.

When she opened the book, a ten-dollar bill fell out of its pages and into her coffee. She stared for a moment, unable even to conceive that it was not a product of her imagination—that the mind that in her grimmest hours often created a job, a boyfriend, a glorious future out of nothing, scarily complete and present, had not just now created the very thing she needed the most, and that when she blinked it would disappear.

She blinked.

The bill settled into her mug, Alexander Hamilton's face just dipping beneath the liquid's surface. She plucked out the ten, wiped it off on a napkin, and leaned it against the sugar dispenser to dry. What would make her feel even better, she thought, was a plate of pierogi. She ordered them.

The first few stories in the book puzzled her. Each time she reached a final page, saw a new title, she thought, Well, surely *that* wasn't a story, was it? She'd always been a fast reader—it was the thing that had convinced everyone in elementary school that she was smart, a snap judgment that, she knew, had shaped her entire life. That she could finish an Encyclopedia Brown book in ten minutes made her teachers treat her as special, made her parents expect more from her, made her peers distrust her; she saw in her personality now the results of those early years. She, too, believed herself to be exceptional in some way; she expected things from herself; she was funny, she knew, and good at winning over those inclined to think the worst of her. Being the smart kid in elementary school had made her a smart kid in high school, where she first found smart peers. Being the smart kid in high school had made her leave Wisconsin for college, where she was no longer exceptional but, thanks to her good humor, surrounded herself with exceptional friends.

Even as her belief in her own specialness had bled away, she'd managed an English degree, and even some modest undergraduate renown as a writer. It helped that she simply read *more* than everyone else, and so while she knew her short stories were as derivative as those of her classmates, they were often derivative of writers her classmates had not yet read. All thanks to a skill that Emily knew was a fluke, an accident of eye-brain coordination, no different from if she could roll her tongue.

"Ooh, a pierogus," someone said, sliding into the booth across from her. She recognized, immediately, the girl from the club. The man she'd been arguing with was gone. Her hair had grown out just a bit, and she was wearing an army jacket. She picked up the table's other fork and pointed at the one remaining dumpling on the plate with its VESELKA logo. "I'll take that." Emily was so surprised she said nothing while the girl speared it and popped it in her mouth.

"Uh, you want coffee with my food?" Emily finally said.

"I only drink Diet Coke," said the girl.

Her name was Emily, too. They agreed immediately that they must be fated to hang out. Emily, still holding her book, suggested it reminded her of characters in a short story.

"If we were characters in a story," Emily said, slurping the soda a waitress had brought, "it would be pretty confusing that we were both named Emily."

"Do you have a nickname?" Emily asked.

"No, I'm only Emily. I'm *definitely* an Emily." She said it so fervently, her cheeks still flushed from the argument, that Emily felt the only gracious thing to do was yield.

"I could be, like, Emmy," she said.

"Oh no, you're not an Emmy," Emily said, crinkling her nose. "You're Em."

"Em," said Em in wonderment.

"'Characters in a story,'" Emily said. She poured the last of her little glass bottle of Diet Coke into the plastic diner cup, sucked the bottom of her straw, pointed at Em's book. "Like those stories?"

Em started to tell her about the author, about how discombobulated the stories made her feel. She showed her the book's sleek cover. "It's part of a whole series," she said. "Modern fiction."

"Oh, from the 1930s?"

"No, from, um, from now."

"So *contemporary* fiction. Modernism is the early twentieth century, before the war."

"I guess that's right," Em said.

"Vintage Contemporaries," Emily said, reading the name of the series off the book's cover. "That's a beautiful contradiction. As a rule, I don't read novels from after 1947."

Em stopped explaining the book. "You want to go somewhere?" she asked instead.

Emily stood up. "I always want to go somewhere," she said.

As they walked up Second Avenue, Em snuck looks at this person with whom she had somehow fallen in league. She had a constellation of freckles across her cheeks and wore leather pants that Em would never have been able to pull off, even if she could have pulled them on. She hunted through pocket after pocket of her army jacket until she found a pack of cigarettes, took one out, and popped it in her mouth. She put the pack in her pocket, then systematically checked every part of the jacket again until she found, in the same pocket as the cigarettes, a lighter. She lit up, took a big drag, pointedly did not offer one to Em.

The silence between them grew to two blocks, then three. Emily seemed unconcerned, sailing so quickly up the sidewalk that Em struggled to keep up. It seemed no matter how fast Em walked Emily was always a step or two ahead of her, ducking her shoulder to muscle past the walkers coming the other way, deftly sidestepping a puddle of vomit of the sort that Em always tripped over herself trying to avoid. A guy with bright red eyes muttered something at them as they walked past and Emily *barked*, like a dog.

Where were they going? Em was worried that Emily thought *she* had some place in mind, when in fact for Em late-night options began with Veselka's and ended around the corner with cannoli from Veniero's. She didn't know any other places to go. But the farther they walked, the more it became clear that to Emily, *somewhere* was just being in motion. Soon Em relaxed a bit and let herself fall into the rhythm of walking just behind Emily, watching her bull her way through the obstacles of late-night Manhattan, sneaking through the breaks she made in groups of drunken guys the way a cyclist drafts behind a faster rider.

She was so close to Emily's back, in fact, that when Emily stopped suddenly in the middle of a block on Twelfth Street, Em bounced off her. "This is me," Emily said, pointing at the steel door to a five-story apartment building. "Wanna come up? I think I have some beer."

Em nodded. She did want to come up.

Two deadbolts, three flights of stairs, and another two deadbolts later, Emily turned on the lights and revealed a narrow studio that didn't answer any of Em's questions. The brick walls were covered in movie posters and the bed was a mattress on the floor and there was garbage everywhere and it smelled like a boy's dorm room, a kind of testosteroney funk. But also, in one corner there was the most expensive-looking stereo system Em had ever seen, with CDs and jewel cases scattered all around it.

Emily threw her army jacket on the tatty couch and crouched in front of a little fridge, the same kind Em had had in her dorm room sophomore year. "Here," she said, and threw Em a can of Pabst. Em made a panicked noise and said the thing she always said when someone threw something to her, which was "I don't catch!" The can bounced off her hands and clattered to the floor. They both stared in silence at the can rolling slowly toward the wall, and Em felt all the goodwill she'd accumulated drain away in a moment of elementary-school shame, but then Emily said in a friendly voice, "Better open that over the sink after it settles down."

Em asked after the bathroom, looking around for a hidden door or something, and Emily took a key ring off the chain attached to her belt, feinted a toss—Em made the same panicked sound—then walked to Em and placed it solemnly in her hand. "Protect these with your life," she said. "Bathroom's down the hall on the right."

The bathroom was large and surprisingly clean. A row of hooks had been screwed into the wall opposite the toilet, each with a name Magic-Markered on the wall directly above it. From five of the hooks dangled towels in various states of threadbareness. On the hook reading EMILY hung a robe so white and fluffy it looked like a polar bear. Em peed and rinsed her hands and stared at herself in the mirror. "Be cool," she said to her reflection. "Please."

When Em came back to the apartment, she hung her coat on a nail in the wall by the telephone. Emily was sitting cross-legged before the stereo, feeding CDs one after the other into a slot in a bulky component with a flashing digital display. "Is that a CD changer?" Em asked. "How many CDs can it fit?"

"Twenty-four."

"But why would you do that?" said Em, who felt very stupid. She opened the beer, which thankfully did not explode. "When are you ever going to play that many CDs in a row?"

"Em!" Emily said. "What we're making here is a *mood*. Let me introduce you to *the shuffle*." She pressed a button and held up a finger, beaming, as the machine clunked, whirred, clunked again. She continued holding up the finger. A voice shouted "Oh!" and Em instantly recognized "Unbelievable" by EMF. Emily dove for the CD player, pressed the skip button, then said, "That was not the mood."

The machine clunked, whirred, clunked again. This time the song was slower, sung by a woman, with thumping drums and a kind of throbbing guitar. *"That's* it," Emily said, and turned it up so the music filled the room and drifted out the open window onto Twelfth Street. The woman sang, "It's gloriouusssss." Em drank her beer and tried to understand what the song was doing. It seemed to be going nowhere, but then all of a sudden it turned out it had been chugging toward a climax all along. She closed her eyes and nodded along as a guitar squalled, a noise that Em liked in spite of herself. When the song ended in odd unresolution, she opened her eyes and saw, to her discomfort, Emily smiling at her, smoking a cigarette.

"That song just fucks me really good," Emily said. The CD player made its noises and moved to a song Emily recognized, Neneh Cherry singing Cole Porter from an AIDS benefit CD Louis owned. Emily turned it back down. She had still not offered Em a cigarette of her own.

Em didn't understand why Emily had invited her here. Was she—Em giggled to herself, a little, when she thought of the word Emily had used at the club—seducing her? Emily obviously was into men, and Em was too, in theory if not currently in practice, but this was New York, and she didn't dare think she understood the mating rituals of someone as obviously *New York* as Emily. She definitely felt a kind of tension that could be sexual. She hoped that wasn't what was happening.

Were they just going to have one crazy night, like in *After Hours?* Maybe it'd be better if it wasn't *that* crazy.

She hoped they were becoming friends.

Em decided that she should take a step to move this in the direction she wanted it to go. "You know, I recognize you," she said.

"Sure, from Danceteria," Emily said.

"No. Well yes, there. But also, we worked together." Emily opened her eyes and raised one eyebrow quizzically. "At least I think so. Did you temp at a mortgage broker a few months ago?"

"I truly have no idea," Emily said. "Those jobs fall out of my brain the instant they're done. Tell me what kind of life-changing work I might have done at a mortgage broker."

"Well," Em said, thinking back, "they had us move a bunch of files from one room to another, and then we had to go through applications and red-flag stuff that was disqualifying."

"Oh! And they gave us *actual* little red flags?"

"Yeah. We would stick them on the application if the person was like, you know, 'Employment: none.'"

"Oh yeahhhh." Emily nodded. "Those red flags were very satisfying, the, the, the"—Emily stared out the window for a moment, searching for a word that seemed like it would never come, but then it did—"the *congruence* between form and function."

"We were on the same team. There were four of us. It was me and my roommate Louis, and some guy from Boston College who couldn't *believe* he was temping, and you."

"I don't remember that guy. He sounds like an asshole. Yeah, go ahead," she said as Em gestured tentatively toward the fridge.

"He was." Em opened the door, with its ANDRE THE GIANT HAS A POSSE sticker, and grabbed a fresh beer. "He kept talking about how he'd gone to school in Boston, and why was the job market so fucked, and I thought he was saying 'Boston' like 'Harvard,' but then it turned out he went to BC."

"Why wouldn't he have just said 'Harvard'?"

"People from Harvard are always like, 'Oh, I went to school at a little place up in Cambridge.'" Em took a drink of the beer, which went up her nose. When she finished coughing she said, "They want to be all casual about it. Then they finally drop the H-bomb."

Emily laughed and lit a fresh cigarette. "I'm sorry I don't remember you. All I remember about that gig is the flags."

Em nodded. "No, yeah, I mean—I'm not that memorable."

"You're really into self-deprecation, huh," Emily said. "That's, like, your kink."

"I don't have any kinks," Em said.

"No, I get it. Wholesome. Corn-fed. Where are you from?"

"Wisconsin," Em said, meaning nowhere.

"You're someone *else*'s kink. You just have to find that person."

"At my job interview, my new boss told me that I couldn't bring boyfriends into the office after hours," Em said. "Like, that was a thing she had to warn me against, because it's happened before. Can you imagine?"

"Sure," Emily said. "I used to wonder if I could hide someone under the counter at the record store. Just to keep me awake. What do you do?"

"Well, I've been, as you know, temping. But I start Monday at a literary agency, working as an assistant."

"So, like William Morris, but for books."

"I guess so."

"But I mean what do you *do*? You're not on the Lower East Side because you want to be William Morris's assistant."

"Well, it's not actually *the—*"

"*Whatever.* I direct plays. So what do *you* do?"

This was a good question. Em took a big breath and said, "I guess I'm a writer. At least, that's what I did in college."

"I knew it," Emily said. "You want some coke?"

"No, I'm good with the beer," Em said, and then muttered, "Oh, you didn't mean, like, Coca-Cola."

"I did not. I meant coke-caine."

Well, this was it, Em supposed, the moment this tentative new friendship ended. She did not want cocaine. She had it tried it once, at college, at Paul's encouragement, and had not liked the snorting or the way it made her heart race. She had become extremely judgmental about everyone else's coke personalities, the way they had once been interesting but now they just made banal observations that they thought were amazing. For a time, she had gotten excited about this point, tried to write it down so she'd remember it for later, and then realized that she, too, was having a boring, derivative coke thought.

She also, obviously, didn't want to use cocaine and then turn into a junkie. Reportedly, that happened a lot.

"No thank you," she said.

"No prob," Emily said. "In fact, if you abstain, I shall abstain. I already am a little"—she made a noise like a jet plane taking off, about which Em would later think, *Well, I should probably have figured that out.* Then she jumped up, pulled her jacket off the futon, dug in the pocket for a little cardboard notebook and a pen. When she finished writing, she looked up and closed the book. "'H-bomb.' Just needed to get that down."

Em felt herself flush. She'd never had someone write down her words before. "I didn't, like, make that up," she hastened to add. "It's just a thing people always say."

"Look, I heard it from you, so I'll give you the credit in interviews. Are you going to use it?"

"Use it?"

"Are you going to write something about that guy, and about Boston and H-bombs and Harvard pricks?"

"Ha. No. No, I grant you this boon. It's all yours to use as you wish. Would you put it in a play?"

"Yeah, maybe," Emily said. "Great character note."

"Are you—is it your plan to direct, like, Broadway plays?"

Emily snorted. "Broadway can suck my big dick," she said. In years to come, Em would often hear Emily say something and think, *Was that really what she said?* "I put up my own shows off-off, in the little theaters downtown." Em had seen some of those little theaters while walking around her neighborhood, and had thought they all looked crappy. But, of course, she understood that the little theaters were where the art got made, not in the big, glitzy Broadway theater where she and her mom had seen *42nd Street*. Emily went on to explain that she was currently working on her breakout piece, a site-specific production of *Medea* on the Brooklyn Bridge. Em had to admit that sounded impressive, if implausible.

An R.E.M. song came on what Em was starting to think of as the jukebox, and Em sat up straight. "Oh!" she said happily. "This is my favorite band."

"Oh yeah?" Emily said. "I know them."

"No you don't," Em said.

"I'm from their town."

"You're *from* Athens?" She regarded Emily with some awe. She had thought she was a creature of New York, but to be a creature of Athens, Georgia, was even more remarkable. A few years ago her sister had given her, for Christmas, a biography of R.E.M. that had made Athens sound like the most amazing place in the world—a wonderland of music and outsider art and happy freaks living extraordinary lives. The only reason she hadn't gone to college there was that she didn't get in.

Emily laughed. It was the first time Em had seen her even a little bit uncomfortable. "This is like the H-bomb but for college radio fans. Yes, I grew up in Athens. My dad taught Mike Mills and Michael Stipe; he's a professor. They came over to our house once."

"Did you freak out?"

"Well, no. I was ten. They weren't famous yet. And anyway, I like them fine, but everyone knows they're not the best Athens band, they're just the ones who got famous." In any other circumstance, Em would have found this statement outrageous, but she was so starstruck at Emily's revelation that she ceded the authority on this question.

"Were you in a band?" she asked.

"Nothing big. You know, I played with some friends at a few house parties. Once at the Downstairs."

Em stared at her. "I have spent this whole night trying to be cool, but it's hopeless. I've never met someone who actually lived in Athens. What was it like?" Emily shrugged. "No shrugging!" said Em. "This is not shruggable."

Emily laughed. "But it was my hometown! So it feels normal to me. What would you do if you met someone who was a huge fan of . . . where are you from?"

"Wausau, Wisconsin."

"Okay, admittedly, that's unlikely. But, you know, the ummm cow farms and whatnot are just second nature to you. I meet people who are super into Athens and I think, *That's the place where I was a miserable teenager.* Just as you were a miserable teenager in Warsaw, Wisconsin."

"Wausau. But," she admitted, "I wasn't miserable."

Emily looked surprised. "What does that even mean?"

"I was basically happy," Em said. "I mean, sometimes I would argue with my mom, and once my boyfriend dumped me. But I played softball and I worked on the literary magazine and I had nice friends. I was pretty boring, but I was happy."

"Well," said Emily, "*I've* never met someone who actually grew up happy." It was true that when Louis and her other college friends complained about their teenage years, Em rarely had anything to add. She understood from everyone's stories that artsy people were miserable by definition from ages thirteen to eighteen, and that from that misery sprung the well of creativity and resentment that fueled their art. Em worried a lot that her own anodyne teenagehood had failed to generate within her the necessary conditions for artmaking, that she had nothing to tap into—no great traumas to process or dismissive family members to spite with her eventual success. Her father had never abused her, and her mother had always been sweetly interested in her writing.

"I'm really lucky, I guess," Em said, shrugging. She waited. She felt that however Emily responded to her teenage happiness would have a lot of bearing on whether they could actually be friends.

"No shrugging," Emily said. "That's cool." Em felt herself smile.

She looked around the tiny apartment. "This is great," she said. "I'm so impressed you have your own place."

Emily seemed to understand what she was trying to say, which was, *How can you afford it?* "Well, rent's really cheap because it's a squat," she said.

"Sure," Em said, nodding. She continued nodding. She nodded a few more times.

"Do you know what a squat is?" Emily finally asked.

"Sure. Like, a dump."

Emily laughed. "It is a dump, that's correct. But no, the building was abandoned, and we're all living here and fixing it up ourselves. We're Sunrise Squat."

"Oh, wow," said Em. "So then who's your landlord?"

"There is no landlord. We all just contribute rent to a central fund and use that to pay for rehab and repairs. And we all have work requirements to get the building up to code."

Em was aware that she was still nodding. "So then, who owns it?"

"Officially, New York City, but they haven't done shit with this building in years. So we just took it over. We're in the middle of negotiating with the city, and if it works out we'll get it."

"You'll get a *building*?"

"Maybe. Or maybe they'll evict us. There are a lot of squats in the East Village. Some of them, the tenants have made a deal and now they run the place. Some of them, the city kicked 'em out to sell it to rich assholes."

Em had finally stopped nodding, because she honestly had never heard anything so crazy. "So you just moved in and, like, took an apartment?"

"Well, yeah. But in the beginning, you know, there was no electricity or water. There wasn't even stairs."

"What do you mean there wasn't stairs?"

"The stairs collapsed sometime in the '80s. Joe and Michael and the other original tenants had to build new ones. By the time I moved in there were stairs and we were connected to water and the electricity worked most of the time. But we still don't have heat."

"What?!"

Emily grinned. "We might have it by next winter. When it gets cold, I have a pile of blankets. If there's a blizzard, I find somewhere else to sleep."

"What do you mean, 'somewhere'"—Emily raised her eyebrow flirtatiously—"Oh."

"Where do you live?"

"Seventh and D. It's me and my best friend from college, Louis."

"Seventh and D! That's deep Alphabet City."

"Yeah, it's a terrible neighborhood. We're, like, right across the street from the projects, basically. I never even really knew what projects were until I moved in." She was not proud of this, was in fact embarrassed, but still it sounded just awful coming out of her mouth. Em attempted to blow right past it. "Wausau, where I'm from, it's really little. There are basically no African American people at all. And when we would go to Milwaukee we would drive through, you know, the bad parts of town, and my dad would never stop until we got to the zoo or the baseball stadium or whatever. And in college I just stayed on campus. I guess I've been pretty sheltered."

"It's not a bad neighborhood," Emily said. "It's poor."

"You're right! I know."

Emily waved her hand as if to say, *Your guilt doesn't matter.* "Michael talks about this a lot. He's sort of a student of history. The Lower East Side's been fucked by landlords and the city for decades. That's part of why squats like this matter. We're reclaiming housing that everyone's abandoned, remaking it for the people who live here."

"That's really amazing."

"You know what happened in Tompkins Square last spring?"

"They closed it."

"But do you know *why* they closed it? It was full of homeless people, because rents go up-up-up, and the cops came and wiped out the encampment and they put a fence around the whole thing."

"Oh, wow."

"There was a riot. A small one. I threw a few beer bottles at cops." Emily lay back on her mattress like that was no big thing and looked up at the ceiling. "Subject change: What's your dad like?"

"He's okay. My parents got divorced when I was in fifth grade. He lives in Chicago with his new wife."

"A wicked stepmother."

"Ehh, she's just my dad's wife. She's fine. She doesn't try too hard. What does your dad teach?"

"He's at the art school. My mom was one of his students. It was very scandalous."

"Whoa!"

"I know," Emily said, sitting up again. "By the time I was old enough to get it, no one cared anymore, but I think it was a big deal. She broke up his marriage."

"I don't know," Em said. "Isn't it more like *he* broke up his marriage?"

Emily smiled. "Yeah, you're right."

Em finished her beer and felt the weight of the silence that had fallen just then. She made a little preparatory noise, the inhale of a person about to speak, but before she could begin her sentence, Emily said, "No reason to leave."

"Oh, I—what do you mean?"

"You were about to say that you probably ought to go. But it's like two in the morning. You really wanna walk home now?"

"But don't you, like . . . need me to leave?"

Emily laughed. "I have nowhere to be tomorrow. Do you have to get up early?"

"I guess not."

"So just stay. I don't have sheets or anything, but the futon's not too bad. Here—" She pulled a pillow off her bed and tossed it to Em.

"I don't catch," Em said as the pillow hit her in the face.

"If I'm not here in the morning, don't take it personally," Emily said. "I don't believe in goodbyes." This seemed like such a ludicrous assertion that Em didn't even question it. What could she say?

What did they each think this was the beginning of? As Em went to sleep, she listened to the unfamiliar sounds of the late-night street outside. (She had never opened, and would never open, the windows in her subterranean bedroom.) She thought about how she'd felt just a step behind all night—lagging just a bit compared to Emily's obvious brains, lagging even more compared to Emily's up-front attitude. She had liked it. Had Emily, too, liked it?

She hoped they would be friends.

She hoped when she woke up, it wouldn't be weird.

It wasn't weird, because when she woke up Emily was already gone. On the wall by Em's coat, she'd written, EMILY & EM. Underneath EMILY was a phone number, and underneath EM was blank, so Em took the Magic Marker off the floor and carefully wrote 595–5245 on the brick. It was rough and uneven and so Em had to trace each line a few times to make it legible, but Emily had done it, and so would she.

— ● —

After her first day of work, she met Louis at a bar by Union Square, where he bought her a drink to celebrate. "To the first of us to get a real job," he said. Louis was permatemping at Baruch, answering phones in the dean's office. Really there was very little difference between their two jobs. In fact, if you did the math, Louis even made a little more money than her. Nevertheless, she felt proud to have been *hired*.

It still felt a little like a miracle. One of her creative writing professors was a novelist who hadn't published a thing since his debut had made a minor splash in the early 1980s. But he had heard that his agent needed a new assistant, and surprisingly had recalled that Em had worked in the department office, and shockingly had tracked her down in New York, which suggested a kind of diligence she'd never seen in his teaching. She'd sent him a thank-you note, of course, when she got the job. He'd written back, "You'll enjoy working with Edith, who is of the old school."

What this meant, as far as Em could tell, was that Edith was old. She tottered around on stick-thin legs and smoked at her desk. But the shelves behind her were filled with American and foreign editions of her clients' books, and the first time Em answered the phone— "Safer Agency, can I help you?"—it was a mystery writer her dad read all the time.

"Didn't you tell him that your dad loves him?" Louis asked now.

"No, that would be weird," she said. "Right?"

"Oh, extremely."

She hit him on the arm. "Anyway, I get paid next week." It was nearly the end of April and she didn't have enough for rent.

"I can spot you," Louis said.

"I'm sorry," she said. "Thank you."

"I'm excited for you. Among the literati."

— • —

The novel Em was reading was very specific on the subject of coolness:

> Phil says, there is one thing, one absolute, irrefutable truth.
> He says, you are either born cool, or you are not.
>   And it is not contagious. You can hang out with cool people, but that will not make you cool—you will simply be

someone who hangs out with cool people. You may go to all the right places, be invited to all the right parties, you may even have fucked all the right people. It doesn't matter, Phil says. The truth remains—you are cool, or you are not. And there's not a goddamn thing that you can do about it. Right? Phil says.

The novel was about young people living in the East Village in the early 1980s, when the neighborhood truly was cool—not now, when the scene, everyone agreed, was past its prime. Em worried on her worst days that Phil was right, because she knew which side of the divide she came down on. Emily, who was born cool—literally, born in the coolest place—said it was bullshit. "Think about the people whose art you love the most," she said. "Is David Byrne cool?"

"Yes," Em said. "He was obviously born cool."

"Okay, sure," Emily allowed. "But Tina Weymouth doesn't seem like she was born cool. She became cool."

They had spent the afternoon pawing the used CD bins on Bleecker before heading south to ogle the skinny artists of SoHo. They'd stopped to pee in the ornate secret bathroom at Portico Bed and Bath. Now they were walking up Lafayette toward Pageant Books, a store where Em had taken to hiding paperbacks on the second floor that she hoped, one day, to be able to buy, once she racked up a few more paychecks.

"Is it just, like, bassists and drummers make themselves cool, and lead singers are born cool?"

Emily considered it. Once again she was barreling ahead of Em, so she was delivering most of her half of the conversation over her shoulder. "No!" she said. "Belinda Carlisle became cool because she hung out long enough with Jane Wiedlin."

"Too bad she stopped."

"Yeah, then she became uncool again. But for one brief moment . . ."

Up ahead were the cartoon babies and dogs of the Pop Shop. "Keith

Haring," Em said, heartened. "Great example. That guy wasn't cool. He made himself cool."

"Yeah!" said Emily. "He didn't even make cool art."

"Right, not at first."

"He tapped into something, and then his art became cool. You wanna know a secret? You think Michael Stipe started out cool, but he didn't."

"Shut the fuck up," Em said.

Emily stopped. Behind her, the rays of radiance shining out from one of Keith Haring's babies encircled her head, giving her a Messianic vibe. "I am dead serious," Emily said. "Everyone from Athens knows this. He had good taste and he was a good singer, but he soaked up fashion and art and style and politics from all the people he met. There's this one guy, Jeremy, he's this great old character who's been part of the Athens scene forever. He used to be part of the Factory with Andy Warhol. And the joke used to be, What will Michael Stipe be wearing? Whatever Jeremy was wearing last year."

"Are you saying he stole this guy's look?"

"No, that's not the point. He found the right people and he taught himself how to be cool."

Em didn't think that could possibly be true, but she appreciated the gift Emily was giving her by saying it.

— • —

As she walked up Broadway toward Union Square, she fingered the key ring in her bag, with its two apartment keys and its one office key, 50 percent more keys than she'd ever had in her life. Even during her work-study jobs at the alumni association (fired for general bewilderment) and in the creative writing department office (where she was also bewildered but, due to the chaos of the place, no one noticed), she hadn't had a key.

Dave at the front desk nodded to her as she walked through the dim lobby and into the elevator. His terrier, Jim, sprang to his feet, yapping at her like the tiny monster he was. That her building had a Dave, a white-haired guy in a uniform who nodded everyone in, made her feel like a New Yorker, as did the fact that Dave had once, when she was wearing her best top, delivered one of those low, approving whistles you hear in the movies. She had never seen Dave out of his chair.

The office, at the back of the hall, faced another building and got very little natural light, so Em turned on the overheads so she could see anything. Edith, her boss, never arrived before ten thirty, but it took Em forever each morning to prepare the office for her inevitably grand entrance. That's why Em had a key.

When Edith swept in, Em knew, she would immediately turn the overheads off, preferring as she did to have the office lit by the several floor and table lamps Edith or some long-ago assistant had placed in impractical locations. Edith's desk, for example, swam in a little pool of warm light like a Broadway star singing a solo, but Em's desk was so dark she couldn't comfortably read submissions unless they came typed in an enormous typeface, a description that unfortunately primarily applied to submissions from psychos. In the gloriously flat, bright fluorescents Em turned on the air conditioner in the window, cleared Edith's coffee cups and ashtrays from yesterday, the cups all half-filled and decorated, like the cigarette butts, with Edith's signature fuchsia lipstick. She pulled the faxes that had come in overnight and sorted them into Junk, Em, and Edith. She eyed the phone handset to which Edith spent the days attached, judged it worthy of a cleaning, and, wincing, scrubbed the encrusted gunk from the earpiece.

As she performed each item on her morning list she thought of what Emily would say about it, or indeed had said about it on previous occasions. The other day Em had told Emily what she thought was an innocuously funny story about Edith tearing out individual pages of an author's fourth draft, balling them up, and tossing them around the office, pelting lamps, plants, the windows, and Em. Emily, however, had replied, matter-of-factly, "What you're describing is a crazy person." Now it was difficult for Em not to view everything about her job through that lens. She had liked her job better when she considered Edith's eccentricities to be charming quirks of the sort she was always reading in publishing memoirs.

When the room was ready for the day, Em guessed she still had twenty minutes or so before Edith's arrival, so she pulled the manuscript she'd started in bed last night from her overstuffed bag and settled down with it on the couch. It had arrived in the slush pile last week, 445 pages long, mailed complete in full-throated rebellion against the standard industry practice of sending an excerpt and delivering the balance of the book only if asked for more. Edith scorned authors who defied the guidelines in the *Writer's Market*—"Send 1st 20 pp, cover letter, SASE. No sci-fi, no romance"—but Em found herself charmed by writers confident that *their* books were the exception to the rule.

This guy was confident, all right. His name was Scot Salem. He was twenty-five and lived in Los Angeles, a city Em had never visited and thought about mostly in the context of Hollywood clichés and, recently, riots. What he was proposing was a complete rethinking of the mythology of the American West. Em knew this from Scot's cover letter, which said, "What I am proposing is a complete rethinking of the mythology of the American West." But she also knew it from the opening scene, two young men driving a Camaro into Joshua Tree with rap music playing on the radio and a body stuffed in the trunk.

She was now halfway through the novel, and she already felt nervous about the conversation she might need to have with Edith about it. Despite all the ways the book was obviously silly, the writing was filled with a kind of energy that thrilled her and frightened her. She didn't really know how to harness that energy in the service of a better novel than this one. She definitely didn't know how to talk about it, especially to Edith, whose list was made up mostly of professors who hadn't finished a novel in years, cozy mystery writers, and guys who wrote thrillers where characters were introduced by name on page seven only to die on page nine, in lines like "and then there was the flash of a rifle, and Samuel Norfenberger knew no more." It was clear to her that for all his faults as a writer and, probably, a person, Scot Salem would rather drop dead than write a sentence like that.

The novel was called *The Big One*. She assumed, eventually, there would be an earthquake. She could already see that title spread across the cover of a Vintage Contemporaries edition, Scot Salem's name with its cool single *t* in the corner.

Edith swanned in a little before eleven, flipped off the overhead lights—"How can you *see*, dear, it's so bright"—and settled at her desk. "Is there coffee?" she asked. Em had made coffee and, sitting in the dark on the couch, said so. There was a long pause in the conversation as Edith waited for her to pour a cup, and Em waited for Edith to ask politely, until finally Em said, "Let me pour you a cup," and Edith said, "Thank you."

The rest of the morning was filled, as always, with Edith on the phone. Em never stopped being astonished by Edith's capacity for telephone calls. The woman was tireless. She called editors and gossiped about scouts. She called scouts and sang the praises of her authors. She fielded calls from her authors and reassured them about their editors. "Taffy," she said, "Louise loves you. *Loves* you. Loves the book. She just had a baby, but she loves you just as much as she loves that baby." She did this four days a week; on Fridays she was at her house in the Hamptons.

Em, sitting across the room, performed triage on the incoming calls: telling Edith when it was someone important, scheduling callbacks, informing writers Edith was avoiding that she was so sorry but

Edith was out today, could she take a message? Before Edith left for a lunch with an editor, she asked Em *her* lunch plans, and Em said, nearly as casually as when she'd rehearsed it in the bathroom, "Oh, I'm meeting a writer from *Grand Street*." Edith had absolutely no idea who wrote for that downtown literary magazine, and therefore Em could write any name she wished on her expense form, thus making lunch with Emily free. Em tried to do this no more than once per week.

When Edith was gone, Em packed a bunch of galleys into a Bloomie's bag. Em got a lot of free books at her new job. People just sent them every day. The twine handle cut into her fingers, and when she reached the diner, she set the bag down with a grateful groan.

"What's in your big brown bag?" Emily asked, sitting down across from her. "Oh, could it be books?"

"I'm going to the Strand after this," Em replied. "Yes, please," she said to the waitress who asked her if she wanted coffee.

"Diet Coke," said Emily without looking up from the bag of books on the floor. "You're going to buy *more* books?"

"No, I'm selling these." The Strand's willingness to buy the advance copies that everyone who worked in publishing had piled around their offices kept Em afloat, as it did every assistant she knew.

Emily held up a Cynthia Heimel book. "Would I like this?" she asked.

"No," said Em. "I love it, though. It's like . . . Dorothy Parker if she wrote about sex."

"Dorothy Parker wrote about sex," Emily said. "She fucked gentlemen—with her pen." Em felt herself blushing. Emily had a great many more romantic partners than she did, and loved to tell Em all about them. Em went on dates, sometimes, with nice, quiet men she met through work or the young alumni association. Emily was currently sleeping with a married sculptor but said she was bored with him. Em could not imagine being bored by such a thing.

Emily ordered a French dip sandwich. Em ordered a salad and, when Emily's sandwich arrived, was jealous. "Are you coming with me this weekend to see Richard's show?" Emily asked her, dripping au jus.

"Yes," Em said. She generally said yes to Emily's offers, because without Emily she'd have little to do at all. Richard was an actor Emily had refused to date because "his work is too interesting." His theater company was based in Brooklyn, a place she had never actually been.

"They're amazing, and I'm not just saying that," Emily added. "They're just, incredibly . . ." She stared out the window searching for the right word for so long that Em started thinking about how to fix the middle part of *The Big One* and, when Emily finally said "angular," no longer recalled what she was talking about.

"Incredible," she said, often a safe way to respond to her friend.

Emily nodded with satisfaction. "I'm trying to cast him in *Medea*, but he says he won't work outside the company, but I think he's just sexist."

"Who do you want him to play?"

"Creon. He's got one scene, plus a spectacular death."

"Don't you think he'd rather be the lead in his own shows than have one scene in yours?"

"Sure, if he's satisfied never being reviewed in the *Times*," Emily said.

While Em fielded Edith's telephone calls, Emily worked as an intern at a feminist theater company on the Bowery. Unspoken between them was the understanding that they each had their own artistic domains, books for Em and drama for Emily. So Em kept her opinion (that it would be a miracle if the *Times* reviewed *medea:abridged*) to herself. In the few months she had known Emily, she had to admit, she did seem to make unlikely things happen all the time through force of will. Her apartment, for example: Emily's squat was barely real by Em's standards, yet she had electricity and water and, unlike Em, a window she could open.

They walked together to the Strand, where the guy at the door asked Emily to check her knapsack. "No way," she said. "I'll wait outside." There she browsed the fifty-cent books while Em handed her Bloomie's bag up to the buyer and waited expectantly. Today, she told herself, she would take the cash the buyer offered her, not the store credit. She would not take store credit. She would take cash. The last thing she needed was store credit, which would only cause her to come back to the store and spend the store credit and then also more cash.

"I've seen you in here before, right?" the buyer said as he removed the galleys from the bag. "I'm Darwin." He was older than her, twinkly, smiling.

"I'm Emily," she said. "Emily Thiel."

"Middelstaedt. That's my last name. You work in publishing, I guess?"

"I'm an agent's assistant."

"That's cool," he said. "You're the gatekeeper." Em felt the peculiar flush of pride she sometimes felt about a job she had only recently managed to explain to her parents. She was a part of things, if only a tiny part.

Darwin held up a slim paperback by Nicholson Baker. "You ever read this guy?"

"Oh, he wrote *The Mezzanine*, right?" asked Em, eliding the question.

"Love that book," said Darwin.

"Isn't it just one guy's thoughts while he rides an escalator?" She laughed. "Seems a little . . ."

"Boring?" He smiled. "It is, kind of."

"No, just, like, *small*. And this one is just about a guy giving his kid a bottle."

"I hear you. But I like that. Like, what even *is* a novel?" As Em considered this question, he finished going through the galleys and said, "Fifteen cash or forty credit." He smiled. "If you take credit, mind if I write my number on the slip? We could go out for coffee sometime."

"That's a lot of store credit," Emily said when Em showed her the carbon-paper voucher.

"No, look at the number! I got his number. He gave me his number."

"Em!" Emily said in an approving tone. "Look at you. What's he like?"

"He knows books," Em said. "He's cute. Maybe thirty?"

"An older man! He shall keep you in the manner to which you have become accustomed."

"He works at the Strand."

"Rich in experience, perhaps," Emily said airily. They crossed the street to Union Square, where Emily walked into the subway without a word.

Back in the office, Em checked the answering machine and sorted the mail. Three of the four phone messages were faxes, helplessly screeching through the line, untranslatable missives from machines set to auto-dial the wrong number again and again. The fourth was from a client whose latest book had been rejected everywhere. Edith, Em knew, would call her back and talk her down, a skill that Edith had once, in one of her expansive moods, told Em was the most important one for an agent to possess.

The slush pile was teetering and Em grimly resolved to spend time today working her way through it. In her first week on the job, she had enthusiastically organized the slush, read every letter and sample chapter, and presented six submissions to Edith, each accompanied by a neatly typed memo enumerating the project's strengths, weaknesses, and market potential. "Honey, I don't need to see six books from the slush pile," Edith had said. "I'll look at one today. And then if there's ever a great one, I'll look at that. But the slush pile is not where you are finding our clients."

To the extent that Edith found new clients, it seemed, she did it by reading *TIME* magazine and by fielding recommendations from her current authors. But as the weeks went on, Em had realized that Edith was not really in the business of representing new authors. She sold books and book proposals by her trusted stable of favorites, many of them to small publishers for meager advances. The agency was financed mostly by the royalties earned by Jack Mortensen, the author of *Futurity*, a book that Em distinctly recalled seeing on the bookshelves of every single one of her friends' parents in high school. It had sold fourteen million copies and been translated into more than fifty languages.

As was often the case, a Jack Mortensen check had arrived in the mail today. It was from his paperback publisher. Sometimes the checks came from his foreign publishers or his audiobook company. Once, the check was from a CD-ROM developer, whatever that was for. As was sometimes the case, the value printed on the check exceeded Em's annual salary of $18,000. Later in the afternoon, Em would walk to the bank to deposit the check into the agency's account; then she would write a new check, for the original amount minus Edith's 10 percent commission, to Futurification, a limited liability corporation based in Wilmington, Delaware.

Jack Mortensen did not live in Wilmington, Delaware. He lived on a ranch in Wyoming. Every so often he would call the office and ask Em, in a deep, genial voice, something absolutely incomprehensible. The last call had been about whether Em was prepared for the coming pre-millennial shift. "2000's gonna be something else," he'd said, "but 1995 is the real 2000, from a futurist's perspective."

And so Em worried that it was somewhat futile for her to get excited about *The Big One*. She worried it was futile to go hunting through the slush that poured into the office every day, dozens of fat envelopes, each of them filled with a writer's dreams and a neatly folded SASE. But she had to keep doing it, because what if she did find a perfect book, and could convince Edith it was perfect, and worth putting into the hands of editors? How else was she supposed to spend her time, anyway? How else could she bridge the gap between what Darwin from the Strand thought her job was and what her job actually was? What else was she supposed to be excited about, while working for a lunatic?

The lunatic called in at three thirty to say she wouldn't be back, she had a meeting. The office was Em's, but she felt restless. She wanted to *have read* Scot Salem's book, but she didn't want to read the rest of it. When the phone rang, Em answered it gratefully. "Safer Agency."

"I love hearing you say that."

"Hi Mom."

"Have you published the great American novel?" She could hear her mother puttering in the kitchen the way she did every day when she came home from the school where she taught. The open and shut of cupboards, the clank of dishes. If she closed her eyes she could put herself there, sitting at the kitchen table, reading a book in the light from the window.

"I've been reading some good things," Em said. She described *The Big One* to her mother a little bit.

"But why do they drive the car into the swimming pool?" her mother asked.

"I guess the whole thing makes more sense if you know that they're on drugs the whole time."

"Oh," said her mom. "Well, I'm sure you'll make it into something wonderful. I was talking to Lucy the other day and she said she hadn't heard from you."

"I didn't call her yet, Mom, I'm sorry."

"You don't have to apologize to me. It's your job, not mine." Lucy was a woman who'd gone to the University of Wisconsin with her mother and who'd later moved to New York and who was—this was the point of her mother hassling her to call—an aspiring writer. Only

two months into this job, Em had already had the experience of literary yentas matching her with friends, all of whom had novels tucked
away in musty drawers.

"Where does she live again?" Em asked.

"Oh, I forget. Let me look." Her mother, she knew, was flipping
the pages of her ancient address book. She could see it: its thick floral
cover, the pages covered in decades of amendments, friends' addresses
rewritten, enemies struck from her mom's life with a single crossout.
The *T* page, she realized with a start, now contained an entry for her,
with her New York address, her home and work numbers, all written
in her mom's familiar script. "Ninety-First Street. Is that the Upper
West Side?"

"Well, is it West Ninety-First or East Ninety-First?" Em asked.

"Oh, don't sound patient like that, you know it drives me crazy.
West."

"Upper Upper West Side, yes." Em had never been north of the
John Lennon memorial in Central Park.

"Well, have her come down to you if it's not safe. I talked to her
the other day and she said that she'd be happy to take you to lunch."

"I'll call her," Em said.

"Emily, honey," her mom said with a chuckle. "I know her book
might not be good. New York seems like a hard place to go undiscovered if you're really something special. But I think you'd like her, and
you could always use another friend, right?"

"You're right, you're right, I know you're right."

"How are you eating, sweetie?" her mom asked, and Em didn't reply. There was a silence, into which her mom clarified, "Are you eating
healthy?"

"I'm good," she said. "I got a salad today. I gotta go—love you Mom."

"Love you." Em hung up and allowed herself just ten seconds to
stew about her mom's food question, and then another ten seconds to
consider just *how* undiscovered everyone she knew in New York still

was: her friends from the English department working miserable internships, Louis temping and sitting in their apartment watching TV, even Emily's production of *Medea*, which surely no one would hike halfway across a bridge for. And Em herself, entirely undiscovered. Terra incognita, observed by no human eye. Except by Emily, who had seen her, picked her out, and declared her worth further exploration.

— • —

When Em arrived at the restaurant for lunch with Lucy Deming, she was surprised to see that Lucy Deming had brought her daughter. "Her sitter's sick," she said, "so we're all lunching together today." She said it not apologetically, as Em expected her to, but matter-of-factly. "Sarah, this is Emily."

Em stuck out her hand, and Sarah shook it, all business. She looked to be six or seven, and wore a pair of overalls and beat-up Keds. Her brown hair came down to her waist. When they arrived at the table, with a third chair pulled up by the friendly waitress—Em was grateful Lucy had picked somewhere casual-ish, and then realized she probably had foreseen this exact situation—Sarah plopped down and started reading a book. "A child after my heart," Em said.

"She'll have things to say, eventually," said Lucy. She was short and jolly, with curly brown hair. She wore a blazer and jeans and moved slowly toward her chair, like a boat docking at a pier. "So! How's Donna Jorgenson feeling about her girl living in the big city?"

"Ha, 'Donna Jorgenson.'" Em didn't know that she'd ever heard anyone refer to her mother by her maiden name before. "She's nervous. She says she's going to visit soon, but I'll believe it when I see it."

"Well, she's never visited me," Lucy said good-naturedly. "It's good to know it's the city she's afraid of."

"When I did my college visits, we stopped in New York for a night, and the only place she knew to stay was the Waldorf, and it was so crummy—just dingy and old. And she didn't want to go anywhere. I had to drag her to a Broadway show."

"What did you see?"

"*42nd Street.*"

"Safe choice."

"It was my big triumph that I got her to take me to Shakespeare and Company."

"I've never known a person who seemed as at home as your mother seemed in Wisconsin."

"I guess," Em said.

Lucy put her hand on Em's. "May we all be so lucky," she said. She turned to her daughter. "Hey, kid, you want a burger?"

"Okay," said the kid.

Em looked down at her hand. Not so many people touched her these days, she realized. Perverts on the subway, and Louis. She and Emily didn't have that kind of friendship.

"Hey, Sarah," Em said to the kid. "What grade are you in?"

"That's, like, *the* question adults ask kids," Sarah said. She pushed her glasses up on her face.

Lucy laughed, a *heh-heh-heh* like a witch's cackle in a movie. "That's not wrong, honey, but it's pretty rude."

Em thought about it. "It's because we don't remember what it's like to be eight or whatever, but we remember third grade."

"What do you remember about third grade?" Sarah asked.

"I remember doing a lot of penmanship. We learned cursive. Oh, and we wrote a letter to our favorite author. I remember I got in trouble for the first time, when Miss Maglio made me stay after school for talking back."

"Well I'm nothing like that," Sarah said. "I'm in *second* grade." She went back to her book.

Lucy made a *what can you do?* gesture. "I just hope she becomes a lawyer and supports me in my old age."

They made small talk until Em attempted the awkward segue: "My mom says that you have a book?"

"Oh boy," said Lucy. "The charity case."

"No, no—"

"It's okay! She knows I write, but she doesn't really know the details. I've written a couple of novels. My first two were published in the '80s." She nodded at Em's surprise. "Real small press, based in Boston. They basically did nothing. First one got some reviews; second one got ignored. They never came out in paperback."

"What was the publisher?"

"Balcony Press." Emily had never heard of it, so she did what she did when someone mentioned a book she hadn't read, which was to nod sagely and say, "Mm-hm." "Anyway, I stopped writing for a long time after those. I had a baby, and I was in love, and then I was in the throes of a divorce, and then I was a single mom. But also, I was pissed—these were good novels, and they mostly disappeared without a trace. Guess the print run on the second one," she said.

"Um . . . five thousand?"

"Four hundred and fifty copies! Can you believe that? And I still have like thirty of 'em. Anyway, the last few years, with her in school, I've been writing again, and I have another novel finally. And half of a maybe-sort-of autobiography kind of thing."

"What's the novel about?"

"Oh boy. I've never been a pitcher. Sarah, honey, what's my novel about?"

Sarah looked up from her book. "It's about Alicia and Kate and their kids and their friends."

"Those are the characters. It's *about* joy in the face of an uncaring world," Lucy said.

"Joy in the face," repeated Sarah.

"That's a good title. Right now it's called *Can't Complain*, but maybe I'll call it *Joy in the Face*."

"How would you describe the plot?" Em asked.

"I would not describe the plot," Lucy said, "because then you would lose interest in reading the book."

Em laughed. "Well, is it a departure from the previous books? Different in some way?"

Lucy considered for a moment. "It's happier," she said.

"Well, I'm happy to read it," Em said. "Do you have a copy ready to show?"

"Yeah," said Lucy, opening her shoulder bag and removing a manila folder with a manuscript in it. "It's a xerox, so it's not, you know, the priceless only copy." She also pulled out two slim hardcovers and placed them on the table. They were called *Hearts and Stones* and *Pleased to Meet You*. "Please ignore the covers," she said. The covers were truly hideous, watercolor roses and young women staring off into the distance.

"So they seem like . . . women's fiction?"

Lucy winced. "Yes, I suppose. Fiction about women, at least. But really, seriously, ignore the covers."

"Why do you want an agent for this one? Were the other two agented?"

"No," Lucy said. "In a nutshell, I would like to make some money this time, so I can stop writing instruction manuals for digital watches."

On the subway back to the office Em read the first few pages of the manuscript. It was a little corny, but it wasn't incompetent or embarrassing. She'd be able to write an honest rejection. The fact was, Edith didn't represent romance, really. As she heard Edith say all the time, the agency wasn't a match.

But she would let her down easy, of course. Her mom had been right—she had liked Lucy. She hoped they could be friends, although she imagined that people didn't usually want to be friends with someone who rejected their writing, no matter how kindly they did it. Lucy had hugged Em in front of the restaurant, and Sarah had once more shaken her hand. "Thank you for reading it," Lucy had said. "You know, when your mom and I were in college, she wrote poetry from time to time."

"No she did not."

"I think I have a copy of the literary magazine. I think she's in it. You'll have to come over sometime for a martini and a quick read of the collected works of Donna Jorgenson."

"Oh, that's lovely. I'd be happy to come over. Although I don't drink martinis."

"That's because you've never had mine," Lucy said.

— • —

The way it worked was: Em would drop a quarter into the pay phone on the corner, dial Emily's number, let it ring once, and then hang up so the phone returned her quarter. Emily would open her third-floor window and drop a key down to the sidewalk. She'd attached the key to a little green army man, who was himself attached to a nylon parachute, so the key would float down gently and Em, who didn't catch, could pick it up off the ground. Em would then let herself in the front door and come up. There was no handrail in the stairwell, and no lights. At night the residents knew to carry flashlights around. Today the tiny square windows facing the back of the building were lit by the sun, casting bright shadows on the metal steps and on the graffiti covering the wall. Em touched her favorite graffito: *This house is an emotional megaphone.*

Emily's building was technically owned by the city, having been seized for nonpayment of taxes early in the '80s. Drug dealers had subsequently taken it over. In 1986 a cabdriver was killed on the fourth floor, and the arrival of the cops momentarily drove the dealers away; at dawn the next day, Joe and Sofia and Michael and Enrique, the founding fathers of Sunrise Squat, took possession of the building and installed a front door. Seemingly that door, painted institutional gray, was a kind of talisman, informing the neighborhood the building was now occupied; the dealers went elsewhere, and the city looked the other way. Over the years, residents had fixed the place up: repaired the roof, tapped the power grid, paid to have the water main repaired, installed a toilet on each floor, jackhammered bricked-out windows. These metal stairs Em was climbing were built by the squatters. There was a community library on the ground floor and a garden next door where some residents, although not Emily, grew vegetables in raised beds.

On the third floor, Emily had unlocked the deadbolt and chain on her door and left it open. As always, she was sitting on her futon, listening to music. "Hey," she said as Em locked the door behind her.

In the apartment it was bright and warm, and Em took off her windbreaker and hung it on the nail by the phone. They had no particular plans, but it had become customary for the two of them to spend Sundays bullshitting tirelessly at Sunrise Squat. (They both agreed Em's apartment was far too grim, even with Louis there.) When Em would look back on this part of her life, later, it was this living room that she remembered herself in, not her bedroom or her office or the streets of New York. The movie posters for *Do the Right Thing* and *Solaris*. The clothes scattered everywhere, the funk of unwashed bras, the blankets piled in the corner for the coming winter. The overfull ashtrays and the odor of cigarettes, the smell of Em's dad transplanted a thousand miles away. The window open if it was even a little bit warm outside, the horns and cars and shouts of the city. The CD changer playing stuff she'd never heard before, and her pleasure when she recognized a song. The tiny bookshelf with its growing piles of books cascading off of it, all gifts from Em, her contribution.

Sometimes Emily had Diet Coke or beer in her baby fridge, which Em had named the State of Denmark, because something was always rotten in it. More often one of them would make a run down to the bodega, with its disinterested cashier and dusty two-liters of Squirt, to buy drinks out of their cooler. (Emily had had to explain to her that the reason the clerks didn't care about her was that it was a drug front.) Sometimes they watched a movie on Emily's ancient TV. But mostly what they did was talk. God, could they talk. Sometimes they argued with each other, sometimes they agreed, sometimes they talked past each other, so eager were they to get their opinions into the air.

"But that's terrible," Em said today. "The whole point of the movie is Tre gets *out* of the hood!"

"That's no happy ending," Emily insisted. "He left his friends to *die*."

"You think the movie would be better if they *all* got shot." Em had been nervous about going but also sort of hopeful that if there were black people there, they would approve of her, a white girl, seeing this black movie. The theater on Second Avenue had been about half-full, and no one paid her any attention at all. Em couldn't believe how much the audience had talked to the screen, as if the characters could hear them and might take their advice.

"Blaze of glory, muthafuckaaaaaa!" Emily said. Sometimes when they talked about racism, Em had noticed, Emily tended to adopt a black accent. It made Em uncomfortable, even though she knew Emily listened to rap music and knew way more African American people than Em did.

"But what about all the stuff his dad tells him?" Em said. "Like, 'Don't let yourself get trapped here.' Isn't that the message of the movie?"

Emily snorted derisively. "You're not reading the movie right." Emily often said things like this, and Em had no good response. "The movie presents Doughboy as the authentic hero of the hood. All Tre and his dad want is to escape. That's a betrayal!"

Em shook her head. "I just don't think that's what the story is supposed to be. It's about, like, their diverging paths."

"Look," Emily said. "You know where the movie's title comes from?"

"What do you mean, comes from? They're boyz, and they're n the hood."

"It's from a song by N.W.A. Niggaz Wit Attitudes. The guy who played Doughboy? That's Ice Cube. From Niggaz Wit—"

"Please just call them N.W.A.!"

"—Attitudes. You think you make the guy from that band, the band that did *this* song"—Emily was pressing the disc skip button on the CD player as quickly as she could—"a song called 'Straight Outta Compton,' like, listen to this—"

"Okay, Emily, I get it."

From the speakers came an aggressive beat. Emily stood up. "This is Ice Cube right here! This is the guy!" She rapped along with the song: "When I'm called off, I got a sawed-off! Squeeze the trigger, and bodies are hauled off! You too, boy, if you fuck with me!"

"I think," Em said, "it's easy for us to say—for *you* to say—that the movie should end with Tre dying."

Emily kept rapping, dropping the N-word several more times. "They wanna rumble!" she declaimed. "Mix 'em and cook 'em in a pot like gumbo!"

"But we're white! The black person who made the movie seems pretty clear on what the message is!"

"Gotta be studio interference," Emily said, sitting down, breathless. "I bet they made him change the ending to make it more *palatable* to suburbanites."

Em didn't think that could possibly be true. Instead of saying that, she said, "*Boyz n the Hood*. More titles should do that. *Raiz n the Sun*."

"*Flowerz n the Attic*."

"*Catcherz n the Rye*."

Emily was laughing. She stood, as if to propose a resolution. "*Alice's Adventurez n Wonderland*," she said.

"*Da Mill n da Floss.*"

Emily doubled over. When she got to laughing, she gave her whole self over to joy. "Da mill n da fuckin' floss! That's good."

Em, too, was laughing. "This is extremely offensive, right?" she said.

"Definitely!" said Emily. She wiped her eyes.

"Just checking."

They went downstairs to the community library, where Emily liked to fulfill her weekly work hours. "What'd you bring?" she asked Em.

"We got a copy of this, for some reason," Em said, pulling a paperback out of her bag. It was Frantz Fanon's *The Wretched of the Earth*, thirtieth anniversary edition, and Emily seized it.

"Oh, this is perfect," she said. "Goes right here." She slid the book onto a shelf marked REVOLUTION.

Unlike most days, the library wasn't empty; at one of the small tables against the wall sat a woman, smoking a cigarette and staring at them with a kind of frank contempt that Em recognized from the women in her building, none of whom responded when Em said hello. Those women were black, and this woman was too. Em tried not to see color, of course, but this woman was very black.

"So, like, *Do the Right Thing*?" Emily said with enthusiasm. "That's a movie that comes down on the right side of the law. You know what Spike said? He said, like, 'People ask me why Mookie threw that trash can. You know who asks me? White people.'" She laughed. She was doing a studied Spike Lee impression. "'No brother ever asked me that question.'"

From the table came a snort. Emily turned to the woman, who had looked back down at her book. "Are you new?" Emily asked. "I live up on three." Em felt her heart thumping in the way it always did when she encountered a black person. She was desperate to prove herself to be one of the okay white people, and knew that her desperation came off her in waves.

The woman looked up again. "I live in See Skwat. Michael said we could come use the library."

"That's cool," Emily said. "I'm Emily. This is my friend Em."

"Like, Em for Emily?" the woman said, shaking her head. "Y'all moms need to get more creative."

In middle school, Em's mom had made her take tennis lessons. She tended to double-fault a lot, because her tosses were very inconsistent. There was a thing she used to do where she would toss the ball in the air, and it would be too far ahead of her or behind her or too low or whatever, and in her head she would think, *That's a bad toss. This serve's going out if I hit that.* But instead of simply catching the ball and trying again, she would continue her motion and, as if outside her own body, watch herself go ahead and hit the serve, which would then soar long or thwap into the net. It was in the spirit of those serves that Em found herself asking the black woman, "Do you have a, uh, a creative name?"

The woman raised one eyebrow. She looked a little older than Emily and Em and was wearing a denim jacket that made her look incredibly cool. "I'm Lisa," she said. "Spelled the traditional way."

"I'm sorry, that was a dumb question," Emily said. Em looked at her in dismay. "My friend's still learning to be a New Yorker."

"Huh," Lisa said. She looked Emily up and down. "Not like you."

"I live here," Emily said. "I know everyone in this neighborhood."

"You even got a voice to use with them."

"That was my *Spike Lee* voice."

"Look," Lisa said. "How does it work here? I want to take one of these books." She held up a book on real estate law. "Do I need to fill something out?"

Em watched Emily write down the title of the book in the library's tattered notebook. As always, she seemed blithely unbothered by her gaffe, while Em could not stop thinking about hers and felt she likely would until sometime in 1992. "If you've got a question about squatters' rights, you should ask Joe. He's a founder and he knows everything. At this point he could probably pass the bar."

"Joe, huh?"

"Yeah, do you know him? When he's not here he's usually playing basketball at the park. He's the Filipino dude."

"The little guy?"

"Yeah, that's him."

For the first time, Lisa smiled. "That motherfucker's crazy," she said. "Okay, thanks. See you, Emilys."

"She's great," said Emily. "We should be her friend."

"You don't think she hates us?"

"Sure, but we can overcome that."

Em spent a lot of her time with Emily wishing that she had even a third of Emily's confidence. She seemed to believe she was prepared to succeed at anything, from charming strangers to staging *Medea* on a bridge or, eventually, becoming an important director. Em knew lots of people who were writers, who were trying to be writers, who said they were writers. If pushed, she might say she was one of them. But so few of them actually *wrote*, Em included. Meanwhile Emily churned out pages of material because, she said, if she was going to make the theatrical work that was most meaningful to her as a director, it couldn't come from someone else's pen. "I'm not a writer," she liked to say. "I just happen to write first, as part of my practice." She often described *medea:abridged* as her breakout project, even though it was not yet scheduled to happen. "It's in development," she often said, and it was true that she was getting notes from other theater people—which she inevitably said were wrong—and negotiating with the city to allow her access. That meant, among other things, firing off letters to her councilman and picking up the responses at her post office box. Em had no idea who *her* councilman was. Why on earth would she? Who had a post office box?

By now it was early evening, and they collected their coats from

Emily's apartment and headed out looking for dinner. "The thing is," Emily said, picking up the thread from long before, "Tre doesn't survive the revolution. College boy, wannabe bourgeoisie."

"Pretty harsh," Em said.

"Name a character. I'll tell you if they survive the revolution."

"Um . . . Alex P. Keaton."

"Are you fucking kidding me?" Emily stopped in the middle of the sidewalk, hands on hips. "He's the first against the wall!"

"Okay, okay. Lloyd Dobler."

"A real hero. Dies saving Diane from CIA goons."

"She-Ra."

"Tough one. I don't care if she's a princess of power, all royals get the axe."

"Um . . . Emma Bovary."

"Ha. Romances a callow lieutenant. They're both killed on the third day of the uprising."

"Sweeney Todd."

"Black ops! Kills like a dozen generals. Totally insane. Lives to a hundred."

"Let me try," Em said.

"Sure. Ducky. From *Pretty in Pink*."

"Ohhh, Ducky. I think he and Andie behead Blaine and ride off into the sunset."

"Homer Simpson."

They were nearing the pizza place. "Blows himself up trying to bomb Springfield City Hall."

"But in the new, glorious future, Lisa rules the Springfield commune."

"Oh, definitely. Bart's her enforcer. A slice with mushrooms and a half order of garlic knots, please. And I'll get a Diet Coke from the cooler."

Emily ordered her slice and they sat down. Em was eager to continue the game, but Emily seemed suddenly to have lost interest. When Em's garlic knots arrived, Emily immediately took one and started pulling it apart.

"I wonder if that's a show," she said, suddenly animated. *"Homer Simpson and the People's Revolution."*

"Wouldn't you have to get permission?" Em asked. "I mean, maybe they wouldn't notice . . ."

"Nah, that's a good point. It would be a huge hit, so they'd definitely notice. But satire's protected."

"You could do it with like old characters. Emma Bovary and Frankenstein and, uh, Paul Bunyan."

"Paul Bunyan!" Emily laughed. "But the whole point is that these corporate characters are breaking their chains. Like, the best version is the Simpsons, the Muppets, uh . . . G.I. Joe, and Snow White."

"You would get shut down in ten seconds."

"I love it. How could we not get press?"

The garlic knots were gone—Emily had eaten most of them—and they retrieved their pizza, scorching hot and puddled with grease, from the guy behind the counter. They blotted the slices with paper napkins until the napkins were bright orange. Em took pride in knowing to fold her slice in half. (Her first weeks in New York she'd eaten pizza with a knife and fork, which she would never, ever admit to anyone now.) She considered, not for the first time, how much of her identity she already had wrapped up in thinking of herself as a New Yorker, and how much that depended on, basically, faking it. Eating pizza the way other people ate pizza. Walking right past the bums on the sidewalk, never revealing how awful they made her feel. Saying oh yes, she read that book, or yes, she knows that movie, and deftly turning the conversation to have you read *this* book, and have you seen *this* movie?

Emily had a clever way of avoiding that problem. If someone mentioned a book or a movie she hadn't heard of, she simply assumed it was garbage. "Saves time," she said.

— ● —

"First of all, I'm sorry, I'm just starting your book. I've been swamped."

Lucy laughed. "It's okay, I understand capitalism. This is what happens when there isn't a robust market for a product."

Lucy's apartment took up the first floor of a brownstone on a quiet street. Incongruously, it was decorated with a Southwestern theme—Navajo blankets, turquoise knickknacks, sere prints of desert landscapes. "We spent a winter in Santa Fe a few years back," Lucy said. "It's the most beautiful place in the world. I'm going to retire there, when I can afford to retire, which is never."

Her daughter was staying over at a friend's house, so Lucy said she was "a free woman." However, "I'm a free woman who feels old and creaky and hates leaving my house, so I hope it's okay if we just stay here and I cook for you."

"Uh, that's fine," Em said. "I am ready to be cooked for."

"What's your kitchen like?" Lucy asked, pushing her way up from the table. Em noticed, again, how deliberately she moved. Lucy was a bit heavyset, and Em supposed she just didn't want to knock into anything. "Do you cook?"

"I *prepare*," Em said. "Pasta, or salads sometimes."

"Your kitchen's small."

Em's kitchen was pathetically small. Their silverware drawer still contained two forks, a knife, and a spoon. The kitchen was also the site of a thriving mouse community, a civilization so advanced they had probably figured out the wheel by now. "I get takeout a lot. I shouldn't, I know."

Em could see Lucy in the kitchen over the half-wall. "I've got some roast chicken in the fridge, so I'm just going to make us some curry chicken salad. Is that okay with you?"

"I don't know, I've never had curry anything."

"Pure Wisconsin," Lucy said. There was the *plonk* of a cutting board being placed on the counter. "Hey, I couldn't find my old literary magazines, but take a look at that book on the table." Em sat down to a thin sorority yearbook, Alpha Gamma Delta, University of Wisconsin, 1964–1965. "I marked some of the pages with your mom and me," Lucy said.

Em turned to the first bookmark. There was her mom, twenty at the outside, younger than Em was now, hairband holding back her bangs. She was standing with a group of girls in front of a sorority house, all of them holding cleaning supplies—mops, brooms, buckets—and mugging for the camera. She found Lucy to her mom's right, holding up a dustpan and rolling her eyes.

Another page: formal portraits, each sister framed identically against a black background, all in matching off-the-shoulder dresses. The hair! Beehives, flip curls, one or two pixie cuts. "Everyone looks identical."

"Individualism was not prized. Do you see me?" Unlike most of the girls, Lucy's smile didn't show her teeth. You might almost call it wry.

"Did you rush in college?" Lucy asked her.

"My school barely had a Greek system. There was like one fraternity, very unsanctioned. They had a tradition of drunken kickball matches."

"My mother told me it was a way to make friends, and I thought I'd never make friends way up north. Your mom, honestly, is one of the only ones I keep in touch with. She was good to me." A knife flashed under the kitchen lights as she chopped.

"No one else moved to New York?"

"Honey, no one else left the state."

"Oh!" A color snapshot had fallen out of the book, her mother and

Lucy in a blue convertible, both of them wearing swimsuits, both laughing their heads off. She didn't think she'd ever seen her mother laugh like this, not when she was little, not in middle school after the divorce, not when her sister was raising hell. She held the photograph up for Lucy to see.

"Oh," Lucy said. "I love that one. We are beautiful, all right."

"Do you remember what you were laughing about?"

"We were a little hysterical, actually. I had a pregnancy scare—getting pregnant, you could kiss your life goodbye. In those days, if they caught you even staying over with a boy, you'd be expelled."

"Expelled!"

"Needless to say, the boy would *not* be expelled. Anyway, I was late, and I didn't want to tell my boyfriend. Donna was going to drive me to the doctor, but then I got my period, so we went to the beach on Lake Mendota instead."

"I love this," Em said. "I love you two."

"You know," said Lucy, "I used to come back to Madison every once in a while, to see friends. But after a few years, your dad got that job in Wausau, and I sort of lost touch with everyone. But I remember meeting you. You were a baby, and your big sister was, what, three? I held you and you cried and cried, like I was pinching you or something."

"I'm sorry about that."

"You were insensate, I forgive you. Here, come and look what I'm doing. This is a recipe you need to know." She saw Em's look of panic and corrected herself. "It's not *even* a recipe, it's just a thing you can do in the kitchen and at the end you have food."

After they ate, Em stacked the dishes in the drainer. "I'm going to go sit on the stoop," Lucy said. "Come on out if you want some fresh air."

The sky between the buildings was sherbet pink and scattered with clouds like confetti. "You smoke?" Lucy asked, pulling a joint from a baggie. Em, surprised and embarrassed, said no thank you. "No problem," said Lucy. Em looked down the street as Lucy lit, puffed, exhaled. She imagined being friends with Lucy for years, imagined Lucy respectfully never offering this kindness again, and turned back to Lucy and said, "Actually, yes, can I join you?"

They smoked down the joint as the light faded from the sky. It was chilly but Em didn't feel cold. "I'm happy," Lucy said. "Can't wait to tell Donna now I've smoked with her *and* her daughter. *Just kidding*," she added before Em could shriek.

"I would die."

"But you should tell her. I think it might actually make her happy to hear." Em didn't tell her mom until much, much later, but it did make her happy.

— • —

It was pouring for the fifth day in a row, and Em's apartment was damp and cold and miserable. Louis was in North Carolina, anyway, so Em felt no guilt about basically setting up camp at Emily's. Emily had a new job, at Kim's Video, so they had videotapes to watch. Em brought beer. They watched a movie called *The Unbelievable Truth*, in which two deadpan misfits sort of fell in love. Em loved it, and could sense that Emily was revving herself up to argue with her about it. To head her off at the pass she asked about Emerson, her sculptor. This turned out to be exactly the right move, because Emily and Emerson had just had a falling-out. There was almost nothing Emily liked to do better than expound upon her turbulent love life.

What had precipitated the current row was that Emily had gone to the sculptor's wife's gallery—which represented Emerson, among a number of more famous artists—and engaged her in a long, critical conversation about her husband's work. Toward the end of the debate, Emerson walked in and was appalled, Emily reported, to find the woman he'd been sleeping with not only talking to his wife but offering a feminist critique of the misogyny embedded in his art.

"I understand why he'd be upset," Em put forth cautiously.

"What a fucking poseur!" Emily said. "He should be grateful to have someone engaging with his work."

It was at moments like this, when Emily was operating at her most Emily-esque pitch, that Em most clearly saw their friendship fitting into a neat template. It was one she knew well from a lifetime of reading: She was Beth and Emily was Jo; she was Melanie and Emily was Scarlett O'Hara; she was what's-her-name, the wallflower, and Emily was Emma. She knew she was the boring one. But she also knew that Emily depended on her for that, and that Emily *was* extraordinary. If sometimes Em yearned to see her friend humbled even a little by failure, she also felt wholly convinced of her eventual success. Yes, only a certain kind of person would say such a thing about her married boyfriend's sculptures. But who among the greats was not, in some way, absurd? She believed in Emily, and the moments when she behaved at her most Emilyish were the moments Em believed in her the most.

For a while they both read their books as the rain came down outside. According to the news, a storm was creeping its way along the coast, heading out to strengthen at sea, then returning to land to dump all that ocean water on New York, where the water would then accumulate sidewalk toxins and eventually flow back into the sea. When you thought about the immense cycles of the natural world in this way, it seemed like a big waste of time.

There was a rumble of thunder like a subway, but in the sky. "Is this the end?" Emily said.

Em quoted the movie: "The world is not gonna come to an end when there's so many people making so much money."

Emily sprang up and headed for the stereo. "We need a song for the apocalypse."

"Apocalypso," Em said, a joke from the book she was reading. Emily barked a laugh and put a disc in the changer. Em had not previously imagined that Emily owned calypso music, but she did. A syncopated beat filled the room, and Emily beckoned her off the couch.

"Dance with me," she said. "Dance a little longer, for soon it will be over, never any more to dance."

"I called that guy Darwin," Em said when the song was over.

"Charles Darwin?"

"From the Strand."

"Oh! That guy! Charles Darwin is dead, I was about to say."

"I called him on the phone."

"Look at you!" Emily chucked her on the arm. Em's lack of romantic courage was a frequent topic of conversation. "What did he say?"

"Well, he remembered me—"

"Fucking of course he did. You looked hot that day."

"I didn't, but thank you. I was all puffy. But whatever, it doesn't matter, we're going out this weekend."

"What are you seeing?"

"We're going to a reading. At NYU."

"Honest to God, you two really are perfect for each other. I'd get a pap smear before I'd go to a *reading*."

She still didn't feel confident, but her New York self *acted* confident, and it turned out that went a long way. Calling a handsome man she'd met in a bookstore? College Emily never does that. But New York Em—she feels scared, but she does it anyway and bluffs her way through the call. "Should we go to that Kathy Acker reading?" he'd asked, and she'd answered, instantly, "Oh yeah, I love her."

That reminded her: "Have you read anything by Kathy Acker?"

"Never heard of her," Emily said dismissively.

"I need to figure out what her story is, so I know what I'm getting into at this reading."

"Get your umbrella," Emily said. (She didn't own one.)

At St. Mark's Books, Em asked the redheaded clerk where she could find Kathy Acker. She was stocked in queer fiction, her books published by small presses, with quotes on the front covers about Kathy Acker's transgressive vision. On the back of each book was a photo of a woman with short blonde hair staring defiantly into the camera. Rather than a rectangle, the photo was a sideways triangle, which Em found striking. She read a few pages of each book, found herself struggling with the language, which was profane but dense.

Up front, the clerk and a still-dripping Emily had joined forces to argue with a customer about the store's X case, where they kept the most-shoplifted books. "It's not there because it's *good*," Emily said, holding up *Naked Lunch*.

"It's there because dumb shits like you steal it all the time," said the clerk.

"I didn't steal anything!" the guy protested. He looked younger than Emily and sorely overmatched. "And everyone knows he's a genius."

Emily and the clerk laughed sharply. "Good luck with this idiot," Emily said to the clerk as she and Em left the store.

Outside, Emily stomped through the rain. "I ought to get a job in customer service," she said.

"You're a natural."

"You bet your ass."

— ● —

Can't Complain by Lucy Deming was quite good, and Em didn't think she liked it.

That is to say, her initial fears—that her mom was forcing her into a situation where she had to read some dreck and be nice to its quote-unquote author—were obviously incorrect, given Lucy's actual history with publishers publishing her books, no matter how small her print runs. But upon reading it, Em found herself smiling at little turns of phrase—laughing at the jokes—caring which young man

Lucy's heroine, Alicia, would find love with. The novel's characters were smart enough, but the novel wasn't about their brains, really. It was about their hearts.

Yet Emily felt herself resisting the manuscript, even as she kept turning the pages, propped up in her bed on the big body-hugging pillow both she and Louis called their husband. *Can't Complain* was set among perfectly nice young people with perfectly normal relationship problems, and thus seemed to have nothing to do with the remarkable time in which everyone was living. It was the *nineteen nineties*. Writers were not writing about a quiet magazine editor trying to decide between her two witty suitors. Writers were penning sizzling tales of debauchery or challenging works that speak to our age like none other. (If those weren't actual blurbs on her collection of Vintage Contemporaries paperbacks, they might as well have been.) Em had recently seen Tina Brown, the editor of *Vanity Fair*, on the *Today* show, describing the new novel by Bret Easton Ellis as "a meteor blazing across the sky of fin-de-siècle Manhattan." Who said things like that?! She'd immediately written it down in her new little notebook.

On the page she'd just read, the two main characters, who had been in a minor fight, resolved their differences in the space of a single paragraph:

> The problem was that both Alicia and Kate expected the other to apologize, when in fact what would have solved their argument was for both of them to apologize, each to the other. And the measure of their friendship was that a day later they saw one another at the diner and, nearly in unison, said, "I'm so sorry." Alicia laughed merrily and dabbed at her eyes; Kate cried through a smile. Kate bought Alicia's cup of coffee, and Alicia bought Kate's tea. To the outside eye, they each spent a dollar, but what mattered was the generosity of the impulse, not the result.

This was no meteor blazing across the sky of fin-de-siècle Manhattan! These people could be apologizing to each other any old year! It felt—Em wrinkled her nose—whatever the opposite of timely was.

Another thing: Everyone in the novel was basically always happy. There were misunderstandings and arguments here and there, but they were always wrapped up, like the one in that passage, with a quick apology or a heartfelt conversation during a walk. There was absolutely, positively nothing transgressive about the novel. She had recently read a short story collection that Darwin had recommended. It was full of sex, drugs, and cruelty. One story was about a sadist who spanked his secretary. The book was called *Bad Behavior*. Lucy's novel might as well have been called *Good Behavior*.

She supposed she should ask Edith, a putative literary agent, about it. There were publishers, assuredly, who would buy something like this and put it in spinner racks in supermarkets in Wisconsin. But wouldn't all the Wisconsin moms who might otherwise be interested in a story like this be put off by the descriptions of New York magazine publishing? Lucy certainly didn't make it seem glamorous—there were no expense account lunches or limo rides to the Condé Nast offices. Alicia seemed, honestly, to be as bewildered by her job as a copy editor as Em was by hers as a putative literary agent's putative assistant. This resemblance to herself made Em like Alicia more, but it made her worry that other readers wouldn't like her at all. What could they possibly find admirable in an indecisive wallflower in over her head?

Now Kate, the friend: She was a firecracker. She was funny, she was confident, she had ambition where Alicia sort of drifted through her job. She didn't agonize over a simple date; she unapologetically went out with whoever she wanted to. She was only in a few scenes, but they were all lively respites from Alicia's head. And there, Em thought. There was her first note. More Kate. Maybe less Alicia? But definitely more Kate.

Over the course of a week, whenever she wasn't sending out royalties or filing correspondence or making coffee, Em toggled between her two vastly different manuscripts, *The Big One* and *Can't Complain*, assembling the material for the two edit memos she needed to write. Having never really written an edit memo before, she was pretty nervous. Edith directed her to a few examples in the files but also said airily, "Oh, you'll feel when it's right." (Em had asked if Edith wanted to read the novels, and Edith said, "It's a little early for that, isn't it, dear?" She supposed it was good that she had autonomy, but that didn't mean she understood what she was doing.)

Her notes for Scot Salem were a bit of a mess. His book seemed so confident in itself that all Em's suggestions felt beside the point. Yes, developing the girlfriend character a little would be satisfying, but would that really transform the novel? Certainly not. Yes, the villain—a police captain simply referred to throughout as The Captain—was over the top, biblically evil, but clearly that was Scot Salem's intention, and who was she to tell him that was wrong? Take the scene in which The Captain pierced a man's cheek with an enormous hook, connected the other end to his police car, and drove through the desert dragging the man behind him, "flopping on the sand like a mackerel desperate to breathe on the deck of a trawler." Like, typing *Is this too much?* seemed absurd. Of course it was too much; that was the point. "Do you need the mackerel part?" she imagined asking, and flinched at the withering scorn with which Scot Salem would surely respond.

Meanwhile, her notes for *Can't Complain* were clear and concise. She explained that she wanted more Kate. She suggested that the novel could benefit from a sharper dramatic arc—an obstacle that Alicia could overcome, something to pierce the soft, contented tone of the book. And she asked Lucy Deming for more signs that the novel took place in the here and now, and that these characters, twenty-somethings in New York, did drugs and went to parties and had sex and just generally behaved more like twentysomethings in New York. (Not like her. Like *interesting* twentysomethings in New York.)

In lieu of getting advice from Edith she'd sought some from Emily—not that she'd asked her to read the novels, that seemed like too much, but she'd described them both and asked if she thought her notes sounded reasonable. "That book sounds rad," she said about *The Big One*, and urged her to resist the impulse to rein Scot Salem in. "He's a genius," she pointed out. "You're gonna tell a genius to spell better?" (It was true that Scot Salem was an atrocious speller.) Em struggled to explain what she found warm and welcoming in Lucy Deming's novel, and when she finished, Emily said, "It sounds like a book your mom would read."

She typed up and mailed her editorial memo to Scot Salem in Los Angeles, figuring it would take a couple of days to get there, and so she had a couple of days before he would call on the telephone. She both dreaded and thrilled at the prospect of that call. The next day she typed her notes for Lucy and put them in the mail; Lucy would get them nearly immediately, she expected. Indeed, Lucy called her the next day.

"I'm very grateful to you for such a thoughtful letter," Lucy said. Em's stomach was in knots, which surprised her; she'd thought she felt so secure about her memo, but now that she was talking to the actual writer, she was struck by her own inexperience. So she felt a tiny wave of relief when Lucy said, "I'm sure you're right that this novel would be more marketable if the characters were a little more exciting. More, as you say, 'of the moment.'"

"Oh, great," Em replied.

"Unfortunately, I just won't be able to do that," she continued.

"Oh."

"So the book's going to have to remain in its current state of un-marketability."

"Well, not *un*marketability, necessarily."

"It's just," Lucy said—"Oh, not now, honey, I'm talking on the phone—I don't really have any experience with drugs or parties or casual sex. I think the versions of them I might imagine would seem pretty foolish to people who do."

"I see."

"At first I read your memo and I thought, *Well, that makes perfect sense*, but the more I thought about it, the more I thought, *These girls in this book don't do that*."

"Well, Kate might."

"Yes, Kate. That was a good suggestion, to add more Kate. I'll try to do that. But Kate just talks a good game. She doesn't do half the things she says she does."

"She doesn't?"

"Oh, no. And I'm interested in this suggestion of yours about the characters not being so happy all the time."

"Did I say that?"

"'I think Alicia would be sad more often.' And you might be right. You might be right! But I was sad for a long time, and right now I just want to write characters who are happy."

"How did you stop being sad?" blurted Em, who felt a long way from her teenage self.

"Oh, honey," Lucy said. "I said, *It is miserable to be unhappy about things I have no control over, so I'm gonna stop*. And I got some good medication. I can give you the name of my shrink. But so you see, I have no interest in writing a bunch of unhappy characters right now."

Em had never considered the possibility that a writer could just choose what kinds of characters she wanted to write. Or that a person could just choose to be happier. Or, really, that you could just tell someone about your medication. She had prepared a number of counterarguments but instead she said, "That makes sense."

"So I understand if you think I should find another agent," Lucy said. "It does seem like we're a ways apart here."

"No," Em said. "I still like the book. I think I like it more now, actually."

"Well, the suggestion about Kate is very good. It needs two more Kate scenes, and I know exactly where they should go."

Em laughed. The idea that Lucy had converted her vague suggestion into a specific quantity of scenes was very funny, but also two scenes sounded exactly right. "Okay, so write those. I'm still a junior agent"—this was not true, she was an assistant—"so I'll need to get Edith's sign-off before I can officially take the book on"—this was definitely true—"but I'd like to."

"Well, that's lovely," Lucy said. "I like you, and I like that you had all these ideas, even if I'm too stubborn to try them."

"I like you too," Em said. She did. She did like her, and she liked saying it.

"And I don't have any other options, agent-wise. So I'm game if you are."

— ● —

Each night before she went to sleep, Emily spent ten minutes or so writing in one of her little notebooks. Em slept over sometimes, when it was late and she couldn't face the walk back down Avenue C, and she'd see Emily, in one of the huge T-shirts she wore to bed, facing the corner of the room, scribbling in the book.

The first few times Em didn't say anything. One night she finally asked Emily what it was she was writing. "Is it, like, your diary?" she asked.

Emily wrinkled her nose. Her T-shirt said STRAITJACKET FITS on the front. She swam in it, but it was likely a men's medium. "I guess," she said.

"Okay, so a journal," Em said, chastened. "Is it for ideas? For working through your feelings?"

"No, no," Emily replied, opening a shoebox on the floor and show-ing Em the dozen or so similar notebooks inside. "I've just always done it. I want to keep a record, you know?"

Em had noticed that Emily often said things like this, statements that left unstated the assumption that someday, someone would want that record. This time, she thought to make a joke of it. "Oh, for the Emily Memorial Library?" she said.

"You can have a wing, if you want."

— ● —

Everyone had produced attractive coats from their closets, except Em-ily, who wore the same army coat she wore in the summer, and Em, whose coat was the same one she had owned since senior year in high school. Em marveled at the array of coats on the subway, on the streets, all worn by impossibly lovely individuals: the brown peacoat on a tall boy whose cheekbones looked like ski slopes, the lustrous blue woolen single-breasted coat that seemed to match the eyes of that blonde reading Hermann Hesse. Even Darwin had a lovely tweed jacket with honest-to-God leather patches on the elbows. He'd worn it out to dinner the other night, and the sleeves had been soft under her hands when he'd kissed her outside the restaurant.

Edith had liked *Can't Complain* and agreed to take on the book, with Em assisting. "Now this book," she'd said, "this book I can sell." (She had not warmed to the pages from *The Big One* Em had finally gotten her to read, calling them trashy, but told Em she could con-tinue working on the book if she liked.) Em had messengered the manuscript (and the cover letter she'd painstakingly composed and revised) to six publishing houses—five chosen by Edith and, at Em's insistence and to Edith's amusement, Vintage. "There's no way," Edith had said, "and anyway, the last thing you want for this is a paperback original," but she'd added Ash Calder's name to the list of editors.

Em had listened with interest to Edith's six telephone calls to the six editors, preparing them for the submission coming their way. To the five women at commercial imprints she stressed the book's romance, its sweetness, the way readers would spark to its good-hearted characters. "I've been calling it a champagne bubble of a book," she said to one editor, taking a line straight from Em's cover letter. "It just hits you like that."

To Calder at Vintage, however, Edith had avoided any real discussion of what the book was about in favor of presenting Lucy as a kind of underutilized resource. "These idiots at Balcony had no idea what they had," she said. "She's writing books that ought to sell, and they couldn't sell her, and now she's got two novels with quotes from the *Times* and the *Atlantic*, and they're yours for a song if you invest in this one."

When Em had asked her about the divergent pitches, Edith had motioned with her empty coffee cup. While Em brought the pot and poured, she said, "I'm friends with those other editors. They know me; they know my taste. Ash Calder doesn't know me from Adam. What he does know, he doesn't like." She sipped the coffee. "He doesn't need me to tell him the book's good. He'll be the judge of that. But a chance to break a writer stuck at a small press? And a bargain? That gets his attention, at least."

Over the phone, Em told Lucy what she knew about the six houses, saving Vintage for last. "Oh yeah," Lucy said. "I have a friend who designs those covers."

"What?!" A person designed those covers? They seemed to Em to have emerged, fully formed, from the head of the zeitgeist.

"Lorraine. You'd like her."

Two weeks went by. Two editors politely rejected the book. One just plain stopped responding to Edith's calls. ("That's normal," Edith said, and Em thought for the one hundredth time at this job, that's *normal*?) But then two offers came through on the same Tuesday, and Em perched on the edge of the couch while Edith called Lucy to tell her the good news. "Ash Calder at Vintage offered five thousand dollars," she said. "Feels low to me, but people tell me that's in their normal range."

"Five thousand, got it." Lucy's voice crackled through the speaker.

"That's for paperback original. That's what they do. You'd do a re-write, Ash editing, and if that goes well and the book sells, they'll buy the two other novels."

"Also for five thousand?"

"Yes, but for both, together. And that would go to Balcony, since they own those rights. I don't know what your contract looks like with them, but you'd probably get half that money."

"It's a big deal that Ash wants to edit your book," Em cut in. "He's considered just about the best literary editor out there. People will really have to take the book seriously."

"It would be a nice change to be taken seriously," Lucy said. "Certainly I don't get any of that at home."

"Ash Calder thinks you have enormous potential as a writer."

Edith, impatient, moved on. "The better offer is from Avon. Hard-cover. Fifteen thousand. That's Vanessa Hyman. She said very nice things about the book."

"I'm going to need to ask you to tell me any nice thing she said," Lucy said over the speakerphone, laughing her *heh-heh-heh* laugh.

"She said the book is charming and urbane."

"Urbane!"

"She loves the main girl, Alicia. She *loves* Kate."

"Points to Emily."

Edith didn't know what Lucy was talking about but was not inclined to award points to Emily. "Sure, sure," she said. "What do you think?"

"Well, this seems like an easy decision," Lucy said. "Fifteen is three times as much as five, according to my crack NASA team of mathematicians."

"Who's that, dear?" Edith said. She didn't really have a sense of humor.

"That's true," Em said. "I had my guys confirm that." She found the section of her notes headed *Arguments for Vintage*. "But Vintage is still a pretty hot publishing house. You'll get reviews. You'll get attention."

"The books they publish are usually pretty edgy, right? Is Ash Calder trying to make this into *Brighter Lights, Bigger City*?"

"I don't think so. He talked with Edith a lot about focusing the scenes. And he said he wanted more of a sense of place."

"Well," Lucy said. "First of all, thank you. This is wonderful news. I can't wait to tell Donna Jorgenson what her clever daughter did."

"I'm really happy for you."

"I bet you want me to go with Vintage, right, Emily?"

"No she doesn't," said Edith.

"It's about what's best for the book," Em said, reading from her notes. "Ash Calder could take this book from good to great."

"You want to talk to the editors?" Edith asked. "We can set up a time."

The next day fall turned, somehow, to winter. By Friday, when Em took the 1 train up to Lucy's apartment from work, the puddles on the sidewalk were sheathed in ice. Em investigated one of the prints on Lucy's wall. "I don't think I knew Georgia O'Keeffe painted things that weren't flowers," she said.

"Yeah, buttes, not vaginas," said Lucy. Sarah, curled on a beanbag chair, looked up briefly from her book, then lost interest.

Outside, the branches of a small tree obscured part of the view from the front window. The leaves had mostly fallen. A gorgeous woman walked by in a long red coat. Jeez, knock it off, New York. Inside, Lucy mixed martinis in a silver cocktail shaker. "I do mine dirty, with olive juice," she said. "You?"

"Oh, I don't really like olives," Em said, and restrained a wince. What a childish thing to say.

"Honey, you have to learn to like olives." Lucy's voice was kind, but Em felt the familiar poke of being corrected by a mother.

While Lucy was rummaging in the refrigerator, Em asked Sarah, "Do *you* like olives?"

Sarah looked at her levelly. "I positively devour olives," she said.

"If you've only ever had olives from a jar you bought at the Piggly Wiggly, you haven't had olives," Lucy said, placing a plate shaped like a bee on the table between them. The plate was stacked with olives in red, green, and black. "This might be the one thing I am truly willing to argue about."

"You love to argue," said Sarah.

"*You* love to argue," Lucy said. "I hate it. But I have to do it, because I'm your mother. The key," she continued to Em, holding up an olive, "is that this is fruit. It's a fruit that has been cured in brine, but never forget you are eating a fruit. And so in each olive you find *that* flavor."

She was still mothering Em, but Em didn't mind it so much. In part it was because her own mother never talked about food this way, as something to deliver pleasure. For Em's mother, food was either something you ate while being good (a salad, salmon, yogurt) or that made you bad (ice cream, potato chips, eggs). So she took an olive from the plate, felt its softness between her fingers, and popped it into her mouth. It was sharp and bitter, yes, but there was something underneath that, something that reminded her of a flower. Lucy was right that it certainly didn't taste like any other olive she'd ever had.

"What do I do with the pit?" she asked, pit tucked into her cheek.

"Put it in here," Lucy said, holding out a little bowl. "Fancy people think you need to take it out of your mouth with your fingers, but you're allowed to just spit it."

"It was good," Em said. "But I still don't want olive juice in my martini."

They toasted Lucy's novel. Lucy held her glass out once more and added, "And to Emily, my agent."

"Edith's your agent," Em said.

"Please," Lucy replied. "Her signature's on the letter, but you wrote the letter. You found the book. You're the agent."

Em felt herself beaming. The martini had cleared her sinuses right up.

Lucy crossed her legs. "I'm going to take the Avon offer," she said. "I liked Vanessa okay. I get that Ash is a genius. But it's just the money."

"I totally get it."

"I want to spend next year writing a new book. I don't want to spend it *focusing my scenes*. Plus fifteen grand gives me six months off writing electrocution warnings for clock radios."

"I'm really happy for you," Em said, and she was. The martini helped with that. Em took another olive. "I guess I do like these," she added.

Lucy drained her martini. "I'm gonna tell you a secret," she said. "At some point, you stop caring about your enormous potential."

— ● —

One evening in November, Em had plans to see the new Terry Gilliam movie with Emily after work. Even though the Bowery was a tree-less wasteland, leaves still swirled around the sidewalk as Em walked south from Houston. The theater company where Emily interned was letting her use their studio space at odd hours to rehearse. She had assembled a cast for *medea:abridged* and said she planned to rehearse through the winter for a week of performances in the spring.

When Em eased the door to the studio open and crept in, an actor and an actress were facing each other while Emily kneeled at their feet. The actress held the actor's hands and seemed to be apologizing. Em sat down and listened.

"I was the fool," the actress said. "I should have been sharing your plans—no, I should have been advancing them."

"What are those plans?" Emily murmured from below.

The actress blinked out of character and looked down at Emily. "To . . ." she said. "To advance the family's prospects."

"But what does that mean?"

"I don't know," the actress admitted.

"This marriage would secure the throne of Corinth for Jason. It's a move that's about *power*."

"So," the actress said, frowning, "I'm telling him I should have been conspiring with him. But why would he believe me?"

"Medea is not some weak *mother*," Emily said, standing up. She started pacing, a sure sign in Em's experience that a potentially brilliant soliloquy was upcoming. She took her notebook out of her bag. "The nurse fears what Medea is capable of. Everyone has heard the stories from Colchis. You betrayed your father, you killed your brother. To these people, you're always an outsider, always a threat, because within you is the cunning of a poisoner and the power of the gods. Why do you think they want to exile you? It's not that you're crazy. It's that you've already shown yourself capable of subverting the dominant power structure." Medea nodded, rapt. "You're trying to convince Jason that you're actually the perfect partner for his plot. That's how you enact your plan. Start again from there."

Medea closed her eyes, then opened them, and when she spoke there was new steel in her voice. She was no longer pleading, Em could hear; she was promising. "No, I should have been advancing them," she said. She dropped Jason's hands and averted her gaze. "I should be waiting in your bed—"

"No!" Emily said. "Don't look away. Give it to him full in the face."

"But it's so humiliating that she has to say that!" the actress protested.

"You slew a goddamn dragon!" Emily shouted. "This worm is nothing!"

The actress laughed in disbelief. But the next time through, as she met Jason's eyes and told him, "I should be waiting in your bed, and happily taking care of your new bride," Em felt a little chill. It was this moment she thought of years later, when she saw the same actress playing a murderous pharmacist on *Law & Order*.

On the way to the movie, Emily, still keyed up, talked her way through her production's final moments, when Medea is supposed to appear in the chariot of the gods holding her dead children. "At first, I thought, *Well, we're on a bridge, the way to do that is to put her on a boat below*. But it turns out the Brooklyn Bridge is a hundred feet above the river. Did you know that?"

"Basically," Em said.

"So now I'm thinking she should be in a pedicab."

Em had been surprised by the Emily she'd just seen, the patient, decisive person who drew performances out of those actors they hadn't felt capable of delivering. Usually when Emily talked about her actors she discussed them as impediments to what she wanted to accomplish, blunt instruments who needed the forge of Emily's focused attention, if only she had time and resources enough. This seemed unkind to the actors, who surely had their own ideas for the characters Emily was asking them to play, but for the first time she saw how Emily's idea of herself might evolve into an actual artistic process.

But why did it have to be on the Brooklyn Bridge! She admired the grandiosity of Emily's vision for her art, for her future. It was just that she feared it might not actually happen. Emily felt no such fear.

The line outside the Angelika wrapped around the corner. "Ugh," Emily said. "I don't want to wait in line for this movie. I'm only seeing it for Amanda Plummer anyway."

"You slew a goddamn dragon!" Em yelled, making a few nearby moviegoers jump. "You can stand in a line with me!"

"That's fair," said Emily.

— • —

Emily didn't like Darwin, and when he broke it off with Em, just before Thanksgiving, she told Em she was better off without him. "He was middlebrow," Emily said over the phone.

Em, sitting in her old room in Wausau, looked around at the posters of bands and TV stars she'd loved in high school and bit her tongue about Darwin's middlebrow-ness. Instead, she complained about his height. "When I met him at the Strand he was up behind the counter and I didn't realize just how *short* he was," she said. On their first date, Em had insufficiently masked her surprise when he arrived, three inches shorter than her, all dressed up like a boy at confirmation.

Her mom had paid for a plane ticket so she could come back to the Midwest for Thanksgiving. She certainly could never have afforded it on her own. Em had asked Edith for a raise, citing the Lucy deal, and Edith had told her it was too early, that she should try again on her one-year anniversary. "But don't worry," she'd said. "You'll get a bonus when that contract is signed. That's standard." (In February, Edith would hand her a hundred-dollar bill, and it would take Em days to find someplace that would break it.)

Emily was still in New York. She had no interest in going back to Georgia, she said, and no money to do it anyway. "I think that's really brave, to keep those people out of your life," Em said. "Maybe for Christmas you should come here." She had assumed the precise position she'd always taken while talking to friends on the telephone in high school: sitting on the carpet, back to the wall, twirling the coiled, springy cord around her finger. She could even see the spots on the cord where her ceaseless twisting had stretched it permanently.

"Ah, Warsaw in winter," Emily said. "I guess at least you'll have heat." Joe and the rest of the guys had not yet managed to install radiators; the money had gone toward the Sunrise Squat legal fund instead, as the city had sent letters to residents threatening a March eviction.

Em had worried that being separated from Emily for a week would hurt their friendship. In fact, they talked even more now than they did in New York. Even on Thanksgiving Em had snuck away from the living room, where her sister's husband was talking about their retirement accounts, to call Emily. Now that the holiday was past—her sister back in Milwaukee, her mom mooning around downstairs—they stayed on the phone for hours. By the time her mom saw the phone bill, Em reasoned, she would be long gone.

On Saturday her mom drove them to Milwaukee to meet her sister for lunch. Such visits had sometimes been torturous, her sister going on about the renovations they were making to their gigantic house. Em resented her sister's husband for making her so boring. But this time Em was looking forward to the lunch.

The cavernous Coffee Trader on Downer was packed with middle-aged ladies. "Do they have places like this in New York, honey?" her mom asked.

"This is pretty big for New York," Em said. Her mother nodded, satisfied.

Her sister bustled in ten minutes late, carrying a shopping bag. "Parking is crazy around here!" she said. "I had to pay for a lot! On the East Side!" She hugged them both, pulled off her gigantic coat, laid it atop the others on the fourth chair. When the waitress came, she ordered a decaf.

"A decaf?" her mom asked.

Anne-Marie lifted an eyebrow at Em. Their mother was hyperalert to any possible sign of pregnancy. All Thanksgiving she'd hounded Anne-Marie about how she wasn't drinking wine, until she'd finally snapped, "Mom, I don't need the empty calories!"

"Em," Anne-Marie said. She'd been conscientious to stick to the name Em had told them all she was now going by. "Tell me about this book deal. I feel like I only heard a little bit about it."

"Lucy is over the moon," her mom said.

Em retold the story, leaving out her disappointment at Lucy's decision against Vintage. "And I've got one other novel that I might be able to convince Edith to send out in the spring," she added.

"Oh, is that the one about the drugs?" her mom asked. "The Los Angeles book."

"How did you remember that?"

"Emily, I remember everything you ever tell me."

"Okay, okay."

"Always listening."

She told Anne-Marie more about *The Big One*. "I don't get it, but I believe you," Anne-Marie said. "Okay, before the food comes, I have an early Christmas present." She pulled a box from the shopping bag and set it on the table before their mom.

"Oh, how sweet!" she said, working a finger underneath the tape. "I don't have anything for you yet. You two are hard enough to buy for—oh!" For inside the box was a T-shirt, and on the T-shirt was printed GRANDMA. "Anne-Marie!" she said, an edge of hysteria in her voice.

Anne-Marie grinned and nodded over at Em, who had unbuttoned her flannel shirt to reveal, beneath it, her own T-shirt reading AUNTIE EM. Their mother looked at them both and burst instantly into tears, like Holly Hunter in *Broadcast News*.

"Mom!" Anne-Marie said.

"I'm j-j-j-just s-s-s-so *happy*," their mother bawled. "My two g-g-*girls*."

Anne-Marie hugged her and Em joined in. "Mom, you look like the Beatles just died or something," she said.

Anne-Marie explained that they'd been waiting for the amnio results—her OB-GYN had been nervous about certain tests, she said—but everything had come through okay, so they were moving ahead. "I had a miscarriage last year," she said to Em. "It was really early, but it was still terrible."

Em put her hand on her sister's arm. It stung that she hadn't known about the miscarriage, but she had been very moved when her sister had called her and asked her what she wanted her T-shirt to say.

"It's just perfect," her mom said, calming down. "One of you building a career in the big city. And one of you with a *baby*."

"I also have a career, Mom," Anne-Marie said. She had just gotten her real estate license.

"And I have a baby! Just kidding," said Em as they both looked at her, horrified. "I don't know why I said that. Obviously I am one hundred years away from a baby."

As they drove back to Wausau, Em looked out the window at the dirty white pastures lining the highway. "It doesn't have to be a *hundred* years," her mom said.

When her mom was her age, she'd already married her father and had Anne-Marie. Darwin was just the third guy Em had slept with, and she'd really only done it because she felt bad about being surprised at his height. "I'm fine, Mom," she said.

When they got home, there was a long message on the answering machine from Emily. She sounded drunk but happy. "I'm at Rob's!" she said. Rob, Em knew, was a guy Emily bought coke from sometimes, one of the cast of characters Emily liked to tell stories about. Rob was notable, she said, for being the politest drug dealer she had ever met. "We're celebrating. Rob. Rob! What's your phone number?" In the background, a male voice said some numbers, which Emily duly repeated into the phone. When Em looked at what she'd written down, she counted nine digits. "That seems like a lot of numbers," Emily said from the machine. "Anyway, I'm good. I'm warm! It's good here. I love you. Okay!"

— ● —

Lucy invited Em to a holiday get-together at her friend Lorraine's house. The cab let them out on a magical street in the Village, a crooked rectangle that looked positively Dickensian, but quaint, not squalid. "Oh yes, I love it here," said Lucy. "Thank Jane Jacobs. Without her this would be an overpass."

Em, who had only recently learned about Jane Jacobs from Lucy, nodded. She got it now, what Jacobs had been trying to preserve.

The front door was hidden in a corner by the Cherry Lane Theatre. "I think this will mostly be artist types," Lucy said as they deliberately made their way up the stairs to the third floor. "That's who Lorraine and Danny hang out with. He's a designer, too." In confirmation, the man who opened the apartment door wore round glasses and a black beret. He greeted Lucy boisterously.

"My dear!" he cried. "What have you brought for us?"

"Just some gingerbread," Lucy said, holding up a paper bag.

"Oh thank the Lord. And a friend, of course?"

"This is Emily," she said, then leaned in confidingly. "She's a fan of your wife."

"Who isn't?" the man said. "I'm Danny. Come in."

Inside the apartment, about fifteen people were crammed into a small living room. Lucy exchanged hugs with most of them while Emily took the coats into the master bedroom and tossed them atop a pile. When she returned, the focus of the party had settled onto the bag of gingerbread, making its way around the circle.

"Shit, that's good," a man said.

"Is it a secret recipe?" someone asked.

"I don't believe in secret recipes," Lucy proclaimed.

The room fell back into a tumult of separate conversations, and Lucy led her over to a small woman with a black bob. She was wearing a beautiful black blouse and bright red pants. They greeted each other with kisses on each cheek, then Lucy turned to introduce Em. "This is Lorraine," she said.

"Your home is beautiful," Em said. It really was: elegantly lit and furnished, careful but not fussy. She'd never really thought of herself as having any particular opinions about interior design, but meeting Lorraine, she suddenly realized that she did, and they matched hers.

In the living room, the various conversations had coalesced into one large discussion of the Soviet Union's fall. The partygoers, all of them older than Em, expressed disbelief at the speed with which the USSR had dissolved. "I think one thing is clear," a man declared. "Reagan was a genius." He laughed as a chorus of boos rained down.

Lucy tugged at her arm. "Come on upstairs," she said. "Lorraine has something to show you."

The fourth floor of the narrow building housed the couple's design studios, two cozy rooms with drawing boards and paper everywhere. In one, a Macintosh computer whirred, somehow both squat and sleek. In her studio, Lorraine stood in front of a flat file, pulling out oversized folders. "Most of my originals for my Vintage Contemporaries designs are in the Random House files," she said. "But I have a few of my concept drawings." She laid the folder down on her drawing table and turned on the lamp.

Inside the folder were a half-dozen variations on a Raymond Carver collection, in colored pencil and marker, photographs and drawings collaged together with type. "You'll see at first I was doing something a lot more homespun, but the more I worked at it the more I focused on this logo here"—she pointed at the little sphere, flanked by horizontal lines, that appeared on every one of the company's books—"and that ended up being the thing that led me to the final design."

"This is amazing," Em said to Lucy, who clapped delightedly.

"Lucy tells me you're a literary agent?"

"I'm an assistant," Em said. Lucy snorted. "I love so many of these books. I'm so impressed!"

"Lorraine, this was almost my book," Lucy said. "Em here wanted me to sell it to Vintage. You could have designed it!"

Lorraine smiled. "Well, it probably wouldn't be me. They've started altering the design." When Em asked her why, she said only, "Tastes change."

A young woman came up the stairs. "Ms. Lorraine?" she asked. "Do you want to say good night to the girls?" Turning the lights off, Lorraine introduced the woman, her babysitter for the night, whose parents were down at the party.

"How old are your kids?" Em asked as they walked back downstairs.

"One's two, and the other was born this summer," Lorraine said. "It's been pretty busy, so in a way it's better that Vintage is having other people design the books right now. Or so I tell myself," she added darkly. "Do you like working in publishing?" she asked Em.

"I think so," Em said. "But I'm nowhere near the level you are."

"Me?" Lorraine laughed. "I'm at no level. Designers are the bottom of the pile. To be honest, I'm getting a little sick of designing for books. I want to be doing something of my own, not arguing with everyone on the sales team about fonts."

"What do you mean?" Em said. "Would you *stop* working with books?"

"There's nothing special about books," Lorraine said. She saw Em's face and laughed. "I'm sorry, you're obviously a true believer! But to me they're intriguing design challenges, dense with information, but also frustrating. I don't mind the idea that I might do something else."

Em shook her head. "But don't you love *making* something that will last forever?"

Lorraine smiled. "Stop by a Goodwill sometime and tell me any of these books will last forever," she said. "What I love about it is when an author feels like I really *got* their book. That's satisfying, to know that you're helping someone feel understood."

"What else would you do?" Lucy asked.

"I've got my hands plenty full now with these two," Lorraine said outside her children's bedroom. "But there are plenty of corporate clients out there who are just as annoying to design for but who pay way better. Or maybe I'll just do something else entirely. Excuse me, I gotta help put these girls to bed."

In the living room, Em poured herself a glass of wine and stood by the door. The babysitter sat on the floor at her parents' feet and held forth on her school orchestra's trip to Moscow a few years before. It struck Em that this college-aged babysitter was undoubtedly more at home with these people than she would ever be. She had made actual friends this year, but she didn't have a community, exactly, not like these people did.

"I hope that wasn't discouraging," Lucy murmured. She clinked glasses with Em. "Cheers, my dear. Thank you for making my year a good one."

Em focused on Lucy. Her eyes were bright and her hair was a frizzy halo around her head. She was positively beaming. Here was a person whom Em had understood, whose writing she was helping into the world. She wasn't getting credit for it, but maybe she could do without the credit—Lucy knew, and Em knew that she knew.

"I'm glad I met you this year," Em said, and drank her wine.

— • —

The next weekend, Emily told Em they were going to Maine.

"Maine?"

"Maine. And bring Louis."

Somehow Emily had gotten hold of a car, a red Toyota Tercel with a curving scar down the passenger side that made the car appear as if it had defeated a samurai in battle. "Whose car is this?" Em asked when she and Louis met Emily in front of the squat at six o'clock Sunday morning.

"Frank from my building. He let me borrow it for the weekend. Hi, Louis." When Em had told Louis about Emily's crazy plan, to protest AIDS at the president's retreat in Kennebunkport, he'd somehow already known all about it and had immediately agreed to come. It was only then that Em got the impression that this was not just some scheme of Emily's but an actual thing.

"They've been planning this for months," Louis shouted from the backseat as they sped across the Triborough Bridge. Em had been nominated to drive, since she had a license and Emily did not. The sky was an intense blue, unmarked by clouds. "They booked hotel rooms, they planned the route. They've been buying supplies for weeks."

"Supplies?"

"Water, stretchers, drums, first aid kits, signs," Emily said. She wore enormous sunglasses. "Speaking of signs—there's a bunch of stuff in the trunk for us to make some."

"Are we actually gonna, like, protest on Bush's lawn?"

"No way they let us get that close," Louis said. "I'm sure there'll be cops all over."

Cops? Em had not thought of this, really. "Are we—are they going to arrest people?"

"Hell yeah," Emily said.

As Em drove Emily fought a constant battle between the noise from the car and the noise she wanted to play from the car's stereo. The result was that it soon became loud enough in the car that no one could talk at all. So they rode across Connecticut and through Massachusetts listening to a series of mix tapes Emily popped into the tape deck. "I'm going for a PROTEST VIBE," she said when side A of one tape ended with Bob Dylan. Side B began with someone hollering, "This is a public service announcement . . . with guitar!"

"This is great," said Louis from the backseat. "Very macho. But I have also brought some tapes."

"You can play your tapes when you drive," Emily replied. "Right now, the ladies are in charge." Em did not point out that she was the lady driving while Emily was the lady choosing the music. At a rest stop north of Boston, they switched seats and Louis put in Madonna.

The farther north they drove, the higher the pine trees seemed to tower over them. When Louis exited off 95 to head east toward Kennebunkport and the sea, they drove through thick marshland and forest. "God?" said Madonna on the stereo, and Emily said, "Yes, Madonna?" and then they all shouted along with "Like a Prayer."

Em imagined that Kennebunkport was usually pretty sleepy this time of year, but today there was so much traffic they couldn't even get to the center of town. Louis parked at a gas station and they unloaded the trunk. The sky was bright and it was hearteningly mild, a late-fall day in early winter. Louis swept his coat over his shoulders and waved cheerily at the middle-aged man in khakis gassing up his sedan. "Act up, you rascal!" Louis called. "Fight AIDS!" The three of them scrawled messages on the blank signs Emily had brought: 1,000 POINTS OF LIGHT, Louis wrote on one side, 100,000 DEAD on the other. Emily's was short and to the point: FUCK BUSH.

Em didn't know what to write but couldn't bear the idea of asking. She finally decided on READ MY LIPS, FIGHT AIDS. "Oh, that's good," Emily said.

"I guess stuff's that way?" Em said, pointing in the direction that everyone seemed to be walking. They joined the crowds headed across the bridge toward the center of town. Most were fit, smiling men Em's age or a little older. But there were also a lot of women, some there with same-sex partners but others who looked as straight and out of place as Em felt.

Soon there were chants, which helped. Chanting was a thing she could do. "We need more than points of light! Health care is a right!" she chanted. Soon that disintegrated and was replaced by "Act up! Fight back! Fight AIDS!" Then a man shouted, "How many more?" and everyone called, "Ask George!"

For Em, AIDS remained a thing she encountered mostly in culture as opposed to real life. She didn't know anyone who was infected, or at least she didn't know that she did. Mostly, what Em knew about was famous people: Ryan White, Rock Hudson, Liberace. She'd read *Borrowed Time*, which she'd found harrowing, and had steered clear of *And the Band Played On*, which was enormous.

Back in Wisconsin AIDS was barely a topic of conversation, a death sentence not to be discussed. At college she'd spent some time with Louis at the campus gay-straight alliance, where boys talked about using condoms and once they'd all picketed a talk by a bigoted preacher. But here in her new city, she knew the disease seemed epidemic; Louis, who was new to town like her but had started volunteering with a care group, told her that people were dying every day. "Aren't you scared to, like, touch them?" Em had asked quietly. "It doesn't spread that way," he snapped. Then a moment later, he said, "Yeah, it's kinda scary."

She worried about him, in people's homes, bringing them food. (She tried not to worry about herself, in her home, with him. She knew the chances of transmission were impossibly low. Still, she didn't tell her mom anything about Louis's volunteering.) And she worried about him out in the city. In college he had had one boyfriend, Tim, who broke up with Louis to go to business school. They'd never been the kinds of friends who talked about their sex lives, such as they were, but one night as he was dressing to go out to a club she'd knocked on his door and asked, tentatively, "Are you being careful?" He put his hands on her shoulders and said, "Emily, I'm too frightened to do anything with anyone." Which was comforting but also miserable in a different way.

So here at the march Em particularly watched the men who were sick as they made their way along with the crowd, afforded space by their fellow protestors not out of fear but out of respect. A man in a wheelchair held a scepter and wore a crown. Several very thin guys walked deliberately, friends hovering at their arms just in case. One wore a shirt that read, STILL ALIVE, NO THANKS TO YOU BITCHES, with a photo of Reagan and Bush.

How determined the set of their jaws, how high their heads! She searched their faces for fear and found none. Em felt certain that in their position she'd be a wreck. She'd be back in Wisconsin in a flash. Ugh, what a thing to know about yourself. Even the bravery it took to care for someone dying—she was in awe of Louis, who was in turn in awe of the men who stayed with their lovers when things went bad. She didn't think she had it in her.

A beautiful man in a fur coat saw Emily's sign, laughed, and started a "FUCK BUSH" chant. Emily was delighted. Em found it liberating to shout "fuck." They were in the center of town now, and the square seemed filled with people. Was it five hundred? A thousand? Emily told them she'd heard someone say that they'd protested outside the Bushes' church this morning, blowing whistles from the street while the president was at the service inside. "Oh, the poor priests," Em said, and Emily rolled her eyes. "Fuck the poor priests!" she sang, to the cadence of "Fuck the Police."

The square was surrounded by police officers. Many of them chatted with locals or protestors, but some stood ramrod straight, stared ahead unsmiling like guards at Buckingham Palace. A few traded barbs with protestors, and one scuffle broke out when a cop said something horrible. As his friends pulled him away, the incensed protestor who'd gotten into it with the officer shouted, "Yeah, and you're a pig!" The crowd booed and oinked at the officer until he left the square. When Em thought about the police at all, which most of the time she did not, it was as friendly protectors, someone who would naturally be on Em's side. It was a strange feeling to see them as adversaries. Their presence on the square felt oppressive, and Em wasn't sure how she should act. As she walked to a deli to get them some lunch, one officer grinned at her and said, "Why are you here, beautiful?" She stared at the ground and walked past him as fast as she could. "Well, fuck you, then," he said, conversationally.

They ate bananas and drank Diet Coke while sitting on a park bench. Emily was in her third month reading something old and Russian and explained it to them avidly. "It's so incredibly *forbidding*," she said.

"Why would you want a book to be forbidding?" Em asked.

"The problem with most books written today—"

"Oh my God," said Louis.

"—is that they're far *too* accessible. You just cruise through it, skimming along, and when you're done you think, *Oh, I'm so smart.* But the great books don't make you feel smart. They illuminate how *little* you actually know."

"That sounds like a nightmare reading experience to me," said Louis.

"Yeah, I mean, you're a philistine."

He sat up, offended. "I'm a *sodomite*," he said.

Then the crowd started moving, slowly, to the south. "We're headed to the compound!" Emily said. "I wonder how close we get."

Wherever it was, they didn't really get close. They marched for about fifteen minutes down Ocean Avenue, a chill wind off the sea blowing Em's sign sideways. Beautiful houses lined the road, tall white homes with black shutters and flagpoles with American flags snapping in the wind. Em thought how much she'd love to have a house like that, right on the ocean. Some of the senior editors Edith did business with had country places; she'd heard from a friend that some summers one woman invited junior staffers up for a barbecue and swim. Em found the idea both thrilling and horrifying.

The crowd massed, stopped moving; up ahead, word filtered back, were barricades manned by Secret Service. The crowd spilled off the road onto the perfect lawns. Organizers arrived at their part of the street and asked everyone to clear more space; men began assembling something with poles and canvas. "Are they making more signs?" Em asked.

"They're stretchers," Louis said.

A man in a shirt reading SILENCE=DEATH approached them, holding two poles. "You're three?" he asked. "Perfect. We're carrying people up to the front, as close as we can get." He handed the poles to Louis.

"It's a die-in," Emily explained. "It's a tactic. People will be bodies out on the street for like ten minutes or something."

"Two of us carry, one of us lies there," Louis said. He looked at them both. "I don't know that you two can lift me."

Em said, quickly, "Um, me either. Maybe it should be Emily."

"Yeah, I'll die!" Emily said, with enthusiasm. Louis unrolled the stretcher on the ground and Emily lay down. Louis took the front, Em took the back. The chants, the whistles, the drums had stopped, and her heartbeat was loud in her head. Her arms burned. Huffing and puffing, she helped carry Emily to the street, then set her down as gently as she could between two men who were already lying, eyes closed, on the pavement.

Louis put his arm around her as they picked their way back up the grassy slope. Below them stretched a sea of bodies, mostly still, arms thrown over eyes to block the sun, heads resting on the bellies of compatriots. They filled the road all the way back to the bend. She could hear gulls in the distance, a news helicopter. One man beat out a funereal rat-a-tat on a bongo drum. She turned for a moment to wipe her eyes and saw police officers standing in front of the perfect white house, and a man and a woman up on the deck, watching the show. She turned her back on them.

In the middle of all those bodies, Emily: impossibly small, lovely, the sun bright on her coat and face. It was the first time, Em thought, she had ever seen her friend completely still.

After the die-in they sat on the rich people's lawn. Now that it appeared they wouldn't be arrested, Em had begun to relax and feel proud of her participation. The sense of occasion had been thrilling, the cause was just, and the people-watching now was unparalleled. Two elegant drag queens walked by, their platform heels dangling from their fingers, their giant feet padding through the grass.

"Thanks for making this happen," Em said to Emily. "I didn't understand, but I understand a little better now."

Emily looked past her, narrowed her eyes. "Holy shit," she said.

"What?" Louis asked.

"That woman walking the dog. That's gotta be Bush's daughter."

"His what?" Em twisted around to look. A woman in her thirties, wearing casual slacks and a striped shirt, was walking a springer spaniel. "Wait, is that Millie the dog?"

"Why do you know that dog's name?" Louis asked.

"The dog wrote, like, a book," Em said. "It was a bestseller."

"You have got to be kidding me."

"We should ask if the dog needs a new literary agent," Emily suggested. She stood up, brushed herself off.

"Emily, don't do anything," Em pleaded. "We don't know anything about this woman."

"If she's really Bush's daughter, she's got Secret Service climbing out of her fanny pack," pointed out Louis.

"We don't even know if she's really his daughter!"

"Oh, she is," Emily hissed. "She looks rich as hell."

"Everyone here is rich!" Em said.

"What a fucking golden opportunity," Emily said. "And you're too scared." She walked away without a word.

"Oh, come on," Em said. But Emily was following the woman, keeping her distance, her hands in her pockets like the illustration in the dictionary for *nonchalant*. The woman and her dog disappeared around a curve, and Emily disappeared, too.

"What do we do now?" Em asked.

"Oh, bless her heart," Louis said. "She is gonna be in such deep shit. All we can do is meet her by the car, right? But first let's get something to eat. I could eat twenty lobsters."

"How many lobsters can we afford?"

"Zero point five lobsters," he said.

They split a lobster roll and a beer in the square. "What does she think she's doing?" Em asked.

"Look, I don't know your girl that well," Louis said. "But she seems like a spark plug."

"It's not going to do any good to yell at the president's daughter!"

"Oh, I don't know," Louis said. "She's definitely doing something."

"If it even is the president's daughter."

"But why should she feel comfortable, whether she's the president's daughter or not?" Louis asked. "I'm proud of that die-in, but I also appreciate a little spicy individual action. Even if the whole reason she did it is for her, not for us."

"She did it because she loves being a pain in the ass."

"Yes. And she loves being the one person who's right."

When they got back to where they'd parked the car around four, it was gone. After a miserable hour, Louis cadged them a ride to the Bronx from a cute nurse who dropped them off at the Grand Concourse. They didn't get home until after midnight.

"I got someone to drive the car back," Emily said when a frantic Em finally got her on the phone.

"Why didn't you wait for us?" Em asked, marveling that she even needed to say such a thing out loud.

"Honestly, I assumed you'd already gone home. You bailed on me, after all."

"You ditched us to harass someone who was maybe George Bush's daughter! What are you talking about!"

"It was her," Emily said. "I fucking gave it to her. A bunch of cops had to separate us."

"Jesus Christ. What did you say?"

"I said her dog may be a bitch, but her dad's a cunt."

"Emily!"

When she told Louis about this, he put his cereal spoon down and said, "She cursed at the president's *dog*?" He laughed. "That girl is crazy. Respect."

2005

The Heart Unstrung

t was their first night out since the baby had been born, and as they stood underneath the cinema marquee, all they could talk about was her. The baby, Jane, was being looked after by Alan's brother and his husband, and she had not cried at all when Alan had handed her over—a sign, Alan declared, that Jane was okay with them having a date. "She wants us to be happy," he said.

Emily pointed out that notion ran contrary to all the evidence of the past few months. They had deceived their child, she said, had failed to prepare her for the separation to come. Now she worried over the falsely cheerful kisses they had offered smiling, drooling Jane, the way they had wordlessly conspired to both simply stand by the door at the same time, *Oh, you're by the door too? And you have your purse? Maybe we'll just*—and then walked out together, as if the idea to step away had just occurred to them. The old Irish goodbye. She always thought of it as the Emily exit, for her former friend, who didn't believe in goodbyes.

"This is the kind of betrayal you never get over," Emily said now.

"I bet she isn't even crying," Alan replied.

They'd been discussing it all week. Dinner and drinks had evolved, when they realized they didn't care about drinks, into dinner and a movie, which had in turn evolved into movie and a movie when they realized that all they truly wanted to do was sit in the dark in a movie theater as long as possible, until Emily's breasts couldn't take it another moment. The Moviefone guy's voice had been like hearing from an old lover.

Alan said, "If I call them right now and say, 'Is she crying?' they will be like, 'No.'"

"They said not to call," Emily said.

"They were very firm on that point," Alan agreed. In fact Derreck, Alan's brother, had interrupted their long explanations of how the baby never ate and never slept to tell them that if they called him even once while they were out for the night, he would turn their baby upside down and just hold her like that.

"Like a rain stick," he'd said.

"Ha ha," she'd said, and Alan had interjected, "But seriously don't shake her."

It was just as well, she thought as the ticket taker waved them through, that they didn't go to dinner. The subway ride down had been nearly wordless—a lovely, exhausted silence that might, if it had continued over a table at a restaurant, have become worrisome. They were both far too tired to make conversation, could barely remember what, just a few months ago, they had ever made conversation about. A conversation implied you had stored some things up to say to the other person, when in their current states they were prone to saying precisely how they felt at the moment they felt it: "I would give anything to take a nap right now," or "We are the worst fucking parents in the world," or "I love her so much I want to die."

The first movie was a sex comedy. Emily had chosen it based on its short running time. She laughed more than he did; during one extremely filthy scene she found her mind drifting to the previous night, when they themselves had had sex for the first time since the baby had been born. "Considering the state of my perineum," Emily had said as they held each other afterward, "that was pretty good." Maybe they would have sex again tonight. Maybe she should have scheduled the sex comedy second.

They skipped the closing credits; Emily had timed their evening precisely, and if they hurried to the theater across the street they'd make it into the second movie in the middle of the trailers. The honks of the cabs on Forty-Second Street seemed just a component of the summer air, thickening it as flour might thicken a sauce. Emily had only been down to Midtown once since the baby had been born, for an unsatisfying visit to her office during which Peter, her boss, had commented on how *easy* a baby Jane was, how she was lucky, because she'd be able to get back to work sooner than the other women at St. Martin's who'd had babies.

The second movie was a nature documentary about penguins: penguins perching on cliffs, penguins gaily slipping over the ice, penguins shitting literally everywhere. Penguin mothers raising penguin chicks so soft and round they looked like Koosh. It quickly became clear that for all their frolicsome waddling about the surf, penguin chicks were at every instant in mortal danger. "This chick can't find his mother," the narrator intoned, "and he's in trouble if he strays too far from the group." The baby penguin peeped with alarm as it scampered across the rocks. A great gull wheeled overhead. A walrus lurked in the dark sea.

As one, Alan and Emily stood and fled down the aisle. Instead of watching the end of the film, they bought Häagen-Dazs.

"Did I choose that movie?" asked Emily on the train back uptown. "Why wasn't there a warning?"

"Three months ago that wouldn't have bothered me even a little bit," marveled Alan.

"A whole new world has opened up," said Emily. "A whole new world of things that will upset us."

Alan took her hand. "I'm really happy," he said. It was true. Emily knew that Alan viewed this essential transformation of himself as a great gift. "I know you're having a hard time, but I'm really happy about us."

"Go team," Emily said wearily. "We should have probably just gone to one movie."

She rested her head on his shoulder from 145th all the way to 207th. She thought about the small life, not exactly a person but possessing definite person-like qualities, that awaited them in their apartment. She couldn't believe she had let her out of her sight for even a moment; she couldn't believe their escape was already almost over. She *was* having a hard time—she felt as though her emotional volume had been turned up two or three notches, so that what might have once provoked a smile now caused a rush of delight, and events that might have once slightly annoyed now made her, for wild moments, unspeakably sad. It didn't help that she'd stopped taking her meds while breastfeeding. She'd need to talk to her doctor about that.

But she also felt as though underneath the messy soaring and diving melody of her emotional state was a steady undertone of—happiness? For the past ten years or so, happiness had often been something she felt she was wearing, not feeling, but she guessed that's what it was. Contentment, maybe. It was solid as Alan's shoulder under her cheek, his leg pressed against hers, rocking with the train's motion.

Their apartment was in Inwood, at the northern tip of Manhattan island, a neighborhood that was in the city but was woodsy and quiet. They lived there because when the broker Alan's old firm had recommended had asked her what neighborhood she wanted to live in and what her budget was, Emily had said "Manhattan" and "maybe $150,000?" and the broker had laughed. He referred them to a junior broker, who also laughed, but said, "Well, there is this *one* neighborhood."

Emily loved it. From the 207th Street station they climbed the stairs into the park, walking from island to island of light. This late on a summer night the park still had a few families running around, the kids working off the last of their energy before bed. Emily watched the moms, watched them watch their kids, tried to imagine Jane turning, as one girl did, clumsy cartwheels across the grass. Could Jane ever be her? Could Emily ever be one of those moms? It seemed impossible, yet just a year ago the idea of having a baby at all had seemed absurd, and here she was.

When they opened the apartment door, Alan's brother greeted them with a chipper hello. The baby, he reported, was great. Everyone said it was so *hard* to take care of a baby, but actually it was a piece of cake. Jane had drunk nine ounces from her bottle and then slept the entire time they were gone.

"The *entire* time?" Alan asked.

"*Nine ounces?*" Emily asked. From the next room, the baby made a noise like a balloon deflating and started to cry.

Emily felt the milk rising at the sound and went into the bedroom, where Jane wailed in the dark. Derreck or Eric had made a game attempt at a swaddle, but Jane had wriggled almost all the way free, except that one arm was trapped against her body while the other, fist closed, stood up in a pose Emily smiled to see resembled a Black Power salute. She picked her up, freed her arm, changed her amazingly heavy diaper, sat in the glider, maneuvered Jane into place, watched with the same wonder she always felt as the baby found the pencil eraser of her nipple and latched on. Mostly she hated nursing, hated how hard it was, hated the blocked ducts and supply problems and the little scale that now sat on their dining room table, as if she were measuring dry ingredients for baking instead of checking every day to see whether she was starving her own child. But when it worked, the first moment was often sweet. She sang a song about all the people who loved Jane. Mommy, Daddy, Grandma. Grandpa, Pop, Julia. Derreck, Eric, Lisa. By the fifteenth verse, Jane's eyes still bright, Emily was reciting people from years before who'd never met this baby. Louis, Lucy, Emily.

She woke to Alan touching her shoulder. He'd placed Jane in the crib, where she breathed deeply. "Ah fuck," she whispered, "I'm drooling." She followed him across the hall and crawled under the covers.

As she nestled against him, she murmured, "You exceed expectations."

— • —

She would, later, never forget the roller-coaster ride she embarked upon every time the baby fell asleep. The pleasure she felt at knowing the baby was sleeping soundly was tainted by her anxiety at the baby's encroaching waking-up. And why was she wasting this precious time, say, watching *The Wire* rather than doing something useful or benevolent (yoga?). By the ninety-minute mark concern for herself was replaced by concern for the baby, and she could no longer think about anything other than her bone-deep knowledge that the baby was dead. During one particularly grim afternoon when the baby napped for two hours, she heard herself say, out loud, before getting up to check on her: "Well, this is it, the last time I'll ever be happy."

Her mother had told them, when Emily was still pregnant, that there would be times when they would want to throw the baby out the window. "No one ever tells you that, but it's true. It's perfectly normal." When her mom had left the room, Emily had wiped her hands on the kitchen towel and told Alan, "I can't believe she would say that to me. I would *never* feel that way about this baby." Now, with the baby three months old, Emily understood exactly what she had meant. Just today Emily had wanted to throw Jane out the window after she refused her bottle, screaming all the while. Her face was so red she looked like a cartoon. She flailed, with intent it seemed to Emily, and knocked the bottle to the floor. Eight ounces of pumped breast milk—forty minutes of Emily's life—splattered over the circular rug.

Luckily, Alan was in the living room. Anyway, the windows all had bars on them. She handed the baby to him and said, "I am going to lie down and cry for a while." This was a thing they said to each other sometimes, as a joke, but a joke that was true.

— • —

They knew one other family in the building with children, Liuba and Nate upstairs. They had Sadie, a baby Jane's age, but also Martin, a five-year-old who loved *Star Wars* and who seemed never to do what his parents asked him to do. Liuba texted Emily sometimes after they both got home from work to invite her over for a glass of wine, after which they would both pump and dump. So every week or so she brought her monstrous pump to Liuba's apartment and sat there, her on the couch and Liuba in her glider, all their boobs out, their pumps honking and wheezing like hydraulic ducks.

"Nate wants a horse," Liuba said to her one afternoon.

"A *horse*?" Emily said in disbelief.

Liuba shouted to be heard over the pumps: "NATE WANTS A DI-VORCE."

Martin came into the living room, wearing his Darth Vader robes. He finished eating a banana and dropped the peel on the floor in front of his mother. "MARTIN," Liuba said. "WOULDN'T IT BE MORE POLITE IF YOU PICKED THAT UP." With a look of steely concentration, Martin thrust his arm out toward his mother, his hand gripping the air like Darth Vader using the Force to choke a hapless admiral. Liuba smiled at him sweetly, resolutely refusing to be strangled to death. Finally he grunted in exasperation, picked up the banana peel, and carried it into the kitchen. Later they found it on the counter *next* to the garbage can.

In the end, sense was talked into Nate by his best friend from college, who flew out from Chicago for an emergency weekend. It turned out what Nate had needed, at least for now, was a few days without children and with a large number of cheeseburgers. He came home chastened, emitting meat sweats and sincere apologies. "Maybe he'll leave me later," Liuba said to Emily the next time she came by. "Anytime but now."

"Will you get a weekend with cheeseburgers?" Emily asked.

"Yes," said Liuba. "It's been agreed. Next month. It's my sister and my best friend from high school. Do you want to come?" And thus it was that upon arriving with Liuba at an awful bar in Cobble Hill Em saw, for the first time in six years, Emily.

Her hair was short and she was behind the bar. She had a nose ring, and the first thought that went through Em's head was an unforgivably hilarious thing Emily had muttered to her, long ago, as they sat by the Astor Place rotating cube and a goth girl stalked past them, her nose ring connected by a chain to an earring: "Gonna grab that and lead her to the feed bin." Em could hear her voice in her head as clear as anything, and then she heard Emily's current voice, the same but just a bit more ragged. She was arguing with a guy at the bar about what was showing on the TV. Then she saw Em and grinned at her, conspiratorially, as if they were still friends.

They were not still friends, of course. *I'm Emily*, she thought. *Not Em.* She accepted Liuba's offer to buy the first round and retreated to a booth where she couldn't see Emily at all. She texted Alan:

How is she?

all good!

Did she eat?

like 3 oz

What are you two doing now?

You need to enjoy your night out!

Emily is the bartender at this bar

Liuba came to the booth, carrying drinks and a newly appraising look. "I gotta say, I'm impressed," Liuba said. "I would not have guessed you knew the bartender in an actually cool bar."

"This place is not cool," said Emily.

"I mean, it's in Brooklyn." Liuba set a glass in front of Emily. "I tried to get you a cider like you said, but the bartender said she knew what you liked." Emily knew without having to sip it that it was a martini, and that it would taste delicious. She sipped it and confirmed. Her phone had buzzed a couple of times and after Liuba introduced her to her sister, Emily excused herself, weighed the option of walking past the bar to get outside, and then called Alan from the bathroom. Maybe things would be okay at home, she thought, but they weren't. Alan was polite and sympathetic but after a few sentences told her, "I'm sorry, babe, I gotta go," which hurt her feelings, even though she could hear Jane crying in the background.

She stared at herself in the mirror. How many times in her old life had she stared in a mirror in a bar bathroom, wondering just exactly how drunk she was gonna get that night? It seemed unfair that on an evening she wished to get well and truly wasted, the person who was the cause of that feeling was the person responsible for making the drinks. But then of course she couldn't get *really* drunk. When she got home she would have to feed the baby, and then wake up, and then feed the baby again, and so on until the morning, and even in the morning she would need to be awake to feed the baby. To lead her to the feed bin. Was it possible she would never get stupid drunk again? It had never occurred to her, before she got pregnant, that this freedom—one she didn't even enjoy that much—would be taken away from her.

She considered how she'd changed since she last saw Emily, the ways she would look different to her. Her hair was longer. Eight years of summer beach vacations showed at the corners of her eyes. She tried not to think of her baby weight, because that was a construct of the patriarchy. (In that glimpse, Emily had appeared to be exactly as thin as she'd always been.)

She gripped the sink, noticed how gross the sink was, ungripped it, and stared at herself. "Just be a grown-up," she said. "For once."

Then she went back into the bar and drank so many martinis that years later Alan would still refer to the rest of that weekend as "the Aftermath."

— • —

On Monday an email from theopenheart@gmail.com appeared in Emily's old Hotmail inbox, the one she used now for online ordering. Where someone else might have used the subject "you" or "Friday night" or "from your former friend," Emily's former friend had employed the subject line as the place for an opening gambit:

Subject: I hope you got home OK because you were TRASHED! Do you remember the

This was Emily's email style, she recalled; once she had gotten an email with the subject, "Meet @ 8pm at Kim's, that's when I'm done, then we can go get" and then the actual body of the email simply read "pizza."

Do you remember the . . . what?

Emily was in her office, in her third week back from maternity leave. Jane was at home with a nanny, a woman named Merle who was so wonderful and loving she filled Emily with unjustified resentment. Jane had only recently developed a personality, was now roly-poly and cute rather than a squalling, pooping meat loaf, and Emily hated to leave her. But on the other hand, she really, really enjoyed sitting in her empty office, absolutely alone, simply doing work.

She clicked away from Hotmail, into her work email, and occupied herself answering questions for next week's sales conference. Yes, this book had sold in Germany, *do you remember the*—Yes, marketing should focus on the author's fame, because God knows it shouldn't focus on the writing, *do you remember the*—Actually, this blogger had upward of *do you remember the*—one hundred thousand readers, so surely they could justify a first printing bigger than ten thousand?

She turned off her monitor and pushed herself away from her desk, casting about for something, anything that wasn't *do you remember the*. There, on the windowsill, next to the photo of Alan and Jane: the self-help manuscript she'd owed notes on since she returned. She picked it up, ruffled the pages, carried it to the coffee machine, poured another cup, told her assistant Lane she was going to be reading, so please, no calls, closed her office door, plopped herself down on the couch, read the first page, and hated it so much she had to write I HATE THIS on her hand just so she wouldn't write it on the paper.

On her first day back from leave, Peter had given her the book, asking her to take it over because the editor who'd acquired it had left for HarperCollins. "Starting you off with a tough one," he said. "No more sitting around at home eating bonbons." She despised the author, Cynthia Margalit, a former Clinton administration mover and shaker who now made her living peddling modesty and self-respect to young women on the lecture circuit. The company had spent nearly half a million dollars on the proposal, so in a way it was a mark of Peter's trust in her that he'd put it in her hands—trust she'd spent years slowly building, dealing with his whims and thoughtlessness so that he understood she was steadfast. She knew that disappearing for months with a baby might have damaged that relationship, so she was heartened to be given the task. But also, she despaired.

Do you remember the what?

Emily shook her head. What did this book need? It needed not to suck shit, obviously, except that wasn't exactly it. It was totally fine for it to suck shit in certain kinds of ways. Her job, then, was to fix the things that needed to be fixed without wasting time fixing the things that didn't matter at all. And she needed to do it—she thought forward, toward sales conference and then to publicity launch and then to the book's spring pub date—in the next week.

So. Fixable: These chapter titles. Too cutesy by half, each of them needlessly alliterative. "The Prim Professional: What You Wear to Work Tells Your Coworkers Why You're There." Ugh. She crossed it out with a careful red line, wrote *CHAPTER TITLE TK*, then chewed her pencil and wondered what it was Emily was asking her if she remembered. Shit! She imagined crossing *that* out with a red line, got up, felt herself leak a little, and said "Thank God" out loud when she realized it was time to pump. When she was pumping, she couldn't make edits; she could only read, and it would do her good to just make her way through this book so she could figure out what she actually *should* be editing, instead of editing everything because everything was bad.

So then she trekked to the kitchen and took her little cold packs out of the freezer and carried them, shamefaced even though she knew there was nothing to be ashamed of, back to her office. Kindly Lane became overly interested in the contents of his file drawer as she carried them into her office and locked the door. She unbuttoned her top, feeling, as she always did, a thrill of disbelief at disrobing in the same office where she'd edited manuscripts and talked to agents and hosted brainstorming meetings for years. Feeling, also, cold in the air-conditioning, as always. She plugged in the machine, hooked the tubes into the cups, attached the deflated storage bags, turned the machine on—felt the breath of the suction on her sore boobs—and at that moment could no longer take it.

As the pump farted away on her conference table, Emily, blouse still open, leapt to her feet, turned on her computer monitor, and clicked Emily's message.

From: theopenheart@gmail.com

Subject: I hope you got home OK because you were TRASHED! Do you remember the

---

There was no text in the body of the email. That subject line was it. Emily stood over her desk, staring at the blank screen until a single drop of milk plunked onto her keyboard.

After she pumped, Emily wrote an email to Louis, and later he called her. It was the end of his workday, five o'clock Iowa time, which meant she still had an hour to go at least.

"Well, how did she look?" he asked. He was walking his dog, and she heard the wind in the background.

"She looked good," Emily admitted into her office phone. "She seemed totally in her element."

"You don't sound happy about it," he said. "Gus, drop that."

"It's not like I wanted her to be unhappy."

"Mmm-hmm."

"I wish her nothing but the best."

"Sure."

"I do!"

"Okay, okay. But there's a difference between wishing her the best and *seeing* her and she's, like, at her best."

"Yes, there's a difference," Emily admitted.

"Hey!" Louis greeted someone off in the distance.

"Who was that?"

"No idea," Louis said. "A neighbor. You just say hey to people here."

"What, like, *everyone*?"

"Sure. You don't want anyone to think of you as that man who doesn't wave and say hey."

"You *wave*?"

"You've been in New York too long."

"I miss you." It had been ten years since they'd lived together, five years since Louis had left for a job in the admissions department of a small college in Iowa, where, he'd once told her, he decided "which sensitive farm boys get to come here and which ones have to go to UW–Eau Claire."

"You too, honey. When do I get to meet the baby?"

"Ugh, I don't know. Are you ever coming back for a visit?"

"No. Are you ever coming here?"

"I used to think no, but now I have these visions, like, our baby running around in a field?"

"She can run already? That seems fast."

"No, she can barely sit up. I just mean, someday she could run through a beautiful field. You have fields, right?"

He chuckled. "Of dreams!" The phone rustled and she heard him say, "Good boy, Gus! Good boy!"

"What did he do?"

"He didn't try to kill this other dog."

"What's the best time of year to come to Iowa?"

"When winter's over, in July. Are you going to write her back? Or call her?"

She sighed. "I want to but I don't want to, is where I guess I am at this juncture."

"Yeah, I get that. Is she using, is the question."

"Unclear. She works in a bar."

"Bad sign." Her email pinged with a new message, from Alan, saying

his boss was keeping him late and could she get home in time to re-
lieve the nanny, which meant she should have left five minutes ago,
and she tuned back in to Louis's voice as he reached the end of a sentence but didn't quite catch what the sentence was.

"Wait, did you say I *should* call her or I *shouldn't*?"

"I said it would make sense if you didn't call her, but that I bet you
will."

"Oh," Emily said. "You know me better than I know myself."

"You bet."

"So did she," Emily said. "Then. But now she doesn't know me at
all. I gotta run. Say hi to Shaun for me."

She took the back stairs down one floor and caught the elevator
there, so Peter wouldn't see her leave. On the subway, as the 1 train
crawled out of the tunnel and into late-day summer sunlight, as she
looked at the time on her phone, certain she'd have to pay the nanny
overtime once again, the phone buzzed with a text. It was from Louis:
But don't you want her to know who you turned out to be?

At home, Merle graciously accepted her apologies. She just wanted,
Emily knew, to get out of there to begin her ninety-minute journey
back to deepest Queens—past JFK!—but Emily needed to convey,
one last time, how sorry she was she was late and how much she appreciated all that Merle did.

Merle left. Emily knew that her appreciation would take the form
of paying her overtime. Where this was going to come from Emily
didn't know; they already paid Merle basically the same amount Emily
earned, though Merle saw much less after taxes and unemployment.
What a privilege, Emily thought for the thousandth time, to work all
day in order to give all your money away so that someone else can
look after your child. It was a good thing she liked her job, or rather
liked having her job, liked most of the people she worked with and
was made anxious by her job most of the time. She did love health
insurance.

Emily took Jane to the living room, the floor of which was festooned with stuffed toys, a bouncer, a swing, a play table, a baby gym mat with dangling animals. They'd put the coffee table into storage because the living room was no longer a place for sustained adult inhabitation. It was a place for tummy time. "Tummy time!!!" she cried as Jane made hilarious grunting noises and lifted her nose up from the rug to look at her. Emily was good at swooping to pick Jane up *just* before she got upset; this time Emily soothed her for a moment then set her down on her back on the baby gym, where she batted sweetly at the plastic turtle, the plastic moon. Emily sat cross-legged for a while, watching her. She laid a hand on Jane's belly and was surprised to see, written on her own skin in her own handwriting, *I HATE THIS.* She licked her hand and rubbed it off. Then she lay down next to Jane to get a better view. When Alan opened the apartment door, that's where Emily was, sound asleep on the floor with a burbling baby on a mat next to her.

"Hey, ladies!" he sang, Beastie Boys–style, with exaggerated good cheer, and Emily loved him blearily, dearly, for the effort he was putting in. He put his backpack down and danced a little cha-cha-cha into the living room. Jane was making happy noises, and when Alan picked her up from the floor she squealed in delight. He swooped her up over his head and just as he said, "Helloooooo!" tiny Jane joyously emitted a stream of spit-up right into his open mouth.

A few minutes later, after he'd cleaned up ("and recovered emotionally"), he said, "Oh man, she is good at barfing."

"It's basically her job."

"Professional barfer."

"It's on her résumé. 'Special skills: Barfing.'"

"'Barfing, sleeping, eating.'"

"'Crying.'"

"'Bein' cute.'"

"'Languages: Baby.'"

"'Proficient in Microsoft Excel.'" They were both laughing so hard they had to sit down. Jane looked from one to the other with polite interest.

"I couldn't even be mad at her, she was so happy barfing on me," Alan said, wiping his eyes. "I wish *I* was that happy about doing my job." The next day Alan spent a not-insignificant portion of his time at the office making a professional CV for Jane and printing it out on fancy paper.

February 2005–present: Baby.
- New addition to a mom & pop in upper Manhattan
- Disrupted the family space, introducing new product lines, tasks, and emotions to a previously stable organization
- Gained weight, eventually reaching the seventy-sixth percentile for babies nationwide

May 2004–February 2005: Embryo/Fetus.
- Conceived after viewing of *Before Sunset*
- Doubled number of cells over and over
- Established circulatory, digestive, and respiratory systems

Special skills
- Barfing
- Being cute
- Pooping rate: 200 PPM

We might survive this whole thing, Emily thought a few days later as she drilled a hole in the bathroom wall to hang up the résumé, which she'd put in an IKEA frame. If we can turn *that* into *this*—if together we can make not only a baby but idiot jokes about the baby—the three of us really *are* a family.

She remembered Em, But Fifteen Years From Now, who didn't have any children.

That night she emailed Emily back from her actual email, not the Hotmail account. "Very funny," she wrote. "Do you want to get lunch?"

— ● —

One Sunday morning they woke simultaneously, as Jane shrieked so loudly from the other room that Alan fell out of bed in surprise. Emily sat bolt upright and looked down at him, amused, as he untangled his legs from the sheet.

"Go ahead and laugh," he said. "You're just jealous that I'm so *alert*."

Jane continued shrieking. It was five forty-five a.m. "If you go downstairs and get the paper," Emily said, "you can go back to bed."

"Are we going to church?" he asked.

"No."

"I'll take that deal." He stumbled out of the apartment in his boxer shorts and a T-shirt.

When he returned from the lobby, Sunday *Times* in hand, she was installed at the dining room table. The nursing pillow—whose name, My Breast Friend, she had at first found mortifying but they now bandied about without a thought—was wrapped around her waist. Jane attached to her right breast, and Emily motioned to the table. "Welcome, traveling merchant," she said. "Your attire is curious. Please lay out your wares."

He pulled the paper out from its plastic sleeve and handed her Sunday Styles. "Here you are, madame," he said unctuously. "I hope you and your breast friend enjoy your morning. And now"—he exited the dining room backward, bowing at her—"Adieu."

Emily allowed herself a moment of thinking about how, tomorrow, *she* would get to sleep in, before she remembered that it was Sunday and tomorrow she had to go to work. Yesterday had been her morning to sleep in, but instead she had foolishly woken up at seven and read manuscripts in bed while Alan dealt with Jane. She'd felt so industrious then, getting ahead of things, but now she just felt like a chump.

Jane wheezed through her stuffy nose as she nursed. She paused sucking, locked eyes with Emily, and farted. "Aww, that feels better, right?" Emily asked. Jane turned her attention back to the breast, and Emily unfolded the style section, only to see, below the fold, a big black-and-white photo of Lucy Deming. She was wearing her overalls and looking away from the camera, laughing at something someone was saying. She was standing in the kitchen where Emily had spent whole afternoons of her twenties.

She closed her stinging eyes for a moment, opened them again to see, behind Lucy in the photo, a ring of measuring spoons hanging from a nail she herself had pounded into the side of the kitchen cabinet.

She looked at the byline first, an old habit: Benjamin Bannon. She'd read his last novel along with everyone else. "A Writer with an Eye for the Domestic Gets Her Due," read the headline. She skimmed the piece, looking for her name. It wasn't in there, but at least Edith's wasn't, either. Bannon praised Lucy's novels, the memoir, gathered a few quotes from Lucy herself. He got his writer friends to say how much Lucy's books meant to them. Anne Tyler thought her view of human nature was gracious. Zadie Smith (Zadie Smith?!) compared Lucy to Jane Austen (Jane Austen?!?!). Dave Eggers said that everyone should dump their therapists and just read Lucy Deming, who knew more about love and happiness than a thousand marriage counselors.

It wasn't that Emily hadn't thought these things herself about Lucy's writing—well, maybe she wouldn't have put it quite like Dave Eggers did. It's just that she had never known that any of *these* writers, serious literary writers who won prizes, thought so. Or expected that, more than a decade later, they would praise these sweet little books that she'd helped bring into print, only to see them essentially sink like stones.

Jane made a sad, congested snort, and Emily took a washrag, wiped Jane's nose, folded the washrag inside out, wiped her own cheeks, shifted Jane to the other side. What she couldn't figure out was why the article was being published now, a random May Sunday in 2005. Lucy's novels were out of print. She got the impression the memoir was a sort of cult success. No one had written about her at all for years. A sentence near the top of the piece caught her eye: "Ms. Deming would have turned 60 this month."

Oh, Lucy's birthday. Of course. It had just happened, and she hadn't remembered.

As far as she could tell this article existed simply because Benjamin Bannon loved Lucy Deming and wanted to write one of those rapturous stories that revives an author's work. (Or, to think of it less generously, he wanted to establish himself as the kind of guy whose praise can resurrect an author's career.) Well, it would work: every editor in Manhattan would read this story today, and the race would be on to buy the reprint rights to the novels. She could see them now: three slim paperbacks, each with a new foreword from Bannon. Emily smiled; she doubted that many of those editors had woken up at the crack of dawn. And she doubted even more that any of those editors knew Lucy's daughter's name. Had she returned to Manhattan? Yes, and there she was in the gosh-darn phone book: Sarah Deming.

Emily ate a bowl of cereal, strapped Jane into her stroller, took her for a walk around the neighborhood. It was going to be a hot one. On the Hudson, a boatful of rowers slid through the water. They all wore sports bras, had their hair in ponytails, and flexed their arms identically on each stroke. She eyed their abs disapprovingly.

Was nine o'clock too early on a Sunday to telephone someone who was—Emily did the math between the girl she'd once known and the year 2005—something like twenty? Yes. It sure was. Emily puttered around the apartment, cleaning things here and there, trying to keep Jane quiet so Alan could sleep, thinking about Lucy. She unfolded

Styles and stared at Lucy's photo. She wished Lucy had been looking at the camera; she wanted to catch her eye again.

Around ten, when it seemed she had been up for eight hours and couldn't possibly spend another minute with this wriggling, fussy child, Alan yawned his way into the living room. "You wanna sleep?" he asked.

"I have a phone call to make," she replied, and headed back to the bedroom.

Before she picked up the phone, she went through her checklist, the one she'd used for every call since Peter taught it to her in her first week as his assistant:

What is my goal?

How do I want to make this person feel?

Her goal, she decided, was simply to *schedule a lunch for early in the week*. Then she could make a formal offer once she'd cleared the money with Peter. She wanted Lucy's daughter to feel *connected to her*.

"Hello?"

"Is this Sarah?"

"This is."

"Hey, Sarah," she said. "This is Emily Thiel. I don't know if you remember me. I was a friend of your mother's."

"Hi," Sarah said.

"I sort of . . . well, I actually took care of you sometimes when you were a kid."

"Oh yes?" Sarah said politely. "I'm sorry, I'm not sure if I remember you." Emily sure remembered that voice, though, higher-pitched, but just as serious. "Are you calling about the article?"

"Oh, it's so great," she said. "I hope you're hearing from all her old friends."

"You're the first, but it's early."

"Ha, yes, I have a baby—sorry, different conception of time here."

"That's okay! I'm excited about the article. How did you know my mom?"

"I was—I worked for Edith Safer, who was Lucy's literary agent. She's the one who sold the books originally." It was easy to say it again, as easy as it had been years ago.

"Oh sure. Edith."

"My mom went to college with your mom, which is how we, like, how initially we made the connection."

"Mm-hm. Edith died, what, three or four years ago, right? She was a character."

"She was, yeah. Listen, I'm calling because I'm actually an editor now, at a publishing house here in New York. At St. Martin's."

"Oh, I don't know that much about publishers. Is that one of the big ones?"

"We're one of the smaller big ones," Emily said. "You're not—what do you—"

"I'm not a writer, no." Sarah laughed. "I saw how that turns out. No thanks." Her voice remained light. "I'm studying urban planning. City College."

"Oh, that's great. Lucy loved that stuff. Why New York looks the way it looks, how it works."

"I know," Sarah said softly. Sure, yes, of course she knew that. In the other room, Emily heard Alan singing.

"So I guess I'm curious—I know the novels are out of print. That's such a shame."

"Oh, definitely," Sarah said. "That's why I'm so happy about Benjamin and Bob."

"I'm sorry, Benjamin Bannon? And Bob . . ."

"Bob um, Bob Fox? Ben's agent?" *Oh*, Emily thought. "Are you not one of the publishers in the thing, the auction?"

"The auction? No, not yet," Emily said easily. Of course Bannon had his hand in the whole thing. It wasn't enough to just write the piece. He had already started working to make the deal. It was admirable of him, or rather Emily would have found it admirable if Bob Fox—Bannon's extremely fancy literary agent—had included her on the submission.

"Well, you should call them. I'm her executor now, but they're handling the whole thing. Do you need Bob Fox's number?"

"No, I have it," Emily said. This wasn't true, but someone in her office would.

"He's the line to Ben. I think he's calling the shots, sort of. I mean, I know I'm calling the shots, but I wasn't on Oprah, you know?"

"I understand," she said.

"Okay, great."

"Hey Sarah? I just . . ." She breathed deeply. "I just want you to know I loved your mother. I loved her. I loved both of you." Sarah was silent and Emily pushed on. "Do you remember a trip to Central Park? You were seven maybe, or eight? We walked around . . ." Emily searched for a memory from that day that she could say to this person she hadn't talked to in over a decade. Mostly she remembered Sarah's hand in her own, the tickle of her hair when she hugged Emily, the coldness of ice—"You got stung by a bee."

"That was you?"

"That was me."

"Huh." Sarah chuckled a little. "I wish I remembered you better. I'm sorry. Do you have blonde hair?"

"Sure, well, blondish brown, light brown. Well, no. Brown."

"Hey, I have to meet some friends for brunch," Sarah said. "You should call Bob."

After she hung up, she sat on the bed, thinking about Lucy and Sarah. Well, if Sarah didn't remember, Sarah didn't remember. Emily sure did.

— • —

On Monday morning, she worked the phones. An old colleague now at the Fox Agency told her that there was no auction yet, but that Lucy's novels were out to the usual high-profile paperback publishers—Mariner, Penguin, Back Bay, Vintage. There was also a collection of previously unpublished essays, letters, and recipes, which could go hardcover or softcover. Bannon published with Knopf, and so her friend said she assumed Vintage had the inside track, which made Emily force herself to breathe deeply for thirty seconds after she hung up so she wouldn't fucking lose it.

A friend at Vintage said the books were circulating and the P&L was pretty good but that Marty wasn't convinced. "They're a little soft for Vintage, aren't they?" she asked.

"Sure seems like it," she said blandly.

Well, if there was no auction yet, she could wait until the afternoon to call, which was good, because she had to lay some groundwork first. Plus, she had lunch with Emily today, which she was nervous enough about. She took the copies of Lucy's books she'd brought from home down the hall, nodded to Peter's assistant Marta, who was on the phone but waved. As the first assistant Peter had ever hired at St. Martin's, Emily had opinions on every young woman who had ever filled that chair, and—as she'd been sure to tell Peter—Marta was one of the good ones. Sharp, hardworking, took direction. Ambitious as hell. Dealt with Peter seemingly effortlessly, no small task. Emily hoped she stuck around longer than the last one.

Peter's door was open, and she saw his high-tops up on the coffee table. "Knock knock," she said at the door.

"Good morning!" he declared. He was sitting on the couch and had the manuscript of the self-help book from the Clinton staffer on his lap. "We gave this to you, right?" he said. "Have you looked at it?"

"It's so bad," she said.

"Oh good, I was worried I was going crazy." In his late forties, with a beard Emily had watched over the years turn from pepper to salt and pepper to mostly salt, Peter was gangly and brilliant. He'd gone to Yale, studied with Harold Bloom, started his career at Little, Brown before taking a left turn—a lucrative one, Emily had always assumed—to acquire upmarket fiction and nonfiction at St. Martin's. He was now editorial director. "Does it need a writer?"

"No," she said, sitting in Peter's office chair behind his desk. She was the only person allowed to do that, and part of the fun of it was remembering how such a move would once have been received. "She can get it up to snuff, I think. I sent a memo to the agent the other week. He said Cynthia was, quote, 'excited about the opportunity to grow in new directions,' unquote."

"How long will it take her to grow?" The manuscript had been almost a year late.

"He says she can turn it around in a month or two. It's more Dr. Frankenstein than a wholesale rewrite. I think she can do it."

"Okay, great. I am *so glad* we gave this to you. I promise the next thing I drop in your lap will be more fun."

"Oh," said Emily, raising an eyebrow. "Are you saying you owe me?"

He laughed. "Uh, to what do I owe the pleasure of this visit?"

She slid *The Watched Pot* across the desk. "Oh, I know this," he said. "Chessie went on a kick where she cooked all the recipes. This is a memoir with recipes, right?" He paged through the book. "Yeah. Oh *right*, that was good gingerbread. There was some special syrup she had to order from Alabama or somewhere insane like that." He looked up. "This is not news to you, I'm sure."

"So Lucy Deming also wrote three novels," Emily said, pushing her copies across the desk to him. "First two with a tiny press in Boston, last one with Avon, back when they did stuff like that. They're all out of print now."

"Ohhh, wait," Peter said. "This is the Ben Bannon piece in Style."

"Right. Bob Fox is out with the novels plus an uncollected works."

"Fox? Bannon must be signed on, then. Can we get this one?" he said, holding up *The Watched Pot*. "Chessie loved it." Chessie was Peter's wife, the WASPiest of WASPs, whom in her assistantship Emily had disdained for the same prissiness she knew others saw in her but who had turned out to be incredibly sweet. She had designed the invitations to Emily's wedding. They had twin boys, eight years old.

"We could try to shake it loose from Avon, but I think we can make a splash without it. The novels are terrific, and people don't even know they exist. But with Bannon intros, fresh covers, they'll do great. You want to read them?"

"Sure, but you don't have to wait for me," he said. "Don't break the bank. Keep it under fifty. Can you get it for under fifty? Bob Fox does not sell a lot of books under fifty." He laughed. "Honestly, he doesn't sell a lot of books to us at all."

"I can get it."

"I believe in you! I'm just saying, if Vintage loves these books like you do, why does Bob choose St. Martin's?"

"Please turn to page seventy-eight of the recipe book," she said. He grinned. Peter loved intrigue, and Emily often found it useful to deliver it, even though it made her uncomfortable. She leaned back in his chair. "Read to me, Peter."

"'Chapter Six: Martinis. The first thing you must know about martinis,' blah blah blah. 'My friend Emily . . .'" He paused as he made the connection. "Hard to believe there was a time you didn't like martinis."

"I've got a personal connection," Emily said.

"This the book? The Edith Safer book?"

"It's not hers anymore," she said, standing up. And she had something Bob Fox would want.

— ● —

She'd chosen the restaurant with some care; she wanted it to be nice but cheap, since if she was certain about one thing about lunch with Emily, it was that she would be picking up the tab. And she wanted them to be in and out in under an hour, in case it went badly.

Walking down Broadway she asked herself why, exactly, she had decided to let Emily back into her life. Maybe it was that her night out with Liuba, the night she'd seen Emily at the bar, had been fun but hadn't made her and Liuba close. Her life was not filled with the kinds of friendships she made when she was in her teens and twenties. Louis had left New York like so many other college friends. Some friendships had faded; some people had died. She had gotten busy and lost track of others. She had Alan, which made up for a lot of it, but she still felt that absence, the absence of a woman her age who knew her to her bones.

Of course, they no longer knew each other to their bones. And she didn't know whether the gap between them was bridgeable; their lives seemed far too different (although she didn't really know that much about Emily's current life yet). And of course her intense years with Emily had been both wonderful and terrible. She'd heard that the whole reason women had second children was that their minds tricked them by erasing the memory of childbirth's pain but retaining the exhilaration of the baby's arrival. She certainly wasn't there yet; she was too close to the event, perhaps, because she still remembered the pain. The same was true of her friendship with Emily. It had been six years since their relationship had finished evaporating, and the bad remained as sharp in her memory as the good.

She was two minutes early to the Belgian place. So here she was, in a position she recalled acutely: standing in front of a restaurant, reading a book, waiting for Emily.

But not for long. At 1:05, she saw Emily approach. Wearing headphones, looking down as in her determined way she darted through knots of tourists and slow-walking couples. As Emily neared, she put her book away.

Emily looked up and smiled. She was wearing plain black pants and a dark gray top, perhaps the most conservative outfit she had ever seen Emily in. She pressed a button on her iPod, took the headphones out, wrapped the cord around the music player. "Hey," she said.

Of course they hugged—how could they not hug?

Inside the restaurant, Emily said, "Give me a second, I have to get something down," and she had her first real chance to study her face as she pulled a small notebook, the kind she still thought of as an "Emily notebook," from her bag and jotted a few sentences. Her hair, dyed a rough blonde, was spiky and parted near a temple. The nose ring she'd noticed at the bar was gunmetal gray. What she recognized most of all was her energy, the way she attacked the page in her notebook, writing with such force that her knuckles turned white.

When she closed the notebook and dropped it back in her purse and looked up at Emily, her eyes were green as ever, with just the smallest lines at their corners. Emily looked good, she realized, and then realized she was glad about that.

"So who were those girls you were with?" Emily asked. "At the bar?"

"Oh," she said. "A neighbor. Another mom in my building, and her sister."

"You guys had a fuckin' night."

"I'm sorry about that," she said. "I know we were—I was a little out of control."

Emily shrugged. "The life and times of a dive bar bartender. I've seen a lot worse."

The waiter arrived, and they both ordered Diet Cokes, then smiled at each other. "This place is all about the *moules frites*," she said, for something to say. "Do you like mussels? I can't remember—are you a shellfish person?"

"I've always been shellfish," Emily replied. "So here is what I know about *you*: You still work at St. Martin's. You let your hair grow out, but then you cut it again. And you have a baby."

"That's all correct. Who's your source?"

"Friendster." Emily laughed. For a hot minute last year, she had indeed been very active on that site, eagerly finding acquaintances at other publishers and people from college. She remembered hovering over Emily's little photo, feeling guilty, then deciding that it was fine—"Friending" was not the same as being a friend, obviously. The post about Jane's birth was the last thing she had written on the site, and she now thought she was pretty much done with it. Everyone seemed to be migrating to Facebook anyway.

"Well, yeah, we have a baby," she said. "Isn't that weird? Her name's Jane. She's five months." She pulled a photo from her purse, the baby sitting up precariously, Alan at the edge of the frame, his hand at her back.

"Wow," Emily said, looking at the photo. "What's she like?"

"Hummm. She's like . . . well, she's like a baby. She's curious. She's sweet. She sleeps okay. She gets angry all the time because there's, like, this big gap between what she wants to do and what she can do."

"Ah," said Emily sagely. "The human condition."

"Do you, um, do you have any kids?"

Emily cocked her head and smiled. "I don't. I don't think that's for me. My mom's given up. What made you decide to have one?"

"Oh, I always wanted kids."

"You did?"

"Well, I think so. I mean, I didn't want kids right away, back when—"

"Sure. But I remember, you loved them, even when we were younger. That girl in my building, the girl downstairs?"

"Oh!" Emily had forgotten about that girl. "Juana! Are you still in touch with her mom? Or with anyone from Sunrise?"

"I see people around sometimes. I don't know where her mom is, though. People sort of scattered."

"Yeah." She sipped her Diet Coke. "So where are you living now?"

It was hard, she thought, to be in a perfectly polite catch-up conversation with a person who once knew everything about you. She had cried in front of Emily about her abortion, for God's sake. She could sense that they both felt it, but that they were powerless to do anything about it. It was the burden of a decade upon them, plus all that other stuff.

Emily lived in Williamsburg, had kept a loft in a semilegal communal warehouse space for years.

Emily lived in Inwood with her husband and her baby.

Emily had been dating the same guy for a couple years, but they just separated amicably.

Emily was a senior editor now.

Emily tended at that bar, did some advocacy work for immigrants and squatters. She still put on shows, most recently in a storefront in Dumbo.

Emily hadn't written anything recently, with work and the baby. She just talked to Louis the other day, actually. He said hi. (This was not true.)

Emily's mom, still in Georgia, wasn't great; "let's not talk about her."

Emily's mom in Wisconsin was easing into retirement. Her dad and his wife had moved to Florida.

Emily was dropping in on police brutality protests and antiwar rallies pretty regularly. She thought Bloomberg was a soulless robot who was better than Giuliani only in that he wasn't a fascist, but he was accelerating Giuliani's work of selling New York off to the super rich.

Emily wasn't paying a lot of attention to local politics these days.

They ate frites in silence for a while, dipping into each other's sauces. She could nearly see, just on the edge of the conversation, the talk that they should have. The talk about how much Emily hurt her when they were younger, about the way their friendship fell apart. She didn't know what that conversation could look or sound like, and she was afraid of it.

"Are you still listening to R.E.M.?" Emily asked. She was not; the drummer had left the band, and though they kept releasing albums as a three-piece—and though she still played their old music all the time—she couldn't bring herself to listen to the new songs.

They worked out that they both loved the Heartless Bastards. They had both attended the same show, it turned out, last winter at a club in Brooklyn—the last concert she had been to. (It had been fun and loud but not as fun as it could have been, because she couldn't drink.) "She's so fucking honest. I love that." "She was incredible up on that stage, just so much raw power." "The songs could have been written thirty years ago, but they also feel like they're about me, now." "My new resolution is to be"—they finished the line in unison—"someone who does not care what anybody thinks of me!"

What would happen at the end of this lunch, she wondered. The waiter would bring the check, she would pay the check, they would walk outside, and then? It's not as if she had room in her life for anyone, really, especially not someone as labor-intensive as Emily. But maybe they could resume, like, a movie friendship? A theater friendship? It would be nice to have someone to go to plays with, should Jane ever commit to actually sleeping at night. It would be nice, she realized, to really *talk* about the play with someone afterward.

The waiter brought the check. She paid the check. They walked outside into the crush of idiots on Forty-Fourth. She tried to figure out what she was going to say, but then Emily said in a rush, "You want to go out sometime? To a show or something?"

"You want to?"

Emily gave a smile. "I do, yes."

"Well, it can be tough, but I'd like that. Do you have a cell phone?" She had vivid memories of Emily scorning the automatons who walked around the city talking on their phones.

"Yeah, I gave in."

Emily gave her the number, and then she typed it into her BlackBerry, and then Emily's phone lit up. Emily clicked a few buttons to program her name into the phone's contacts. "Em," she narrated. "Ee em. Save."

"Emily," she said. "It's Emily."

Emily shrugged. Already walking away, she said, "That'll confuse the readers, but sure."

— • —

Back at work, Emily scanned the first page of a short, typewritten manuscript on the huge office printer/scanner. She'd brought the manuscript from home after an increasingly desperate early-morning search through their file cabinet. (She finally found it tucked into a folder helpfully labeled PAPERS.) She carefully laid the well-thumbed pages on the glass and waited patiently for the green light to slide across, the machine to ingest the words to its memory. There, waiting for her in her email, was a pretty good PDF. Magic!

Then she prepared to call Bob Fox. She closed her email, turned off her computer monitor, readied a notepad. She jotted down a few phrases: *Edith Safer's assistant. I know these books better than anyone. I'm in the memoir. Bring Lucy's legacy into the 21st century.* (She scratched that last one out; too stupid.) *What is my goal?* she wrote. *How do I want to make Bob Fox feel?*

Then Lane called from his desk: "Emily, Bob Fox is on the phone for you."

Shit! *My goal is to get these fucking books. I want Bob Fox to feel like selling me these fucking books.* "Hey Bob," she said, then "Hi Bob," then she picked up the phone and said, "Hello, Bob, how are you."

"Hi, Emily." His voice was warm and smooth. "I don't think we've met before, have we?"

Well, he had hit on her long ago at a party, when she was young and hot, but she didn't mention that. Bob Fox was a superagent, with a list that was basically a who's who of contemporary literature. She should have realized he was involved. All those other authors who appeared in the *Times* piece were his, other than Jane Austen, and she assumed he was working on her.

"Sarah Deming tells me I should talk to you," he said.

Oh, bless Sarah. "I used to see a lot of Sarah when I worked for Edith Safer. We—Edith made the original deal with Avon."

"You were her assistant?" he asked.

"Yes."

"I knew Edith," he said. "I never saw Lucy as her kind of writer, exactly. She was more meat and potatoes, as I recall." Emily kept quiet and hoped he would connect the dots.

"Well," he said finally. "Candidly, I hadn't really thought of St. Martin's for these books."

"Oh, I think we're a natural home," she said. "We can handle literary fiction, but we also know the women's fiction marketplace better than anyone. I've always thought Lucy should be selling to Lorrie Moore readers but also to Jan Karon readers."

There was a short silence, and then Fox laughed briskly. "That's good," he said. "She didn't sell to *any* readers the first time around."

"No, she sure didn't. Except I guess to Benjamin Bannon."

"Well, I'm happy to broaden the field a bit on this submission. We're proposing a four-book deal, the three novels plus a new book of letters and essays. Benjamin will write an introduction for *Can't Complain* and help secure introductions for the others. We're looking to bring Lucy's legacy into the twenty-first century. I'm sorry?"

Emily had stifled a laugh into a cough. "Excuse me," she said. "This sounds exactly right. I'd be really delighted to be the one to do this. I know these books as well as anybody."

"Terrific," Fox said, in a tone that said he had already turned his attention elsewhere. "That means we don't have to send you fresh copies. I'll have my assistant email you the cover letter."

— • —

When Emily opened the door, Alan was aiming a spoonful of mashed something at Jane's face. The baby turned her head at her mom's entrance and emitted a squeal of delight that turned instantly into a howl of protest when Alan poked the spoon into her ear.

"Mommy's here!" he said, filling his voice with hearty joy. "She's been a little monster," he added to her.

"Are you a *little monster*?" Emily said, tickling a giggling Jane under the chin.

"Oh, *now* you're happy," he said. She knew she shouldn't revel in her daughter preferring her to Alan, she knew it was a meaningless phase, she knew it hurt Alan's feelings even though he pretended it didn't, but for a moment she let herself swim in Jane's obvious delight at her arrival. She would make it up to him later.

They agreed, for the fourth or fifth night in a row, to get delivery. "I'll cook tomorrow, I promise," Alan said.

"We live in the greatest city on earth," Emily said. "We can just not cook!"

Alan brought out a bottle of wine and said, "I think it's time." She had not touched booze since the Aftermath, but with a solemn nod accepted a glass, which then sat tantalizingly out of reach as she nursed Jane. Once Alan took the baby away and she could hear him singing through the dining room wall, she picked up the glass and sipped. Their favorite delivery guy brought dinner—the one who whistled so loud you could hear him from the elevator.

"Was that our favorite delivery guy I heard?" Alan said in a low voice as he came out from the bedroom. "Oh my!" For Emily had lit candles, set the table with their wedding china, and laid out his mapo tofu as elegantly as one could lay out a dish that was radioactive red.

"To what do I owe the pleasure?" she asked him, an old game. He smiled.

"Why, we're celebrating," he said.

"What are we celebrating?"

"Our handsome daughter will bring us a dowry of many goats!"

She giggled. One glass of wine was probably all she needed tonight. "Tell me a thing," she said as she pinched a piece of chicken with her chopsticks.

"Hmm, a thing," he said, then held up a finger as he finished chewing. His cheeks were already darkening with the heat of the dish. "Okay. Today I learned that the executive director doesn't send his own emails." Alan was an attorney at a housing rights nonprofit.

"What do you mean?"

"He dictates them to his secretary, like . . . like I don't even know what. Like a *New Yorker* cartoon."

"That," Emily said, "is remarkable. Is he one hundred years old?"

"Sixty maybe. I went into his office today, and his monitor is completely covered with taped-up photos of his kids."

"Aww, that's sweet."

"His kids are little. Second wife."

"Fuck him," she said.

Alan raised his glass. "Fuck him," he proclaimed.

"Fuck him."

Outside, the sky had gotten dark, and thunder cleared its throat across the river in New Jersey. The wind had picked up and the trees in the courtyard sounded like ocean waves. Emily told him about her lunch, about being in the running for Lucy's books. "Those are two very notable things to happen today," he said. "Do you feel good?"

"I think I do. I have to convince them to pick me."

Alan got up, took her plate, stacked it atop his, kissed her forehead. "You'll just need to dazzle them." He walked toward the kitchen. "Find us something to watch. I'll do the dishes."

"No!" she protested, getting up. "I refuse to make a decision. *You* find us something to watch."

"Okay, okay."

"Nice try, pal."

From the kitchen she heard the friendly *ba-boop* of the TiVo. She Tupperwared the leftovers, washed the plates, and took the wine bottle out to the living room, where Alan was sitting cross-legged on the couch. On the screen he'd highlighted an episode of *Numb3rs*. "We got a Numthers," he said.

"Oh, I don't know that I can handle a Numthers tonight," she said.

"Okay, we're watching *Dancing with the Stars*."

"Yeah we are."

Emily thought maybe she would, after all, have another glass of wine.

That night, Jane gave them the gift of not crying while they were having sex. The sex was good, and after was good too, lying in the crook of his shoulder, listening to water dripping through the leaves on the tree outside their bedroom window.

"You didn't say how you felt about your lunch," Alan said into the silence.

"It was fine. I mean, it was good."

"How is she?"

"You don't have to care about her," Emily said. She propped herself up on an elbow, arranged the sheet so he wouldn't see her saggy belly, left one breast exposed as a treat. "You barely know her."

"But you care about her, right?"

"I guess I still do," she said.

"So." He shrugged. "I'm gonna care about what you care about."

They were quiet. A siren went by down on Broadway. "I think she's good," she said finally. "I liked talking to her. I'm sure she'll do something that drives me insane the next time I see her. But I spent so long, like, making her not my friend in my head, so it was weird that we just fell right into it."

"I mean, that's good, right?"

"I guess. I guess we speak the same language, still."

"If it turns out you can't stand her, then just say goodbye. You did it once."

They lay there breathing together in the dark. *Had* she ever said goodbye? She wasn't sure. When Jane cried from the other room, she let Alan pretend to be asleep and went to her. She'd said she'd make it up to him, after all.

— • —

Jane didn't ever get through an entire church service, but they liked dressing her up and showing her off. They'd been attending Holy Trinity for a few years, nothing big, just stopping by on Sundays if they didn't sleep too late. Now that Jane was always awake at six a.m., it was easier to make it.

And having a kid changed the church equation. Before, they went because it was calming, because they liked the sermons, because it was a way to meet neighbors, albeit mostly elderly ones. None of those reasons were particularly serious. Now going to church was all wrapped up in questions about whether they were, actually, Episcopalians, for example. Whether they intended their daughter and any future children to be Episcopalians. They had named Lisa, Alan's sister, the baby's godmother, but had thought of her as the secular kind of godmother, who would one day take her goddaughter out for mani-pedis. Religious education had not been insisted upon.

The good news was, all the old Inwoodians *loved* Jane. On this windy June morning they crowded around on the steps to the front door, reaching out to touch her perfect little socks, her bald head encircled with a headband that Emily knew was gender essentialist but was still preferable to explaining to everyone that she was a girl. Here in Inwood, a lot of Dominican and Puerto Rican parents pierced infant girls' ears, a decision Emily found horrifying even though she knew that was pretty culturally insensitive of her. No one ever got confused about *those* babies' gender, though, you had to give it to them.

The Episcopalians could really stretch a service out. Jane got antsy in minutes, so they sat in the back row and traded off who walked her around the hallways. (It was amazing how much of partnered parenting was trading off: trading off sleep, trading off working late, trading off sitting in church. That only one parent at a time could do normal life things was a real testament to how thoroughly the simple presence of a baby could obliterate normal life.)

(Of course, she loved her. She often found herself reflexively saying this after complaining about the baby. Sometimes she complained so much about the baby that people looked a little horrified.)

Today Alan took Jane for a walk after the first hymn, to which Jane had stridently objected for reasons of her own. An ancient lay reader delivered the Old Testament passage from Song of Solomon, and the Gospel, which was from Luke. Emily often told Alan, who had a beautiful voice, that he should volunteer as lay reader sometime. "Give the old ladies a thrill," she said. He declined—he was actually very shy, one reason he'd abandoned journalism for the law—but he would sometimes, at home, say something authoritative ("Five months is a great age to start yogurt because it activates the gut flora") and then follow it with a solemn "The word of the Lord." "Thanks be to God," Emily would reply.

The second hymn was a doozy. She'd never learned to read music, so her version of the melody always sort of meandered near the notes everyone else was singing, and this one really went all over the place.

But she found herself transfixed by the lyrics. It was called "Spirit of God, Descend Upon My Heart."

> Spirit of God, descend upon my heart;
> wean it from earth, through all its pulses move;
> stoop to my weakness, mighty as thou art,
> and make me love thee as I ought to love.

She liked the idea of God stooping to *her* weakness. Certainly most days she felt nowhere near Her level.

> Teach me to feel that thou art always nigh;
> teach me the struggles of the soul to bear,
> to check the rising doubt, the rebel sigh;
> teach me the patience of unanswered prayer.

Boy, did she not know the patience of unanswered prayer. Or just in general the patience of not knowing what came next.

Alan returned, and wordlessly she took the baby from him and found a bench in the shady courtyard. The birds chirped somewhat in time with the reggaeton thumping out of someone's speakers on the street. She could hear the cars zip down Seaman, but here, where you couldn't see them, you could fool yourself into pastoralism. She set Jane down in the grass and gave her a toy, after making a visual sweep for dog poop. While Jane squeaked delightedly, she hummed a little of the hymn, or perhaps some completely different melody that PhDs in musicology would not be able to identify as the hymn. It was with Jane that she felt her lack of patience most acutely. She wanted so desperately to know what her baby would be like at one, at two, at three. What kind of kindergartener would she be? What kind of *teenager*? How amazing would it be to have a teenager who could have whole conversations with you, and watch PG-13 movies? Yet she knew that when that time came, and she was watching PG-13 movies with her daughter and laughing about Goldie Hawn sitting on a GOT MILK? billboard, she would yearn for a return to the roly-poly, portable, squashable baby she was now. She ached already with the loss of that wonderful baby, and then laughed and thought, *Pull yourself together, she literally is that baby.*

Apparently, this was what parenting was: feeling preemptive nostalgia.

Jane, on the grass, fussed, and though Emily knew she was supposed to let her learn to self-soothe she swooped down and grabbed her and lifted her high in the air and said, "Wheeeeeee!" because when she was an old lady this is what she would remember.

— • —

What she always told Lane and Marta and every other assistant when she took each one out to lunch was: Just make the call you're afraid of. Be prepared, be ready, but once you're prepared and ready, don't sit there worrying about the call. Just make the call. At least then, however it goes, you'll be done with the call.

Of course, she herself was not making the call.

She sent an email to Alan about baby music classes in Inwood, she replied to an email from Peter about budgets, she read *Gawker*, she went to the bathroom, she chatted with Lane about the book he was reading. Finally, embarrassed by her cowardice—this was always what it took!—she closed her door and sat down and just dialed the fucking numbers.

"Emily, hey," Bob Fox said. "This is a hell of a thing you sent me. Ben is astonished."

"I've had it a long time," she said.

"Yes, I imagine. Why isn't it in *The Watched Pot*?"

"We just decided it didn't fit the tone."

"'We,' meaning you and Edith." She didn't reply, but let him think for a moment. "Well, I suppose you had your reasons. You just sent me the first page. How long is it?"

"Two thousand or so."

Finally he said it. "Ben really wants the piece for the collection."

"I would love nothing more," Emily said, "than to include it in the St. Martin's edition of Lucy Deming's unpublished work."

"If Lucy wrote it, the estate controls the copyright."

"Of course," Emily said. "But I've got the only copy."

Fox chuckled. "Okay, okay," he said. Control your breathing, Emily. "Your offer is very competitive. I'd love to be able to come back to Sarah with another ten, which would make this an easy decision."

"I would be delighted to give another ten to Sarah."

"And Ben's fee for the introduction is a little low," he added. "Can you do any better there?"

"I cannot. Not if I'm bumping it up for Sarah. Tell Ben I'm so sorry."

"He'll be fine. Well, let me talk to them, but I'm confident everyone will be thrilled. What a pleasure to do business with you, Emily."

"Terrific," Emily said. "And I feel the same."

"I'm going to have my assistant schedule a lunch. I want to hear the whole story."

See? she thought, dancing around her office. *Just make the call.*

— • —

Alan and Emily talked about it for a long time and finally decided that if Emily's mom came out for a week, it would be, on balance, more helpful than it was a pain in the ass. It was the first time she'd come to New York since 9/11 scared her off, and so picking her up at LaGuardia would be more complicated than when Emily had just double-parked the car and run in to meet her at baggage claim. This time Emily called her mom a week ahead of time and taught her how to text, a thing she had never done before, so Alan could pick her up on the curb as opposed to parking a hundred miles away and then trying to find her in the terminal.

"I got her," Alan reported as he drove across the Triborough Bridge. "She was smart. She wore a bright red hat."

"I was very visible!" she heard her mom say in the background.

"Give her the phone," Emily said.

"Hi, honey," her mom said. "I'm being driven by a very handsome chauffeur."

"Okay, Mom."

"*Driving Miss Daisy 2* in here," Alan said in the background.

"That is *not* what I meant!" her mom said. "I'm not that old yet."

"We're excited to see you," Emily said.

"I can't wait to get my hands on that baby."

"Jane, tell Grandma how excited you are." In her exuberance, Jane knocked the phone out of Emily's hand and it broke into pieces on the floor. Luckily, it was the landline.

Alan dropped her mom off and went to park, so her mom rang the bell and Emily buzzed her in. She bounced Jane around the dining room, certain the baby could read the anxiety coming off her in waves. It would be fine. Her mom was here to help. She was not judging Emily's parenting choices. The very term seemed absurd. As if she were making choices! As if she weren't simply flailing, at every moment!

There was a knock on the door and there she was, her mom, already crying, and then Emily was crying, and of course Jane started crying, and when Alan struggled through the door with a suitcase he looked so instantly miserable at the tableau of these three weeping women that Emily started laughing through the tears.

"It's okay, it's okay, Alan," said her mom. "We're not rending garments or anything."

Anne-Marie had told her that their mom was an ideal grandmother, and she was right. She did not judge, or if she did, she said nothing about it. Emily and Alan *knew* that their strictures on screens and allergens must baffle a mother of the 1970s, but Donna accepted and obeyed the rules without a word. She slept on the fold-out couch and took the baby for walks at the crack of dawn and, when Emily and Alan stumbled out of their bedroom at eight, stunned by sleep, she served them eggs over easy. Only once did Emily bristle, when her mom made some offhanded comment about the baby weight, but hey, this week she managed to get to the gym not once but three times.

Her mom had limitless patience for tummy time, for peekaboo, for sitting Jane up and watching her slowly, slowly topple over. Daily activities that Emily and Alan had started to take for granted—nap time, or the nightly bath—became sweet all over again through her mom's eyes. Jane's hams filling up the little plastic bathtub! How could she have lost track of how wondrous that was?

— • —

The worst part about her heroin addiction, Emily said, was the constipation.

"The *worst* part?"

"Well, no. But it's definitely an aspect I don't miss at all."

None of the places they used to eat dinner in Union Square still existed. Indeed they'd all been replaced so long ago that the restaurants that supplanted them were now themselves out of fashion, and two women in their late thirties could walk in at seven p.m. and get a big table to themselves.

Would she ever, she wondered, stop being surprised about how old she was? Surely her mother, right now watching the baby so she could go out to dinner, did not feel that way. Surely those wizened ladies of a certain age you saw feeding pigeons didn't spend all their time thinking, *How am I not twenty-five?*

"It was awful," Emily said. "I would just go a week, two weeks, without crapping."

Emily stared at her friend, horrified. But also thrilled, in a way, that she was telling her this. In its shocking familiarity, it seemed like an artifact of their former friendship, not commensurate with their current tenuous connection. But she was hungry for details of this dark period in Emily's life, which coincided roughly with the time she'd distanced herself from her. In Emily's stories she saw hints and clues to mysteries from the past, all the times she'd flaked, all the broken promises, all the casual cruelties.

"I did not know that was, like, a side effect."

"There was no instruction manual!" Emily said. "So I had no idea. And when I did take a dump, it was horrible. Eventually I just learned that what you do is you just mainline laxatives. Over the years, I probably used as much baby laxative as I did actual drugs."

"That's crazy!"

"I was crazy, in a way," Emily agreed. "It became what my life was, though. You know how you get used to impossible things? Like what you were saying about babies waking up a million times in the middle of the night. You don't think you could get used to that, but when it's your life, you just do it."

"I guess so."

"Sorry to compare your baby to heroin. I'm just saying, I would get up, I would pop laxatives as if they were multivitamins, I would go to work if I had a job, I would get high. That was my day." It struck Emily how odd it was for her friend to deliver the story of her years of addiction as comedy. But then she always had been a showman.

"Can I ask you," she said, "what happened with my wedding?" By the time she was getting married, they never saw each other, but she had not been able to conceive of *not* inviting Emily. In the days before the wedding, she had carefully composed a note telling her how much her presence meant to her.

"Oh God," Emily said, and now the comic tone she'd assumed disappeared. "That was so inane. I was angry because you didn't give me a plus-one, even though, in retrospect, of course you didn't want him there. But I decided I would go. I was proud, I remember. I thought I was taking the high road."

The wedding had been at a farm in Pennsylvania, a few hours' drive from the city, and guests had been put up in painstakingly selected country inns. She and Alan had packed little welcome bags full of local soaps, bug spray, and beef jerky for all the guests' rooms, stamped them with the logo Chessie had designed.

She had spied Emily, the day before the wedding, checking in, and had waved on her way to a luncheon thrown by her mother. She'd thought Emily looked pretty good—dressed stylishly in black, a city mouse in the country. But then she never showed up at the wedding, her seat at the table with Louis and Joe empty.

"My supply ran out," Emily said now. "I just couldn't face everyone without some cushion." The day after the wedding, the manager of the inn gave her Emily's welcome bag. The note she'd written to Emily was still inside, unopened. She remembered being most upset about that.

"Was it a good wedding?" Emily asked. "I bet it was a good wedding."

"It was a terrific wedding," she said. "We had a swing band."

"Oh yeah, what was that, 1999? I bet you did." That was the year everyone had a swing band at their wedding. "I'm really sorry I missed it."

"Louis got really drunk and danced all over Alan and yelled, 'Emily, I'm gonna fuck your hussssssbannd!'"

"Amazing."

"My parents were unamused."

"Oh, I can just imagine Donna's face. They don't do that in Warsaw."

Emily pinched the last of her noodles between chopsticks and slurped. "Part of the whole thing," she said, "is to apologize to people you've hurt. I had this big long list, everything from your wedding to the *Angels in America* tickets." She winced; she hadn't thought about that fiasco in years, but she still remembered what Emily had said to her. "But you're not supposed to do it if you don't think the person would not welcome your reaching out. For a long time, I told myself that you didn't want to hear from me, and that made it easier to let that slide."

"I'm glad to hear from you now."

"Good," Emily said. She smiled. "Okay, tell me about this book deal. You got in the *New York Times*!"

"I did! They love to cover deals that they had a hand in. It's a whole power thing."

"You know, I meant to tell you, I finally read that book," Emily said. "*No Complaints*, is that what it was called?"

"*Can't Complain*." She felt herself instinctively bracing.

"I liked it," Emily said. "I thought it would be corny, but that lady could write a book, my, my, my." She would later tell Alan that hearing Emily say that felt more satisfying than any apology could have been.

— ◆ —

The night before her mom's flight home, Emily took her up to the roof and they sat in lawn chairs, drinking wine and looking at the stars. It was one of those evenings that was the reason there was a whole song about liking New York in June.

Her mom was spending her retirement savings on travel with a group of ladies who called themselves the Red Hat Society, named for that poem about being an old woman and wearing purple. She told Emily about a few of the trips, to the Badlands, to Toronto, to the Potawatomi casino in Milwaukee. "But this is my first visit to New York," her mom said, "where I really get the appeal."

"Well, it's pretty different than when I moved here."

"That's true. It's pretty different when you have a little money."

Emily looked over at her mother, who was gazing upward contentedly. They rarely talked about money, but it did not escape her that her book publishing salary, meager by New York standards, must surely be more than her mom had ever made as a Wisconsin public school teacher. She had looked up MLS listings in Wausau and knew that their apartment with its two tiny bedrooms—so far north in Manhattan that Lisa, who lived in Brooklyn now, referred to their neighborhood as "Upper Canada"—was worth more than the house she grew up in.

"We're doing all right," she said.

"I'm glad, honey."

They talked about Lucy, about Emily's deal to publish the books. "That would be just wonderful," her mom said. "I bet she's up there smiling at us."

"That's a nice thought."

"Actually, you know what Lucy would say if she saw us sitting out on a beautiful night. She'd say, 'This is pot-smokin' weather!'"

This is some kind of milestone, Emily supposed on her way down the staircase. She quietly let herself into the apartment. Alan paused his video game and turned to look at her. "My mom," she said, "wants me to bring up my pot."

Alan burst out laughing. "Sorry," he said. "I was just trying to imagine my mama saying that, but it gave me a stroke."

"I think it's nice. And weird. Nice and weird." In the bedroom, she rummaged around on the shelf in her closet, pulled out her pipe and a lighter and the Tupperware in which she stored the weed she bought from the brother of her assistant, three assistants ago. On her way out, Alan said, "Enjoy your white-lady night!"

Her mom lit the pipe, held it, released the smoke smoothly. "Are you . . ." Emily asked. "Do you smoke at home very often?"

"I'm divorced and I live in Wausau," her mom said. "Of course I do."

"You know, Lucy told me that she loved that she'd smoked with you *and* with me. That tickled her."

Her mom giggled. "That's just lovely," she said. She blew a cloud of smoke into the sky. "Here you go, Luce."

— • —

Ben Bannon was on a research trip to the Maldives so would not be joining them for lunch. Before leaving for the restaurant, Emily tried saying those words out loud a few times, making Lane laugh. "Oh, I'm on a research trip to the Maldives." "Oh, I'm so sorry, I shan't be joining for lunch. Research trip to the Maldives, don't you know."

She and Peter shared a cab. He'd asked if he could come to lunch. "This is your deal, I'm not bigfooting in any way," he'd said. "I just want Bob Fox to know I've got your back." She saw the wisdom. The editorial director making an appearance was a statement of support that Fox might remember when it came time to submit other authors, big-name authors, living authors even. Peter had dealt with Fox in his old days at Little, Brown, but they hadn't made a deal in Peter's entire tenure at St. Martin's.

His assistant Marta had a job offer from Penguin, Peter told her in the cab.

"What a drag," Emily said.

He shook his head. "I cranked up the charm, but I think what she wants is money. It is really hard to hold on to diverse employees. They all get hired away!"

Emily thought about the face Alan would make when she told him what Peter had just said. "It doesn't help that she's almost the only person of color in edit."

"Hey, look, I'd be happy to keep her," Peter said. "Feel free to look at the budget and see what magic you can work."

"I'll talk to Lane. Those two are close. Maybe he'll have some insight."

"Honestly, we'll be all right. She was smart and all, but she had bad taste."

"Peter."

"I'm serious!" She was used to this, his *grapes were sour* impulse when someone might depart. When she had left St. Martin's for the associate editor job at Houghton, he'd been unbelievably bitter, and when she'd returned a few years later for a senior editor position he'd created for her, all was forgiven. He put his hand to his mouth as if telling a secret. "I saw her the other day eating a salad and reading *Barbara Kingsolver.*"

"You're awful!"

"Middlebrow as hell."

"If you ever publish a book as good as *The Bean Trees*, you can die fulfilled."

"Yeah, fine," he said. "But the salad looked bad." He looked at her, anticipating a response to his punch line, then shrugged. "What's Lucy's kid's name again?"

"Sarah. I haven't seen her since Lucy died."

"Oh, wow." He patted her shoulder. "That's intense. Well, you reconnect with her. I'll wine and dine ol' Bob Fox."

"Nice try," Emily said.

Ol' Bob Fox was in a booth at Café Gray, a young woman tucked next to him. "Sarah?" she said, though there was no question this was a larger version of the girl she'd known, and the gulf of years this exposed gave her vertigo.

The way Sarah got up to greet her made Emily certain that Fox was being a pest. Well, kid, welcome to publishing. She was taller, of course, and had turned out pretty, which at age eight had still been in question. Lucy had been striking but not pretty. But Sarah had big eyes and gorgeous hair to go with Lucy's chin.

"Is it okay if I hug you?" Emily asked.

"I recognize you!" Sarah said. "I know you! Yes!" And they embraced, laughing.

"What a story," Bob Fox said.

"This had all better be in the press release," Peter added.

"Exactly!" said Fox. "Good to see you, Peter."

"I recognize you! I know you!" said Peter.

"Very funny," he said. "It hasn't been that long, has it?"

Sarah was still standing, uncertain, so Emily asked her, "Do you mind? I'm just going to slide in next to Bob and you can sit here on the end. Hello!"

"Hello!" Bob Fox said. They kissed on both cheeks. "Such a pleasure."

The waiter took their drink orders, and Fox asked for a bottle of champagne to toast the deal. Emily wasn't sure if Sarah was even legal, but this wasn't the kind of place where they asked. Peter wasn't a creep the way Fox was, but he showed off for Sarah, the way confident men can't stop themselves from performing for pretty girls. Men their age, honestly. She might as well have been at a four-top at Odessa again, two guys competing with each other for who got to talk to Emily.

"We're looking at spring 2007," she said to Sarah to give her a break from the boys. "May or June. I think they're perfect for summer, these books."

"Will you use the same covers?" Sarah asked.

"Oh my, no," said Emily. "I hated those Balcony jackets, and the Avon cover for *Can't Complain* wasn't much better. Pastels and flowers." She made a face and Sarah smiled. "I want something that speaks more clearly to the literary qualities, and that points to the smartest fiction of that era. Because that's what Lucy wrote."

"Hear, hear," Peter said, raising his glass. They all clinked.

Sarah cleared her throat. "I just wanna say, thank you for this. It really means a lot to me that my mom's books are alive again. And that it's you doing it, someone who knew her. I think she'd be really happy about this."

"Well, she was pissed they were published so badly the first time," Emily said. "But she'll love what I'm going to do with them."

In the cab on the way back Peter chucked her on the arm. "This is a really good thing you did," he said. "Great for the company, great for that kid, great for you. We're gonna sell the hell out of these books."

"I think so."

"And Bob Fox loves you. While you and the girl were in the bathroom he goes, 'Hoo, she is a sharp one.' I told him not to even try to get one over on you—you'd eat him for lunch."

"Oh, good, I'm a bitch."

"No, no, he appreciates it. I think we'll be seeing the next big submission from the Fox Agency."

He looked at his BlackBerry, and Emily took the opportunity to slouch in her seat. She was exhausted. It was exhausting, being on all the time. In the bathroom Sarah had asked to see a photo of her daughter, and they'd smiled together at the shot of roly-poly Jane sitting on her lap, staring directly at Alan's camera with a skeptical look. That was the only moment Emily had let her guard down all day.

— • —

Now she knew why Marta and Lane, work spouses, had been huddling a lot the past few days. When she arrived in the office the next morning, Lane's coffee cup was full and steaming, his computer was on, but he was nowhere to be seen. She closed her door most of the way and answered some emails. Then she crept to the door and swung it open. Lane froze, mid-sip.

"Hey," she said. "Got a second? I wanna hear what you think of the Cynthia Margalit marketing plan."

Lane's coffee mug had not moved. "I, uh, I haven't had a chance to read it. I was talking with Marta . . ."

"Oh, no problem. Glad you're helping her. Do me a favor and give it a quick read and then come in? I'm open till eleven." God, these kids. They were as transparent as windows.

Lane was gay, awkward, and sweet. He'd gone to a SUNY school and had zero connections, but she had hired him because his cover letter had made her laugh really hard. It had been the right move. He worked his ass off.

When he came in, she saw that he had filled a notepad page in preparation. His handwriting was legendarily atrocious. Once Marta and another assistant had taken a note he'd written around the office and asked everyone what they thought it said. They then posted the results on the wall of his cubicle, where he still proudly displayed it under the original note:

> Did yogurt must lawns 7
> D. Boon must launch!
> Dan, you aren't loose
> Do you shit [something???]
> Do you want drugs?
> Dogs yak wolf llamas

The original note had said, "Do you want lunch?"

"Okay," he said, perching on her couch. He always sat at the very edge, leaning forward, like at any moment he might need to leap up to help an old lady across the street. "It's a pretty good plan, considering, you know. The book." Lane did have good taste, happily. He hated the right things.

They ran through it, and she made note of a couple of his ideas, which were certainly no worse than the ones the marketing department had come up with. He said he'd type them up in a memo and email them to her. "Before you go," she said, "let's talk Marta."

He froze. The kid had no poker face whatsoever. "Umm, sure," he said, "what about her?"

"I know you two are tight. Is there anything we can do to keep her?"

"Oh! So you know about, um—"

"Peter told me about the offer, yes."

"Look, I don't want to mess her up."

"You love working with her, right?"

He looked glum. "Yes."

"So it's in all our interests to find a way to make her happy. Do you think this is a money thing?"

He sat up, if possible, even straighter. "I don't think there is anything you can give her that would convince her to stay," he said carefully. "I'm gonna go write that email, okay?"

"You're a good friend, Lane."

"The best," he said on his way out.

— • —

Now that her mom knew how to text, she wouldn't stop. Almost every day she wrote, Good morning! Emily knew she should find it oppressive, but she mostly found it charming, because her mom didn't seem to care that sometimes she failed to write back. And she had not abandoned any of her other communication modes; she still mailed Emily clippings from the local paper whenever they mentioned someone she'd gone to high school with, and she still sent her a check for her birthday.

A thin man in a bowler hat held the door for her at the ATM. His earlobes were spread wide open but were empty of gauges. His eyes, heavy-lidded, tracked Emily as she entered. He rattled a cup at her. He looked like a hundred different guys from Sunrise. He even looked a little like Emily.

She deposited the check from her mom: fifty dollars. In the memo field, she'd written *xoxo*. She didn't need it the way she once had, but she did love money.

She dug a couple of quarters from her purse and dropped them in the man's cup on the way out. He tipped his cap and winked, an oddly old-fashioned gesture.

In Emily's chronicle of her bad years, she hadn't outright said that she'd spent time panhandling, but she got the impression that there were really lean months, months when all her money went to drugs, months without a job when she was entirely dependent on Rob. Emily had mentioned, in passing, being fired from a job selling subscriptions to Lincoln Center Theater because she fell asleep in her cubicle, being fired from a job at a restaurant for stealing from the till. She herself had never been fired and found these admissions—which Emily had relayed ruefully but not ashamedly—more shocking, almost, than the stuff about actually doing drugs.

Emily was always smart enough that if she could just be straight for two hours she could talk her way into nearly any job. She even got rehired at Kim's after her old manager left and lasted for a solid six months; she really was a natural there, with her encyclopedic movie knowledge and withering sarcasm.

She wondered if Emily had been forced to beg, and where. She fast-walked through subway stations every day, mind elsewhere, headphones in, the panhandlers invisible. Had she walked past Emily, ever? Had Emily seen her? Had she even said her name?

Emily had been working at the bar, she said, for a couple of years.

She loved it. Booze had never been her thing, she said, and the owner was a fellow addict and kept the place clean.

— ◆ —

Alan and Emily got home together. "I have such good news," Merle said. "Today she ate *two* bowls of cereal at lunchtime."

"That's amazing," Emily said. "What a big girl!"

Alan picked Jane up and tweaked her nose. "That's so many Cheerios!"

"No, the Lucky Charms," Merle said.

Emily stifled a laugh and went to the living room, leaving Alan in the kitchen to tell Merle and Jane, "Actually, the Lucky Charms are *Daddy's* cereal."

— ◆ —

Marta's goodbye drinks were at a dive bar Emily would never have chosen in a million years but which, after a cocktail, she really warmed up to. There was space for everyone and the music wasn't too loud to talk and if the floor was hideous, well, in the aftermath of the Aftermath she certainly didn't intend to drink enough to see it up close.

Peter gave an eloquent toast, seemingly off the cuff but which she knew he'd rehearsed this afternoon. "Marta came to us two years ago," he said. "I've never seen anyone ace an interview like that. She knew our list better than I did. For her edit test, I gave her the Franklin Donaldson book"—there was a chuckle from the older employees—"and her memo was really very good, but during the interview I asked if she had any other thoughts, and I remember what she said." Here he went into an adroit impression of Marta's serious, quizzical affect, though thank God he had the wisdom not to put on her Salvadoran accent: "'If it were me, I would just cancel the book. Why aren't you doing that?'"

The room exploded into laughter. Marta covered her eyes. "And what did you answer?" Chessie asked. She was standing next to Peter wearing a lovely pink Tory Burch dress that Emily would never in a million years have worn someplace this dirty.

"I said we weren't canceling because we'd already spent three hundred thousand dollars on it and there was no way in hell we were getting that back!" Peter said. "And then I hired her." Everyone applauded.

"Marta, in all seriousness, you're remarkable. We'll all miss you so much. Those chumps at Penguin don't know how lucky they are. Of course they're getting a hard worker, a genius organizer, and the baker of the best chocolate chip cookies in New York." More laughter. Marta had once brought in cookies to an office birthday party, and when Lane had teased her about bringing in Chips Ahoy!, she had delivered an impassioned, *Slate* magazine–quality pitch about how Chips Ahoy! represented the Platonic ideal of chocolate chip cookies and anyone who made their own was a fool. "But they're also getting a brilliant editorial mind, as every one of my authors can attest. She's going to be a star. Marta, I believe that—in the traditional words of the El Salvadoran people—*contigo, creo que hasta un pingüino puede volar.*"

Marta broke into laughter. "What did he say?" someone asked.

Marta lifted her glass. "'With you, I believe even a penguin can fly.'" Big cheers. Peter beamed. He didn't speak Spanish.

Later that night, after Chessie steered Peter away from the usual gaggle of assistants soaking up war stories ("Your actual children call," she murmured, smiling) and out the door, Emily sat with Lane, Marta, two other assistants, and Marta's roommate, a wiry librarian with a full sleeve of tattoos who somehow made a mullet look cool. In her day, librarians did not look like that. She got a real Emily-and-Emily vibe off Marta and her roommate, with Marta, of course, as her. Or maybe she was incapable of seeing any pair of twenty-five-year-old girls and not framing their friendship that way.

She was reading a text from Alan and neither listening nor not listening. She needed to go, anyway. The young people deserved to have time without her skulking around.

"A penguin can fly," one of the assistants said. He laughed again. "Man, Peter was great. You really earned that."

"Yeah, all that and more," the roommate said. "After what he—"

Suddenly no one was talking. Emily looked up from her phone. Lane and Marta looked guilty, the roommate looked angry, and the other two assistants looked confused. Christ, she should have left half an hour ago. She got up from her chair and gave a casual little wave. "I'm gonna head out," she said. "Marta, I'm really happy for you. Don't get in too much trouble, everyone."

— ● —

Anne-Marie had a screened porch, so they could sit outside in the afternoon without Emily or Jane getting devoured by mosquitoes. From her seat in an uncomfortable wicker chair, Emily could see the twins in the backyard with their father. He pitched a wiffle ball to Hannah, who swung way too early. Olivia, playing catcher, picked the ball off the ground and threw it back to Mark.

While Anne-Marie rocked with the baby, Emily told her about their adventure at LaGuardia, where ten minutes before boarding a fussy Jane, sitting in the umbrella stroller, had finally exhaled an audible sigh while pooping so hard that it squirted out the legs of her shorts. They'd left her clothes in the bathroom trash and abandoned the reeking stroller in a corner of the terminal, where it had surely been detonated by a hazardous materials team.

"I bet you didn't miss *that* part of having babies," Emily said to an aghast Anne-Marie. She and Mark had adopted the twins from Korea just after the girls' third birthday.

"Actually, they were still in diapers then," Anne-Marie said. "No one had ever potty trained them."

"Oh, gosh." Outside, Mark chased a wiffle ball toward the fence while the girls ran around screaming.

"Yeah, that was a challenging time. Basically, we oversaw four years' worth of development in one year."

"I wish I'd known." When the girls arrived, already so old, Emily had felt like she could never catch up, and didn't really have the money to visit anyway, so she hadn't seen a lot of her nieces for the first few years.

"We all had a lot going on," Anne-Marie said gently. "And anyway, no one really understands about kids until they have kids."

The screen door smacked open as the girls ran inside. "It's raining!" they announced.

"Are you helping Daddy clean up?" Anne-Marie asked, pointing to Mark gathering their toys in his arms.

"He said we should come inside!"

"I heard thunder," Mark said from the yard. "It's okay."

Olivia, the twin who was infatuated with her little cousin, put her hands on her hips. "Mom! Don't let Baby Jane get wet."

"I'll come in if it starts raining hard," Anne-Marie said. When the girls went into the house, she said, "Boy, if you moved here you'd have all the babysitting you could handle."

Emily smiled. "You let me know when Milwaukee gets a publishing house."

"I keep telling Mom there's no way, but she really holds out hope."

"I want to visit more, though. It would be great if we could get the cousins together every August." She was aware, as she said it, that she had not shown the same devotion to family togetherness when it was only Anne-Marie who had kids. To try to gloss it over, she added,

"And you should come out and visit sometime. We'd love to show you around."

"We should do that, honey," Mark said, shutting the screen door behind him. "I'd like to see those memorial pools, you know, at Ground Zero." He sat on the chair next to Anne-Marie.

"No thank you to that," Emily said. "But I could take you to some great museums."

While they talked, Mark kept craning his neck to look up at the sky. "There's been some storms out toward your mom," he finally said. "I guess they had a big tornado by Madison."

"I should call her," Anne-Marie said, starting to get up.

"She's okay. I talked to her. They didn't get hit."

"Aw, Mark," Emily said. She was filled with warmth for this rumpled tax accountant who made her sister so happy. "Thank you for taking care of everyone."

He glanced at Anne-Marie. Emily saw her meet his eye. "No thanks necessary," he said, flustered. "I'm gonna go in and check the TV. If it gets windy, you three ladies come in, all right?"

Anne-Marie kissed the top of Jane's head. The baby was getting squirmy, so she stood up and walked around the porch, pointing to things and naming them. "That's a door! *Door*. That's a tree. *Tree*." The limbs of the tree were starting to creak and bend as the storm approached.

"Mark's really great," Emily said.

"I agree," said her sister. "You didn't used to think so."

"What are you talking about?" Emily said. "I've always loved you two together. You're perfect for each other."

"Emily, come on. You would volunteer to do dishes just to get out of a room he was in."

"I'm just helpful!"

"He's not cool," Anne-Marie said. "So yes, we're perfect for each other."

Outside, a siren began blaring, the tornado warning Emily knew intimately from her childhood. "Uh-oh," Anne-Marie said. "Here we go." Jane started crying, her pitch almost perfectly matching the siren. They went inside to find Mark deputizing the twins. "Olivia! What's your job?"

"Find Dora and bring her downstairs!"

"Hannah! What's yours?"

"Get the lantern!"

"Go! You've got one minute!" Mark looked up from his watch and said to Anne-Marie and Emily, "You'd better get into the basement."

"Yes, sir," Emily said.

Emily had never been in her sister's basement, the only part of the house that did not look perfectly charming. Instead it was filled with exercise equipment and massive 48-packs of toilet paper from Costco. In one corner lurked a foul kitty litter box. The kitty, Dora, arrived shortly afterward in Olivia's arms. Jane stopped crying, intrigued by the bustle around her. They waited by the washing machines. They could see through the tiny windows up near the ceiling that there was a lot of lightning, but the house was so sturdy they could barely hear the wind. Mark played cards with the girls. When the storm passed and the all clear sounded, Hannah was disappointed that the power had never gone out, so Anne-Marie took Jane upstairs while Mark and Emily stayed in the basement with them for a while, the lights turned off, playing Go Fish by lamplight.

— ● —

On her first day back to work after vacation, she walked over to Peter's office when she knew he'd be in. His new assistant, Kim, was sitting outside the door. Emily saw on her desk the packet of detailed notes Marta had left behind. She remembered writing a similar bible for whoever it was who replaced her with Edith, for the assistant Peter hired after her. No matter why you leave, you want to make it as easy as possible for the next person.

"Hi," she said. The girl looked up, startled. She was black, young, pretty. They were always pretty. Emily was definitely the least pretty woman Peter had ever hired as his assistant. She needed to tell him to hire another plain girl, for a change. "I'm Emily. Thiel. I'm a senior editor here."

"Oh wow, hi!" Kim said, standing up. "I'm Kim. Hey." She still had that first-day bubbliness.

"Hi Kim. My office is right down there. Lane's my assistant. You should reach out to either of us if you have any questions, okay? I used to sit in that chair, many moons ago."

"Oh my God, really? That's amazing."

"Well, it's a better chair now. Are you excited?"

"Yes, of course! It's such an opportunity to learn."

"You're learning from the best," Emily said. "Try to remember that when he's calling you Sunday morning to photocopy something for him. That's what I always used to tell myself."

The girl laughed uncertainly. "Here, let me buzz Peter and see—"

"It's fine! Just let her in!" Peter called from the office. Kim sat down.

"If his door's open, it means he'll see visitors," Emily murmured. "He usually does it for an hour or two every morning."

"Thanks," she said. "Uh, go on in."

She smiled her most winning smile. "I shall, thank you."

Peter was on his sofa, a dozen book jacket designs laid out before him. They were all for the same book, a nonfiction immigration chronicle, but the designer had delivered a variety of looks. "I always love this part," he said, gesturing at them. "All these different ways to express something! All these different versions of a story."

"Which one does Sam like?" she asked.

"I told him not to tell me, but it's this one," he said, pointing at a severe, dark treatment on the right side of the table. "That guy's a good editor, but he's such a Republican on design." He picked up another, this one a riot of monarch butterflies. "God, this is great. Maybe I'll send this one back just to fuck with him."

Emily closed the door. She saw Peter notice, but he didn't say anything, just kept moving the book jackets around like a sliding puzzle. "How was—where were you?"

She sat down in the chair opposite. "Wisconsin. Letting the cousins get to know each other."

"It was good you called in to that budget meeting," he said.

"Of course."

He looked up from the table. "What's going on?"

"Why did Marta quit?"

He pursed his lips. "Other than, she got a great offer from Penguin."

"Yes, other than that."

"You'd have to ask her. Did you ask her?"

"I'm asking you."

"Whew!" he said, showily wiping his brow. "You scared me with that door thing, I thought *you* were leaving. Over my dead body!"

"What happened with you and her?" she asked.

He rolled his eyes. "Nothing happened," he said. "You remember being twenty-five, everything's the end of the world. Remember when you quit? Why did *you* quit?"

"Was there something that was the end of the world for her?"

"Not one thing, no. I think she just got tired of me. You know better than anyone that I'm an acquired taste."

"What would Marta say if I asked her?"

"I'm not putting words in that young woman's mouth," he said. "That would be very *problematic*."

"Peter, come on."

"You come on. I'm *attentive*. I pay *attention*. That's what makes me a good boss. That's what makes me a hard boss, too, because you can't fuck up without me noticing. You remember that."

She did remember. For the first six months here, she'd been positive she was about to be fired every day. Peter directed a lot of personality right at you. He shouted, he told jokes, he said outrageous things to get a response. It was like being directly in the sun. At first, she'd burned.

"And you survived, right?" he said. "Marta was a little bit uptight, frankly. You know how this generation is, they're all so fragile. A stiff wind can knock 'em over. And I'm a stiff fuckin' wind!"

She had survived. She thought often, with pride, about how after those awful six months she had pushed back, started to give as good as she got. She remembered one day, in the old building, when Peter was needling her about something he was sure she'd gotten wrong, how could anyone be so foolish, what the fuck was wrong with her, and finally she'd snapped, "I'll bet you fifty bucks I'm right." He'd looked shocked, then laughed and said "You're on." She'd been right, and he'd paid up. When she got promoted off his desk, a year later, he'd had one of the designers draw a $50 bill with his face on it and framed it for her. It still sat on the bookshelf in her office.

"Look," he said. "I'm sure she got her panties in a wad—sorry, sorry—about some fucking joke I made, but she never said anything about it. When *you* were pissed about something I said, you just told me. Maybe Marta was afraid to do that. But what am I supposed to do with someone like that?"

"Peter, you've got to dial it down a little," she said. "You're right that these girls just don't know what to do with you. But we can't keep losing talent."

"Babies," he said. "We can lose babies."

"Do you promise?"

"Look, can you talk to this new one? Just tell her what she's in for. Tell her what kind of guy I am. Give her the best version of me. And maybe give her some tips."

She folded her arms. "Promise, Peter."

"Fine," he said. "I'll keep it in my pants. I'm kidding! I'm kidding. I'll be good."

"Thank you."

"Thank *you* for being my guy." He picked up the most colorful dust jacket design, the one with the butterflies. "Look at these little fuckers! They're beautiful. Sam's just gonna have to suck it up."

— • —

Alan used to be a Deadhead. That was the most embarrassing thing about him. But over the years, he had played so much of the band around the house that Emily, to her surprise, had come to know and even like some of the songs.

Just after Thanksgiving, Jane had the flu and was feverish and sad and, after an incredible diaper bomb that rivaled the Great August Airport Blowout, she absolutely would not stop crying. In the end Emily, covered in poop anyway, simply turned on a warm shower, stripped both of them naked, and stepped in holding the baby, who instantly stopped crying and gaped at her with utter astonishment. The water splashed everywhere, the mess ran off them both, and Jane twisted her body around, trying to figure out where the water was coming from.

When they were both dry, a robed Emily held Jane in the glider. The lights were low. She'd been rediapered and wrapped in blankets and was finally not fussing. Emily wasn't a medical professional, but she got the sense that maybe her fever had broken a little. She rocked back and forth, singing a Grateful Dead song that made for a good lullaby. "If my words did glow with the gold of sunshine," she sang. "And my tunes were played on the heart unstrung."

"It's 'harp.'" Alan peeked around the door, home finally from a late night at work.

"Harp?"

"The harp unstrung."

"Let me go ahead and correct whatever Grateful Dead guy wrote this—"

"Robert Hunter," he said, instantly.

"A 'harp unstrung' wouldn't even make a sound."

"Well I think that's the point of the—" She held a finger up to her lips and gestured to the sleeping baby. "He's saying that nonetheless the magic is conveyed—" She shushed him, shaking her head solemnly. "Okay, okay," he said, laughing. "Don't let me interrupt you. What could be better than my beautiful wife singing the Dead to my beautiful baby?"

"With my beautiful voice."

"Life is perfect."

"Don't look in the bathroom, then."

He disappeared, looked in the bathroom, and peeked back around the door. "Ah," he said. "I'll get to work diverting the rivers." He stood in the doorway a moment more. "I like your version better. The heart unstrung. That would make a good title for something."

Emily looked down at Jane, sleeping eyes, red cheeks, pinkies the size of Good & Plentys. "It's how you make me feel all the time, kid," she said. "The heart unstrung."

"I'll clean up," he said. "I brought home dinner when you're ready."

"Wash your hands!" she called after him.

"I'll never stop washing them!"

— • —

When she and Emily had first reconnected, she had wondered what her former friend possibly had to offer her, what Emily could add to her full and complete life. But as the months went on and Emily seemed always to be interrupting something interesting to hang out with *her*, she started to wonder the opposite: What did *she* possibly have to offer Emily, whose life was packed with theater and men and late nights at bars?

One thing that she didn't have to offer Emily was the joy of spending time with a small child, because Emily didn't care about small children. She had never known someone so unmaternal in her life. In December, she invited Emily up to Inwood to get to know Alan and Jane. Emily arrived bearing a pie and gripped it with profound alarm when she was offered burbling, squirming Jane to hold. "No, that's okay," Emily said. "I've, uh, I've got this pie."

It had taken her some time to get over this seeming rejection of Jane, the most important thing in her life. What did Emily mean, she didn't want to hold the baby?! But as the evening went on, she came to find it an interesting challenge to find things to talk about that *weren't* the baby, a challenge neither she nor Alan had faced recently. Well, what *did* they think of *Brokeback Mountain*? (They hadn't seen it yet.) Well, how *did* they feel about the new *Sweeney Todd*, where the actors play instruments? (They'd missed it.) (They had a baby!) Well, their guest tried, what *did* they think would happen in the new season of *The Sopranos*? Ah! On television she was absolutely prepared to argue passionately. She also had opinions about *The Wire*, and *Six Feet Under*, and *Extras*. Emily and Emily agreed Ricky Gervais was a genius and that the American *Office* would never match up to the British one. Alan, who thought the British *Office* was too mean, abstained. Soon they were talking about Hurricane Katrina, and Kanye saying George Bush didn't care about black people, and whether Kanye was a genius or an idiot. ("Why not both?" Alan cracked.)

Alan excused himself to bed, Emily smiling gratefully at this tacit offer to get up with Jane in the morning. They finished around midnight, Emily trying to call her friend a cab, Emily declining. "I like the time on the subway," she said. It wasn't exactly like their long nights in the squat, but it wasn't entirely unlike it, either. After Emily left she felt herself buzzing—not buzzed, not exactly, she'd only had a few beers, but *buzzing* with ideas and enthusiasm. The last part of the night had been Emily telling her about the theater project she was working on, Chekhov in a subway station, and Emily had surprised herself by asking some sharp questions that made her friend stop to really consider the answers. They were editorial questions, she told herself—the kinds of questions she would ask about a novel or a book proposal. What is the shape of this material? What does this art do that other work can't? She got the impression from Emily's bemused response that she didn't get asked these kinds of questions very much about her work.

"Will you come to rehearsal?" Emily asked before she left. "I could use your eyes." She had a quick vision of Emily holding her eyeballs in her hand, like in *Beetlejuice*. She agreed to stop by next week after work, a promise that would entail some further spending of spouse points to pull off. Then she went into the kitchen to wrap up a slice of pie for her friend, only to hear the door shutting behind her.

She rolled into bed, where Alan was snoring lustily; she was about to nudge him to get him to roll over when she heard Jane crying. She rolled right back out of bed and crept toward Jane's room.

She crouched outside the door, as if she were a SWAT guy preparing to enter a hostage situation. She was listening. Sometimes, very seldom, almost never, Jane would cry briefly but then go back to sleep. It wasn't impossible that this time was one of those times. She had a vivid memory of a night when they both had nine a.m. meetings the next day and it had been her turn and Jane had started crying and then, for some reason, simply stopped and slept through the rest of the night. What if it happened again? The bards would sing of it.

This time she heard her daughter's cries sputter and trail off, and there were four seconds of incredible hopeful silence, and then Jane *screamed* in rage and Emily was through the door in a flash. Jane was standing in her crib in the dark, holding the bars like a prisoner, livid.

The night-light reflected off her tears. "MAMA," she said sternly, and Emily picked her up and sank into the glider, unsettled at being scolded by an eleven-month-old.

The goal was to rock her to sleep without having to further feed her, because they were trying to sleep-train her—an awful term, as if Jane was a dog, although in her most exhausted moments she wished they could get her to be half as obedient as a dog. Emily had found the most useful mindset for getting her back to sleep was to become totally blank, to rock mechanically back and forth while not engaging with her daughter's many attempts to change the object of their inter-action from *sleeping* to *eating* or, for that matter, *playing* or *talking* or *tickling*. To maintain that blankness, she found it necessary to steer her thoughts away from the present or the future, and toward the past. She thought of her and Emily's first friendship, those few years in the East Village. She thought of the way that they became, for a certain time, like two halves of one whole, a shared brain their friends thought of as Em-and-Emily. There had been such comfort in knowing her place in that ecosystem: she was the one who hadn't read Dostoyevsky but who *did* know to send a thank-you note, the one who would dazzle no one with her intellect but who would also offend no one with her obstinate belief in the power of that intellect. She was the one who was less of a genius but more of a human.

For a while Emily's genius had been enough. More than enough. She'd been happy to catch just a little bit of the reflected light. Happy to benefit from it, in fact. But she also found herself exhausted at the work she had to do to repair all the harm Emily did to her, to everybody. Granted, right now, gliding with a blessedly quiet toddler radiating the heat of sleep in her arms, the harm felt far away in her memory, and the light felt bright.

This evening had made real the possibility of a kind of return of that part of her, the part that was illuminated. She felt, a decade later, like she could focus that light in ways that might be useful to Emily, to her. The question was, could the rest of her life accommodate that new piece? She thought perhaps so. It would require her to be someone a little different, but she'd always been able to be different people when she needed to be.

She gently dumped her sleeping daughter back into the crib, Jane's brand-new curls sticking to her sweaty forehead. She left a hand on the girl's stomach, slipped an index finger in between the buttons of her pajamas to feel her smooth, round tummy. Jane stirred, cooed, stayed asleep. Part of her was here with Jane, feeling the baby's pulse as her own. Part of her was building ideas about Chekhov in the subway. Part of her was with Peter, steering him, making the most out of his particular genius. Part of her was with Lucy's books, guiding them slowly through the machine, so at the other end they would come out as she'd imagined them. Part of her was in bed with Alan, curled into his apostrophe in the dark. She knew that later she would feel doubts, would feel frightened, but at this moment she thought she might be big enough, she might have enough within her, to be all those things at once.

1993

The Emotional Megaphone

Em had begun to think of herself as an anthropologist whose research focused solely on Emily.

On the subway, Emily loved to give up her seat for the elderly. The very appearance of a gray beard or a stooped back got her to her feet. Often, Em saw, the riders to whom she offered a seat did not yet think of themselves as elderly, and resented Emily's overtures. Emily didn't care.

On the subway, Emily never got up for pregnant women, or people with babies. It was like she didn't even see them. She asked her why and Emily said that once she'd given up her seat for a pregnant lady and the husband—the husband!—took her seat, leaving the wife standing next to her. She still seemed indignant, months or years later. "Breeding doesn't make you special," Emily said.

On the subway, Emily often took out one of her little notebooks and made notes about her fellow riders. There was nothing surreptitious about it: she would stare right at someone, squinting as if to bring them into focus, then scribble something in the book, then stare again. Sometimes she even made little sketches that Em found very acute in their choice of details. Emily was not a trained artist, but in her sketches as in conversation she was a kind of expert caricaturist with a knack for finding a person's defining feature: a gaudy ring, legs crossed at the ankle, a scornful frown. Once, on an N train, the man across from Emily stared back, pretended to preen and pose, then said, "Okay, show's over," and moved farther down the car. Emily silently transferred her attention to a woman sitting nearby.

On the subway, Emily refused to give money to people who sang, or danced, or sold candy bars. She scorned the homeless who had worked up a whole patter, the ones with clever signs. But when they entered a car with a sleeping bum taking up a whole row of seats, Emily often waited until they reached their stop and then, on the way out of the train, sidled past him and slipped a dollar bill under his hand.

On the subway, Emily spread her legs like a man twice as tall, her backpack slouching on the floor between them. Next to her, Em was acutely aware of her own presence on the seat. She was proud to be with someone who so assertively demanded her fair share, and more, but nonetheless she tucked herself into the space Emily left over. Between them—a small person making herself big, and a big person trying to make herself small—they occupied about as much room as two people ought to.

On the subway, Emily bit her nails. It was a habit she pursued as assuredly as she did everything else in her life, and so even though she took care of her hair and her clothes her hands looked just awful. Often in the corners of her fingernails tiny scabs would reveal the places where Emily had picked at the cuticles until they bled. Em got used to seeing Emily working over a finger, eyeing it, tucking it away in a pocket for a while. Over the years of their friendship, it got so that Em never even noticed. But then one rainy Sunday they were supposed to meet at the Seventy-Ninth Street station, and as Em waited under an awning for the terminally late Emily, the umbrellas and raincoats up and down Broadway all smeared together. Everyone looked the same in a New York drizzle. But then she saw a figure standing kitty-corner to her, looking the wrong direction. The person's hood obscured their eyes, but Em saw the hand creep up, the teeth worry at the nail. For a moment, she could see her friend as strangers might see her, a young woman at sea in the city, as uncertain as everyone else. Em wasn't fooled.

Em was desperate for stories about growing up in Athens, but her enthusiasm only embarrassed Emily, or, more accurately, made Emily embarrassed for her, for her uncool enthusiasm about this cool place. It seemed to Em that long before Emily herself actually attended

UGA, her life in the college town had already revolved around the school and its denizens. Her father's students were forever slouching about her kitchen; she hung out on campus or on Broad Street or in the university's black box theater. She told stories that sounded like college stories—stories of house parties with bands who would later become famous playing in the backyard, or stories of friends making great artistic leaps forward—before passingly mentioning that at the time she was, like, thirteen. If she'd ever had a curfew, she never mentioned it. She often spoke with affection of Charlie, a boy who'd loved Emily so much he carved a V in his chest. ("V for . . ." Em inquired, and Emily said, "Van Gogh.") Charlie was one of her father's favorites, she said, a very promising painter, and it was not clear what age she'd been when he, besotted, flipped open his penknife. "Old enough," she'd say.

And so pinning Emily down on what her actual college experience had been like was difficult for Em, whose own narrative of college was sharp and linear, a story with a beginning, a middle, a junior year, and an end. Sometimes Emily mentioned idiot professors she'd fought with; sometimes she alluded to wild experimental productions that in some oblique way must have fulfilled a course requirement. She referred often to the "pink house," an in-some-way-legendary falling-down Victorian in which she had lived for months—years?—together with other artists in ever-shifting configurations. Someone got a job in Atlanta; someone else was staying with her girlfriend a lot; someone else invited a guy he knew from back home. One roommate dealt drugs and another roommate had given her the CD changer and another roommate was the son of a famous poet, who once sat in the living room, observing her son and his roommates with distaste, before being awarded an honorary degree.

Emily had left Athens under stormy circumstances, that much was clear. Was it about her parents? Was it about the higher-ups in the college's drama department, for whom Emily expressed nothing but the purest scorn? Was it about the record store she worked at, a workplace where everyone had been cool except for the stalker? "I was just done with that place" was all she would say. Em didn't even know if she'd graduated. She'd mentioned with some bitterness an aborted honors project, a production of Fornés scuttled by actors who didn't get it, an administration that only wanted to cut her down to size. But Em had trouble with the math. Emily was only a year older than her, but seemed to have lived in New York since the beginning of time.

— • —

Em let herself into Lucy's apartment and called out, "Hello?"

"I'm in here!" Lucy said from the tiny alcove off the living room she called an office. Em heard the slow *clack-clack-clack* of Lucy typing at Lucy speed.

"Don't get up," Em said. "Do you need anything from the kitchen?"

"Coffee? Sarah made me some before she went to school, but I drank it."

Em would have to tidy up the kitchen or there would be roaches. While the new pot brewed, she washed the breakfast dishes and put away boxes of cereal, packets of granola, a half-full bag of penne pasta. She poured milk in Lucy's coffee and brought her the mug, sitting down on the wooden chair perched just outside the alcove. "Your hair's a mess," she said.

"I tried washing it, but, you know." Lucy sat back in her chair. "Let me finish this page and then you can take over." She went back to the typewriter: *clack, clack, clack.*

"Won't the nurse wash it for you?"

"Well, that's not her job." When she finished the page, Lucy carefully rolled it out of the typewriter, set it atop the pile on her desk, and took hold of her cane.

"Want help?"

"I think I'm all right," she said. She maneuvered herself up and made her way into the living room, easing herself onto the couch. "Ah, I left the coffee in there," she said with a comic-strip slap of the head. Em moved it to the end table.

It was six months since Lucy's diagnosis. When she had called Em at the office to tell her the news, she'd said, "Can Edith sell a funny memoir about a terminal disease?"

Can't Complain got good reviews and, according to Vanessa, was selling all right, helped along by an essay that Lucy placed in the *Times*, assisted by a junior editor at the *Book Review* Em had met at a party.

A Happy Novelist Faces a Sad Story
By Lucy Deming

I've always written about the good stuff.

There was a time in my life, a bad time, when I was a pessimist. The glass wasn't half-empty, it was nearly gone, and the bottle was already in the trash. But as a writer, I've always written optimistically. I love writing about characters who are living the best they can, who are in love, whose circumstances may be complicated but whose days are full of joy. I love writing about the food they cook, the wine they drink, and the hangovers they don't regret.

I once went to a reading by a very famous writer who said, "The job of an author is to make life as difficult as possible for his characters." The idea was that in those terrible circumstances, character is revealed. But I never agreed with that. Life is already difficult. God knows I've made life difficult for the people I love: my mother, who worried about me all the time; my daughter, whom I browbeat to study, study, for God's sake; my husband, who found life with me so difficult he considered drugs but settled for a new girlfriend and a new apartment in California. When that happened, I got very sad for a very long time before I finally shook myself out of it.

When I finished my latest novel, *Can't Complain*, a friend asked if the novel was just a little *too* cheerful. "Shouldn't your characters be sad more often?" she said. What she meant was: Shouldn't things be a little harder for them? They live, they love, they dispense witticisms. Where's the suffering?

But I don't want to write the hard stuff. I like my characters. I made them, after all. They're like my children, except that they actually do what I say. Things are hard enough for everyone, even fictional characters; they don't need me making it harder on them. And I find that they reveal just as much in their passions and predilections as that famous writer's characters did when he put them through the wringer.

Last summer, I was having a lot of trouble with my legs. They'd always hurt when I walked too far—I've never been petite—but they went from being angry with me to simply being unresponsive, as I did to my mother when approaching adolescence. I would tell my legs to walk over there, and they would ignore me, or do such a half-hearted job of it that it was barely worth it. On one of those occasions, my right leg decided, midstep, that it was done communicating with me for the day, and I fell down and broke my ankle. (*I sure showed you, leg*, I thought as the pain rang through my body.)

Well, like most problems I've tried to ignore over the years, the news didn't get better. A doctor told me I had amyotrophic lateral sclerosis, better known as Lou Gehrig's disease. A Yankees disease! Bitter news for anyone, but worse for me, a

Southerner and a Mets fan. Why couldn't I have simply blown out my elbow, like every Mets pitching prospect?

I still don't want to write about the hard stuff, but more and more of it is hard stuff these days. I'm walking with a cane. I can still enjoy cooking and food and drink and conversation, though the doctors assure me that before long those abilities, like all abilities, will fade away, as if I'm a baby in reverse. (Thanks for the assurance, Doc.) I still can play with my daughter, although our pastimes are getting more and more quiet: reading together, cooking something simple, watching movies. Luckily, she's always been an indoor cat, so spending time together isn't the hard part. Knowing that I'm going to have to say goodbye to her, and she's going to have to say goodbye to me, that's the hard part—which, as I've said, I don't intend to write about, so let's move on.

My friend says, "The hard parts are what sells books." Scarlett O'Hara's torments. Sylvie and Ruthie's struggles in *Housekeeping*. Even that madman Stephen King is writing about the hard parts—loss, sadness, sickness, heartbreak— though he distracts us with ghosts and space aliens. And given that I have a daughter to feed and send to college and push out into the world, even though I won't be there to do it in person, I guess it would behoove me to write about the hard parts.

But I'm my own character. I created me, from scratch, and I've been building myself for forty-*ahem* years, and I'll be darned if I'm going to put myself through all that. It took me a long time not to be unhappy, and I'm not going tell a sad story now, just because of a plot twist as hacky as a fatal disease.

Every day friends come to see me, so I'm writing about them. Yesterday I made a delicious risotto, so I'm writing about that. This morning my daughter came into my bedroom and the sun streaming through the window lit up her hair like the halo on a Renaissance painting. It was just about the most beautiful thing I'd ever seen. So I'm writing about it. I'm going to keep writing about the good stuff, just as long as I can. ∎

"Being a writer is good sometimes," Lucy had said when the essay was published and long-ago friends and family sent her dismayed letters, "because it helps you avoid a lot of sad conversations."

Now Em settled down at the desk and read the page Lucy had finished. "Are you at the end of a thing, or does this continue?" she asked. Lucy and Em had explained this new book to a dubious Edith as recipes, with a memoir.

Lucy very, very carefully picked up the cup of coffee. "Let's start fresh," she said as Em rolled a new sheet of paper into the typewriter. "I just remembered a cobbler."

— ◆ —

On the train, Emily was quieter than usual. She had headphones and a book, and she'd skim a few pages and then close the book, distracted, and look out the window at the silver blur of the northeast, her fingernails at her mouth. Outside Baltimore, the batteries on her Walkman died, and Emily, out of character, had packed a baggie full of fresh AAs in her duffel.

They couldn't afford the sleeper car on the Crescent, so dinner was à la carte. They waited until after the train left Washington and crossed the Potomac, when other passengers were starting to turn off their lights, to walk through the rocking train to the dining car. Em convinced the attendant to just let them order grilled cheese off the lunch menu rather than spring for a steak. They found two empty seats across a table from a middle-aged man in a suit nursing a Budweiser. "I won't be here long," he said.

They sipped glasses of water and read their books while they waited for their food. When the man asked what they were reading, Em showed him her book, *The Secret History*, with its striking clear plastic cover. "It's about a group of classics students who get wrapped up in a crime," she explained. He asked if it was exciting like John Grisham, and she said no, it wasn't really. She wished he would just let her read.

"How about you over there?" he asked Emily. "Looks impressive." When Emily didn't answer, he waved at her. "You hear me in there?"

She didn't take off her headphones, so she was very loud when she said, "My friend was raised to be polite to random assholes, but I wasn't." The man's expression when he left soon after reminded Em of a batter looking at the sky in disbelief as he walked back to the dugout after strike three.

They'd been friends for nearly two years, and Em had never really seen Emily like this. When they finished their sandwiches, Em hesitantly put a hand on Emily's. Emily started. They almost never touched. Even last summer, when Emily had accompanied Em to Planned Parenthood after a poorly thought-out one-night stand with a poet, she had talked Em through it, not hugged her through it.

Emily seemed to understand Em's intent and pushed her headphones down around her neck. The sound of a squalling saxophone leaked out until she pressed stop on the Walkman. "Hey," she said.

Em thought about asking what was wrong, but instead said, "What are you listening to?"

"Morphine," Emily said. "It's too bad we can't listen together. That would be cool." Em knew that what she meant by this was that she wished she could control what Em was listening to, too.

"I think you'd like this book," Em said. "Lot of intense intellectual debate. Plus murder."

"This can be my one if you want," Emily said. She'd agreed to take one post-1947 book recommendation from Em per year. "It's only January, though."

"When was the last time you saw your grandma?" she asked.

"When I left Georgia," Emily said. "That was '89."

"What's the party going to be like? Do you know?"

"Not really. They're having it at my aunt's house in Conyers." This was the first Em had heard that they wouldn't be going to Athens. Maybe Conyers, wherever it was, was close. "My grandma loves barbecue, so I think they'll probably have someone roasting a pig or something."

"A whole pig?"

"Yeah. They don't do that in Warsaw?"

When the invitation for Emily's grandmother's seventy-fifth birthday celebration had arrived, Emily surprised Em by asking if she would come with her down to Georgia for it. Emily rarely asked Em to do anything. Usually she told Em what they were doing.

Emily had called to RSVP from Em's office, where long distance was free; when she said what time their train would get into Atlanta, her aunt suggested she'd tell Emily's mom to pick them up. Emily had hung up the phone and said, "What a nightmare this is going to be."

"What's your grandma like?" Em asked now.

"She's great. Can we get some beer, maybe? Do we have enough money for that?"

They carried their beers back through the dim cars, bracing themselves against the backs of seats as the train rolled to and fro. This time Em took the window.

"She's an archetypal grandma," Emily said finally. "Bakes cookies, the whole shebang. I stayed with her a lot while my parents were off at artists' residencies and stuff." She pulled from her beer. "Once they went to Greece for three months and I spent the whole summer at her house. That was outstanding."

"I can't imagine spending a summer with my grandparents. I would get so bored. What did you do?"

"I read, basically. And watched old movies with her. I was ready to get away from all the bitches in my neighborhood in Athens." Em felt as though she'd told Emily dozens of stories of her own childhood but knew almost nothing about hers. She made a vaguely encouraging noise and Em continued. "I'd take her dog for walks. Sometimes we would visit the apparition site."

"Excuse me?"

"Yeah, this is weird," Emily said. "In Conyers, there's this lady who says she gets visited by the Virgin Mary, and once a month her farm gets just flooded with crazies who want to hear the word of God. We'd go sometimes. Grandma Catherine's really into it."

"Was that, you know, terrible?"

"It was wild. Mobs of people on pilgrimages from all over the place, and they're all praying the rosary. And my grandma would just hang out for hours, listening to the prayers and watching people. But then one time I met a guy whose parents dragged him down from Missouri or something and we made out behind the porta-potties. Nothing like getting fingered while a thousand people recite Hail Marys in the background."

"That seems, uh . . ."

"Formative."

Em had brought a deck of cards, but Emily didn't like games. She dealt out Solitaire but lost every time. Finally she just cheated. In the window Em's reflection looked puffy and tired. Next to her, Emily was dead asleep; she'd already gone to the bathroom to brush her teeth and then conked out. Her headphones lay tangled on her lap, so Em gently removed them, put them on, and pressed play. A low saxophone moaned over a bass line. "Somedaaaaaay," a man's voice sang, "there'll be a cure for pain."

She slept fitfully, hearing in the twilight of a dream the conductor's voice announcing the names of little Carolina towns: High Point, Salisbury, Gastonia, Spartanburg. In Charlotte the train stopped for twenty minutes, and through half-shut eyelids she watched the man from the dining car walk from light to light along the platform, head down against the cold. After that she finally conked out all the way and awoke to dawn, the crimson sun shining directly into her window as they crossed a bridge. The berm was thick with kudzu, and in the distance tall pines speared the sky.

Emily stayed asleep, or pretended to be asleep, until the conductor announced Atlanta. Em thought the train trip would be an adventure they took together, but Emily had had other ideas.

Inside the station a woman wearing a jean jacket waved at them and then hurried over. She stopped short in front of them. "You made it!" she said. Though Emily had told her their moms were the same age she seemed younger, dressed in a flowing skirt and boots, her hair conspicuously blonde. Despite the differences, she was so obviously related to Emily that it seemed almost embarrassing, like seeing two people wearing the same top to a party. She hovered for a moment, then hugged Emily, who hugged her back. Then she opened her arms up to Em. "You're Em!" she said. "I don't know you yet, but come here!" She smelled expensive.

In the car, Peggy—"Call me Peggy"—kept a steady stream of questions coming. How long was the train, had they slept, was it too cold up there in New York, how did they meet? Emily's answers were guarded, Em could tell, but not unfriendly. Em had expected Peggy to have more of a Southern accent, but her voice had only a lilt, like a drop of pigment in a watercolor. "Are you girls hungry?" she asked, and they both blurted, "Yes."

They stopped at a funky little diner with retro décor and a menu full of tofu scrambles. "We should try to be fast," Peggy said as they sat down at a booth. "Traffic's going to be bad into Conyers because it's an apparition day."

"Oh, Emily told me about that," Em said.

"If you'll pardon me asking—are you religious?"

"Christmas and Easter," Em said. "I did youth group in high school."

"Well, this town turns into a nuthouse on these days. I can't stand to visit. It is just full of Christian wackos."

"Like your own mother," Emily said tartly.

"Please, don't remind me," Peggy said.

The waitress arrived, her hair an honest-to-God beehive. Emily and her mother looked away from each other. Em ordered first.

"Who all is coming to the party?" Em asked once the waitress disappeared behind the swinging doors to the kitchen.

"Some cousins, a few neighbors. Some of the ladies from her church." Peggy swirled her Diet Coke in her glass as Emily sipped hers. "My brother, Emily's uncle."

"Uncle Walter is coming?" Emily said. For a moment, she and Peggy made the exact same face, and Em fought back a giggle.

"I'm just planning on avoiding him. Please, Emily, please do the same. Not at Grandma Catherine's party."

"We'll see," Emily said.

"Oh, Jesus."

Peggy drove a two-lane highway the rest of the way into Conyers. Sometimes they'd pass under or over the interstate, and though the traffic didn't seem bad, each time they did, Peggy made a little noise of satisfaction. Em asked how far they were from Athens, and nodded when told it was an hour away. She was here for Emily, she reminded herself, not for her own fantasies of coolness.

Emily's aunt's house was a wide brick rambler surrounded by so much lawn it might better be described as a field. A dozen cars were parked out front. The front porch had big white columns, for some reason, like Monticello. At the side of the house, smoke blew in tangles from what looked like the biggest grill Em had ever seen. "Is that—is there a pig in there?" she asked.

"Oh, you bet," said Peggy.

Inside, the house was full of smoke and sound and people who shared qualities with Emily but seemed, nonetheless, totally different from her. There were freckles, there was thin brown hair, there were voices turned up just a bit louder than appropriate. But there were also baseball caps and polo shirts and bangs that looked straight out of Em's high school yearbook. Everyone who wasn't Peggy greeted them with an accent straight out of *Gone with the Wind*.

The living room windowsills were as packed with Precious Moments figurines as the room was with well-wishers. In the corner, installed in a big brown easy chair, was a thin woman holding a Miller High Life. "Emily Catherine!" she called as soon as she saw her granddaughter, and the room parted.

For the next few minutes, everyone else hung back respectfully as the two women reunited, Emily crouching in front of the chair. They were having what would have been a private conversation except that Emily had to say everything every loud and distinctly. "YOU'RE THE ONLY ONE WHO COULD GET ME BACK TO GEORGIA," Em heard her say, and Emily's grandmother slapped the arm of the chair with delight. Em loved her right away. She knew from experience that Emily would never think to introduce them, so she stood in front of them until Emily's grandmother looked over Emily's shoulder and said, "Well, who is this?"

Later, she went outside to look at the smoker, only too late realizing that the man tending it was the fabled Uncle Walter. He was perfectly nice to her, though, at first. He offered her a cigarette, which she declined, and asked after her trip. "I took that train up to New York once," he said. "Years ago. I love that city, man. Always somethin' going on."

"Yeah, there sure is."

"Next time I come by, I'll look you two up. You and Emily roommates?"

"No, I live in a different apartment. Is grilling the pig your job?" she asked.

"Smoking, we're smoking her. Low and slow," he said. "Low heat, slow cook. I'm about to take her off—you wanna see?"

He pulled on a pair of big protective gloves and lifted the lid of the smoker. Inside was a long, heavy mass, inarguably the shape of a pig's body, wrapped in aluminum foil. It smelled, Em had to admit, delicious. He plucked the foil off to reveal dark, wrinkled skin, disconcertingly recognizable as such, like her own leg cooked brown. "Em," Walter said, "meet Hillary. Hillary, meet Em."

"Hillary?" Em asked.

"Hillary Rodham, that's what I call her—no offense if you're a feminist," he said, throwing a wink. "Man, she cooked up perfect, look at that." He rooted around in the pig's midsection, pulled out a few strings of meat. "You wanna try this?" Em looked away, said "No thanks" as loudly as she could. "Hey, just a joke," he said.

In the kitchen, Emily's father was holding forth on Georgia football, singing the praises of some running back or another. Roger was a tall man in his sixties with a ruddy face and neat gray hair. He didn't look or sound like any art professor Em had ever seen. When he spoke, he gestured exuberantly with his hands. "I saw this boy hit the line and *bam*"—a punch of the air, his drink spilling on the floor—"Oh, sorry about that, Kent, he was ten yards downfield before they knew what hit 'em."

Peggy sat at the table, holding a cocktail as some neighbor talked to her. Grown adults were usually better at masking their boredom, Em thought, and in her inability to do so Emily's mom resembled her daughter, whose face also became a mask of impatience when Em wasn't being interesting enough. Em thought suddenly that she ought to check on Emily. This seemed like a situation where she might need a supportive hand.

Emily, however, was fine. She was helping Grandma Catherine to her feet and leading a group who were planning on heading to the farm where the Virgin Mary appeared. "Oh good," she said, tossing Em a key chain, "can you drive my grandma's car?"

Now *here* was the adventure, Em behind the wheel of a Chrysler—yes, as big as a whale—leading a convoy of cars from the party, filling up more than her share of the lane up the highway north of town, Grandma Catherine directing from the passenger seat. Each time they approached an intersection, she said, "No, no, no, no, don't turn here, oh YES, oh no, no, this isn't it." Finally she just said, "YES, this is it," but Em already knew because she could see hundreds of cars parked in a field.

"We picked a good day," Emily said as their group of twelve made their way toward the house where everyone seemed to be assembled. She was carrying a lawn chair she'd pulled from her grandmother's trunk. "It's not a weekend, so it's not a total zoo." She explained that the house was visitated on the thirteenth of the month, every month. The woman who lived there was the center of it all. "She smells roses, sometimes she collapses. It's very menstrual, in my opinion."

"Now hush," her grandmother said, laughing. She was flanked by Emily's aunt on one side and one of her church friends on the other, each of them with a light touch on her arm as she picked her way up the hill.

"Grandma, you can't deny it!"

"She's right, Catherine," declared the church friend. "Womanhood in full flower."

Emily unfolded the chair at the edge of the crowd, so far away from the house that Em could only sort of make out the figures standing on the porch. Banks of speakers were arrayed around the house, but at this distance whoever was speaking sounded like a Charlie Brown teacher. There was a familiar liturgical rhythm to it, though, and when the congregants in front of them began chanting along she realized everyone must be doing the rosary. Em watched her friend, standing next to the chair, smiling, her hand on her grandmother's thin shoulder.

On the way back to the house, she tried to reconcile the Emily she knew—who made fun of "Jesus freaks" often enough that it made Em uncomfortable—with this person dutifully taking her grandmother on a pilgrimage. There was so much Em was still figuring out about Emily, but her commitment to her prejudices was one thing she'd thought immutable.

"Oh, good, you're back," Emily's mom said. She was pulling on her coat in the front hall.

"What'd we miss?" Emily asked.

Peggy rolled her eyes. "Ugh, *Walter*. We've been fighting for an hour. I can't take him anymore. Hi Mom," she said as Catherine stepped through the door.

"You're leaving?" Emily and Catherine said, nearly in unison.

"Yes—sorry—we're just so busy, and Roger has an evening class. Did, uh, did Mary appear?"

"Everyone said she did," said Catherine. "We couldn't hear."

"Hey, I think you need to be careful going out in the cold," Peggy said. "You're in the middle of chemo!"

"Mom, she's fine."

"And, you know, to stand in a field, that doesn't seem worth it."

"I was sitting down," said Catherine. "I prayed for you."

"Well, thanks for that," Peggy said, rubbing her eyes. One of the church ladies led Catherine back toward her chair. "Emily, where are your bags?"

"I'm gonna stay here," Emily said.

Peggy looked at her. "You haven't been home in four years," she said. In the living room, conversation had died down.

"I didn't come down here to be *home*. I came to see Grandma."

"You can't spend a little more time with your father and me?"

"You're the ones who are leaving!"

"Yeah," called Walter from the living room, "why you leaving, Peggy?"

"Jesus Christ," Peggy said.

Em said her awkward goodbyes to Emily's parents. On his way out the door, Emily's dad looked at Em blearily and proclaimed, "That's not Emily." (Emily was on the back porch, not saying goodbye.) Walter stuck around long enough to collar Em in a hallway and speculate with gruesome specificity about the sexual relationship he was certain Emily and Em were having. She twisted away, her face red, angry at him, angry at herself for being scared to respond.

In her chair, Catherine dozed. Emily's aunt took the beer from her hand before it could fall to the floor. "I think your grandma's drunk," Em said to Emily as they sat on the back porch.

"I hope so," Emily said. She lit a cigarette. "She's definitely an alcoholic, but at least she's a sweet drunk."

"Not a mean one."

"Not like some people."

That night Em held Emily while she cried. She'd never held her before, never seen her cry before. She could tell, from the way Emily turned her head away even as she twisted her body into Em's, that Emily felt humiliated. Finally Emily calmed down, sniffed a few times, and got up from her aunt's guest-room bed. "Thank you for being normal," she said. She carried her things into the bathroom and closed the door.

Em lay on the bed, listening to the water run. She thought back to when Emily had asked her to come to Georgia. What had surprised her was that Emily had *needed* her at the party for some reason. Emily always seemed to enjoy her company, even respected her, but had never needed her. She portrayed herself, Em realized now, as a person who never needed anyone.

She knew she should feel flattered—she *did* feel flattered—but she also felt frightened. While Emily had cried into her sweater, she hadn't known what to do with her hands, or what to say. She wasn't sure she was prepared for this kind of responsibility.

On the train home, Emily took Em's copy of *The Secret History*. "I thought you said this book was smart," she said outside Charlotte.

"It is smart."

"It's dumb as hell," she said, "but I can't stop reading it."

"Well," said Em, stung, "I'm glad you like it."

"All I can think of is how much better *your* version of this story would be," Emily said.

— • —

As she walked out for lunch, Dave at the front desk of her office building looked so chilly and miserable that she brought him a cup of coffee on her way back. He brightened and asked her to sit down. "Join me for a spell," he said. "We haven't talked in how long?"

She wasn't sure she wanted to eat lunch in the lobby with her weird doorman, but Edith was in quite a mood today, so it wouldn't hurt to stay out of the office, she supposed. "I'm so sorry about Jim," she said. His poorly behaved dog had died over the holidays.

"Oh yeah," he said gruffly. "He just seemed to know his time had come. I bought him a steak, even, at the diner, had them cook it up rare, but he turned away from it. In the end, I took him to the vet, and they gave him an injection. They were very kind about it."

"Well, he had a good long life."

"Yeah, fourteen years."

"Are you going to get another dog?"

"Oh no," he said seriously. "I'd never replace old Jim." A tear had formed in one of his eyes, and with a red-and-white handkerchief he unselfconsciously wiped it away. "I think I might take up a hobby, though."

"Just take one up?" Em had always assumed a hobby was something you had a preexisting interest in, but maybe she was going about it all wrong.

"Oh, sure and all. I thought I might want to learn to cook."

As she took the elevator up, she rubbed her hands together to warm them. In the light of Dave's simple grief for his terrible dog, she felt her emotions surging every which way. She thought of a photo she'd once seen of a canal system in Amsterdam, the water from the sea given dozens of channels to flow down, so that no one surge could overwhelm any one passage. She felt all her canals rising at once, and felt uncertain she possessed the capacity to keep them from overflowing their banks.

Before she'd left, Dave had described to her a dish "a woman friend" had made for him: chicken wings in a lemon sauce. "And she put 'em on rice," he said. "And I asked her, 'What's in this rice to make it taste like that?' Well do you know, she'd grated a little lemon into it." He beamed. "Imagine!"

— • —

Em didn't live in Sunrise Squat; she still lived with Louis, but in a less-horrible apartment on Fifteenth Street, next to a Chinese restaurant called Yummy Food. But she spent so many days and evenings in the squat that she knew pretty much everyone by name, and it had become generally understood that Em would often join Emily for her service hours. "Two Emilys for the price of one," Lisa said once when she saw them laying tile in the lobby. Sometimes, when Emily couldn't make it, Em just did the work herself and signed their name to the log sheets.

They didn't talk about it much, but Em had come to see Emily's position in the squat as one of the most exceptional things about her, and about her own life in New York. She looked back with embarrassment on the times she'd so confidently declared the Lower East Side was over, that it had stopped being revolutionary a decade before. It was so easy to live in a place without understanding what was bubbling under the surface, but she got it now. The Sunrise community was stormy, fluid, messy—the family downstairs straight out of "Luka," the hooker down the hall who was forever in a fight with the squat about sneaking johns into the building, the endless debates about what to do with the city's demands. The squats tended to attract people without great options, people who'd been, as Michael liked to say, "rumbling and tumbling through life," but people looked out for one another, and the longer she spent there the more people looked out for her.

Emily wasn't so enamored of the squat, even though it was actually *her* home, not Em's. This was because everyone gave her a hard time about Rob. It was the universal opinion of everyone in the squat that Rob was bad news. He was a small-time dealer, so no one felt endangered, but they eyed his proximity to Emily—and his frequent presence in her apartment—warily.

"Look, I've seen it a lot," Joe said to Em as she helped him install a radiator in a second-floor hallway one early spring afternoon. "Anytime you got a chick stuck to a dealer's side like that, it's no good. Like, what is their relationship?"

"He's her boyfriend."

Joe scoffed. "Boyfriend!" Joe was a drummer in a hardcore band, and Em liked to watch his muscled drummer's arms at work. She and Emily had gone to one of his shows once. It had been so mind-bendingly loud that Em had to leave after two songs, but she still daydreamed sometimes about running a hand along his bicep. He was older than her, maybe thirty-five, and reveled in his position as the sage elder of the squat. "Does she even like him?"

"Sure she likes him." But did she? It was true that Emily liked drama, and Rob delivered in that department. They were each always storming out of the other's apartment and stormily reuniting and having stormy reunion sex that Emily would tell her about later.

"Hey, hold this here," Joe said. "What do they have in common?" He flipped down his protective visor and Em did the same. The torch was too loud for them to talk, so Em just thought about his question for a while. Rob didn't really care about theater or movies or art. They were both funny, when they were straight. The thing they most had in common, Em supposed, was that they both really enjoyed drugs.

When she tried to explain the squat to her parents, they were as baffled as she had once been. She liked to think of her dad in his beautiful apartment in Wicker Park. He was a handy guy, and had always seemed frustrated with his bookish daughters, who showed no interest in working around the house. What would he say if he saw her now? Grimy jeans and bulky protective gloves, holding a radiator steady while her friend welded it into place with bright blue flame. "I'll show you the life of the mind!" she shouted.

Joe turned off the torch. "Pardon?"

Joe was married, anyway, which should have made him less suitable as a subject for Em's fantasies but didn't. Well, not married—he and Sofia had never gotten around to a ceremony, but they'd been together forever. Joe called her his old lady. Together the two of them had led the first wave of residents in the squat in the 1980s, lived the first hard years, when snow would fall through the roof and settle in the empty stairwell, when guys peed in beer bottles because there weren't toilets yet. Em loved to hear Joe and Sofia tell stories of those years—the face-offs with the police, Joe and Michael and Enrique menacing drug dealers with wrenches when they tried to do business out of the basement, the hectic autumn when everyone quit their day jobs and worked 24/7 to fix the roof before the winter. It was exhilarating, the freedom to take a perfectly blank slate and transform it into something new just as you were transforming your life, too. In those days, Joe liked to say, every night was a party, and punk bands played shows in the basement. Everyone was older and chiller now. They left that shit to the newer squats.

Emily had moved in after most of the heavy lifting was done, after there were bathrooms on every floor, after a punk kid named Sammy rehabbed the third-floor apartment where she lived now, scrounging drywall from work sites and two-by-fours from Dumpsters. Sammy OD'd, was saved in the middle of the night by paramedics. His parents dragged him back to Houston. He never even came back to clean out his clothes and tapes. Joe and the other old heads still called the third floor Sammy's floor, still did double takes when they saw Emily wearing his Oilers sweatshirt.

There were three nonnegotiable house rules: no stealing from your neighbor, no violence against your neighbor, and no drug dealing from the building. One day Joe and Michael took Rob aside and reminded him of that third rule, warned him that if he broke it even once Emily would be kicked out. Em wasn't there but could imagine Rob, hands up, saying, "I get it, man, I get it." She could imagine his slippery smile.

— • —

Jack Mortensen was in town, and Edith was beside herself. When Em arrived at the office, Edith was already there, burrowing through the files. "I can't find it!" she moaned, holding her head. "Where have you been?"

Em considered a number of different ways to say *This is when I always come in*, discarded them all, and finally said, "What are you looking for? Can I help?"

"I'm looking for"—she pulled out a file folder—"Jack Mortensen's"— she dropped the folder atop the file cabinet—"first book proposal"— she pulled out another file folder—"from 1982. I want to show it to him at lunch. Oh, he's taking us to lunch. Are you wearing *that*?"

Em considered a number of different ways to say *This is what I always wear*, discarded them all, and finally said, "Yes."

"Well, can you change? Jack likes girls in dresses."

"Excuse me?"

"He's old-fashioned. Oh, don't look at me like that. I'm not asking you to sleep with him. Just show the guy a little leg, will you?" In Edith's opinion, Em behaved like a nun and needed to cut loose once in a while. Her previous assistant had hosted boozy salons in the office on Saturday nights; when one turned so raucous the police were called, she was fired, but Edith still spoke admiringly of her guts, and the quality of the boys she dated.

"I'll find the proposal," Em said. She shooed Edith away from the files, which were her domain, not Edith's. Edith never opened the file cabinets, which had been carefully organized by past assistants for the benefit of assistants yet to come. The files were where Em learned about Edith's authors and their various quirks and neuroses, immortalized in memos and faxes and, often, explanatory letters-to-the-future written by the assistant at the time. Through the files, she became acquainted with those predecessors. She knew them all now: Jenny, Edith's first assistant a million years ago, who conducted long, passionate arguments with Edith via memo; Ethan, whose contract markups were thorough and precise; Tom, whose editorial notes verged, in Em's opinion, on moronic; Claire, whose memos often included asides so funny that she was not surprised when Edith said she was now writing for television; Susan, who made payout mistakes Em was still cleaning up.

The MORTENSEN file took up almost an entire drawer. Em replaced the folders Edith had removed and scattered around the cabinet, then fingered her way patiently through the tabs. She believed in her fellow assistants. One of them had filed the proposal in the correct place, she knew it. It ought to be in the earliest correspondence folder, 1980–1984. Inside she found scores of flimsy faxes, the ink so faded that they appeared nearly blank; carbon copies of notes from Edith on the agency's terrible letterhead; a sheaf of rejections from editors who she had to assume kicked themselves every day; four Christmas cards, all with messages identical to the card she'd opened just a few months before:

EDITH—
  Here's to the future!
Jack

Oh, and here it was, the proposal, toward the back of the folder. She had missed it the first time because it was only a few pages long and had a couple of memos stapled to the front. There was a long note from Jenny, the first assistant, explaining what *Futurity* was, who Jack was, how he was well situated to promote the book through his speaking and business consulting networks. Then there was a long note from Jenny that Em recognized instantly as the second memo you have to write when it becomes clear that Edith never really read your first memo. Below that was a third memo, in which Jenny had forcefully made the case that Edith was wrong and the book would definitely sell. On that third memo, Edith had handwritten: "This seems like nonsense to me, but make a list and we can send it around."

Em carefully photocopied the proposal, then put the whole original packet back in the correspondence folder so that it would be there when some future assistant needed it. "Oh, bless you," Edith said when Em handed her the copy. "Now go change."

The apartment was empty but for Dolly, their cat, who darted away when Em opened the door but then wove through her legs as she stood at the rolling rack where she hung up her clothes. (She'd given Louis, who wore much nicer things than her, the closet.) She took off her work pants and stood glumly before the mirror. She did not particularly want to show Jack Mortensen some leg. She didn't like her legs. She supposed she could do her best with her cleavage, which in her experience men found distracting. She *did* have the right dress for that. She rummaged in her dresser and found a pair of control-top pantyhose, which she held up to the window to make sure there were no runs. After she peed so she wouldn't have to do it at the restaurant, she wrestled her legs into the hose and put on the dress. She looked okay, still borderline professional. No, she would *not* put on more makeup for Jack Mortensen. She scratched Dolly, locked up, set off the three blocks back to work.

What Em also saw in the files were the occasional examples of previous assistants agenting books of their own. Sometimes the books didn't sell. Sometimes they made small deals. But it didn't happen very often, and sooner or later those assistants went somewhere else, leaving the books behind.

At other agencies, bigger agencies, young employees could build their own stables of writers. A girl Em had met at a writers' conference had done that—she'd made a niche for herself working with children's books, and now was a kind of junior partner at her agency. (At the writers' conference, where they both were on a panel about agenting, the girl was blithe and confident, while Em found she had almost nothing helpful to say.) If such a thing had ever happened to an assistant at the Safer Agency, Em could find no evidence of it.

When she got back to the office, she was grateful to see that Edith was on the phone, which meant she could direct her craziness at people besides Em. She had to work through some slush and make notes for Lucy, who'd asked her for her thoughts on the memoir so far.

The notes first. She had a hunch Edith or Jack would insist she have a drink at lunch, and she could face the slush better with some wine in her. In her nearly two years at the agency, she had gone from finding the slush exciting to finding it a drag to finding it actively depressing.

(She understood, from her acquaintances who also worked in publishing, that this was the natural progression all assistants went through.) Most of the submissions were just so awful, yet so much energy and care had been given to their preparation. Painstakingly self-addressed envelopes accompanied sample chapters full of hokum and ghastly sex scenes, evidence that most would-be writers simply had no idea how bad their writing was. As a would-be writer herself, she found this a nerve-wracking observation. She hadn't yet turned on the fancy word processor her sister had given her for Christmas.

She knew the solution to writer's block was supposed to be to read great books, but she found those no more helpful than reading the slush. Reading great books just convinced her that she was absolutely right about the hopelessness of toiling away at anything. How had this middle-aged man written so beautifully in the voice of a fifteen-year-old girl? This short-story writer: How was each one of her sentences so alive it seemed to spark? How did Cormac McCarthy come up with this shit?

Reading Lucy's writing, though, didn't depress her. In part this was because Lucy was sticking to her declaration to only write about the joy in her life; there were chapters on Lucy's happy childhood, her Iranian grandmother, Sarah's birth, dinners with friends, a blind date so terrible that by the end neither she nor the guy could stop laughing. (The chapter ended with them shaking hands and solemnly agreeing never to see one another again.) Each chapter was named after a certain meal—the grilled cheese and whiskey sour Lucy had consumed the night before Sarah was born, or the Manhattan clam chowder she spilled on herself during the blind date—and as much of the book was devoted to recipes and discussion of the food as to Lucy's own story.

Em also found reading Lucy invigorating because she was starting to see that a book didn't, in fact, have to be a bewildering work of genius to be something she loved. Reading Lucy wasn't like reading Denis Johnson or Joy Williams, who were basically from another planet. But she understood now that it was okay for her to like, even love, something that made her feel good, that comforted her. Emily would scoff, of course.

Mostly, though, Em loved reading Lucy's book because she knew she was part of it. She was in it, yes—the day when Lucy had taught "my friend Emily" to like olives appeared in a chapter about martinis— but she was *part* of it even beyond that, because she was making it better. As Lucy talked through the stories in her apartment, Em did more than simply type. She weighed in on phrasing, made suggestions on organization, warned Lucy when she was straying from the book's tone. And now Lucy wanted her to give notes.

The chapter she was reading now was about how one of the pleasures of living in New York was the way you saw famous people and great artists being just as annoyed by the everyday problems of urban life as you. Even Susan Sontag has to sit in the terrible chairs at the Anthology Film Archives. Even Kurt Vonnegut needs to wait for the bathroom at Town Hall. One summer day, Lucy was driving with a friend down Twenty-Third Street, trying to turn right onto Ninth Avenue, and there was a young woman standing in the turn lane waiting for the walk sign to change, and the windows of the car were down, so the friend just yelled at the person to get out of the way, but in the middle of yelling realized who it was, and so ended up yelling, "Hey, move it, Mary Louise Parker!"

Most of the chapter was devoted to a potluck baby shower she had attended at "my friend Lorraine's apartment" that was also attended by Bobby McFerrin. When Lorraine had issued the invitation several months before, her old friend Bobby had been a little-known a cappella jazz singer. When the time of the party came around, however, he had become the superstar performer of a ubiquitous number one song. He still came to the baby shower, though, and brought a peach cobbler, which he was upset about, because it hadn't turned out the way he wanted. Lucy tried to reassure Bobby McFerrin about his cobbler, which she thought was pretty good. However, she had to stop herself, over and over again, from saying things like "Don't worry about the cobbler," or "Be happy about your cobbler." Together, they worked out what had gone wrong with the cobbler—he had tried for a biscuity topping, which had gotten soggy, so Lucy suggested something more oaty, with self-rising flour. Later, Bobby McFerrin sent her a card telling her his next cobbler had turned out wonderfully.

Here was the recipe for the cobbler, which she called Cobbly McFerrin:

Find some fruit. Firm fruits work well, such as apples or pears. They can be a little underripe. Peaches are just splendid in this recipe, especially mixed with blackberries. In fact, you can make this recipe with nearly any kind of fruit, or combination of fruits. If you would enjoy it in a pie, you can put it in Cobbly McFerrin.

If the fruit has a peel, remove the peel. If it has a pit, remove the pit. Slice all the fruit up and put it in a square or rectangular baking dish. Continue until the dish is about half full of fruit. I often think of the quantity of fruit suitable for this recipe as six apples' worth of fruit.

Now it's time to make the oaty streusel topping. In a bowl, combine the following:

1 cup self-rising flour
½ cup sugar
½ cup brown sugar
½ teaspoon cinnamon
Dash of salt
Then add:
½ cup (1 stick) butter, melted
Dash of vanilla
1/3 cup rolled oats

You might as well mix it all up with your hands, because you're going to get all gooey doing the next step, which is scattering the streusel mixture over the top of your fruit. No one in the entire history of the earth has ever complained that their cobbler had too *much* topping on it, so if you want to make more, that's just fine.

Bake at 375 degrees until it's golden brown and bubbly, about 25 minutes. Serve hot while whistling a jaunty tune about maintaining a positive outlook.

Em didn't have a lot of notes. She wanted the Bobby McFerrin story to be longer. She wanted to know more about Kurt Vonnegut. She rearranged the recipe a bit so that someone like her, who couldn't cook, wouldn't be caught by surprise by things like an unpreheated oven. It was fine not to have a lot of notes, because the chapter was good. It did what Lucy wanted it to do. She just knew it, the way she knew which pair of her shoes were best for walking.

Jack Mortensen was not a lech, thankfully. When Edith and Em walked into the restaurant, he showily marveled at his good fortune, to be dining with *two* beautiful women!, but then mostly spent lunch talking about The Future. Em had guessed that he would be wearing either a cowboy hat *or* cowboy boots, but she was wrong; he only wore a bolo tie. As she'd expected, they both ordered martinis and made a whole thing out of insisting that Em have one too. (She silently thanked Lucy for teaching her how to order a martini.)

Before the entrees arrived Edith pulled the old proposal from her purse and showed it to Jack. "I remember the day I first read this," Edith said. "I loved it immediately."

"Aw," Jack said, moved. His cheeks reddened over his beard.

"I'd never read something that explained to me, so clearly and inspirationally, how to think about the coming decade."

"Boy, I know I owe you a new proposal," Jack said.

"I only need a page or so. What about the millennium? Is there something there?"

"Sure," he said. "As the great cosmic clock turns over, the human soul, that seeker of order, hungers for a commensurate reset. For those who embrace the age, the millennium offers a remarkable opportunity to tap into that elemental desire with images of renewal and rebirth."

"Great, write that," Edith said, and the waiter arrived with their food.

As they ate, Jack asked Em how she spent her time in New York. Well, what he said was, "A young person, the city laid out before you like a buffet; surely you partake!"

"I see a lot of movies," Em said. "Plays when I can afford them. I don't get to a lot of restaurants." She was grateful when her entirely boring answer sent Jack off on an aria about how in the future, audiences would hunger for experiences unattainable by the earthbound human form, which was why he was investing heavily in pharmaceutical companies.

"It's been a great pleasure," Jack said as they bid farewell at the door, bestowing one lingering glance to Em's breasts. At least she hadn't changed for nothing. He kissed Edith's hand and said, "My dear, I pledge to have that one-pager on the millennium to you by Memorial Day."

"That's exciting, a new Mortensen book," Em said as they walked back to the office. She was taking it slowly down the sidewalk so Edith didn't fall behind.

Edith snorted. "He's promised me a new proposal for ten years," she said. "If he sends anything, I'll eat my hat."

"Wasn't Jenny the one who originally championed *Futurity*?" Em ventured. "I feel like I remember hearing that."

"She liked it, too," Edith said. "She wrote a really dynamite cover letter for that proposal. I knew we had gold then."

"Where is Jenny now?"

"Connecticut, I think. She quit and got married. Beautiful children."

"And you were the agent on *Futurity*, not her."

"Oh, sure," Edith said. "She'd only been here two or three years."

— ● —

The wind picked up and Emily and Em ducked into a vintage store on Greene Street to warm up, only to find themselves in a wonderland of weird furniture. Here a bamboo bar, there an art deco sofa. They wandered the floor, heating up inside their ugly coats. The girl at the counter, impossibly beautiful in horn-rimmed glasses, read a magazine and ignored them.

The store was called the Second Coming. Upstairs they found racks of broad-shouldered dresses of a different era, their mothers' time or maybe their grandmothers', they didn't know. "These are perfect for *The Open Heart*," Emily said. The *Medea* project had fallen apart after a bitter argument between Emily and the actor playing Jason, after which the cast took Jason's side and quit en masse. For much of the previous year, Emily had been prepping what she now called her breakout show: a site-specific work about surgery and ghosts, meant to be performed before the ruins of the Smallpox Castle on Roosevelt Island.

They shrugged their coats to the floor and tried dresses on, or attempted to. "This was made for someone eating Depression food," Em grunted. Emily, thinner than ever, managed to slip into a dress. She looked like the ghost who appears in the background of a photo.

— ● —

That March Em was added to the eviction phone tree, so that when the city was planning an action against one of the squats, she could join the emergency mobilization. Early one Saturday, Michael, Emily's

downstairs neighbor, called and told her that police were surrounding
Dos Blocos, another squat on Ninth Street. She called the two people
down the tree from her, got dressed in her warmest clothes, and woke
up Louis, who was always up for a protest.

They hurried through silent, gloomy streets, hands stuffed in
pockets, to find chaos on Ninth. Michael was just outside the police
cordon, holding a bullhorn and directing traffic. With his long strawberry blond hair and big glasses, he looked androgynous and unas-
suming—he reminded Em of another Michael, Stipe—but in fact he
burned with an inexhaustible white-hot rage at cops and landlords
and the city. "You two join that group there," he told Em and Louis.
"Tell everyone: Our goal is to bother the cops from the sides. Be loud
as hell, shout for the cameras if the cameras come. But don't engage
physically, don't get arrested—we're gonna need all the bodies we can
get." He raised his bullhorn. "FUCK THE PIGS!" he chanted, and
soon everyone had joined in.

Fuck the pigs! Em was delighted by the old-fashioned simplicity
of the slogan. She could imagine her parents shouting it at a Viet-
nam protest in Madison, if they had been the kinds of students who
protested. (She'd asked her mom once if she'd joined in the uprising
at UW, and her mom told her that in 1969 they were four years out
of college. "I was too busy having you.") The pigs themselves stood
around, chatting casually with one another, a counterpoint to the organized protestors and their red-haired drill sergeant. At the center of
everything, two cops negotiated with three Dos Blocos residents who
had chained themselves to the steel front door.

A news crew pulled up in a van, and Michael changed the chant.
"WE WILL ALWAYS FIGHT!" he called. "HOUSING IS A RIGHT!"
From an upper window of the squat, two young women in parkas
unfurled a bedsheet on which they'd painted THIS IS OUR HOME. The
neighbors, nearly all Puerto Rican or black, were starting to appear
in doorways and windows. A few shouted at the squatters—"Pay some

rent!" "This is our neighborhood!"—but most seemed to be on the squatters' side, or at least not on the side of the cops.

After half an hour, the cops moved out, as coordinated and as inexplicable as a murmuration of starlings. A cheer filled the chill morning; protestors filled the space the cops had occupied, began disassembling the barricade. As the cops filed past Em and Louis, one mustached face smirked at them, and Louis said, "Call me, you bitch." A woman brought hot coffee to the chained-up residents while the guy with the keys worked on the padlocks. They found Emily, who'd been on the far side of the cops with Joe and Frank and Lisa.

Most of the protestors, cold and anxious about their own homes, dispersed, but a handful, including Lisa, Em, and Emily, followed Michael to Life Cafe for breakfast. The waiters cheered as they paraded in and settled into three booths. Em and Emily ended up sitting back to back to Michael and one of the Dos Blocos leaders. Amid the revelry, she heard Michael's clear, frustrated voice: "They weren't really serious. They didn't even bring a ram."

"So what's the point, then?" another person asked.

"Just harassment. A show of force."

Around the tables, others joined in. "They want us to know they can do this anytime they want," Lisa said.

"NYPD's got a five-billion-dollar budget."

"Every one of those officers is thrilled to get the overtime."

"Come scare some squatters on a Saturday morning."

"They'll come back and clear that place out."

Friedrich, a German squatter who'd spent the winter staying with Michael, interrupted the darkening conversation. "Remember our chanting, yes?" he said. "Housing is a right. It is not a privilege to have shelter. You must fight for that right when they try to take it. You are citizens, and you deserve a home."

"Some of us aren't citizens," someone said.

"You deserve it, too," Michael said. "We made these places when no one wanted them. We turned ruins into housing, for us and for anyone in Loisaida who needed it." In fact, Em knew, this was a stumbling block to the mission of the squatters, most of whom were white: Puerto Rican squatters were rare and often didn't feel welcome. Lisa talked all the time about how badly many of the squatters treated their nonwhite neighbors, who had been here before them and weren't thrilled about the new faces on their blocks. Many of those families had been through so much in the '80s that all they wanted, if they earned enough money, was to get out to New Jersey or Yonkers, not to put down roots in a building without a roof. Michael continued: "We saw value where the city saw none. Now the city sees the sweat and the money we've put in, and they see dollar signs. But they won't take our homes without a fight."

Em, moved, grabbed Emily's arm. Emily started. She'd fallen asleep.

— • —

Em had the opposite problem with Lucy as she did with her parents: Lucy thought the squat sounded amazing, romantic even, and Em felt she had to disabuse her of her more fanciful notions of communal living. "Some of the people are sort of psycho," Em said one day after lunch. "Maybe from three years of peeing in buckets."

They'd spent the morning with Lucy talking and Em typing. Now Lucy was in bed and Em was sitting at the dresser, experimenting with Lucy's makeup. She turned to show off the results and Lucy laughed, *heh-heh-heh.*

"Is it too subtle?" Em said. She'd given herself Kool-Aid mouth with the lipstick.

"When can I see Sunset Squat?" Lucy asked.

"Sun*rise.* Sun*set* Squat is the assisted living center for elderly squatters."

"Send me there when I'm peeing in a bucket," Lucy said.

"Stop it. We can go! It's a lot of stairs," she warned. Just getting Lucy out of the apartment was getting to be a whole production, much less getting her through the squat. But she was less and less inclined to leave home at all these days, so Em thought she'd better seize the opportunity.

They decided to bring Sarah along. Like any eight-year-old, she complained extravagantly when informed that she had to stop watching TV and *do something*. But once they were all in the cab she perked up, asking questions about the squat and Em's place in it. "But why do you do all this if you don't even live there?" she asked finally.

"Well," Em said from the front seat, a little stuck. "At first I was just helping my friend, who does live there."

"The other Emily," Sarah said. They'd met a few times. Emily talked to her like she was an adult, which she appreciated.

"Right. But I really like the people who live there, and I really believe in what they're doing. And I don't like the way the city and the police are treating them." Sarah nodded. In the wake of the LA riots, she was just starting to get the idea that the police were sometimes the problem. "And the thing is, when I'm in a meeting and they're making plans, I always have an idea that seems good, and they usually use my idea. So I like that part, too. I like helping them do this amazing stuff."

"People who make things," Lucy said to Sarah, "sometimes don't realize how much they need the people who help them make things." Em turned to look out the window just in time.

When they pulled up to Sunrise Squat, Lucy looked up and down the street. "Will we be able to get a cab back?" she asked. "I have definitely never been in this neighborhood before."

"I can wait," the driver said. "I'm not gonna catch a fare around here anyway. How long will you be?"

"Probably half an hour," Em said. The cabbie nodded, turned the meter off, and pulled his hat down over his eyes.

Em had a key now. The lobby was dark in the late afternoon, and they stood in the gloom for a moment, letting their eyes adjust. Lucy moved across to the wall by the stairs and checked out the graffiti.

"This house is an emotional megaphone," she read. "Good title for a novel. *The Emotional Megaphone*."

"It's true."

"In fact, sort of describes all novels, if you think about it. Should we say hi to the other Emily?"

"She's at work," Em said, hoping she'd made it there. "Here, I'll show you the library instead." In the library, Sarah took one look at the tiny shelf of picture books and pulled her own book out of her backpack. Lucy ran a finger along the shelves marked TENANT LAW, REVOLUTION, RACE AND GENDER. "Is there an Emotional Megaphone section?" she asked. In Fiction, she was delighted to find a copy of *Can't Complain*. "A lot of these novels came from me," Em said. "Before there was, just, like, a *lot* of Bukowski."

They left Sarah in the library to go outside to the garden. Here Lucy was in her glory. "Oh, these are going to be beautiful," she said, running her finger along the beanstalk climbing a trellis. "Will you sneak a few uptown?"

A little girl and her mother were weeding, wearing identical floppy hats. "Hi Juana!" Em called and the girl waved. "They live right downstairs from Emily," she said quietly. "She kicked out her husband. He used to abuse them both. Last year he broke in and was yelling, you know, he was gonna kill them, and some of the guys from the house threw him out. It was amazing. Like, this righteous flood descended upon him."

"Oh!" Lucy put her hands on her hips. "Is he dangerous?"

"He won't be back," Em said.

Frank came over and Em introduced him. "This garden is his baby," she said.

"Well," Frank allowed, "me and a lot of forced labor. Emilys included."

"This is an exceptional garden," Lucy said.

"Yes, it is," he replied.

"I think what I loved most about your squat," Lucy said as their cabbie, awake again, sped back up the West Side Highway, "was its incongruity. The garden is the most obvious example."

"What's incongruity?" asked Sarah. She was leaning against her mother as they both looked out toward the water.

"It means something that seems out of place. The garden is like a little jewel in that streetscape. But so is the whole building, the whole squat."

"Everything's pretty rough for it to be a jewel," Em said.

"So you're all cutting and polishing it together," Lucy said, pleased with her metaphor. "But what a wonderful thing. I hope you're proud of what you're accomplishing there."

"I am," Em said.

— ● —

Last summer Edith had allowed her to submit Scot Salem's novel as her first official book as a junior agent. Every step had been terrifying: the calls to editors introducing herself and pitching the book; FedExing manuscripts all over town, each with a carefully proofread cover letter; Scot Salem calling every day as soon as he woke up on the West Coast to ask if anything had happened yet. Then the slow dribble of rejections, each as empty of meaning as the last. So many *alas*es. The phone call from Ash Calder asking to talk to Scot had been a godsend, the last of the editors to respond but the one whose response she was most eager for, finally with some good news.

The editor had talked to the author for half an hour, Scot reported afterward.

"What did you talk about?" Em had asked.

"Surfing, mostly," Scot said, bewildered.

"He's a good kid," Calder had told her the next day. "I'll send some notes. If he wants to rewrite it, I'll take another look."

Em had told Scot she could send the book out to the second tier of publishers, or he could take the shot Vintage was offering him and rewrite it. Scot loved the idea of being published by Vintage, loved getting an edit memo from the legendary Ash Calder. He'd spent six months revising the book. But it had all gone wrong, and Calder had sent Scot a rejection letter, and now Scot was on the phone, furious.

"This letter is . . . like . . . have you ever seen a letter like this?"

This is the first book I've ever agented, she wanted to say. She had no idea what to do about the letter from Calder, which had arrived earlier in the day. In it, Calder thanked Em for sending the revised version of *The Big One* but said that, alas, it was still a pass for him.

"What does he mean, 'still a pass'?" Scot was reading from the letter, which Em had faxed to him. "He was the one who said I should revise it! He sent me that whole memo telling me what to do with it!"

"I know," Em said.

"He said it was great! He said all it needed was another pass!"

"He never promised to publish it, Scot. He said he'd be really interested to see the revision."

"I spent all winter on that rewrite. I cut like half the novel! I cut the whole migrant worker subplot! Did you talk to Ash?"

"I did call him, yes." What Ash Calder had said, on their phone call, was, "Look, you know as well as I do that sometimes the rewrite just shows what was wrong with it in the first place."

She knew no such thing. "The sections with the migrant workers were very different in style," she'd said. "Should we consider reinstating those?"

"Oh God no—that was shitty. I was right about that."

Now, to Scot, she said, "The market is really tough for first fiction right now," which was a thing that she'd heard an older agent say on a panel at the ABA conference.

When she finally got Scot off the phone, she avoided eye contact with Edith—who had listened to her side of the whole thing—and headed to the bathroom to cry in frustration. Em had felt throughout the whole process that things were occurring at a level somewhat more elevated than she could truly understand. She'd managed to fake her way through, repeating things she'd heard Edith say to clients and editors, but her relative ignorance was now being revealed. Scot Salem thought she knew something, but she didn't. Ash Calder spoke to her like they were buddies, but in fact every time she talked to him on the telephone she saw white at the edges of her vision and felt on the verge of a panic attack. Edith *knew* she didn't know anything, but just let her fuck it up. Had she conveyed Calder's ambivalence appropriately? Had she given Scot false hope? How had she transformed him from a confident new voice in fiction to a needy, desperate writer just like all the rest? How had this poor sap thousands of miles away come to depend on her?

How could she extricate herself from this mess?

What would happen if it was Lucy, who was her friend, and Lucy's book?

— • —

In April, Lucy's health took a turn. Her nurse brought a wheelchair to the apartment. Her speech was getting noticeably slower. Also, she couldn't type anymore.

The nurse, a kind Trinidadian woman named Molly, also brought over a high-powered blender, and gave a little presentation to Lucy and Em about eating options when Lucy was no longer able to chew solid food. "For example," Molly said, "you can blend sweet potatoes and chicken broth, and get a lot of nutrients that way."

Em looked at Lucy, apprehensive. Lucy, sitting in her new wheelchair, smiled and said, "No fucking way!"

Over the next few days Lucy worked on her end-of-life instructions with Em. There would be no feeding tube. There would be no hospital stay. Sarah was not to be around for the very end; her father was on call to take her away when the time was right. Lucy's will was up to date: Edith would be in charge of her literary estate ("such as it is," she said grimly) and would place all proceeds ("if there ever are any") in a trust until Sarah turned eighteen.

"And I want you to sell this memoir," she said. "Think of a good title and sell it for a ton of money."

"I'll try," Em said. The royalty statement for *Can't Complain* had not been promising; after decent first-month sales, the book had mostly disappeared from stores. "Not to beat a dead horse—"

"Yes, please don't beat me," Lucy said.

Em gave her a courtesy laugh. "I just mean, I think a chapter about being sick might be necessary. It's what editors will want."

"Yes, editors will love a recipe for pureed sweet potatoes," Lucy said.

"It doesn't have to be that."

"Well, come on," Lucy said, pushing herself away. She was still working out how to use the wheelchair, and Em had shoved various end tables and armchairs against the wall so she wouldn't be forever bumping into them.

"What are we doing?"

"Making a last meal," said Lucy.

Lucy's kitchen was much too small to accommodate the wheelchair, so she sat in the dining room. "Get an apron. We're making *tahdig*," she said.

"What is that?" Em, never a confident cook, was made even less confident to see Lucy's head just barely staring at her over the half-wall between the kitchen and the dining room.

"Persian rice," she said. "My grandma Habib made it for me and my sister." There was a chapter in the memoir about Grandma Habib, a feisty Iranian immigrant who married a good ol' boy furniture maker from Hickory, North Carolina, learning to make fried chicken the way her husband's mama did. But Lucy hadn't told any stories about her making actual ethnic food, and Em's disquiet increased.

"Am I really the right person to make Persian rice?" she asked.

"No one else is here," Lucy said, although at that moment Sarah got home from school.

At Lucy's direction, Sarah set a pot of water on the stove to boil while Em rinsed a strainer full of rice until the water ran clear. Sarah poked impatiently with a wooden spoon at the steaming but not yet boiling water.

"You know what they say about a watched pot," Em said.

"It has to boil sometime," Sarah replied. Lucy laughed, *heh-heh-heh*. Sarah stood in one place, staring directly at the pot, until the bubbles began popping to the surface. "There," she said.

Em poured the rice into the boiling water. "Shouldn't I cover it?" she asked, and Lucy shook her head no. After just a few minutes, Lucy said, "Now pour it all out into a colander." Em took care of that part, and then Sarah ran cool water through the rice.

Em melted butter in an unbelievably heavy cast-iron skillet while Sarah mixed some of the rice with yogurt in a bowl. "Do I have any herbs in the refrigerator?" Lucy asked. She did not; Em did most of the shopping now, and was oblivious to herbs. "If I did, you could chop them up and mix them with the rice, but oh well." Em added oil to the butter and then, when it was hot, carefully scraped the goopy yogurt-rice into the pan. A little oil splashed on Sarah's arm and she yelled, "Ow!"

"That always hurts," Lucy said. "I'm sorry, honey."

They mounded the rest of the rice in the skillet and Sarah got to use the end of her wooden spoon to poke holes all over the mound. "That lets steam escape," Lucy said.

Em frowned. "But don't we want to trap the steam, so the rice . . .

uh . . . engorges? Shut up!" she added helplessly as Lucy laughed. "Isn't that what you do with rice?"

Lucy waved her hand at them for a moment. When she stopped laughing, she said, "Nope, you want the steam to escape so the bottom gets crispy."

"What do we do while we wait?" Sarah asked.

"You do the dishes," Lucy said. "I sit here making fun of you."

Little tufts of steam burped out of the holes in the rice as they washed the pot, the colander, and the bowl. "How long do you cook it?" Em asked. "How do you know when it's done?"

Lucy did a thing with her shoulders that resembled a shrug. "It's done when it's done. You just hope for the best when you flip it over."

"When you what?"

Indeed, once they took the rice off the heat, Lucy's instructions were to set a big platter on top of the unbelievably heavy (and now very hot) skillet and then somehow to flip the whole thing over in one quick motion. This Sarah and Em completely failed to do, and the result was a messy pile of fluffy white rice covered in chunks and shards of crispy, deep brown crust. Additional fragments were scattered across the counter. "It's okay," Lucy said. "That's what happened to Grandma Habib, too. Try it."

Em picked up a triangle of crust. It was hot, crunchy, nutty, salty. It was the best thing she'd ever eaten.

— • —

Louis and Emily and Em and Rob went to church. It was a joke, really, the product of them all talking about their childhood experiences on Sundays. Emily and Louis had grown up in very religious families; when Em had first met Louis at college he wouldn't even say "goddamn," just "G. D." For her part, Em grew up attending a Methodist church in Wausau, the theology of which mostly revolved around making sure everyone was out in time for kickoff of the Packer game.

"How great would it be," said Emily, with a familiar spark in her eye, "to just show up at church tomorrow morning?" It was very late Saturday night, and Emily and Rob were wired on something. They all riffed on that for a while, the way they did, and then the riffing wound down, and then Rob was shaking Em awake. He was wearing a plaid sport coat and a tie with a palm tree on it.

"Where did you get that?" Em asked blearily.

"Where did I get what?" Rob said.

Emily was wearing the vintage dress, the one with an impossibly small waist. She tossed Em a dress she used to wear all the time but that was now too big, one that Em still wasn't convinced she could fit into. "I'll just wear my jeans," Em said, eyeing it.

Louis met them outside. He was wearing a suit. They passed an Iglesia Católica and a synagogue before they reached St. Patrick's on Mulberry Street. Emily, Em noticed, did not look great as they stood outside the door. "Are you thinking about your grandma?" she asked, and Emily nodded.

"Does she speak in *tongues*?" Rob said, tossing his cigarette into the street.

"Shut up," Em said.

The service was already going on as Emily pushed open the door. Shuffling and giggling, they made their way to a pew in the back of the dark sanctuary. A few old Italian ladies looked back at them, but most people ignored them, the way they'd ignore a bum. It was warm in the church, and it smelled like wood and candles. Rob muttered a joke, and Louis shushed him. After a little while, Rob fell asleep. Soon the other three kneeled on the rail in front of them, shamed by the hush of the service into reverence. When they said the Lord's Prayer together, Em felt as content as she'd felt in Lucy's kitchen, before the diagnosis.

The next week, Em went back, without telling Emily. When the time for silent prayer arrived, she prayed for Lucy.

— • —

The teenager who lived on the first floor of Sunrise Squat had a clarinet. In an environment of hardcore and punk bands, such an instrument stood out. It was black and brass, and he kept it polished to a shine. He said he'd taken lessons where he grew up in Missouri, and no one could doubt him, because he put not just a sound but a whole personality through the mouthpiece.

The problem was, no one wanted to hear it in the middle of the night, which was when he always seemed to be playing it. A meeting was called—a full squat meeting, on the subject of this sixteen-year-old kid living alone with his clarinet. The teenager sat with a mutinous expression as his neighbors complained about his late-night music. Em thought it was a little unfair that this bastion of independent thinking was coming down so hard on a kid's weird habit, but on the other hand it was pretty annoying to be woken up in the middle of the night by otherworldly woodwind sounds. Finally Enrique, with the wisdom of Solomon, suggested that if the teenager wanted to play in the middle of the night, he should go up to the roof.

When Em and Emily returned to the squat late, they would sometimes hear, as they turned onto Twelfth Street, not just the sounds of distant car alarms but the wail of a clarinet, like a distant loon. She thought it sounded like the boy was calling out for others of his kind.

— • —

When the weather started turning, Em's sister and her embarrassing husband came for a visit.

Well, they came to New York City, but they sure as hell weren't staying in Em and Louis's apartment. There was no room, and also they wouldn't be caught dead. They stayed in Midtown. (Mark traveled often for accountant conferences or whatever and had a lot of "points," Anne-Marie said, which Em guessed were like frequent flier miles, but for a hotel.) They flew in on Midwest Express for a long weekend of art museums and tourist crap, plus a carefully demarcated Saturday-night dinner with Em and her friends. Em tried not to take offense that Anne-Marie didn't seem to have an hour to spare for just her alone. It was only three days, she reminded herself, and she had a needy husband who wanted her around, and anyways if she only saw Anne-Marie with a crowd it would mean she wouldn't feel so bad about not knowing what to say.

It had been her mother who'd called her, sobbing, to tell her that Anne-Marie had lost the baby. They'd shared one difficult phone call, the next day, when her sister was still doped up, and then Em sent Anne-Marie a long, heartfelt letter. She barely remembered what was in it, she'd written it in such a late-night fever. Hopefully it had not made things worse. Whenever they talked afterward, they both steered clear of the subject of the lost child, of children in general. She couldn't imagine what it was like, and in her inability to imagine felt her own failure as a sister.

After, Anne-Marie had thrown herself into her real estate career, selling the hell out of houses in Whitefish Bay, to the point that at Christmas she'd told Em that she'd made more money that year than her husband. Which meant that together they basically had more money than God. Em still didn't like Anne-Marie's husband, who wore a tie to work and often forgot he was still wearing it when he got home and would just be sitting there on the couch, watching the news, necktie still knotted. How could her sister, who in high school had dated the most dangerous skater at Wausau East, be married to a guy who didn't even *notice* he was wearing a tie? But she tried to separate her distaste for Mark, for Anne-Marie's whole domestic settling, from her feelings about Anne-Marie herself and her grief. Maybe this wasn't the life Em wanted her sister to be living, but she still mourned the baby who was supposed to be part of that life.

On Friday she left work early—Edith was already gone—and cleaned her apartment's gross kitchen and gross bathroom. She had to borrow a mop from a neighbor and then, faced with a mop bucket and a bottle of Pine-Sol, admit she didn't even really know how mopping was supposed to work. The cat perched atop one of the bookshelves, watching scornfully as Em poured too much cleaner onto the tile, splashed it with too much water, and then pushed the puddles into every corner. In the end, she was left with dirty, pungent ponds all over her floor, which she sopped up with paper towels. When Louis got home, he said, "It smells like you had a threesome with some pine trees."

Anne-Marie had insisted she and Mark wanted to see Em's apartment, and she was perversely excited to discover how much they would hate it. What kind of face would Mark make when he sat on the couch? How dire a report would Anne-Marie bring home to their mother, who, Em had finally realized, would never visit her? "They *shouldn't* understand the way we live," Emily had said, which was exactly right. Em wasn't letting them see the squat, though. She had limits.

On Saturday morning, her sister called her. "The concierge got us a reservation for six thirty," she said. "Is it still four of you?"

"Yeah," Em said. Emily, Louis, and Lisa would certainly never turn down a free dinner at a presumably expensive restaurant.

"What about Lucy?"

"She's not feeling well enough." She probably wasn't, but in truth, Em hadn't even asked her. She didn't like mixing friend groups. The times Lucy and Emily had ended up in the same place had made her deeply uncomfortable. It didn't help that Lucy found Emily adorable, which drove Emily crazy.

"That's too bad. Mom wants me to send her something. Some flowers, maybe?"

"That'd be nice." She gave her sister Lucy's address.

"Hey, do you want to come to the show with us tonight? It's on me."

"What are you seeing?"

"I don't know, I gave Mark your list. He's getting the tickets." Em despaired of Mark choosing a good play, but nonetheless said sure, she'd love to.

"So is it okay for us to come over at five thirty? I'm really excited to see you. Mark too."

"I'm sure he is."

"Emily."

While Lucy would not be there tonight, Em was making one of her recipes, an artichoke dip she swore by for entertaining. She'd described it in the new book as "easy as a Monday crossword," but it was by far the most involved cooking Em had ever done in her apartment. Louis offered to help, but the kitchen was too small for him to join her, so he ended up chopping bread crumbs at the table. When Lisa arrived, holding a six-pack, she said, "It smells great in here."

"That's my artichoke dip!" Em said with pride.

"And the Christmas tree orgy," added Louis.

"I don't know what means, but get it out of your system before the grown-ups get here, honey."

Em worried her sister and Mark would be babes in the wood in her neighborhood, but they arrived on time, buzzed up, worked the lobby door like pros. When she saw Anne-Marie's face, embraced her sister, Em felt a wave of joy and sadness come over her. She was so happy her sister was here, and so sad her sister was usually so far away.

They left their wet umbrellas out in the hall. Mark, holding a bottle of wine, gave Em an awkward hug with the other arm. "Smells like Christmas in here!" he said. Behind him, Louis raised an eyebrow.

Anne-Marie and Mark knew Louis, who air-kissed them both, and Em made introductions with everyone else. With the couch, the rolling desk chair from her room, and the chairs from the dining table, there were just enough places for everyone to sit. "Where's the other Emily?" Anne-Marie asked, pointing to the one open seat.

"Oh, she's never on time," Lisa said.

"She's *sometimes* on time," Em said. "Her boss just makes her stay late a lot."

"Uh-huh," Lisa said. "What time did you tell her things were starting?"

Em glared at her. "I mean, five." Everyone laughed, and she felt herself flushing. "I just don't want her to miss dinner!"

"It's really generous of you to take us out," Louis said.

"Oh, we're so happy to meet all of you," Mark said. "What would a trip to New York be without feeding some starving artists?"

"They're not *starving*, Mark," Anne-Marie said.

"I could eat a little something," allowed Louis.

"Artichoke dip!" Em said, standing up. She got the warm dish from the kitchen and set it down on the coffee table. "And there's crackers and carrot sticks."

"Can I pour drinks?" Lisa asked. (This was a graceful way of telling Em she'd forgotten to pour drinks.) "Mark, what have you got there?"

"Oh, we just picked it up on the way," he said, holding up the bottle, which he'd set between his feet on the floor. "New York City! There's a really good wine store right there on the corner." Em knew the place; she had walked in, once, and immediately walked out when she saw the prices.

Lisa took the bottle into the kitchen and called, "Em, what do you think? Am I pouring into the coffee mugs or the plastic cups?"

"Maybe it's also time for your housewarming gift," Anne-Marie said, holding out a big Bloomie's bag.

"Oh, you didn't have to do that," Em said. She pulled out a box of wineglasses.

"Obviously, we'll take them," Louis said.

"Rinse them out first," said Anne-Marie.

The doorbell rang. Em buzzed Emily in while Lisa poured the wine. They were about to toast when Emily shoved open the door and burst into the living room. She was dripping wet, her hair matted to her brow. When she saw them, glasses raised, she said, "To the bourgeoisie!"

"To the Big Apple," Mark said.

"To my big sister," Em added. Anne-Marie smiled.

"You know," Emily announced, drying her hair with paper towels, "the name 'the Big Apple' comes from a whorehouse." She had their attention and continued happily. "Yeah, there was a brothel down in the Bowery in the 1800s. The woman who ran it was named Eve, Eve Something. She was French. Very fancy. She liked to call her girls 'Eve's Apples.' So then, when people called New York the Big Apple it was usually disparaging—the city of whorehouses. I suppose that's not how you meant it." She looked at Mark. "Who are you?"

"This is Emily," Em said into the silence of the room, and introduced her sister and her husband. "Did you lose your umbrella?" she asked. "You're drenched."

"Who the fuck carries an umbrella around?" said Emily.

"That's fascinating, about the Big Apple," Mark said. "Where did you read that?"

Emily shrugged. "I've done a lot of research for a piece I'm working on that's about New York history. But that's just a thing that New Yorkers know." It wasn't a thing that Em knew. For years afterward she would bring this amazing fact up in conversation at parties, until a historian told her it was completely untrue.

"What are we listening to?" Emily asked, heading over to the stereo. "Are we in a speakeasy?" Emily liked to be in charge of the music wherever she was, and was known for commandeering the stereo at parties, even ones where she had never met the host. Now she ejected the jazz CD Louis had picked out.

"Make yourself at home," Lisa said.

"I always do." Emily dropped a CD in the tray and pressed play. Sometimes Emily decided she was going to put on a show, and there was nothing you could do about it. You just had to wait her out.

The stereo emitted machine-gun drums and squealing guitars. Everyone except Emily jumped. It was the Ministry album that had been the most misbegotten choice of Em's twelve-for-a-dollar BMG CD club deal last fall.

"Now, does this count as grunge?" Mark asked, speaking loudly to be heard over the song. Louis winced, and Anne-Marie saw him.

"No, this is not grunge," Emily said, returning to the living room. "It's industrial." When Em stood and turned the music down, Emily laughed. "This album is meant to be played *loud*."

"I don't think everyone's loving it, though," Em said.

"So," Emily said to Mark, "what show did you decide on?"

"We got tickets to *Guys and Dolls*," Anne-Marie said.

"What about that whole list I made you?" Em asked. "What about *Angels in America*?" She'd also suggested *Falsettos*, *Fool Moon*, or *Kiss of the Spider Woman*. She supposed Mark had vetoed them all. If only she could just take her sister to a real show!

"That just opened, and it's a real big hit, I guess." Mark shook his head in amazement. "So that was a good suggestion, but the concierge basically laughed when I asked him about it. No tickets to be found."

"I think the concierge suggested *Guys and Dolls*, right, honey?"

"Oh yeah," Mark said. "He said it's really great. Great song and dance numbers."

"*Guys and Dolls*," Emily said.

"Well, I trust the experts," Mark said. "That's his job, to recommend Broadway shows. Have you seen it?"

"Have *I* seen it?" Emily said. "I don't go to Broadway."

"Except you're coming with us to *Angels in America* this summer," Em said.

"You got tickets! Wow," Mark said. He admired access.

The rain ended about the same time the Ministry album did, so catching cabs to the restaurant was not an ordeal. Mark gave them the address but said, "You can just tell your driver to follow our cab. It'll be like a spy movie."

"They're adorable," Louis said in the cab. Now that the rain was over, the windows were open to let some fresh air in. They were cruising up Third Avenue, trailing Anne-Marie and Mark's car.

Emily snorted. "'Does this count as grunge?'"

Em snorted, too, despite herself. "That was really embarrassing."

Emily did her best Bugs Bunny. "What a maroon!"

"Oh shit!" Lisa said from the front seat, pointing. Up ahead, the other cab swerved to the right, hitting the brakes, only to have a rollerblader wham into the car's side. The cabbie laid on the horn. "Fuck you!" the rollerblader shouted from the pavement. The other cabbie yelled something back, then pulled away.

"Wow, welcome to the big city," Louis said.

At the next intersection, they stopped at a red light. "Ah, look what he's doing," said their cabdriver, as the rollerblader skated past them. He grabbed on to the first cab's rear bumper just as the light turned green. Now the rollerblader was surfing behind the cab like Marty McFly, his hair flowing behind him. They must have been going thirty up Third Avenue, but the guy was cruising. He pulled himself up the car, hand by hand, toward the driver's door. "What is this, what is this?" their cabbie said, and honked.

What they figured out later was that the driver's window was closed, but the back windows were open, so the rollerblader, desiring revenge, did the only thing he felt he could: he swung his fist through the open window, smacking Mark in the head. "Oh my God!" said

Louis. Then the rollerblader peeled away, skating in the wrong direction, right past their cab. He looked totally satisfied.

They pulled up next to Mark and Anne-Marie's cab at the next stoplight. "Are you okay?" Em asked Mark through the window.

He was holding his ear and looked bewildered, mostly. "Why did he do that?" he asked.

When the light turned green, Emily said, "That's the most incredible thing I've ever seen."

"Like a Metropolitan Diary," agreed Em. "Welcome to New York, Mark."

"Y'all are pretty harsh on that poor man," Lisa said. "He seems like he's trying."

"That's the problem," said Emily. "He's *trying*. I'm sure he's a great . . . what does he do?"

"An accountant."

"A bean counter."

"*Total* bean counter."

"What does your sister see in him?"

"I have no idea," said Em.

"I guess there's no accounting for taste," Emily said, and the two of them burst into laughter.

"I can't believe you," Louis said.

"If she can't make fun of her sister's boring husband, who *can* she make fun of?" Emily asked.

The restaurant Mark had chosen was not boring at all. It was a big, loud, pink-and-rose Mexican restaurant with a packed bar. There were flowers everywhere, and the whole place looked like the inside of a piñata. While Mark was in the bathroom, Anne-Marie told them he had special-ordered a Zagat's guide from Schwartz's Books and spent hours looking through it for places to eat on the trip. Em had to admit this was one of the most fun restaurants she'd ever been to. And one of the most expensive—some of the entrees on the menu cost $20.

Mark insisted they all drink margaritas, a cocktail Em had always found way too sweet. These, though, were salty and sour and totally satisfying. And he ordered guacamole for everyone. Lisa was the only one of them who even knew what guacamole was, but they all oohed and aahed when the waiter brought three avocados to the table, turned them inside out, and mixed them up with a bunch of other ingredients in a huge stone pestle. Everyone devoured the dip; only Emily, who hardly ate anything most days, wrinkled her nose and turned it down.

Em loved *Guys and Dolls*. It had great song and dance numbers. It was about the Big Apple. Everyone in it was beautiful and funny. The margaritas had been strong, so she dozed off during one of the slow songs in Act II. She awoke at a squeeze of her hand and saw Anne-Marie smiling at her with tears in her eyes. On the other side of Anne-Marie was Mark, grinning at the stage like a doof. She wished, thereafter, to be a better sister. It took her a while, but she was.

— • —

When Em let herself in, the apartment was dark. Lucy must be asleep. She slipped off her shoes, opened the blinds on the front windows to let in some light, and immediately stepped on a Lego. After she put all Sarah's Legos in their bin, she cleaned up the markers, the tea set, the glass with a single lemon wedge sitting at the bottom (wait, was Lucy drinking?), the ashtray (what the hell?!).

She would need to talk to Lucy about that. *You cannot be smoking cigarettes at this point! You're in enough trouble!* Although on the other hand, she could imagine Lucy pointing out, what's the worst that could happen?

Oh no! Heh-heh-heh, I could die!

She checked the calendar for the week. The nurse would be in today, Wednesday, and Friday. Lucy had a doctor's appointment tomorrow, Tuesday. She'd need to get here plenty early to get her dressed, out the door, and into a cab. In fact, she should schedule the car today. Fuuuck, why hadn't she made the doctor's appointment for a day the nurse would be here? She needed to remember to do that next time. Sarah had a choir concert on Thursday night—she should go to that, right? Otherwise she wouldn't have anyone. Or maybe Lucy would want to try? She'd have to ask her.

How was the food situation? The freezer still had a lasagna and a seven-layer dip ready to go. She took the lasagna out to thaw. Lucy's friends were bringing casseroles, and Sarah's best friend's mom had paid to have Zabar's salads delivered every week. Other than those, though, the fridge was pretty bare. Maybe Em could go shopping before Lucy woke up.

She was standing in the kitchen, staring into the refrigerator, making notes in her Emily notebook, when there came from the front door the sound of a key rattling into a lock. The handle turned. The door began to open. *It's Lucy*, Em thought for one intensely happy moment. *She's been gone, but now she's back, she's home.*

It was not Lucy. It was a woman, older than Lucy, her hair a newscaster's helmet. She backed in, opening the door with her rear, carrying two big paper bags of groceries.

"Hello?" Em said. The woman let out a tiny shriek and whipped around. A single apple flew out of one of the grocery bags, sailed across the room, and landed perfectly on Lucy's favorite armchair. Em said, "It's okay! It's okay! I'm a friend of Lucy's!" Then thought, *Wait a minute*. "Who are you?"

The woman sat down, breathing heavily. "I'm Lucy's sister," she said. "Good Lord, you scared me to death. Are you . . . Em?"

"I am . . . Em."

"Lucy told me about you. Sarah did, too." She put the shopping bags down on the floor. "I'm Joanie. Pleased to meet you. Swear to God, I thought you were a murderer."

"I'm sorry I scared you."

"I've been in New York City one day and I'm already getting murdered."

"Usually it takes longer," Em said.

She stood up and smoothed her skirt. "I flew up from Charlotte. I'm here to help. I'm here as long as y'all need me to be here." Her voice, Em realized, sounded just like Lucy's, if she had never lost the Southern accent she must have grown up with. Em looked at this woman in her sensible shoes and began to cry.

"Oh honey," Joanie said, and hurried around the half-wall into the kitchen to embrace her.

"I'm so glad you're here," Em sobbed. She was wrecking this poor woman's nice blouse, she just knew it. "Lucy's so sick, and I've been the only one, and . . ." Joanie patted her back. She smelled like really good hair spray, just like Em's mom, and that just made it worse.

"I'm sorry," Em said, pulling away. She tore off a paper towel and wiped her face. "She's *your* sister. I can't even imagine how you're feeling."

Joanie waved her hand, an eloquent movement that contained within it an acknowledgment of her own sadness but also the recognition that sometimes things like that had to wait. For a moment, Em forgot how upset she was, so remarkable was this gesture. It was like one of those German words expressing a philosophical notion so complex Americans wrote dissertations on it.

"You sit," Joanie said. "Do you drink coffee?"

Em sat. She looked out the window. From the kitchen came the sounds of coffee percolating, of groceries being put away. It was one of the first really warm days of the spring, the first day that felt like summer. Everyone was showing their arms.

Joanie brought her a coffee and sat down. Because Em had shoved all the furniture to the walls, they were all the way across the living room from each other, separated by a handwoven rug from Santa Fe. Em saw a red Lego she'd missed stuck in the rug.

"Is that really true?" Joanie asked softly. "Have you really been the only one?"

"No," Em said, sniffing. She told her about the casseroles, the bagels, the frequent visitors after the diagnosis. "But Lucy's started telling people not to visit anymore," she said. "And there's been no one else to just help, you know, with the day-to-day. Well, there's the nurse. She comes three days a week. I try to come three days, too." She took a deep breath. "We've been working on a book, but Lucy's sort of lost interest in that. I think it makes us both too sad."

"Is this the recipe book?" Joanie asked.

"Yeah. There's enough, I guess. I just always want her to write a little bit more."

"Can I read it?"

"Oh, gosh. I don't know. You'd better ask Lucy."

"I will," she said. She reached down, dug the Lego out of the rug, and rolled it between her finger and thumb. Em realized in that silence that there were no chapters in the book about Joanie.

"Okay," Joanie said authoritatively, and it was as if a machine had just been turned on. "I'm here and I can help with all this. You tell me all the things you've been doing and we can divvy them up. You might need to do the really New Yorky stuff. This city scares the bejesus out of me."

Em still came uptown three days a week, but it made a huge difference having Joanie around, her smoking in the house notwithstanding. Aghast that her eight-year-old niece walked to school alone in Manhattan, Joanie started going with Sarah in the morning and picking her up in the afternoon. Though all Sarah's classmates also walked alone, she didn't seem to mind. She adored her aunt and was just sorry that her teenage cousins had not also traveled from North Carolina.

Joanie's arrival also encouraged Lucy to make more of an effort to get out of bed and be in the rest of the apartment. Em could tell this was partly due to the activation of her good-host instincts—she was forever asking Joanie if she needed something to drink—but also partly out of a desire to put on as good a face as she could for her sister. One afternoon they were all sitting in the living room, and Lucy, haltingly, told a story about how her older sister had liked to dress little Lucy up like a doll.

"Oh yes," Joanie said, laughing. "That just made you miserable. But I was so happy to have someone to take care of!"

Lucy looked at Em with a raised eyebrow. "I did not want to be taken care of," she said.

But it was Joanie, now, who would sometimes bring a bedpan in to Lucy's room and then carry it out when Lucy wasn't able to get out of bed. Em had been terrified of that eventuality, and the fact that someone else was doing it—that she could concentrate on calling cabs and dealing with the telephone company—made her feel simultaneously relieved and ashamed.

But what Em could do was go out with Sarah. They went to the library, or got a snack at the diner, or visited the Museum of Natural History, which Em had obviously never seen but to which Lucy had a family membership. Sarah liked the halls of gems and minerals, dark and quiet compared to the bustle of the rest of the museum, the jewels laid out on black cloth.

On one visit, an older woman told them that the Star of India had been stolen from the museum once, in the 1960s, because no one at the museum had changed the battery on the enormous sapphire's alarm. Eventually it was found in a locker in a bus station in Miami. "So the lesson is, never forget to change your batteries!" the woman said, which Sarah and Em later agreed was a completely inane lesson to take from that story. The lesson was, you never knew who wasn't doing their job.

— ● —

As far as Em could tell, Edith's preferred situation with her assistants was to have the assistant quit or get fired right before Memorial Day, so she didn't have to pay them while she was gone. Em refused to quit and was too valuable to be fired, so for the second summer in a row, she would work alone in Manhattan while Edith repaired to her house in Montauk.

Last summer had been gloriously stultifying—three months of slush and answering the phone. Edith seemed to start drinking around lunchtime and never once called in after two. On afternoons when Emily didn't have a shift at Kim's, she would come to the office and play movies on the VCR by the couch.

This summer was turning out different. There was Lucy, for starters, and the greater and greater responsibilities Em had at Sunrise Squat. And Emily was less available: picking up more hours, spending more time at Rob's, working furiously, she said, on her *Open Heart* script. She came in to the office about once a week, whenever she needed a printer.

Today she'd brought in *My Own Private Idaho*, a movie they'd watched together many times after Emily duped a copy on Kim's dual-deck VHS. They sat together on the couch, each reading, half watching a movie they knew by heart. But when River Phoenix and Keanu Reeves sat by the campfire, they both put down their reading and gave the men their full attention.

"When I left home, the maid asked me where I was off to," Keanu said, reclining, gorgeous. Here Em and Emily joined in joyously: "'Wherever, whatever, have a nice day.'"

On the screen, River curled tighter and tighter into himself, lit by firelight. "I could love someone, even if I, you know, wasn't paid for it," he said. "I love you, and you don't pay me."

"Mike," warned Keanu.

"I really wanna kiss you, man," River said, and as they always did, they gasped at the beauty of it.

"Talk about an open heart," Em said.

"God, he'd be perfect," said Emily. The lead role of her show was a young surgeon who gives himself up to the ghosts who haunt his hospital. "A guy I knew said he knew his brother—Leaf?—and I gave him a script, but who knows if he ever saw it. I bet he's dying to do theater, though."

"Probably. He's a serious actor."

"He only looks like a god."

— • —

Sarah and Em made the cake. Sarah was an excellent young baker, though she tended to overdo it with the rainbow sprinkles.

Joanie handed Lucy a birthday hat, which she refused to wear. Joanie wore it instead. It perched precariously atop her hairdo.

Em turned out the lights and brought in the cake. The three of them sang—the adults hesitantly on the first line, but then, inspired by Sarah's enthusiasm, finishing strong. It was very difficult to dampen an eight-year-old's spirits on a birthday. "Can I blow out the candles?" she asked her mom, and Lucy said, "Go for it."

"Make a wish!" Sarah said to her mother, then blew.

Em thought, *Fuck it,* and cut the entire cake into four enormous pieces, cake slices from a cartoon, the size she'd always wanted when she was little. She remembered protesting bitterly against her mother's thin slices, her declarations that there would be more tomorrow. (In fact, she often threw leftover birthday cake away while Em was asleep.) Sarah's eyes widened when she saw her piece, and she said, "Yes!"

The cake was delicious. Sarah, giggling, fed forkfuls to Lucy. Joanie ate exactly one bite, praised it extravagantly, and set her plate aside. Em finished her whole goddamn piece.

While Joanie cleaned up, Sarah and Em sat on the floor in the living room watching television. A kid named Doug got in trouble with the principal because of his cartoon making fun of the cafeteria's mystery meat. "This show is *really* good," Sarah said to Em. Em had to admit it wasn't bad, but mostly it just felt amazing to lie on a rug and watch cartoons while grown-ups did the dishes.

About halfway through the episode, it became impossible to ignore the fact that Lucy and Joanie were having an argument.

"He flew here from California," Joanie said. "How can you say he doesn't care?" Lucy's ex, Duncan, had come back to town, leaving behind his second wife and a new baby, and was staying in a hotel nearby. He stopped by sometimes to take Sarah to piano lessons or the library.

The rhythm of the fight was odd, because Lucy talked so much more slowly than Joanie did. "He flew from California to get Sarah," she said. "Not because of me."

"He's not *stealing* her. He's trying to help! And you said you *wanted*—"

"Well, he can just stay away from me."

Last summer, when Lucy had invited Em to come upstate for a week, they had been sitting on the dock reading while Sarah played in the water, and Em read Lucy a line she loved, about the dissolution of a character's marriage: "There had been no intrigue, just a gradual wearing down of the mechanism for concern." "Oh yeah," Lucy had said. "That's exactly what it's like."

"He *told* me he wants to see you," Joanie said now. "He was married to you for ten years!"

"Yeah, he left just in time."

Sarah moved closer to the TV. Em tried and failed to catch Joanie's eye. "You cannot shut him out," Joanie said. "For Sarah's sake, you need to let him—"

"I can die any way I want to!" Lucy snapped. Sarah stood up and, without a word, walked out the front door.

"I'll get her," Em said to the sisters, who weren't looking at each other but had the good grace to appear embarrassed at least. She grabbed her shoes and ran out the front door of the brownstone. "Sarah!" she called to the child, who was already halfway down the block. She hopped down the sidewalk, trying to pull on her shoes, then followed her.

She caught up at Columbus, where Sarah, a rule follower, was waiting impatiently for the walk light. When the sign changed Sarah set off across the street, and Em walked alongside her. Neither of them spoke. The city was alive with city sounds: cabs zooming past them, a police siren a few blocks away, the bodega guy commiserating with a customer about the Yankees. An old lady with a pinched face walked her pinched-face little rat dog toward them. Em nudged Sarah's arm, pointed the dog out. Sarah nodded and kept walking. As they crossed Central Park West, Sarah took Em's hand, then dropped it when they got to the park.

They walked down the bridle path, the reservoir invisible to their left. "Where are we going?" Em finally asked.

"The playground," Sarah said, to Em's surprise. Sarah, old beyond her years, was not much of a playground kid.

On this beautiful June day the playground was filled with insane children, most of them younger than Sarah. Instead of going in, she sat on a bench outside the fence. Em sat next to her. Sarah was looking straight ahead. In profile her chin looked exactly like her mother's.

A bird trilled in a tree nearby; fat, stupid bees bumped drunkenly into soda cans in the trash can at the playground's entrance. Behind the fence a boy was chasing a group of girls across a wooden bridge, all of them shrieking happily.

"This used to be my favorite playground when I was little," Sarah said.

Em held back a smile. "When you were little, huh."

Sarah cast a glance her way, alert for mockery. "Yes," she said.

"When I was little." She pointed at the bridge. "That was there, but all this stuff here"—the blue-and-red playground apparatus—"That's all new. It was fine before. I don't know why they changed it."

"You sound like a real New Yorker," Em said. "Complaining about how the city's different now."

"Before, there were more things to climb, and—OW!" She smacked her arm and a smashed bee tumbled to the pavement. "SHIT!" She leapt to her feet and stomped away, holding her arm. Em hurried after her. She remembered crying piteously when stung by a bee as a child, but Sarah seemed absolutely furious, stalking around and cursing under her breath. She really was a New Yorker.

Em got some ice and a plastic bag from a nearby hot dog stand. Sarah's cheeks were bright red and her eyes gleamed, but her face was set as they sat in the grass. Still the children played.

"What's California like?" Sarah asked. Lucy had not let her visit him there.

"I don't know," Em admitted. "I've never been west of Missouri."

"I guess it's all sunny and beachy, like *Baywatch*."

"How do you know *Baywatch*?!"

Sarah gave her an incredulous look. Who doesn't know *Baywatch*?

"There's Disneyland," Em said. "That seems awesome."

Sarah snorted. "We have *Central Park*," she said.

When the ice melted, Sarah got up and walked around the playground, touching the apparatus. Who was this child, who was courting nostalgia at the age of eight? At one point another kid directed a jet of water toward her and she screamed delightedly, dancing out of the way. Then she collected herself and walked on, dignified as a cat.

They walked back to the apartment, Sarah's sweaty hand in Em's sweaty hand. At the bodega, Sarah deigned to allow Em to buy her a Bomb Pop. A few days later, at Lucy's insistence, Duncan took Sarah back with him to California. Em wasn't there when she left, but Joanie told her it was the worst thing she'd ever seen in her life.

— • —

The city was auctioning off five community gardens on the Lower
East Side, vacant lots that locals had made beautiful over decades.
Em sat in the back of the room with Louis, their backpacks on their
laps. The city employee running the auction introduced her favorite
garden—"Twenty-five hundred square feet, undeveloped, at 237 East
Seventh Street." This was the garden where she had scrounged cinder
blocks for her bookshelves, where she had ducked in to cry one afternoon on the way home from work, only to have a woman in overalls
pat her shoulder and hand her a pot of cilantro. Its winding paths, its
butterflies. She remembered walking past at night and hearing the
sound of crickets, as if a tiny bit of the country had been transplanted
between tenements.

Several developers had sent bored representatives to make a play
for the properties, but for this garden the auction was joined by several new bidders in suits. The long strawberry blond hair should have
been a tip-off, but none of the city officials who regularly did battle
with Michael were at the auction. Soon the bids reached a million,
then two million. The developers dropped out. Michael and Joe were
bidding against each other, scowling across the room through the
incongruous monocles they both wore. Em felt the thrill of disobe-
dience, the delight of seeing everyone else in the room realize something was going on, the pride of knowing she helped make it happen.
The monocles had been her idea.

When Michael said "Two-point-five million dollars!" Em and Louis
and others scattered around the room opened their backpacks, and
ten thousand crickets filled the air.

— • —

Someone broke into Frank's Tercel in front of Sunrise Squat and stole the big canvas case of cassettes he had inside. Years of mixtapes from friends and lovers, gone. "If that happened to me," Emily said to Em, "I swear to God."

Emily and Em joined others from the squat, watching Frank duct-tape cardboard over the broken window. When he finished, he tossed his cigarette into the gutter and turned to face his audience. "I guess someone just needed all those tapes even more than I did," he said. "I hope whoever it is, he's okay."

That night there was a meeting in the community library. New York HPD—"the Department of Housing Prevention and Destruction," Michael liked to call them—had put forth an offer. If the residents could get together the cash and financing, they could buy the building and live as owners. Otherwise, the city warned, they would all be evicted.

"They can say they'll evict us, but it doesn't mean it's true," Michael said at the meeting. "We can always file an adverse possession suit. But this is still a pretty big deal. Not every squat gets this."

"It's because of all the work we've done," Joe said. "They see an opportunity."

"What about people who can't afford to buy in?" Emily asked. The xeroxed packet Sofia had handed out at the door listed a per-square-foot price that would be a real stretch for most residents, Em guessed. Emily paid only $75 a month to live in Sunrise; residents with bigger apartments paid $100. And if you couldn't afford that, you could always work extra hours to make it up.

"It's not the cash up front that's the issue," Sofia said. "It's the mortgage. We'd all need to contribute to that each month, and it's gonna look a lot more like market rent than it does right now."

"And that would be real," Joe said. "The bank wants that money every month. The bank don't take hours in the garden." Slowly the discussion wound its way around to the inescapable truth: if they bought the building, some of them would end up having to evict their neighbors.

Sunrise Squat rejected the city's offer. Emily and Em went door to door, handing out cardboard so everyone could black out their windows. Late one night, Joe and Michael pulled down some iron fencing from Tompkins Square and hauled it into the entryway, to be ready.

— ● —

"You don't have to come out as often," Joanie told Em on the phone. "There's really not that much she needs anymore."

"Of course I'll come," Em said.

— ● —

They'd all read Part 1 of *Angels in America* in Shakespeare & Company, sitting side by side by side on the floor in the basement, but to see it was a whole other thing. On a hot Tuesday night at the end of July, they took the subway uptown, handed their precious tickets to the man at the door, made their way up, up, up to the fourth row of the top balcony. When the angel crashed through the ceiling and hovered in all her glory over Prior at the end, Ellen McLaughlin was still lower than they were.

Afterward, buzzing, they walked west to a brightly lit diner on Tenth Avenue, where they split a sundae and argued about the play.

"How dare he," Louis said. "Everyone I know, your partner gets sick, you stay."

"You're just mad because he has your name," Em said. Secretly, she'd watched the character of Louis and his betrayal of his sick lover with woozy recognition.

"I'm not thrilled about that, no."

"But isn't it the job of the artist to make us see ourselves at our worst?" Emily asked. "Otherwise, what's the point?"

Hard things, Em thought.

"It's just—it does nothing for the struggle," Louis said.

"Come on," Em protested. "The theater was full of ladies from Jersey watching a beautiful man in drag! Hearing Little Sheba jokes!"

"Well, it does a little for the struggle," Louis allowed. "But it's annoying that this is *the thing* about AIDS. Like, no one else has to do an AIDS play because you could never do a two-part extravaganza with an angel coming through the ceiling."

Emily went off on a tear about how much she hated the production's direction: "Slow it down, George C. Wolfe! You don't need to make everyone come all at once!" Louis confessed that his coming out to his parents had closely resembled Joe's awful phone call to Hannah. Em said that she loved Harper most of all, which made Emily say, "What a psycho bitch!" All disagreements aside, they were desperate to know what would happen next, but Part 2 wouldn't open until the fall. Even as they argued, they knew, Tony Kushner was somewhere in New York hectically trying to finish writing it; they'd read all about his struggle in the *Times*. Anyway, none of them had enough money to buy tickets.

Em called her sister. "Anne-Marie," she said. "I need an early Christmas present." A week later, an envelope from a ticket broker arrived in the mail, enclosing three tickets for a Sunday show in December. She marked it on the calendar in her and Louis's apartment, wrote the date in Magic Marker on Emily's wall underneath Rob's telephone number.

— ◆ —

Through July and August Em came uptown about once a week, burned out from her spring of caretaking and overwhelmed with helplessness at how little she could do now. Joanie was right: Lucy didn't need anything anymore. Sarah was in California. Joanie could heat up lasagna for herself just fine.

Lucy died in the middle of August, August 15. It was a Sunday. Em wasn't there; she was working in the garden at Sunrise Squat.

Joanie told her that it had been a quiet day. She had sat with Lucy for a while, then read the newspaper in the living room. The hospice nurse had told her she ought to come back in, so she did. She played some music in the bedroom, songs she remembered Lucy liking when they were kids. A little after two, she just stopped breathing. "Nothing dramatic," Joanie said.

At the funeral, a week later, Em had the unexpected task of introducing her mother to Edith. Her mom, in from Wisconsin for the first time since Em had moved to New York; Edith, in from Montauk. She was touched that they both came, angry that they hadn't been more present throughout.

Lucy's ex-husband was short, with a bushy mustache. He looked dazed. Sarah held his hand for the entire service. It was the first time Em had ever seen her wear a dress. Em didn't get a chance to talk to her. She saw Lorraine and Danny and a group of the friends from the Christmas party. Em stood with her mother and with Emily and Louis, who had ridden out to Brooklyn in Frank's tapeless Tercel, air blowing in through the broken passenger-side window. Louis had loved *Can't Complain* and had been delighted by Em's friendship with its author; Emily had never stopped thinking the book must be boring and conventional. Until Lucy got sick, Emily referred to Em's lunches with her as "your dating-your-mom time." But for the past few months Emily had been sweet and solicitous when the subject turned to Lucy, and at the funeral she kept her hand on Em's shoulder. Em was grateful for that.

After the funeral, she gave her mother the sorority yearbook. "Oh!"

her mom said when she saw the snapshot of Lucy and Donna at the beach, and pulled a Kleenex from her purse.

"I love that photo," said Em. "Lucy told me about what happened."

"She told you?" Her mom gave a sad little laugh. "That's okay, I suppose. I still remember that day. I was so relieved."

"I know. Lucy told me girls got expelled for this?"

"Oh yes," her mom said. She lowered her voice, even though they were alone in Em's apartment. "Do you know I never told your father?"

"Well, it wasn't any of his business," Em said, but then looked at her mom, freshly crying, and understood. "Mom?" she said, touching her mother's leg. "Lucy told me it was her."

"That was sweet," her mom said. "She was always very protective of me."

The last time Em had seen Lucy had been three days before she died. The hospice nurse had been there. Lucy was awake but was long past speaking. Em didn't know what to do, so she read aloud from the book she was in the middle of.

> Above the entrance to the courtyard there's a beautiful pediment with a Greek inscription, a long inscription. I wanted to know what it said, because the courtyard was lovely, peaceful, and the doors were lovely, and the pediment—well, I went to find a guard, to see if he could tell me what it said. But on the wall opposite the courtyard I saw a card with the translation. It said: ART IS FOR MAN A HAVEN FROM SORROW. And it cheered me so. I hadn't known how sad I was, I think.

She'd stopped for a moment. Lucy was still, her eyes facing the ceiling. Emily felt angry at the connections her mind wouldn't stop making, drawing lines between the words on the page and her own life that felt intrusive. Emily felt angry that this author had described precisely how she felt about art most of the time, angry that she'd read it in a circumstance where it was beyond incorrect, nearly outrageous.

After a half hour or so, Em had gotten up. "I'll see you next week, okay?" she said. The hospice nurse cut her a look. Em took Lucy's hand, dry and thin against her own soft, sweaty skin. "Goodbye," she said.

— • —

A few days after the funeral, Em traveled uptown one more time, to help Joanie clean out the apartment. When she got there, most of the furniture was gone, but the shelves were still full of books and the kitchen was still full of, well, of everything. Years later, when she did finally learn to cook, Em would look back on this day as one of the great missed opportunities of her life. Lucy had assembled a kitchen full of perfect culinary equipment, everything a New York cook needed—nothing unnecessary to clutter up the small space, no trendy bread machines or tagines, just well-balanced, well-cared-for knives, beautiful pots and pans, a bright red stand mixer. Joanie didn't want any of it. "I have my own kitchen," she said. "I can't wait to get back to it. Take anything you want."

But she lived in a tiny apartment with Louis. Neither of them cooked. Where would she put a deep blue enamel casserole dish? That stand mixer was bigger than their counter.

The books, though. The books were another matter. With books she didn't care how crowded her apartment already was. She could already imagine the look of dismay on Louis's face when she showed up, but that didn't stop her from filling six big file boxes full of books and wishing she could take more. She secured three copies each of Lucy's first two novels, the Balcony Press editions. (Joanie, who loved Lucy's books, would take home the rest of those.) She took all three of Lucy's copies of *Sense and Sensibility*, even though she already had her own. She took home authors she'd heard of but never read: Lucy's Shirley Jacksons and her Iris Murdochs and her Angela Carters. She took authors she'd never heard of: Elizabeth Taylor and Grace Paley and Rachel Ingalls and Ursula Le Guin. She took Lucy's two Vintage Contemporaries.

Joanie helped her carry the boxes to the curb, along with the one kitchen item she'd taken, the incredibly heavy cast-iron skillet. After they loaded all the boxes in the trunk of the cab, Joanie hugged her. "There's one other thing," she said, pulling a paper-clipped packet from her purse. "Lucy had me type this up. Before her—before she couldn't talk anymore. She said I should give it to you after she passed."

Em took the packet and looked at it. At the bottom of the first page she saw a handwritten *L*. "The note's from her, too," Joanie said. Em felt Joanie hug her once more and put her in the cab. She heard Joanie tell the cabbie her address. She managed to wave goodbye as she pulled away.

The note read:

Emily,

You can decide whether to include this chapter or not. I didn't tell Edith about it. It's up to you.

I think the book should be called "The Watched Pot." You'll see why.

I love you. Goodbye.

L

The chapter was called "Tahdig (Persian Rice)."

Em looked out the window of the cab as they crossed the transverse. A stone wall, a riot of trees. The blank face of the park police headquarters. The darkness of a tunnel, and the light of the sun.

"That's a lot of books in the trunk," the cabbie said finally. "You gonna read all those?"

Em looked up, surprised, as if waking from a long sleep. "Yes," she said.

— ● —

On the Tuesday after Labor Day, Edith walked into the office at eleven and turned out the lights. Em sat at her desk, glad it was suddenly so dark Edith couldn't see the expression on her face. "Well now!" Edith said, rubbing her hands together. "Welcome back!"

— ● —

"Dumpster sighted," Michael said over the phone. "We need manpower." Em was at work, Edith staring at her from her desk, so she said, "I understand. I can be there at six or so."

"Fuck," he said. "Can you call your people?"

"I'm heading to the post office," she said to Edith when she hung up. "Anything outgoing?" From the pay phone on the corner, she made her phone-tree calls. "The city parked an empty Dumpster in front of Sunrise," she told them. "When they put one in front of 319 the cops came at the building the next day. When they evict everyone, that's where all the furniture and things will go."

"Everything all right?" Edith asked when she got back to the office.

"Got a date," Em said, to Edith's delight.

Edith knew that Em had spent much of the summer at Lucy's; that was a sanctioned activity. Em had not told her how much time she was spending fighting for an apartment that she didn't even live in. Edith had lived in the same two-bedroom in the San Remo for forty years. Em had seen it once—it was a hoarder's playground.

That evening she ran from work to Sunrise, afraid she'd arrive to squad cars and chaos, but the street was quiet. The empty Dumpster lurked like a sentinel on the curb. She called Emily from the corner, like the old days. "What's going on?" she asked.

"Come around the back," Emily said. "The front's blocked."

Em steeled her courage and walked briskly through the urine-scented alley, ignoring the skitterings of rats or whatever the hell those were. A ladder was propped against the back wall up to an open window. When she climbed in, she was in Michael's apartment, his bougie squat, with its wallpaper, its art deco lamps, its honest-to-God *piano*. It made Emily's apartment look like a dump, and Emily's apartment was nicer than almost anyone else's in the building.

Michael wasn't here, but the door to the hallway was open. She heard music and voices from the entranceway, where Michael and Joe were coordinating a team welding the iron fence bars across the front door. Despite the grim circumstances, it was like a party—everyone had beers, and a boom box played They Might Be Giants. "Everybody dies frustrated and sad, and that is beautiful," one of the Johns sang.

Upstairs, Emily and Rob were sprawled together on the futon. "Hey," she said, not trusting their reclined position. "Are you guys okay?"

Emily sat up with theatrical energy. "We're great!" She grinned. "I've got funding for *Open Heart*."

"What?" Em said. "That's amazing! Should we be, like, moving your stuff, though?"

"If the cops come, I'm set," Emily said, waving toward the corner of the room, where the CD changer was unplugged and sitting in a milk crate atop a suitcase. "But listen to this. Do you know who the Wooster Group is?"

"Sure, the Wooster Group," Em said, from the habit of two years of book parties, then realized she didn't need to do that. "Actually, I don't know them at all. Who are they?"

"They're a downtown theater ensemble. You know Spalding Gray? Who did that monologue we saw about trying to write a novel? He started out there."

"Sure, I remember," Em said. She had not enjoyed the show; Spalding Gray's procrastinatory ordeal writing his novel had felt like a dark preview of what it would be like to write one of her own.

"It turns out Rob here"—Rob, still slouched, lifted a beer in belated greeting—"sells to one of the company's founders! He told him all about the show, and they want a meeting."

"*Rob* told them about the show?" She had not been aware that Rob knew anything about *The Open Heart.*

"'Tis the beating! Of his hideous! Heaaaaaaart!!!'" Rob sang.

"And you think they might be able to produce it?"

"Are you kidding?" Emily said dismissively. "This show is in their *wheelhouse.* Literature, tech, embodied performance—I've been trying to get it to them for years, and it turns out this motherfucker hangs out in Ron Vawter's loft once a month!"

Rob gave a salute, acknowledging that yes, he was that motherfucker.

"It's a go production," she said. "Ron told Rob he's taking it straight to Elizabeth LeCompte."

"That's incredible," Em said. "Let's celebrate!"

"The State of Denmark," said Emily, "is strong. We got some beer in through the front door just in time."

Em tapped the Andre the Giant sticker, opened the fridge, opened a can. "Yeah, this is crazy," she said. "Aren't you worried about everyone?"

Rob sat up. "You gotta get a new apartment. This welding-the-door thing is bullshit."

"I know, I know," Emily said. "Em, should we live together somewhere?"

Em, shocked, said, "You'd leave Sunrise?"

"Well by tomorrow I might not have a choice. But it's not normal to have to protest every weekend just to live in an apartment! You don't live here, you don't know what it's like."

Em was stung. "I kind of know what it's like. I protest with you!"

"Right, yes, I'm sorry. But every day it's another argument, another eviction. It's too much."

"Wouldn't you want to live with Rob?" Em asked. Rob laughed.

"Come on, Rob likes his space," Emily said. There was something weird in her voice, an unconfident note Em wasn't used to hearing from her friend. "And you and me, imagine us living together! Imagine the work that'll come out of that apartment. People will talk about that place for decades."

"They'll have to put a replica in the Emily Memorial Library," Em said. Rob laughed again. He got up, grabbed his backpack and the bathroom key, and left.

It was quiet but for the sound of clanking far below. "Think about it, okay?" Emily said.

"I can't just leave Louis in the lurch like that. We still have six months on our lease."

"Louis can come, too," Emily said. "I didn't want to say in front of Rob, but my dad sent me some money. Enough for a broker's fee. Or to break your lease."

"Your dad?" Another surprise.

"He says he's worried about me," she said. Then she got up, walked over to the window, lifted up a corner of cardboard to look outside. Em finally identified what she'd heard in her voice, that unfamiliar note. Emily was afraid.

The cops didn't come that night, or the next day. Everyone had to use the ladder until the guys managed to remove the bars from the door. The Dumpster remained outside, waiting.

— • —

Sometimes on the train, Em and Emily liked to play Twenty Questions. As Louis said, they shared a brain, so it rarely took either of them all twenty questions to guess the person the other was thinking of. One time Em said, "I have a person," and Emily said, "Archbishop Desmond Tutu?" and Em said, "Goddammit."

Today, though, Em was stumped. They were headed to the Cloisters, and as the train rattled toward 125th Street, Em had sailed way past twenty questions and was thoroughly confused. Here were the things she had ascertained about the person whose identity she was supposed to guess:

- She was a woman.
- She was nonfictional.
- She was American.
- Other characteristics the mystery person suspiciously shared with Em: she was straight and white, she was born in Wisconsin, she went to college in Connecticut, she lived in New York City.

However, *unlike* Em,

- She was between thirty-five and forty years old.
- In addition to New York, she also lived in London.
- She was famous for her writing.
- She had written three novels and a screenplay that had been nominated for a Golden Globe, but not an Oscar.
- She also worked in the theater. In fact, Emily claimed *she* had collaborated with her before.

"You worked with someone who's written screenplays?"

"Just the one screenplay."

"I didn't know you collaborated with"—Em was about to say "real people," but instead she said "anyone prominent like that."

Emily smiled the silent, merry smile of someone who knows she is driving her friend crazy. Em wanted to hit her. "Okay. Jesus Christ. Does this person have children?"

"No."

"Is she married?"

"She is."

"Is her husband famous? Or her partner, I guess."

"No. Remember, she's straight."

"Right. Have *I* met this person before?"

"You see her all the time." Emily giggled.

"I don't know any famous people yet! Um . . . when was the last time I was with this person?"

"Yes or no questions please."

"Was I with this person in the past six months?"

"Yes."

"The past three months."

"Yes." Emily bounced up and down on the plastic subway seat.

"The past month."

"Yes!"

"The past week!"

"Yes!"

"The past day!"

"Yes!"

"Excuse me. I have seen this person *today*."

Em couldn't stop laughing. "You have indeed."

"Uh . . . since noon."

"Yes."

"In the last hour."

"Sure!"

"Emily, am I somehow with this person right now?"

"You are."

Em looked around the subway car. In the middle of a winter

weekend afternoon, it was about half-full. "Is one of these people White Toni Morrison?"

"No."

A terrible notion had been scratching at Em's mind for a few minutes now, but it had made her so mad that she had tried to ignore it. Now she asked: "Emily. Is this me?"

"Yeeessssss . . ."

"Is this, like, somehow future me? Me *in the future?*"

Emily hooted. "It's you—fifteen years from now!"

Em looked at her with horror. "You can't do that!"

"Why not?"

Em thought about all the times Emily had presumed, on her behalf, the kind of person she was, the kind of artist she would one day become. She was furious but couldn't think of how to explain why. "You made up a bunch of shit," she said. "How was I supposed to guess it?"

"It's all going to be true," Emily said in what she clearly hoped would be a winning manner.

"Shut up! You don't know. Three novels. A *Golden Globe.* Give me a break."

"Why not? You'll—"

"It's embarrassing!" Em said with sudden passion. She saw Emily pull back in surprise. Several faces on the subway turned ever-so-briefly toward her. "That's never going to happen. I'm an *assistant.*" Her eyes welled up. "Stop saying things like that. *My future?* You don't know my—" She stopped, turned away, pulled a Kleenex from her purse. Why did Emily's steadfast belief in her make her so angry? Why was she so convinced she herself was a fraud when she'd always known Em, for all her faults, was the real thing?

They pulled into 125th Street and station light flooded the windows. Em could see families standing on the platform: a Puerto Rican lady holding a toddler so bundled up he looked like a snow cone, a

Chinese mother with a baby in a sling, a woman in a headscarf and her sullen teenager. As the last two got on the train, she snapped something in some other language and the teen sat next to his mother, visibly mortified.

They pulled out of the station into the dark.

"It's just a Golden Globe *nomination*," Emily said. "You don't win."

Em saw herself in the subway window cracking a smile. She wiped her face.

"You lose to John Sayles."

"John Sayles?"

"He writes *Driving Miss Daisy 2.*"

"There's no way John Sayles would ever write *Driving Miss Daisy 2.*"

"Miss Daisy gets hit on the head and gets amnesia. Poof! She's racist again. Her nurse (Oscar nominee Whoopi Goldberg) has to teach her that we're all the same."

Em stared at Emily, who was looking into the distance, as if reading a poster. Finally Em relented and slouched down in her seat. "Probably *I'll* end up writing *Driving Miss Daisy 2*," she groaned.

"Em," Emily said fervently. "You will *never* write *Driving Miss Daisy 2.*"

— • —

After a year of calls and letters, Emily had a meeting, finally, with someone at the Landmarks Preservation Commission who could approve her use of the Smallpox Hospital. Em asked her if she could help her prepare—if she wanted to run her pitch by her, or think through the answers to some questions. "I don't need practice talking about *Open Heart*," Emily snapped. "I've spent my whole life preparing to make *Open Heart*."

Mornings when Em didn't stay over at the squat, she had taken to calling Emily on the telephone before work, just to make sure she was up and ready to go. She'd missed a shift at Kim's, and her manager was a hard-ass. Em's calls weren't something they talked about; they were just a thing that Em did. On the morning of Emily's Parks Department meeting, though, Em was swamped running royalty statements and didn't get a chance to call. Around three, when Em finally took her sandwich out of the fridge, she suddenly remembered her friend.

"How'd it go?" she asked when Emily answered the phone.

"Did you know the Parks Department isn't even in Central Park? It's just in an office building."

"Did you go to the wrong place?" It was just like Emily to make a drama out of something as simple as a meeting with some government bureaucrat.

"No, I didn't go to the wrong place. It was fine. I'll convince him eventually."

"I'm surprised you're bothering," Em said. "Why not just do the show and ask forgiveness later?"

"Well, maybe that's what I'll do, in the end."

"I'm sorry I didn't call you to wake you up."

There was a silence, and Em worried she'd overstepped. "I wasn't home anyway," Emily said finally. "I was at Rob's."

— ● —

When she came out to the living room, drying her hair, Louis was on the couch watching the *Today* show, their cat on his lap. River Phoenix's photo was behind Katie Couric's head. "Oh God, did you hear?" he said. She watched with him for a few minutes and then went back to her room to dig Rob's number out of her purse.

"Fuck!" Emily said when she told her.

"I know," Em said. "It's horrible. His poor family."

"He *had the script*," Emily said. "I finally got his assistant's information. FUCK!" In the background, she heard Rob saying, "Whoa, dude."

"Emily, the boy is dead!" Em said. Emily viewed every person, every event, through the lens of her own prospects. "Was he really going to be in your play? Did he even see the script?"

"Well, I'll never know now, I guess," Emily said darkly.

"What's happening with the Wooster Group?" she asked.

Emily groaned. "They're taking forever. Rob says that Ron says they're really deliberating. But I don't want someone who *can't decide* if they want to do this play."

"Sure."

"I want someone who *gets* it, like you get it."

"Of course." This was familiar, comfortable, being the last person who was still on Emily's side.

"I'm thinking about just withdrawing it. You know, fuck them."

"Sure."

— • —

When the cops finally came, it was a rainy Tuesday at the beginning of November. For days before, many of Sunrise Squat's residents had been moving their things out, finding safe places for their possessions. The families with kids were long gone, exhausted from weeks of uncertainty. Emily was spending most of her time at Rob's; she had even moved the CD changer there.

Overnight, lit by streetlights and a half-moon, Em had helped her friends pile furniture, trash, and two-by-fours across Twelfth Street. They pushed the Dumpster over and filled it with concrete rubble. At about four in the morning, they flipped over a car that had sat abandoned in front of a fire hydrant for months. Her hands joined everyone else's as they rocked the car, rocked it farther, tipped it completely over into the middle of the street. Breaking glass, cheers, laughter. A bouquet of parking tickets fluttered away on the wind.

At dawn, Em sat on the curb by the overturned Dumpster with

Lisa and her brother Alan, who had come up from Maryland, where he was in journalism school. His yearlong reporting project was about the battle for the squats. He hadn't told his professors that he was no longer simply interviewing but had gone ahead and joined the barricades. He was tall and funny but right now looked shrunken and exhausted, as shrunken and exhausted as Em knew she looked. She'd never worked so hard in her life. She was eating a granola bar and drinking one of the Cokes the clerk at the drug-front bodega had passed out to all the protestors.

"You know they're gonna come when they wanna come," Lisa said. She had a job with the city's parks department, but now—"To my parents' dismay," she'd said once—spent much of her time working on her own squat and organizing protests with Michael and the other fair-housing leaders.

"Maybe the judge will stop it," Em said. A court case was active; they hadn't gotten an injunction, but the judge had said there was sufficient evidence to suggest the squatters might have an adverse possession claim. Michael said the lawyers were downtown right now, filing a second injunction request.

Lisa snorted. "You think a judge is gonna stop the NYPD? Girl, that's the whitest thing you ever said."

Alan said, "You never know."

Lisa got up and flexed. "Sun's out, guns out," she said. "Let's get back to work."

All morning squatters rode around the neighborhood on bikes, carrying walkie-talkies. "About fifty cops on Avenue B." "Someone at 204 just called me, cops came in the front door and are up on the roof. You see 'em?" Em was standing near Michael when she heard his walkie-talkie buzz and a voice say, "Michael, there's a motherfucking tank driving down Avenue C."

Michael laughed. How could you not laugh? "Jesus Christ," everyone agreed. And then there it was, a big old tank with NYPD printed on its side in white block letters. The *Times*, in its story the next day, would call it a "tanklike armored vehicle." Em would remember that forever.

Michael got on the walkie-talkie and said, "I'm going inside. This building has protected us for years. Now it's our time to try and save it, or to fight to the end." He climbed into a second-floor window and pulled the ladder up behind him. He would wait behind the same front door he'd helped install years before, to show the neighborhood the building was being reborn. The door was welded shut and barricaded from the inside with iron bars and freshly poured cement.

At noon, floods of police officers came from both avenues, nightsticks locked and loaded. Em linked arms with the people on either side before the western barricade. They backed up as far as they could, women spreading wet cement in the street in front of them so the cops would have to wade through it. She saw Louis, Sofia, the hooker from down the hall. She saw Lisa wearing a bike helmet. She saw the teenage clarinetist from the first floor. He looked as frightened as she'd ever seen a person look. It took no time at all for a police officer to tear her away from the line, his hands on her arms, her waist, her ass, wrestling her to the wet ground, and all the time she was *hollering*, the things coming out of her mouth! She never thought she would ever say such terrible things, but she lost her mind a little bit, and only when her hands were cuffed behind her back and the cop's knee left her shoulders and she was left there with wet hair and gravel embedded in her cheek did she understand she was crying "Emily, Emily, Emily."

Soon the cops began to work on the front door with power saws, and Michael and Joe and Frank stood behind the door with hammers, whaling away at the saw blades as they poked through. The cops swore as their saws broke, retreated, were replaced by more, like zombies. They'd never stop. When the door started to fail, Michael and Joe and Frank retreated into Joe's apartment on the fourth floor and barricaded that door and listened to their screaming neighbors pulled from their apartments and drank the last of his Scotch and watched live TV news coverage of the whole thing from Chopper 4 up in the sky. Eventually they were the last ones dragged out of the building, and as they were hustled down toward the lobby, Michael would later say to Lisa's brother, he wished they hadn't done such a fucking good job building the stairs. He wished the stairs groaned and collapsed under the weight of dozens of boots, that they all hurtled down in a great apocalyptic cloud, and that every single one of those cops died screaming.

And Em returned late that night, when it was all over and she'd been bailed out and she'd checked on Lisa and Louis in the hospital. In the moonlight, she looked in the Dumpster, now upright, and in it she saw a child's bed, crates full of records, the books from the library, soaked and bloated and ruined. Below them, a minifridge, open and empty, with a sticker of Andre the Giant on it.

— • —

Lisa had a shattered leg. The cops said she got it resisting arrest, but everyone knew they hammered her after she went down, hammered until they heard her scream.

Louis had a broken collarbone. "Fuck yeah I was resisting arrest," he said to his parents on the telephone.

Everyone was in the same hospital, so on Thursday morning Em woke up, ignored the annoyed messages from Edith on her answering machine, and walked across town. St. Vincent's towered, brown and ugly, over Seventh Avenue. Louis was watching TV, surrounded by friends. He'd been to St. Vincent's countless times, of course, volunteering in the AIDS ward. "Everyone loves visiting me," he told Em. "I'm the only one in this place who's not dying." And then Emily appeared in his doorway.

She hugged Em and they stepped out into the hall. She was crying, apologizing, but Emily barely heard her. Rob had gotten this really amazing shit, she said, and she was so upset about the squat and everything, and so she just disappeared. She was basically not on this earth for a week. Kim's fired her, but she knew she could get the job back. "But I'm so sorry, Em, I'm so sorry I wasn't there fighting."

You could walk through the halls anywhere in that hospital and no one would ever ask who you were or what you were doing. Suddenly they were in Lisa's room. Lisa's brother was sitting by the bed. "Hey Alan," she said. "Emily lived in Sunrise Squat. Interview her. Ask her where she was when the cops came." Then she walked out the door. She didn't talk to Emily for a month.

— • —

11/11/93
Edith:

Attached find the complete manuscript for "The Watched Pot," Lucy Deming's posthumous memoir with recipes. This includes all the chapters she wrote, and the ones she dictated to me, before her death.

It's a beautiful book. It is as funny as Lucy's novels, full of wisdom and kindness. Readers will find joy and solace in these stories of childhood, child-raising, dinner parties, and bad dates.

They'll also find eleven wonderful recipes, from the perfect martini to wonderfully crisp fried chicken. There's even a recipe for the best gingerbread you'll ever taste. I've learned so much about food, comfort, and life from this book.

I know this is an option book for Vanessa at Avon, but I think we should push hard for "The Watched Pot" to go to the open market. This feels like a breakout book to me, and I think it could do really well with a wide submission.

-Emily

11/13/93

Edith:

Lucy always thought of this as a memoir, with recipes. To her, the recipes and the stories behind them—and teaching people who don't know how to cook how to make these delicious dishes on their own—were just as important as the autobiographical elements.

You're right that this style of book is very uncommon. I don't know of any other memoirs that mix cooking with storytelling like this. But to my mind that's an advantage. The book will stand out in the marketplace. It's a little bit memoir, a little bit life lessons, a little bit cookbook—perfect for appealing to multiple audiences.

I strongly feel we should not try to cut out the recipes. Lucy didn't want that, and in addition I think it would weaken the book, artistically and commercially.

-Emily

11/20/93

Edith:

First of all, thank you for deciding to leave Lucy's recipes in "The Watched Pot." I think it's the exact right choice.

I think we should reject Avon's offer. This book is worth much more than $15,000 on the open market. Vanessa views the offer as a favor to Lucy's family, not as an investment in a book she's motivated to make a success. In your conversations with her, do you get the sense that she is passionate about the book and its chances in bookstores? I know she told you she wished there was a chapter about Lucy's illness, but to me that betrays an unwillingness to accept this particular book in the

spirit in which she wrote it: a celebration of the good stuff, even
when life is hard.

In my opinion, Avon is the wrong home for this book.
They have no profile in the culinary/cookbook world. The
perfect publisher would be someplace like Harper or Random
House, publishers with strong programs in both memoir
and cookbooks. The right promotion plan for this book,
for example, would combine a first serial deal that makes
the most of Lucy's literary flair and second serials in Good
Housekeeping, Gourmet, etc. I have little confidence that
Avon could execute such a plan, especially considering how
badly they did with Lucy's novel. (You'll recall her only major
publicity hit was engineered by us, through my connections to
the Times Book Review.)

This is Lucy's last chance to break out. She needs to be at a
publisher who's excited about her. Let me submit the book on
the open market. You won't be sorry.
-Emily

11/25/1993
Dear Peter,

I'm not sure if you remember me, but we've met at a few
different book events over the years. We had a terrific
conversation at the Random House party last spring
about our shared love of the Vintage Contemporary line. I
still can't believe you said your favorite cover was
"Airships"!

I saw that you've just moved to St. Martin's and I'm writing
to express my interest in the position as your assistant. As
you may recall, I've been working as an assistant at the Safer

Agency for about two years, and I'm ready to take the next step in my career. I believe my strengths lie in working with authors and in advocating for great books, and I've long dreamed of pursuing the editorial track.

As the only assistant at Safer, I've excelled at scheduling, filing, budgeting, and managing the slush pile—all tasks I'd happily take on for you, in addition to whatever else you require of assistants. I've also worked with the head of the company, Edith Safer, in client development, proposal writing, and providing notes to authors. While I haven't sold any books of my own, I was intimately involved in the deals for Lucy Deming's novel "Can't Complain" and her memoir "The Watched Pot" to Avon, including closely editing both books in conjunction with the author, writing cover letters and managing the submission of the former book, placing her acclaimed essay in the New York Times Book Review, and finalizing the latter book after her untimely death this summer. I'd love to tell you more about that experience, and what I've learned from it, in person.

I've attached my CV and look forward to speaking with you.

Best wishes,

Emily Thiel

12/11/1993

Dear Scot,

I'm so very sorry I wasn't able to place "The Big One." I continue to believe that the book is terrific. I'm confident that whatever you write next will find a home.

Unfortunately, I won't be able to be the agent for that book, because I'm leaving the Safer Agency for another opportunity. It's been a pleasure working with you, and I wish you the best of luck.

Sincerely,

Emily

— • —

On her first day at St. Martin's, she wore her only blazer and her nicest shoes and noticed immediately that all the women in the office dressed like her while Peter, her new boss, walked around in Chuck Taylor tennis shoes. He wasn't a slob—his shirts were ironed and his beard was neat—but he seemed to take pride in being able to flout the unofficial dress code.

After two years with Edith it was like suddenly being teleported into the fastest level in Frogger. She went from near-total inattention to an attention so fierce she cried in the bathroom almost every afternoon. Twenty times a day he shouted for her to come in and barraged her with questions. He demanded that she think three steps ahead but was always himself five steps ahead. He asked for her opinions, insisted that she *have* opinions, took her opinions seriously enough to witheringly critique them. She went home on that first Friday feeling, as she had never felt with Edith, as if she was part of something extraordinary. Peter was the one who had made that, and Peter was taking her along for the ride.

For that whole first week her desk had a different nameplate on it, JOHN GERHARD. "They gave me an assistant but I didn't like him," Peter told her. "I wanted my own guy." When she came in on Monday, the new nameplate read, EMILY THIEL.

— • —

They were barely speaking, but what could they do? The tickets for Part 2 were stuck to Em's fridge with a magnet, and who knew if they would ever have this chance again. She thought it was extremely possible Emily would flake. If so, Louis said, they'd be fine. He had a friend whose boyfriend had dumped him before their date for Part 2 and the guy brought the second ticket with him to the show, sold it to a hopeful waiting outside, and slept with the guy afterward. "Plus, he *made* fifty bucks on the ticket," Louis said.

Emily hadn't gotten her job back at Kim's and was, Em thought, unfortunately dependent on Rob. When she called, though, to tell her their plans for the night of the show, Emily said, "I'll meet you at six." And there she was, standing outside Yummy Food at 5:58.

If they walked to the theater, they'd have enough money to split a cab home, Louis and Em had decided. It was a pretty winter evening, crisp enough for coats but not too cold. North, north, north on Broadway they walked, through a holiday market, past sidewalk Christmas tree vendors, past restaurants they couldn't afford and stores full of clothes. It was a long way to walk without a conversation, so eventually they talked about movies. Em and Louis had cried through the final fifteen minutes of the new Merchant Ivory movie, with Anthony Hopkins as a butler and Emma Thompson as a maid. "It's just beautiful," Em told Emily.

"I don't know," Emily replied. "It's not just a bunch of repressed English people biting their lips?"

"That's my sexuality," Louis said.

At Bryant Park, they realized they'd need dinner before the show, so they all bought hot dogs and Snapples from a cart. "In honor of the other Louis, should we also chug some Pepto?" said Louis.

"You have the tickets?" Emily asked. Em patted her coat pocket. She'd even confirmed all three tickets were in there when she removed the envelope from her fridge door.

It was 7:20 as they crossed Broadway, plenty of time before curtain.

"No one's even here yet," said Louis as they approached the theater, but Em felt an awful squirming in her gut—something about the empty street, the dark doors. She moved her Snapple bottle to her other hand, pulled her tickets to the Sunday-night show from her pocket, and saw that in fact they were tickets for the Sunday matinee. For the rest of her life, Em would remember the sound her Snapple bottle made after she tossed it over her shoulder in despair and it shattered in the middle of Forty-Eighth Street.

"Are you kidding me?" Emily said. "How could you fuck this up?"

Em would think of *that* moment—not the destruction of Sunrise Squat—as the instant their friendship was broken, though like the glass all over the pavement, it would take a while to be ground into dust and disappear. She thought often of the way Emily said that, the cruelty in her voice, and felt each time a fresh outrage to have been called untrustworthy by the most inconstant person she had ever met. Yes, the tickets were her fault, but what were the tickets amid the cavalcade of disappointments and outrages to which Emily had subjected her? As the years went by, Em began to think of the tickets not as a thing *she* did, but as one disaster among many, the overwhelming balance of them instigated by Emily.

Emily got less and less reliable and more and more mean. She demanded to know why Em wasn't writing anything and refused to read the books she edited. She scoffed at Emily's career and called her new boss a creep because he put his hand on her back at a party. Once, during a fight with Rob, she crashed with Em for more than a week and the whole time did not wash a single dish. She alienated Louis, pissed off Lisa, drove away the old crowd from Sunrise. When Alan started law school, Emily called him a sellout. She later described Em and Alan's engagement as a moment of capitulation Em would eventually regret. She seemed forever angry at Em, forever disappointed in her.

Em found excuses not to see her, stopped going to her shows even before there stopped being any shows to go to. Em unplugged her phone at night so she wouldn't have to deal with the calls from Emily who was stuck somewhere and needed cab fare, Emily who needed a place to stay, Emily who was upset about some unknown slight and needed to tell her about it at midnight. Emily needed, needed, needed. Em could feel them heading in different directions, and Emily's direction was down, and for her own self-preservation she kept her distance. In the end there was no dramatic event, no all-night argument that ended their friendship. There was just a gradual wearing down of the mechanism for concern.

— ● —

All winter long cops guarded Twelfth Street and Sunrise Squat, but still, late one night, Michael and a bunch of the young guys snuck in. No one knew how they got through. In the morning, there were new barricades and new signs hung from windows, FOREVER OUR HOME, and every news crew in town was there filming as the furious cops had to go back in and haul everyone out again.

2007

It's Done When It's Done

Louis left New York because his job was going nowhere and too many of his friends were dead and his ex-boyfriend got him a job in admissions in Iowa.

Philippe left New York because he felt crazy all the time, like the city put crazy in the water.

Frances left New York because he got sick.

Jamilah left New York because she wrote novels and then a university in Louisiana gave her a job.

Max left New York because he kept getting cast in touring productions and never on Broadway, so he figured, why pay New York rent?

Ashley left New York because the boy she loved lived in Virginia.

Terry left New York because he could never find a place to live that felt like Sunrise Squat.

Joe and Sofia left New York because a friend started a co-op farm in Hudson.

Simone left New York because a guy got murdered on her block, and her parents told her that if she came back to Phoenix they'd pay for a year's rent, and then someone got murdered on her block there, too.

Jonathan left New York because if he got a job in Durham he would only need to do it eight hours a day, not every single hour he was alive. Now he spent his evenings and weekends reading books and watching TV.

Erica left New York for California, hated California, moved back to New York, and then went back to California. "It was the lesser of two evils," she told Emily once.

Don left New York when most of his coworkers died on September 11.

Rachel said she didn't even mind leaving New York because she was a Red Sox fan and she was sick of being surrounded by smug Yankees fans. Matt, a Yankees fan, said he didn't even care because the Red Sox would never win a title. This conversation occurred immediately after Game 3 of the 2004 American League Championship Series.

Penelope left New York when a firm in her hometown recruited her and she realized that even though they paid half as much she could afford twice as much house there.

Phuong left New York when she was standing on a corner waiting for the light to change and a guy approaching in the crosswalk said, very quietly, "Excuse me," and then less than one second later shouted, "I said GET the FUCK outta my WAY, BITCH."

Kirsty left New York because she loved New Zealand so much she just stayed there. Luckily, she was rich.

Derreck left New York because he wanted to live someplace where he didn't think the cops were gonna kill him all the time.

The following people left New York because they had kids, and they just couldn't take it anymore: Liuba and Frank, Matt and Pete, Claire and Dave, Alia and Dan, Shauna and Frank, Laura and Greg, Julia and Ben, Matt and Cora.

— • —

I'm at the top of the hill, Alan texted her, so she hoofed it up the stairs, splashing all the way, and found him standing under his umbrella, under a big tree, in the middle of the Isham Park lawn.

"Aw, you didn't have to wait for me," she said.

"This way we get"—he looked at his watch—"three minutes and forty-five seconds to talk to each other before we get home." She laughed. "Go!" he said, then looked at her attentively.

"Oh uhhhhhhh I got galleys of Lucy Deming's books."

"That's great! Can I see them when we're not standing in the rain?"

"For sure. What did you do today?"

"Absolutely, positively, unquestionably, nothing interesting at all. Oh, wait! I had a good lunch."

"I had leftovers. Didn't you bring the leftovers?" She'd made a big pot of risotto the night before and had loaded two Tupperwares with the excess.

"I did bring the leftovers."

"Oh, is that the good lunch you're talking about? That's sweet."

"That *would* have been sweet, you're right. But I meant that we had a goodbye lunch for the interns and I put myself in charge of ordering, and so we had awesome sandwiches from 'Wichcraft." She smacked him on the arm. "I'll eat the risotto tomorrow!" he protested. "I wanted to give the flavors another day to really meld."

Inside the lobby, she grabbed the mail while he shook out his umbrella. She kissed him on the elevator and he said, "You have little drops of rain in your eyelashes."

Merle and Jane were in the kitchen washing dishes. Jane said, "Mommy Daddy!" She ran over to them, losing her balance for a moment, grabbing onto the bar cart, letting go in alarm when it rolled into the wall.

After Merle left, they all played a game where Jane carried her sock from one to the other and then back. The rain had stopped, so they agreed to go out for dinner. They should have saved the money but they both wanted to see Jane in her rain boots and slicker too much. While she dressed her, Alan loaded the diaper bag. Then Emily said, "Do you have her turtle stuffie?" So he grabbed that. Then she said, "Do you have some applesauce? A sippy cup?" He went to the kitchen and grabbed those. "Do you have bibs?" she asked. He had one bib, so he got another one. "Diapers and wipes?" she said.

"I did successfully put diapers in the quote-unquote 'diaper bag,'" he said.

Outside it was cold and wet but Jane sure didn't care. Alan pushed the stroller, and she walked alongside. When she saw a puddle, she would sally forth to stomp in it and scream with joy. Then she would retreat to Emily's or Alan's side.

At the café, Emily pulled the galleys from her bag and laid them on the table. They were to be published in June, accompanied by a collection of remembrances in *New York*. "They look great," Alan said. "Very '80s."

"I tried to get the woman who did the original Vintage Contemporaries, but she's not designing anymore," Em said.

"Those books you keep on the shelf by the front door?"

"So I told our designer, 'Like Vintage Contemporaries, but not legally actionable.'"

"I see it. No, honey," he added, deftly sliding *Hearts and Stones* away from Jane's grasping hands and placing a spoon in them instead. She threw the spoon on the floor. He put a ring toy in front of her and she swept it off the table. He laid out seven Cheerios and started counting with her. "One! Two! Three—well now there's only three Cheerios left. Now there's zero."

"Jane!" Emily said in her most Jane-inviting voice. Jane grinned a toothy grin. Alan picked up the new collection and said, "I like this one the best. Oh, look at Lucy on the back! That's your photo!"

"I smile every time I see it."

"'Photo: Emily Thiel.'"

"Yes, I'm now a professional photographer."

"Well, they didn't pay you."

"That's true," she admitted. "I remain an amateur photographer. Speaking of which:" She pulled her new phone with its fancy camera from her bag and snapped a few shots of Jane, who had absolutely cleared the table in front of her of all objects and was casting about for something else to throw to the floor.

"Here, give it. Let me get you two."

"Ugh, I'm a mess."

"I don't care! You two look just like each other."

"Hold on," she said, and took out a hairbrush.

"Just let me take a stupid photo of my baby and my wife who I love!!" he whispered, not mad exactly, but.

"Here," she said, and handed him the phone. She leaned close to Jane, who gamely attempted to pull off Emily's ear.

"That's perfect," he said. "You look like you're being tortured." (She loved her, she loved her.)

She took the phone back and put it in her bag. "Do we have plans Saturday?" she asked. "Emily wants to know if I can come downtown. I said maybe we all three could come."

"To do what?"

"Um . . . to shop for props."

Alan looked at her, then looked at Jane, who at that precise moment flung her sippy cup backward. It skittered across the next table, sending silverware flying, and whacked into a pillar, knocking a chalkboard menu to the floor. Jane said, "AAAAAAAAHHHHHHeeeeefr."

"Sounds great," Alan said. "Hope we go to a china shop."

That night the rain turned to sleet and then to snow. Emily lay in bed, thinking about Sunrise Squat, how miraculous it had been when Joe turned on the heat. Their radiator in this apartment hissed and clunked like a locomotive and put out so much warmth that they had to prop the window open. Snowflakes breezed in and then melted in midair.

— • —

What became clear after a few texts was that what Emily really needed was not her but her car, in order to transport props to her performance space. Given the likelihood of endless driving around and the unlikelihood of playgrounds, they decided that Alan and Jane should just stay home.

When they met outside a weird scrapyard-cum-junkshop on Houston Street, "Where'd you park?" was the first thing Emily asked. Ah yes, *this* was a feeling she remembered, Emily making full use of the accoutrements of other people's adulthood.

"What are you trying to get here?" she asked Emily.

Emily was wearing a truly remarkable ensemble, bib overalls and a body stocking. The overalls appeared to be seersucker. She tossed her cigarette to the curb and said, "I need stuff from the New York City"—she made her voice like an old-time radio announcer's—"*of the future.*"

"So, a jetpack?"

"No, no." Emily laughed. "It's postapocalyptic. We're doing it on the top floor of one of those expensive new condos in Williamsburg, but because of global warming it's surrounded by water, and they have to scavenge the city to survive." She immediately knew that this was a good idea, and she felt her annoyance with Emily leak away, replaced by curiosity. This, too, was a familiar feeling.

"Oh, so you need *de*tritus."

"I thought that was pronounced *deTRYtus*," Emily mused. "I suppose I've never said it aloud. Oh this is perfect," Emily continued, pointing to a big MTA sign for the G train.

Together they filled a broken shopping cart with old magazines, diner menus, a bunch of iron hooks, a poster showing a woman with feathered hair beatifically holding a gyro, an ornate locksmith's sign that clanged and clanked. Emily hefted one of those triangular sign/lights that sits atop a cab, the gentleman's club ad on its face making sultry eye contact with everyone in sight.

She went out to check her phone—nothing from Alan—and when she came back inside, Emily was standing in front of a disconnected pay phone, hand on her chin.

"What would postapocalyptic New Yorkers use that for?" she asked.

"That's a good point," Emily said. "Nothing."

They loaded everything into her car. The cab thingamabob took up her entire backseat. "Did you ever learn to drive?" she asked Emily as she pulled out of her spot.

"Yeah, a couple of years ago," Emily said. "I have a license now. I even drove a moving truck for a little while."

"*You* did."

"Yeah." Emily looked at her and laughed. "What do you mean, '*You* did.'"

"You told me once that you would never get a driver's license because there were always people willing to give you a ride."

Emily turned to the window and said lightly, "Well, eventually I ran out of people."

Over the Williamsburg Bridge, into a part of Brooklyn that she never went to, a part that she understood from *New York* magazine was now extremely trendy. Dilapidated storefronts sat side by side with new luxury buildings, many of them still under construction. Driving past young people dressed in ugly clothes that somehow did not disguise their dewy beauty, she thought about how once she had been the young person in the neighborhood old people never visited. Back then, she spent months having no idea she was neck-deep in political ferment and cultural transformation. She was just trying to keep her head down and avoid embarrassing herself.

Now she was the visitor. Emily, for her part, still belonged. When they parked behind one of the new condo buildings, a tall young woman wearing jeans so skinny she looked like a cartoon bird embraced Emily. For a moment she stayed in the car, checking her phone. Three texts from Alan, each one recording something funny that Jane had said. I interrupted her while she was saying something and she yelled STOP ERUPTING ME.

When she got out, the woman with the impossible jeans shook her hand politely. "I'm Soleil," she said. Soleil?!

"We got such great stuff!" Emily said.

"Can't wait to see it. Ohhhhhhhhhhh," said Soleil as she spotted the taxicab triangle thing. "Look at *her*!"

"She's beautiful!"

"I can saw this in half and lay a two-by-four across and that's the table," said Soleil.

"I love it," Emily said. "She's our designer," she added as she carried the sign through the service entrance. "Total genius."

On the fifth floor, the elevator opened into an unfinished space, rooms framed but no walls, pipes and wires threaded across the ceiling. Bright, enormous windows looked out over Williamsburg to the river beyond. Two women were talking to a guy with a man-bun by the windows, pointing at the ceiling above.

"They're trying to figure out where to install the screens," Emily said. "And then getting power to everything is a whole nother issue."

"Where did you get the money to produce all this?" she asked. "How on earth did you get this space?"

"Oh, funny story. Well, not the money, that was just a lot of grant-writing. But do you remember that advertising executive I went out with a few times?"

"Sort of." She remembered, sometime in the mid-'90s, a fancy steakhouse in Murray Hill, a delicious baked potato, cocaine she politely turned down. She remembered it all ending with a calamitous return to Rob.

"Well, anyway, he bought this for his son. They're building out the whole floor into a single apartment. I know. Obscene. But he and his son are in a fight, so the whole thing's on hold, and he told me I could use it for a show."

"Marco? Was that his name?"

"Marcus, yeah. Good guy. Rich asshole."

"And you're still friends?"

"Sure," Emily said. "We see each other every once in a while. We have similar schedules." She had deciphered similarly vague statements in the past as being references to twelve-step meetings.

"Once upon a time, the idea of you being on good terms with an ex . . ."

"Ha ha, yeah. Well, I don't have to burn them *all* down."

While Emily went off to talk to another of the young people, she walked carefully around the empty space. Tape on the floor seemed to indicate the spots where the audience would sit. She lowered herself onto a blue X and watched her friend move from person to person, looking for all the world like the woman in charge.

Her phone buzzed with a text. It was Alan, asking where *Hippos Go Berserk* was. The next text was Alan, saying never mind, he found it. She swore to God, he needed to just save up all these texts and tell them to her when she got home.

When they had known each other, the first time, she'd seldom seen Emily in a theater. In part, she knew, because she had been intimidated and avoided the long process of production, only attending the show itself, if there even was a show. Often, there wasn't a show. But she also thought she remembered, back in those days, Emily doing most everything on her own—not collaborating with designers and technicians and the guy with the man-bun, who appeared to be an honest-to-God carpenter, if such a thing was possible? Her memory of Emily's collaborations in those days was that they always ignited in a blaze of recrimination and betrayal, Emily announcing with great disgust that she was done with so-and-so forever, fuck *her*.

Emily looked over at her, smiled, gave a wave. It was possible, she realized suddenly, that Emily might have viewed her lack of participation in those years as a lack of support. But she had spent so long fearing that one day it would be *her* with whom Emily was done forever, that she would be the so-and-so.

Oh, Emily wasn't waving, she was beckoning. She got up and walked to where Emily and man-bun were looking at their scripts. "The question is, what's the initial image?" Emily asked her. "The audience comes up the elevator and what do they see?"

She considered the question. What would she do if she faced a manuscript with a problem she didn't know the solution to? She'd ask a question right back.

"Do you want them to feel comfortable, and then you overturn that?" she asked. "Or do you want them to feel uncomfortable from the start?"

"Comfortable," Emily said, while man-bun said, "Uncomfortable." Everyone laughed.

"Well, you need to know the answer to that," she said.

"That's exactly right," Emily said with animation. "Because there's a version where you come in and there's spooky lights and music. And there's a version where you come in and it all looks normal, but then you notice that out the windows it's just water and rooves."

"Maybe Ken's in here already when the audience comes in," man-bun suggested. "Sitting at the table, doing something totally ordinary."

"Reading a book," she said.

"Yessss," said Emily to her. "And your job, my friend, is to tell us what book." She hailed a small woman in a baseball cap. "Makena, can we give her a script? This is Emily, she's our dramaturg."

When she got home that evening, she was still chewing on the question. "Mommy!" shouted Jane when she walked in the door.

"Did she nap?" she asked Alan. "Did you take a nap?" she asked Jane. Often the answers were different.

"I took a nap!"

"She did, once we found the ol' hippos." The thing was, they did a bit where *Hippos Go Berserk* was only available at naptime, and the rest of the day, it simply disappeared from the house. As a joke they had once told Jane that the book traveled to other people's houses to help *those* children take naps, and returned when Jane took a nap, but Jane could not decipher gentle absurdity, and so she now resolutely believed there was one copy of *Hippos Go Berserk* in the world and that it appeared at their house around two thirty every Saturday and Sunday afternoon. And now they couldn't get out of it. The Sandra Boynton book was far too crucial to their weekend sanity to risk up-ending its efficacy with the truth.

She had no idea how Merle got Jane to nap on weekdays. It certainly wasn't via *Hippos Go Berserk*, which was hidden like pornography under the mattress of their bed.

They ate curry chicken salad for dinner and went for a walk. Jane saw a firefly and lost her shit completely. After Jane went to bed that night, Emily told Alan about her sudden appointment as dramaturg to a site-specific science fiction climate change play. "That's cool," he said. "What does that mean?"

"I think I'm another set of eyes on the script, and I'm supposed to contribute ideas and do research and make suggestions."

"So you're an editor."

"I'm an editor but without, you know, the institutional authority."

He raised an eyebrow. "So then where does your authority come from?"

She thought about that for a moment. "I guess Emily just gave it to me. With those guys in the performance space, it was like she knighted me and everyone just agreed, *Oh yes, she's a knight now.* And then everyone just went ahead and asked me questions and scheduled me into rehearsals and things."

"Tell me more about this schedule," he said, drinking his beer so she couldn't quite see his face.

"I know." They both had limited capacity for extracurriculars. He jogged occasionally. He played basketball at the park on Saturdays, bodying teenagers with bad attitudes, he said. He had a fantasy foot-ball league that required one boozy in-person draft and one boozy end-of-season party each year. She went to the gym twice a week and tried to see a play with Emily or with friends from college once a month. She and her sister took a spa weekend every winter. They both had occasional work events, which didn't count unless they seemed *too* fun. Anything more taxing to their calendar than that, it was tac-itly agreed, required formal spousal approval.

Emily didn't resent this, and she didn't think Alan did either. This was just the way it was. If they slept the hours they needed to sleep and worked the hours they needed to work and cared for Jane the hours she needed caring for, that only left so many hours. Emily thought a lot about Saturdays when they were first married, when they would leave the apartment at noon, take the subway downtown, walk to a movie theater, and just buy tickets to whatever was playing next. Sometimes they would sneak into the next auditorium and watch the end of whatever was playing there! That was why once they wandered into the last ten minutes of *The Banger Sisters* to see Susan Saran-don and Goldie Hawn, apparently the titular Banger sisters, having a tearful heart-to-heart, and then the camera pulled back, further and further, and to their amazement the two actresses were sitting atop a GOT MILK? billboard.

For a while, when Jane was extremely portable, they still went to weekend brunch. The good thing was they would get to restaurants when they opened at nine a.m., and get out just as the bleary-eyed child-free people lined up outside. But once Jane was ambulatory, forget it. It all ended last summer, when they met some friends in the Village and Jane fussed in her high chair, walked all over the restau-rant touching things, then started vomiting like a fountain. Alan had picked her up, desperately trying to cover her mouth as she barfed her way past horrified brunchers, and sprinted to the sidewalk. When she was finally done Alan had to throw his shirt into a trash can on the corner. Emily had carried her sleeping, feverish daughter while Alan pushed the empty stroller back to where their car was parked. It was a hot morning just before Pride, and Alan later told her that walking shirtless up Christopher Street was the first time he'd ever understood the inherent cruelty of the male gaze.

Needless to say, their friends from that brunch would never have children. The number of people who'd surely been convinced never to procreate by Emily's child! She would single-handedly achieve population control. (She loved her, she loved her.)

"I think it's doable," she said now. "It'll be a little bit of a drag for two or three weeks in September. But she'll be in nursery school by then. And I thought I might have my mom come out."

"I love your mom," he said, "but you understand that she's a poor substitute for you."

"We could do your mom instead."

"Noooo thank you. Your mom is great."

"Honey, say the word and I'll turn it down. I know it's asking a lot."

"I would never say that word," he said. "We'll work it out."

Emily found this dissatisfying, even though technically it fulfilled the requirements of a completed conversation. What she wanted was for Alan to be overjoyed, so that she could feel joy, too. Instead, she worried he was annoyed, she got annoyed at him hiding his annoyance, she felt guilty about being unfair to him, she . . . *Get a grip*, she thought. *This is going nowhere.*

Tonight was her night to go to bed early and wake up with Jane, and she took a shower to try to snap herself out of her bad mood. After the shower, she wiped the mirror and stared into it, examining the tiny lines around her eyes, which put her right back into the bad mood. Finally she shook her head and went out to the living room. He was at the desk, staring at the computer in his familiar position of perplexment, left hand on his forehead, right hand on the mouse. "Good night," she said.

"Night."

She waited there to see if he'd look up. Finally he did and smiled. "You okay?" he asked.

"Yeah," she said. She was not, exactly, but she needed to stop making that his problem. "Yes. I'm good. Come to bed soon."

"I would love to," he said, "but the Internet is filled with idiots."

"The word of the Lord."

"Thanks be to God."

— • —

They were trying the Atkins diet, which meant they were eating a lot of steak. They owned a tiny charcoal grill they kept on the roof of the building. One Saturday they climbed the three flights up in the dark stairwell and then blinked at the brightness of a brisk, perfect early spring afternoon.

They set up chairs and Alan lit the grill. Emily rolled a ball to Jane, who also rolled it, though not back. The walls around the terrace were adult-armpit-height, but that didn't stop Emily from panicking very slightly every time Jane ran anywhere near them.

The eighth-floor apartments had their own private roof space, and one of their neighbors, a musical theater composer, was sitting up there, separated from them by a short wall, smoking a joint. "Should I put this out?" he asked.

"Nah, she doesn't know what it is," Emily said.

"You want?"

"Yes, thank you," she said. Alan rolled the ball with Jane while Emily leaned over the wall, took a drag, and blew the smoke out toward the Bronx.

"She's really big," he said, pointing at Jane, who was busy cracking herself up by sneaking up on Alan and shouting, "Boo!"

"I know," said Emily. "She just keeps on growing."

"You sort of wish you could freeze 'em," he said. He had a three-year-old, a boy.

"I don't," she said honestly. "I'm ready for her to be a creature of reason."

Alan came over, holding a squirmy Jane. "Steaks are ready," he said.

"Steaks is high!" chuckled the composer. Alan smiled. Emily didn't get the joke but couldn't focus on it because all she could see was Jane, wriggling in Alan's arms as he stood near the edge. She knew there was no way she could suddenly throw herself away from her father over the wall, but it was impossible to get herself to stop thinking about it, and she felt faint from the effort.

"Please," she said. She was crying? "Please, please, put her down, put her down."

The previous year, their refrigerator had stopped working, but not all at once. First she noticed that sometimes stuff in the freezer wasn't as frozen as she would have liked, and then she noticed that the milk didn't last as long as it should, and then one day the ice cream was melted. The repairman told Alan that they could special order a new condenser for the twenty-year-old fridge, or they could just buy a new fridge for slightly less money. The one they bought was resolutely middle-of-the-line, but when it was installed she couldn't believe how *cold* everything got in it, and by extension how not-cold everything in her fridge had been for so long. It had happened so gradually she'd never quite noticed how everything was not the way it was supposed to be.

When Alan asked her, as kindly as he could, whether she might need to go back on her antidepressants, she knew immediately that the same thing had happened. She hadn't known how sad she was. She couldn't believe how grim she had gotten without really noticing.

When she started taking her pills again, she was filled with gratitude that she could feel things in appropriate ways. She'd forgotten what that was like, and forgotten that she'd forgotten.

Being herself, she wasted countless brain-minutes feeling guilty about putting her husband and her daughter and coworkers through the bad time. "You didn't put us through anything," Alan said. "You were the one going through something," and she knew he was right, but she couldn't help but notice that she believed him more after a week on the meds. But this was progress, such as it was.

And as the summer approached she felt, in her bones, the days getting longer, the mornings getting warmer, the light lingering into the evening.

— ● —

Lisa called to tell them that Michael died. He'd been sick with cancer, and in those final years he had clashed with some of his old compatriots, but that didn't matter now. "There's a memorial Tuesday at Tompkins Square Park, then an East Village march Wednesday. All-night dance party Thursday at See Skwat, then a rally Friday. Saturday they're doing a benefit concert."

"Jesus," Emily said. They were standing at the kitchen counter with the phone on speaker turned way up to counteract the sound of their daughter dancing to Laurie Berkner in the living room. "That's a lot!"

"Oh, and they're staging his squat opera, too. What can you two do?"

"Definitely the memorial, right?" Alan asked. "I don't know if we're the target audience for a dance party."

"The concert's gonna be insane," Lisa said. "Joe's band is getting back together."

"I couldn't even listen to them with twenty-five-year-old ears," Emily said. "I'd like to see Joe, though."

"He'll be at everything," Lisa said. "I'ma go to the rally. You know apartments in Sunrise are renting for three grand a month?"

"Is that what we're protesting?"

"I think we're just generally protesting. Protesting against it all."

"Against the march of time," said Emily.

Alan nodded. "It does seem unfair, when you think about it."

The memorial was a little sad, but it was also a reunion, a rally, a celebration of a guy who packed a lot of living into forty-five years. It was held in a little plaza near the dog park. (A dog park, in Tompkins Square!) Someone had mounted dozens of photos from Michael's various squats to posterboard, and Emily and Emily spent a few minutes browsing through them, reminding each other of people's names. There was one photo taken inside Emily's old room, blown up huge on its own piece of posterboard: Michael and Emily sitting on the couch laughing about something. The wall behind them was covered in notes and slogans in Magic Marker. Getting up close to the photo, she could see the section of the wall by the telephone devoted to phone numbers. There was her old phone number, the last four digits of which were now the PIN she used for everything. There was her number at the Safer Agency, and Rob's number, and Michael's number, and Lisa's, and Kim's Video. All the numbers were seven digits, not ten; the 212 went unstated. Above all the numbers, near the ceiling, she saw what one or the other of them had written late, late one night: VINTAGE CONTEMPORARIES.

Framed on its own was a photo of Michael in the window of Sunrise Squat. It was the day that he had led the reoccupation of the building, and he leaned out a second-floor window, his long arms crossed, shouting down at the unseen cops below. Above him hung a bedsheet sign reading NO TANKS IN OUR CITY.

Emily sat in a folding chair next to Emily and Lisa. Alan pushed the stroller in a loop around the sidewalks, listening, and Emily smiled each time she saw him trundle behind the speakers' stand.

Friends from Sunrise, from the other squats where he'd lived before and after, took the mic. "Michael didn't count sheep at night," one said. "He counted politicians, figuring out how many he'd have to kill to get title to his squat." Laughter rippled through the crowd. There were no politicians here, but Sofia said she recognized a lawyer from the city who'd squared off against Michael through the '90s.

After about forty-five minutes, one of the speakers said, "Let's take a walk, huh?" People started beating drums and trash can lids, making a glorious racket. Everyone got up and stretched. It was cloudy, but the rain had held off. The mourners, two hundred strong or more, set off down Seventh Street, blocking traffic, pissing off truck drivers. She picked Jane up from her stroller and had Alan click her into the backpack so she could see what was going on. The toddler pounded on Emily's head in time with the drums.

Emily couldn't remember the last time she'd walked down Seventh, once the main street of her life and the focus of her daily anxieties. They passed the squat at 209 where Michael moved after Sunrise, got sick, and died, and the crowd chanted, "Michael Sammons! Rest in peace!" They passed Emily's beloved garden, now condos, and chanted for that. They passed The Germans and 278, where Michael had lived for a year or two, and cheered for squats still standing. 278 was on the other side of the street from Emily's first apartment, but all the buildings looked the same and now she couldn't pick out which stoop had been hers, which subterranean windows she'd hid behind those first frightened months in New York, before she met Emily. She wondered if the mushroom had ever grown back.

Up Avenue D, back west on Ninth Street. Serenity, still standing. Dos Blocos, rest in peace. Fetus Squat, rest in peace. See Skwat, still proud on C Street. At Twelfth, they turned left and Emily took Emily's hand. The facade of Sunrise still stood, but the building had been gut-renovated and upgraded. Joe mentioned he'd gone to an open house once and couldn't believe how nice the countertops were. She could

see the window where Michael had hung his sign, and above it, the
window from which Emily had dropped keys to her. She remembered
the way the keys drifted down on their parachute, fluttering and turning like a leaf from a tree.

When she was first seeing Alan, after he'd quit reporting, gone
to Washington for law school, and come back—and Lisa had rein-
troduced them, and their first official date had concluded two days
later—she'd asked him why eviction had ended things, why no one
had appealed the adverse possession case for Sunrise. He'd written
about it for his law review. "It's hard to pursue a case without a home
base," he'd said. "People were scattered and exhausted. And the cops
trashed everyone's docs, anyway. A lot of the paperwork proving continued occupancy ended up in the Dumpster."

On the other hand, he'd pointed out, the fact that a judge had even
suggested the tenants *might* have a claim spooked the city, which was
why for the most part they didn't forcibly evict squats anymore. These
days, they negotiated. No tanks in our city. Many of the old squats
were working through the process of transferring ownership—and,
yes, debt—to the residents. That had its own pitfalls, as seen in the
debates that had driven a wedge between Michael and many of the
other early squatters, but it was a kind of victory in Sunrise's name,
nonetheless.

"Sunrise Squat! Rest in peace!" they chanted, and chanted, and
chanted. The drums got louder and louder. The horns of cars stuck on
Twelfth added to the cacophony. Alan took a photo of them and then
showed her the screen of the camera, and she knew instantly that she
would get that shot printed: she and Emily, fists raised, mouths open
in angry protest, and behind her head in the backpack Jane, floppy
hat on her curls, raising both hands above her head and grinning like
a maniac.

When it was over, she said goodbye to Joe, to Sofia, to Frank, to
Lisa, to Juana and her mother, to the punk kids and Michael's friends

and people whose faces were familiar but whose names she had long forgotten. She couldn't say goodbye to Emily, though. She had already taken off.

— • —

Emily's new phone also shot video, and she spent a lot of time pointing it at her daughter, taping—she'd need to think of a new word for this—everything she did. One night she and Jane were having a dance party in the living room, a frequent rainy-night activity. She was playing her music on shuffle—Emily's invention, as she always thought of it—and a Spoon song came on, and Jane loved it. "Again," she said when it was over, so Emily played it again and taped her singing along, sort of phonetically: "You gano fearada underdogs!" she sang, shaking her naked booty with abandon. They weren't exactly potty training but they *were* letting her go around without a diaper sometimes, to see what happened. She positively snarled: "Thass why you willna surVIBE!" In the video Emily took, Jane appeared to be furious, but in fact she was so happy singing the way the man in the song sang.

When Emily showed the video to Alan, he said, "We should get one of those coat of armses"—

"Coats of arms?"

"Right, like viscounts have. And that would be the family motto written along the bottom. 'The Underdogs.'"

Emily put the video up on the Internet for her family to see. The next time she talked to her mom, Donna said something about Jane still looking a little chubby, and Emily surprised herself by telling her mother, clearly and firmly, that under no circumstances was she allowed to discuss Jane's weight or her eating choices. She would not bring them up to Emily, and she was not to discuss them in front of Jane. She would not give Jane a complex about her body the way she'd given Emily one. As far as her mother was concerned, the topic did not exist.

"I'm sorry, honey," her mom said.

"I accept your apology," Emily replied. "And I'm serious about this."

Many years later the video of Jane dancing was taken down by YouTube as algorithm-identified child pornography, and Emily mourned its loss as she would that of a favorite photo album, lost in a fire.

— • —

The best thing about book parties was seeing the incredible apartments of every author's richest friend. Lucy Deming's richest friend, posthumously, was Benjamin Bannon, and it was into his gorgeous SoHo loft that Emily and Peter stepped, directly from the elevator, on a June night. The air had been disgusting outside, but here it was cool and dry. Central air in an *apartment*. She was aware this was the least of the extravagances she was about to witness, but it still felt decadent as hell.

On a table near the front were stacks of the four books, each with their perfect covers. Even having held them in her hands before, she couldn't help but pick up a copy of the new collection. "Hey, did I tell you I took this photo?" she asked Peter.

"About a thousand times. You took it at a book party very like this one, as I recall."

"Not that much like this one." Lucy didn't have any rich friends when she was alive. It was too bad. She would have been a fun person to be rich with. "It was at her friend Lorraine's house. Nice, but modest. Oh shit, there's Bob Fox—how do I look?"

"Like a hot mama. Let's go get him."

"Bob!" she said, kiss, kiss. In his perfect suit jacket and just-so unbuttoned top button he looked entirely at home in this beautiful apartment, which, come to think of it, was probably a dollhouse by the standards of wherever the hell he lived.

"Hello, my dears," he said. "Congratulations. Emily, you look stunning."

"Thanks for making this all happen," she said. He'd convinced Bannon to host, though St. Martin's was footing the catering bill.

"Bob, level with me," Peter said. "How close did we get on the Jonathan Safran Foer novel?"

Fox laughed. "Oh, shop talk right off the bat!"

"I've been itching to ask," Peter said, dancing around as if scratching a dozen mosquito bites.

"You were very competitive," Fox said. "Jonathan loved you, Emily. He just felt more comfortable where he was."

"Well," Peter said, putting his arm around Fox, "at some point you've gotta let us win. You can't just use us to jack up the price forever."

"Why, Peter, that's not the only thing I'm using you for," Fox said, with a look at Emily.

Well, she had made an effort tonight, she supposed. "You should see me most days. I'm covered in cheddar bunnies. Want to see a photo of my two-year-old?"

"Oh, let me introduce you to Benjamin," Fox said smoothly, steering them over.

In contrast to cartoon Fox, Benjamin Bannon seemed positively asexual, a brain still uncomfortably adjusting to the body it carted around. He shook Emily's hand and told her how grateful he was for her rediscovery of "the *tahdig* essay." (He pronounced it with a careful Persian accent.) He paused frequently while speaking, making a repeated circular gesture with his hands, seemingly to haul forth each new noun from the depths. "It's such a transformative . . ." (hands circle) ". . . *piece* in our . . ." (hands circle) ". . . *consideration* of Lucy's . . ."

(hands circle) ". . . *body of work*." She wanted desperately to finish his sentences, but he was a Pulitzer Prize winner.

Sarah was there, too, and offered her an olive off her plate. "It's a fruit, remember," she said. *"Heh-heh-heh."*

Emily worried Benjamin Bannon was going to give a . . . (hands circle) *toast*, but he demurred. Peter called for everyone's attention and introduced himself. "I'm not going to go on and on, because there's someone else who should speak to you tonight." Emily felt herself blushing. "I've worked with her for more than a decade, and I've watched her grow into one of the best editorial minds around. Emily Thiel is truly an *editor*, what do I mean by that, I mean she's not one of those editors who thinks of himself as an author." This got a laugh. "And maybe she'll write a book someday, I don't know, I'm sure she'd write a fabulous book. But she's also no Gordon Lish, imposing her voice on a project, cutting a story to her vision. What she does is she finds people with great stories, and she helps them tell those stories the best they can. She has great eyes. She sees the best version of everyone she works with, and puts that version out in the world. I've benefited from this myself, and I can tell you, anyone who gets the benefit of Emily's eyes is lucky indeed."

Emily saw Lane, her old assistant, standing near the bar. He'd left for his new job back in 2005, a few months after Marta. She gave him a wave, but he was listening to Peter, arms crossed, frowning. Well, he had never been Peter's biggest fan.

"A lot of people made this book happen. Let's run down the list. Benjamin Bannon, whose incredible *Times* essay started the ball rolling; Bob Fox; Sarah Deming, Lucy's daughter, who's here with us today. She's this lovely young woman right here. Say hi, Sarah." Sarah did a whole *ta-da* wave to the crowd. "But no one is more responsible for this book than Emily. Emily knew Lucy, she cared for Lucy. Emily helped her shape her work the first time around, Emily saved an essay for fifteen years, and Emily packaged these four books brilliantly. That's all the work of an editor. Everyone, please give a hand to my colleague and friend Emily Thiel."

Emily was a little dazzled as everyone applauded. She stepped forward, concentrated on looking as normal as possible. If her armpits could stop it with the sweating now, that would be fantastic.

"Well, thank goodness Peter didn't go on and on," she began, and it got the laugh she needed to collect herself and remember her speech. Peter clutched his chest as if to say, *A palpable hit!*

"First of all, Lucy loved a good cocktail party. She loved people talking, sharing, eating, and drinking. She loved staying up late. As she wrote, the last half hour of a cocktail party is when people *really* tell the truth. So with the blessing of the great Benjamin Bannon, we're not putting a cap on this party. It's done when it's done."

"Hear, hear!" someone called, and there was a smattering of applause. She was counting on the fact that almost everyone was even older than her to keep from going too far over budget.

"When I first read *Can't Complain*, I sent Lucy an editorial memo I hope is never unearthed, in which I asked her, basically, to sex it up a little." Everyone laughed. "I wanted more conflict, more desperate unhappiness. I was twenty-two, in my defense. It took me a while to understand what these novels were. Back at twenty-two, I wanted the book to be more timely. I forgot that the opposite of timely is *timeless*.

"I guess what I mean to say is that I don't view these new editions, or this party, or all you wonderful, fancy people at the party, as evidence that Lucy has somehow reached the exalted halls of literature. What's happening is that literature is finally broadening to include Lucy. I think that's good news for everyone who loves reading, who loves writing, and, yes, who loves literature. Thanks for coming, everyone, and thanks for your support of these books."

"A manifesto!" Peter said in her ear as everyone clapped. "I love it."

Emily made a beeline for the bar, but was interrupted so often by kind people that she despaired of ever getting a fresh drink. One person who stopped her was Lorraine Louie, who hugged her. Her bob was gray now, but she looked otherwise unchanged. "Oh, I'm so glad to see you!" Emily said. "I wanted to hire you for these covers, but our art director said you're, like, a doctor now?"

"A nurse," Lorraine said, laughing. "I had a cancer scare about ten years ago, and I decided to change things up completely."

"Wow," Emily said. "You really did get out of books."

"You really got into them," Lorraine said. "Which was clearly the right thing to do. This is such a gift you've given Lucy."

"What do you think?" Emily asked, holding up one of the new paperbacks. "Have you ever been the subject of an homage before?"

"I don't think I ever have," Lorraine said. "They look really good. Has anyone at Vintage said anything to you?"

"A friend told me they're a little chapped."

"Well," said Lorraine cheerfully, "screw those guys."

They chatted for a minute more, then Emily excused herself. To her great relief, the next person she saw was Lane, offering her a martini. "My hero," she said. "How are you? I miss you!" He had taken a job at a nonprofit doing housing advocacy. How could she resent him for that? She could not.

"I'm doing okay," he said. "I saw Alan at a work dinner last week. He said you were good."

"I should have thanked *you*!" she said in sudden horror. "You did so much on these books!"

"It's fine," he said. "It was a good toast!"

"That means a lot. Thank you."

"Peter's still Peter, I see," Lane said. He gave Emily a searching look.

"I think that's unlikely to change," she said. "The man's fifty, he's a genius, he is who he is."

"And you're still putting the best version of his story into the world," he said.

"Well," she said, but he was shaking his head. "What—"

"Marta said to say hi."

"How is Marta? Is she still at Penguin?"

"She's still there. You should give her a call."

She pulled Lane over to the side of the room. "Stop talking like you're in a spy movie. Just tell me what happened with Marta and Peter."

"It's not my story to tell," he said with wounded dignity.

"Yes, yes, you're the best friend. Will you just tell me: Is it something I should have known about?" He stared at the floor. "I wish she'd talked to me. Why didn't she just talk to me?"

"I don't think she ever seriously considered talking to you," he said. She looked at him, offended. "You're just, you're close to Peter. You were his assistant! You talk all the time about how he was so tough on you but you got through it."

"Well, but he didn't *harass* me. Is that what we're talking about here? I'm not trying to pressure you, but what are we talking about?" Lane was silent, and she kept on talking. "Is she sure, though? He loves to hear himself talk. He believes in his own charisma. I think that reads sometimes . . . more inappropriate than it actually is." She was gesturing vaguely at the window, but when she looked back at Lane he appeared absolutely crestfallen.

He composed his face, but she'd seen it. "I wonder why Marta didn't talk to you," he said.

"Hey," she said. "Should I call her? I'll call her."

"It's up to you," he said. "I gotta go. Congratulations on the books. I love them. I mean it." He left, grabbing a slider on his way out. Once an assistant, always an assistant. She'd always done the exact same thing.

— ● —

It was a Saturday morning, and Emily had a brunch date. "We almost ready?"

"If this child ever puts on her shoes," Alan said.

"I'm doing it," said Jane, who was reading a book.

Alan finished packing the diaper bag. They had a big day planned, visiting Aunt Lisa in Brooklyn and then meeting Mommy after her brunch. As Emily kneeled in front of Jane, applying sunscreen to her face, Jane placed a hand on her shoulder and said, "I love you, Mommy."

"Aww, that's sweet. I love you too."

Alan opened the apartment door and they headed into the hall. "I love you, Daddy," Jane said.

"I love you too, boo."

Jane pressed the down button on the elevator. When it arrived with a *ding*, she said, "I love you, elevator."

"Alllll right," said Emily.

Emily rejected the oppressive weight of traditional gender assumptions except that she let Alan drive everywhere, because she liked to sit in the passenger seat and close her eyes. Jane, too, fell asleep during car trips, and they'd scheduled this forty-five-minute drive to coincide with her midmorning nap. It wasn't quite enough sleep, but she probably wouldn't be a nightmare.

"How did it happen that all the good brunch is in Brooklyn?" Emily asked as they approached the tunnel.

"Was that rhetorical?" Alan said. "Because I have an answer, but it's fifteen minutes long and it's about gentrification."

"Okay, okay."

He dropped her off in Park Slope on his way to Crown Heights, and she walked a few blocks south to the restaurant. Marta stood outside. "I'm on the list," she said. "I think maybe ten minutes?"

Marta seemed nervous; it had taken a lot of back-and-forth to secure this brunch. She remembered that Marta loved talking about work, so Emily peppered her with questions about life at Penguin. The publisher had a line of mysteries that no one was paying that much attention to, and Marta didn't know anything about mysteries but was having a good time building that up. She said, "I remember you told me once, find something that should be doing better, but no one's giving it enough love, and you can have a big impact right away. That's exactly what happened."

The restaurant was loud, filled with exuberant twenty-five-year-olds, and once they had mimosas Marta seemed to relax. Emily passed along what office gossip she knew, acknowledging that as a middle-aged mom she no longer had access to the really good shit. She asked after Marta's mom, who'd undergone cancer treatment while she worked at St. Martin's.

Marta and Lane were going to a lot of protests, she said. "Environmental, gay rights, economic inequality." As Marta described her gradual political awakening, Emily thought of herself and Louis, all those years ago, figuring out what they believed in. Louis had emailed the other week. He and his partner were thinking about flying to Massachusetts to get married. This was the kind of news that once would have occasioned an hour-long phone call, but instead she'd written a heartfelt email in between meetings.

"I'm glad you two are still so close," Emily said as their Benedicts arrived. "I'm sure you know—I asked you to brunch because of Lane." Marta's face darkened. "He was cool!" she hastened to add. "He just said it was time I talked to you, and he was right. Long past time, really."

Marta broke the yolk of her poached egg. "And what do you plan to do after we talk?" she said.

"Honestly, I don't know. I want to start by listening to you." Marta made a little noise, not quite a laugh. "I mean it, Marta."

"The first month I worked for Peter," Marta said, "we were in a meeting about *libros en español*. You were there. He said I should help because I was a hot tamale. Do you remember what you said?" She didn't remember any of it, in fact. "You told me it was a great opportunity."

"But it was a great opportunity," Emily said.

"Right, a chance to make a big impact."

"Wasn't it?"

"But this is how it always was with you," Marta said. "It was worth it if I could turn it into something. But what he said to me didn't matter."

"It mattered!" Emily protested. "Your first week I told you, you've got to have a thick skin. That's how I made it through."

"Oh, I heard about your thick skin," Marta said. "Peter loved talking about your thick skin."

"I have always tried to look out for his assistants."

"That's not looking out for us!" Marta put down her fork. "That's telling us how to put up with him like you did."

"But that's life!" Emily said. "You get past the bullshit so you can do something real!"

"You're proud of your thick skin, that's the thing," Marta said. "That's why you can't listen. You're proud you made it through. I don't get that. I feel sick whenever I think about working for him."

Emily took a breath and let it out. She finished her mimosa and said, "I think I want another one of these, do you?" Marta nodded. "Look," Emily continued. "We're coming at this from different places. And I recognize that my place made it hard for me to listen. I'm really sorry about that. But you've gotta tell me: Did he harass you? Should I be reporting him?"

"Of course he did. But reporting him won't do any good."

"But what did he *do*? Did he threaten your job?"

"That would have been easier," she said. "Or if he'd just grabbed, you know, grabbed me. But no, he talked about my outfits all the time. He spoke shitty Spanish because he thought it was funny. He shouted, you know that. He told me I was too stupid to see why a book was bad."

The waitress brought them new mimosas and Marta looked out the window. The noontime light was fierce outside the glass. When the waitress left, Emily almost spoke, then shut her mouth.

"When my mom was sick," Marta said, "he acted so nice, like, oh, of course you can take care of her, don't worry about it. And then he just piled on the work. When I fell behind he told me how you checked in every day during maternity leave. And then finally, at Book Expo, he tried to follow me to my hotel room."

"Oh no."

"But see, that's what you hear and, I can tell, all your alarm bells went off. But honestly that was a relief. Nicole and Belle, the old assistants, they told me how to deal with that. The other stuff . . . that was every day, and he wasn't drunk. He was being the exact kind of boss he intended to be."

Emily felt miserable enough that she couldn't look at her plate. Finally she said, "I'm really sorry I didn't listen."

"So what are you going to do?" asked Marta.

"I guess first I need to listen to Nicole and Belle, too."

A summer storm blew through Brooklyn while she was in the cab on the way to Lisa's. Along Eastern Parkway, people scattered ahead of the downpour. One woman's umbrella blew inside out and flew right out of her hand. The woman looked up at the sky and shook her head. As Emily passed her, she didn't move at all, just stood in the rain and took it.

Lisa, now an engineer for Prospect Park, had the second floor of a brownstone. Her boyfriend worked weekends, so it was just her and Alan and Jane when Emily came in, dripping wet. "It's raining, Mommy," Jane said.

"How'd it go?" asked Alan.

"Oh," said Emily. "I don't know. Bad. Good, you know, she talked to me."

"Alan told me about her," Lisa said. "You sure she isn't just a baby? Like, get grown and join us in the real world."

"I'm sort of down on the real world right now," Emily said.

Lisa and Jane were drawing with markers at the dining room table. "You got washable, right?" Emily asked.

"Please," Lisa said. "I'm an auntie, but I'm not an amateur." Her boyfriend had a kindergartener with his ex.

The plan had been to go to the park, but instead they sat in Lisa's living room while Jane drew pictures and presented them, with great ceremony, to the adults of her choice. "I hear you're doing a play with Other Emily," Lisa said. "Oh, thank you, baby, it's beautiful."

"It's been good so far," Emily said. "No big eruptions or anything."

"Not like the old days."

"No, definitely not."

"You know," Lisa said, "she emailed me out of the blue a couple of years ago with an apology."

Alan said, "You never told me that. Is this a horse? Oh, a *crocodile.* Scary!" He held up the drawing, which looked like neither a horse nor a crocodile. They all oohed and aahed and Jane went back to the table, satisfied.

"Was it, like, a twelve-step thing?"

"Sort of, although it wasn't really about the drugs. It was about racial shit."

"What?"

"Yeah, like, she knew she'd been insensitive way back when. She said she was sorry for all her microaggressions."

"Really!" Alan said. "Girl's been reading up."

"I'm sorry to make you explain things to me," Emily said. "But what is that?"

"Just like the little things that white people do that they barely notice but that add up," Alan said. "You know, mispronouncing a name, or 'Can I touch your hair?'"

"I had to look it up," Lisa said, "but as soon as I read it I was like, 'Oh yeah, I'm familiar.'"

"Oh sweetie, I love it," Emily said to Jane. "It's a puppy? Thank you. Yes, I'll keep it forever. Was that weird?"

"A little. I mean, she was one of those girls who just sometimes dropped an N-word in, because she thought she was down."

"More of a macroaggression," said Alan.

"Huh." Emily considered. "I don't do those microaggression things, do I?"

Lisa and Alan laughed in unison. "Honey, just because you're married to a brother doesn't mean you have a get-out-of-whatever-free card," Lisa said. "When Alan first started dating you—"

"Come on, now." Alan held up his hands.

"Oh, is this a secret?" Lisa asked her brother. "I just remember how she would always be, like, 'I don't see color.'"

"Oh God," Emily said.

"Not so much anymore," Alan hastened to add. "But you would do that white people thing of, 'Hey, you know Jerry? Tall guy, curly hair, Sagittarius, wears high-tops, you know . . .'"

"'He really likes basketball?'" Lisa said. "'Listens to rap?'"

"And finally I'd have to be like 'the black guy'?"

"Ugh, I'm sorry."

"Also, there was the time you assumed I grew up in the projects," said Lisa, who in fact grew up in the suburbs.

Emily remembered that moment well. She still could feel the hot flush of humiliation. "Can you forgive me, Lisa?"

Lisa smiled. "Understand, baby, that's not a thing you ask for."

Alan asked, "Did Emily ever apologize to *you*?"

"Basically," Emily said. "She didn't reach out before. She said there's a rule where, if you think the person wouldn't want to hear from you, you're supposed to leave them alone."

"Did you ever apologize to her?" asked Lisa.

"For what?" Alan said.

Emily pointed out, "She was the one on heroin."

"Y'all came apart before it got really bad for her," Lisa said. "When a friendship falls apart like that, I bet she was feeling it, too, that's all."

"You don't owe her shit," said Alan. "Oh, what a beautiful elk!"

— • —

Sniffling from a summer cold, Emily was working from home, so her assistant Sondra called her on the phone with the news. "We made the list!"

"You're kidding."

"Number eight!"

"Number eight?!" She did a brisk, triumphant lap around the living room, stepping on Jane's favorite stuffed bee, which let out a terrified squeak.

"They're emailing it over now. I'll forward it to you."

The package in *New York* had looked great, but what really took Lucy over the top was a very surprising full-pager in the *Times Book Review*. She had thought the novels might get a mention in New and Notable Paperbacks, but instead, Meg Wolitzer gave the royal treatment to the collection. "The book does not read like an assemblage of odds and ends from a long-dead and out-of-date writer," the review read. "Instead, it arrives speaking urgently to life as we live it today, part blessedly funny essay collection, part candid second memoir from a writer whose first is a touchstone for every smart woman I know." A friend at the *Times* told her it would have been on the cover except that they got stupid Henry Kissinger to review a stupid George Bush biography.

She refreshed her email, refreshed it, refreshed it, refreshed it. And there it was, the paperback nonfiction list.

8. IT'S DONE WHEN IT'S DONE, by Lucy Deming. (St. Martin's) Essays on friendship, illness, and food from the late author of *The Watched Pot.*

It wasn't her first bestseller. It wasn't even her first bestseller she actually cared about. (Stuff like Cynthia Margalit did not count in her personal tally.) But a few days later, it *was* the first book of hers to achieve something she'd always dreamed about: on the A train, a woman got on at 125th Street, stood in the middle of the packed car, carefully pulled a book out of her tote bag, and when she opened it Emily saw her own photo of Lucy staring at her from the back cover.

— ◆ —

Runners on the corners, and Bloomsbury's shortstop was playing shallow. Every literary softball team had one guy who had played in high school. He was always twenty-eight, he always played shortstop, and he always crept in during each woman's at-bat. Emily lined the first pitch straight over his head. He turned, hands on hips, to see it land in left-center. Zack scored; Carlton advanced to second. "Yeah!" Peter shouted from the St. Martin's bench. "What a poke! You can't play in on her, short!"

Emily eventually made it to third before Evelyn, Peter's new, willowy assistant, sort of desperately waved the bat and gently booped the ball back to the pitcher for the third out. Peter liked to call Emily the team's secret weapon. Most girls in publishing were a certain type, the high school literary magazine type, game to come out to Central Park but unlikely to put the ball in play. Emily wasn't exactly athletic, but she sure wasn't willowy. She played JV softball before she quit for the literary magazine, she had a low center of gravity, and she could hit slow-pitch just fine.

Each summer, St. Martin's played five or six softball games on the big fields of Central Park. The games were played against other publishing houses and magazines. Random House had two separate teams; the team from *Vogue* wore custom-made softball shirts that said, on the back, YES, WE ARE SILENTLY JUDGING YOU. Literary softball games were, as a rule, casual and unskilled, an excuse for friendly competition and a few beers in paper bags. The exception was the team from *High Times*, who were ironically not the tiniest bit mellow, who hired an umpire to call balls and strikes, and who defeated everyone 16–3. They did share their weed afterward, though.

Peter loved to pitch and took pride in writing the team's lineups. He couldn't hit worth a damn, but in literary softball could usually hustle his way to an infield single or two. Mostly he enjoyed peppering the game with old-timey baseball chatter, which his coworkers found mildly annoying but which drove other teams insane. Once, Emily was standing on base and the exasperated first basewoman from the *Paris Review* said, "Why does he keep saying, 'can of corn'?"

The game ended as the lights started coming on in the big apartment buildings surrounding the park. As they walked west with the Bloomsbury team, Emily spotted the San Remo, where Edith used to live, right by the Dakota, where John Lennon and Rosemary's baby lived. They often invited the other team to a bar in the west 80s, where Peter would hold forth and where, occasionally, junior editors would begin star-crossed romances. Sometimes, the opposing shortstop would flirt lightly with her, which she enjoyed. This happened less and less frequently, now.

Tonight she could stay for one beer, she thought. Peter had already had a few at the field and told Evelyn to order pitchers for everyone. Like many new assistants, Evelyn did not have the kind of credit limit that allowed her to plunk down a card for the night and expense it later, so Emily gave the bartender hers instead. "Thanks," Evelyn said. The problem was now she was stuck for longer than she wanted to be stuck. She texted Alan.

I gotta stay another hour or so, I'm sorry

> no problem! We're food
>
> *good

Kiss my baby for me

> Mission Accomplished

She talked to a nice senior editor at Bloomsbury about a book they'd both bid on recently and lost. Then she checked on Sondra to make sure she was having a good time. Finally she judged the pitchers emptied enough to order four more and close out her tab. It was less fun being the grown-up, she found, than she'd thought it would be when she was a kid. She'd thought she wanted to be in charge, but mostly that meant cleaning up messes a lot.

She looked around the now-crowded bar for Peter to say goodbye. He was holed up in a booth, close-talking Evelyn, who was laughing hard but also trapped against the wall. She came over, slid into the booth across from them, and threw Peter a glare. "Hey," she said to Evelyn. "Sondra wanted to explain the expense system to you. She's over by the bar."

Peter got up and gestured gallantly to Evelyn. "Right this way, my dear," he said. She got up and headed across the room. Peter slid back into the bar with a guilty schoolboy's look. "Sorry, Mom," he said.

"Don't 'Mom' me. What are you doing?"

"I'm keeping it in my pants." He giggled.

"Peter, I talked to Marta."

"Oh no, *Marta*," he said with mock horror. "What did *she* tell you?"

"She told me you made her feel like shit. She told me you wouldn't stop commenting on her outfits."

"She wore amazing outfits! She didn't want me to say anything?"

"Come on!" she said fiercely. "You are making a fucking fool of yourself!"

"Ah, mind your own business," he said, waving her off.

"I talked to Kim. I talked to Nicole."

He rolled his eyes. "Oh, Jesus, Girl Detective."

To keep from saying something else, she said, "I'm going home."

"That's a good idea," he replied.

"You should go home too."

He looked uncertain, finally. "Maybe I will."

"Come out with me. Here, here's your bag. Come on." She picked their way through the bar, told Sondra she was leaving, asked if anyone wanted to share a car uptown. Thank God, no one did.

She put Peter in a cab and flagged down her own. She checked her bag, her wallet, her phone. She had everything, just like always.

— • —

Over the summer she'd been researching climate change and structural engineering for Emily's show. "By then New York will be basically subtropical," she said over the phone during the design conference call. "More like how coastal South Carolina or Georgia is now. There should be cypress trees."

"Oh, that's fascinating." Emily said.

"The fun thing," she said, "is that actually that part of Brooklyn is gonna be more of a swamp, with a mixture of salt and fresh water."

"Tell me there will be alligators."

"You could make a case for alligators. Eventually, anyway."

"You hear that, Soleil?" she crowed. "We got our gators!"

— • —

Emily apologized for all the time she was spending on the phone; there was a little bit of a mess at work, she said, and she was trying to clean it up.

"Are you or are you not available to eat crabs?" Derreck said.

"I can fit that into my schedule."

They were staying in Annapolis, where Alan's family had gone for summer vacations for years, with Derreck and Eric and their new baby, who was named Tariq. *The stress is on the second syllable*, their birth announcement had assured everyone.

Tariq was adorable but very, very fussy. Jane enjoyed holding Tariq on her lap, but immediately gave him back to his dads whenever he started crying. "You got it, kid," Alan said. "That baby is somebody else's problem."

"Noooo, we all love you, Tariq," Emily said, but the day they went out for crabs, she felt enormous relief when it was Tariq who wailed so piteously that Eric had to walk him down the pier, out of earshot. She loved it when her child was good, but in a dark way she loved it even more when other people's children were bad.

"Why is Baby Tariq so sad?" Jane asked.

"He's a baby," said Alan.

"It's hard to be a baby," Derreck said, sucking Old Bay off his fingers. *"Dur dur d'être bébé."*

"He wants to talk with us and eat crabs with us, but he's too little to do anything," Emily said. "He's frustrated!"

"He doesn't want crabs," Jane said. "Ew!" She was entirely grossed out by all the cracking and tearing and scooping involved in a crab feast. She didn't even like to look at the piles of shells on the table.

"Isn't it better being a big girl?" Alan asked. "You can talk to us, and walk around and do things."

"I can eat hush puppies," she said.

"You bet."

"They're not real puppies," she confided to Derreck.

Emily was often surprised how much of her time as a parent she spent trying to make deadpan eye contact with Alan, as if she were Jim in *The Office* and he a camera.

They heard the approaching cries of Tariq. Eric stood on the sidewalk, helplessly bouncing the inconsolable infant. His forced jollity was reaching insane-asylum levels.

"Being a daddy is hard!" Jane announced. "Being a mommy is easier, because the baby can just drink your milk from your nipples."

"It didn't work as smooth as all that, kid," Emily said.

"Uncle Derreck doesn't have any milk in his nipples," said Jane.

"I better get him," Derreck said, glancing mournfully at the bucket of crabs, still half-full. He got up, cleaning his hands with a wet wipe.

"I'll leave you one or two, don't worry," Alan said as his brother left.

"I don't miss that," Emily said.

"It is crucial," Alan said before Eric came back, "that we never forget what it was like."

"Like the Alamo," said Emily.

— • —

After dinner, the phone rang. "Hi Peter," she heard Alan say. There was a short pause. "Let me get Emily for you."

Emily picked up in the bedroom. "You told him," Peter said.

"Of course I did. He's my husband. You told Chessie, right?"

"Yes. She's upset."

"She has every right to be."

"She's upset at you."

Of course she should have anticipated this. "I'm sorry she feels that way. I love her, still."

He snorted. "I wouldn't offer her your hand anytime soon, she's liable to bite it off. She thinks this is a power play."

"Is that what you think?"

"No. I don't think you want my job. You're not ambitious like that."

Though he was right, she didn't and she wasn't, it still stung. Fifteen years and he could still hurt her when he wanted to.

"What did Eileen say?"

"She's hiring an outside firm to do an investigation. Until then I'm working from home."

She heard the clink of ice in a glass. She even knew what he was drinking right now: Jack on the rocks. He always had money, but he never cared about expensive liquor.

"I never harassed you," he said. "I never propositioned you, not once."

"You never did."

"Quid pro quo, I never did that. So what is this?"

"You spent three years yelling at me, Peter, until I left for Houghton."

"I *saved* you," he said. "I saved you from a batty old bitch who stole your work. I put you in a place where you could excel and every single thing you accomplished was *you*. Sure, it was hard. Shit is hard in the real world!"

"I don't know, Peter," she said. "I don't know why you made it hard that way for me and why you made it hard this way for Marta." He scoffed. "I *do* know that in the past eight or nine years every one of your assistants has left, and they've all left unhappy. And the ones who aren't white, they were even unhappier. I could barely get them to talk to me. But now I know a little bit more about the different ways you made it hard for them."

"What are you doing, Emily? You're just telling a story here."

"No," she said. "I'm helping other people tell theirs."

He laughed, a short sharp bark. "Just because they couldn't take it. Not like you could take it."

"I took it. It was not a sign of my talent or my strength of character that I took it."

She heard him sip his drink, up there in his big house in Westchester. His kids were in fifth grade now. She hated this. Alan cracked open the door to the bedroom, caught her eye, sat down on the bed, held her hand.

"The investigation is not gonna turn anything up because there isn't anything," he said. "I'm a tough boss. I tell dirty jokes. Big fuckin' deal."

"I don't know what the investigation will turn up."

"I always thought we were partners," he said. "When you came back, I thought, *This is it*. I had my guy, finally."

"I wish I could be your guy this time, Peter."

"Ehhh," he said. "I'll forgive you, someday."

"I wasn't apologizing."

— • —

"It's a perfectly constructed narrative," she said. Emily laughed. "You could teach it in an MFA workshop. Rising action as ever-larger groups of guests arrive. Finally the house is filled—"

"With hippos."

"It seems to be a large house."

"I assumed so. Ow FUCK that's hot." They were sitting in a park near Emily's apartment in Brooklyn, across Smith Street from the hole-in-the-wall bar from which they had procured a bag full of deep-fried cheese-and-prosciutto balls. They were incredibly delicious, but the insides were still near-nuclear in temperature.

"Not yet, honey, they're too hot," she said to Jane, who had run up, eager for a snack. Alan followed, also eager for a snack, and she said, "You and Daddy can share one. He'll blow on it for you."

"So the house is full of hippos," Emily prompted her.

"Right. And then, there's an incredible climax, right in the very center of the book: ALL THE HIPPOS GO BERSERK!"

"Hippos go baserk!" Jane cried out in delight. She and Alan wandered back toward the swings.

"They're dancing around, swinging from chandeliers. The works. But then when the party's over, the hippos begin to depart. First nine, then eight, then seven."

"Falling action. Aristotelian."

"Right. And then they're gone. And the final hippo sits at home alone, missing all forty-four of her friends."

"Then what happens?"

"That's it."

"That's the end of a children's book?"

"Yes. One hippo sitting alone at a table."

"Wow," Emily said. She sat back and took a meditative bite of a prosciutto ball. "That's intense."

"I sincerely love it."

"What a lesson for children. 'Your friends will eventually leave you.'"

"Well, Jane doesn't see it that way, I don't think. When you read a book over and over and over, it's less like"—she made a single up-then-down motion with her hand—"and more like"—she made a continuous wave, up and down and up and down and up and down. "It's like the difference between Beckett and, uh . . ."

"Joyce."

"Yeah."

"Hippos come and hippos go."

"Such is life."

— ● —

What she should have been doing, with Peter out, was consolidating power, managing the narrative of his absence in a way that would make things easier for her when he inevitably came back. Instead, she spent two weeks of vacation time in rehearsal with Emily and all the twenty-year-olds. Emily had lost all objectivity, so she had no idea if she was right, but the show seemed really good. In the old days her friend's scripts had been full of posturing and long agonizing speeches and obviously autobiographical score-settling, but the scenes between the three women and one man in this loft in Williamsburg were quiet, practical, elusive. The relationships between the four of them were revealed through how they treated one another, the secrets they kept and shared. They were like children in a fort, but with adult desires. In Emily's favorite scene, one of them brought back a container of Swiffer wet wipes she'd found in an abandoned building, and the four of them spent an intent, nearly silent five minutes cleaning their home, a place they'd only ever seen filthy. All fights were forgotten, all resentments forgiven. The instantly identifiable smell of Swiffer made its way through the loft as they worked.

Then one of them was eaten by an alligator! Emily couldn't believe it when she read it in the script. But in this weird mix of realism and science fiction and punk rock and fairy tale, with these four young people as Lost Boys, it totally worked. Hoo boy, she'd drunk the Kool-Aid, she guessed.

To the work friends she'd told about this production, it was difficult to explain what a dramaturg actually did. Basically, she was the person who watched, asked weird questions, and made weird suggestions. The Swiffers were her idea. So was the sound of rain, which soundtracked nearly every scene. When everyone was racking their brains trying to figure out how the loft could be breached from the outside by the raiders who attack at the end, it was Emily who said, "It's like other kids raiding the tree house, right?" Soleil found some panes of safety glass, rigged up an incredible air cannon kind of deal on the outside of the building, and now at a crucial moment a ratty old baseball came crashing through the window to land at the actors' feet.

During tech week, her mom came out from Wisconsin to stay with Alan and Jane. Each night they all stayed in the loft late, long after the actors were gone, fixing technical problems, working out light cues, tweaking the sound. She loved working with all these women—it was almost all women—and she loved most of all watching Emily put it all together. She couldn't believe Emily's patience, her calm, her openness to others. She had always had a sense of a director as the voice of God, like in *A Chorus Line*, she guessed, but Emily spent most of her time in the loft sitting on the floor, surrounded by the other artists, soaking up their words. She thought of her friend all those years ago, boiling over with countless ideas, alienating countless collaborators. Maybe we're all frauds at twenty-five. But in our fraudulent selves we see the seeds of the artists we might become, if we can overcome our worst tendencies.

One morning she was woken up by Jane running into her room and climbing up on the bed between her and Alan. "Sorry, sorry," her mom said from the door. "I was just making her breakfast, and I turned around for a *second*. She's a slippery one."

"It's okay," Emily said, and her mom went back to the kitchen. Jane burrowed under the covers, squirmed around. Alan, well experienced by now, turned his body so he was not directly facing Jane, whose little feet were precisely at nut level.

"Don't you want to *snuggle* with us?" Emily asked, trying to get Jane to stay still in a hug.

"I want to *wiggle*!"

"Whoa, careful there," she said.

"Mommy!" she said, surfacing. "You got no pants on!"

"Silly Mommy!" Alan said. "Where are her pants?" Last night she had gotten home at midnight, crawled into bed wearing only a

T-shirt, woken Alan up by rubbing his dick through his boxers, and climbed on top of him. She was currently off the pill on the advice of her psychiatrist and her OB-GYN, so every time they had sex was a little bit of an adventure. Would they manage to get the condom on this time? She was not loving the current shape of her body, but Alan sure seemed to like it. They had turned into horny teenagers, stupid with lust, right down to shushing each other so as not to wake her mother.

The dress rehearsal went great except that none of the lights worked. Emily was surprisingly sanguine about it. "You guys were so good, I barely even noticed," she said to her actors. To Emily she muttered, "If that happens tomorrow night I will murder every single person here."

On opening night, she and Alan took the elevator up together with two complete strangers. People she did not know, coming to their play! The doors opened on the loft, dark and quiet. Through the full-wall windows, lightning appeared to flash in the night sky. Alan looked at her in surprise. When they'd entered the building from the sidewalk, it was a quiet autumn dusk. It was all projection work, designed by Soleil and a video artist Emily had met while on an artists' retreat in Georgia.

Ushers in black led them, with little flashlights, to their cushions on the floor and told them to please turn off their phones. (Scattered here and there were chairs for those whose backs couldn't take it—an addition she'd suggested at the last minute, when she'd imagined her mom trying to sit through the show.) The actor playing Ken sat on-stage already. An oil lantern illuminated, on the table beside him, a stack of water-stained children's books: *Goodnight Moon*, *The Little Fur Family*, *Peter Pan*, *A Wrinkle in Time*. Disheveled and intent, he was reading *Hippos Go Berserk*. Alan turned to Emily and said, "There's another copy?!"

Each time the elevator dinged, a square of fluorescent light opened in the wall and new audience members stumbled out, bewitched. As Emily and Emily had discussed, with each ding Ken shifted a bit, as if he didn't quite hear it, but he heard *something*. The lightning got closer; the thunder got louder. Rain started to patter on the projected windows. Soon it was a full-on storm, the thunder rumbling through the floor, and then there was a huge crash and the lantern went out. In the dark, the sound of morning birdsong. Dim light revealed four bodies sleeping in sleeping bags on the floor around them. The projectors illuminated the windows: morning on a vast and misty marsh, the crumbled bridges dangling, the spires of Manhattan poking out of the water far away. Someone near Emily whispered, "Oh my God."

— • —

Jane was sitting on the floor, half playing with her toy piano and half watching the Backyardigans. Emily found that if she plugged her ears with her fingers and held the book down on the chair's arm with her elbow, she could just barely tune out all the noise in favor of the Anita Brookner novel she was trying to read.

It had been a tough couple of years for Emily's pleasure reading. Manuscripts at night, a screaming kid during the day. But Jane was finally old enough to play on her own, at least for a little while, and also old enough that the American Academy of Pediatrics grudgingly admitted that looking at a TV for a little while wouldn't kill her. Emily had also realized, finally, that when Jane called something to her attention, she didn't really care if Emily actually looked up, as long as she emitted words from her mouth.

"Tasha's singing!" Jane said now.

"She sure is," Emily said.

In the novel, Christine and the old window-washer, Mr. Crickmay, were having a cup of tea and talking about his dog who'd just died, and then they fell into a lovely conversation about food—chicken on lemon rice and lamb cutlets *forestière*. Emily couldn't shake a nagging feeling of familiarity about the scene. She'd never read the book before, though.

> Finally he stood outside the door.
> "Never give up, Mr. Crickmay."
> "Never, Madam. That's what I say to myself every morning. You never know what's round the corner. Nice seeing you, as always, Madam. And that was a lovely cup of tea."
> They shook hands, as they always did, and then Christine was alone again.

She laughed a little at the corniness of it, the sweetness, the way their familiar friendly ritual masked their sadness. *Oh*, that was it. The scene was just like the one in *Hearts and Stones* where Clara drinks coffee with the super of her building. There was even a dog in that one, she thought. She'd reread it last year in preparation for republishing it. *Good one, Lucy*, she thought.

Then she turned the page and laughed loud enough that Jane said, "What's funny, Mama?"

"Oh, it's Austin all covered in swamp goop!" she said, pointing at the TV.

"Swamp goop!" Jane repeated.

Emily put her finger on the margin, on the note written in Lucy's handwriting in what she realized only now was Lucy's old paperback of *Latecomers*. STEAL THIS, the note said.

Later, she remembered that they owned noise-canceling headphones, so she put those on.

— ● —

Sarah's father had made a fortune doing Internet something-or-other, so Sarah lived in a big apartment in one of the new buildings in the East Village. It was there that Emily, Alan, Jane, Lisa, Emily, and Sarah celebrated Thanksgiving, though Sarah ceded official hosting duties to Emily.

In the stainless-steel kitchen that Sarah admitted she rarely used, Emily and Lisa made all their favorite sides. (No one cared about a turkey.) Sarah joined Emily to make *tahdig* in her mom's old skillet, straight from her mom's book. "I remember this," she said. "I'm sure I do."

While the rice was steaming away and everyone watched a movie on Sarah's comically large TV, Emily washed her hands and picked up the book. She remembered reading the essay the first time, the day Joanie slipped it to her. She remembered thinking it was hers, no one else's. She had been right, then, that it didn't fit the happy book Lucy wanted *The Watched Pot* to be. And it felt right, now, to let it go, to include it in this final book, to let everyone else read it. She'd had it to herself long enough. And she still held the things that could only ever be hers: the note from Lucy, the scrawled *L*, the "goodbye."

She read:

Dying people want comfort food, of course. I've learned this through the unfortunate act of dying myself, slowly, from what my people in North Carolina would call "a wasting disease." The disease is putting my mind and body under greater and greater pressure until, I suppose, one or the other will pop, and then I'll be dead.

One day in the middle of my decline I found myself wanting to make *tahdig*, the crusty Persian rice my grandma Habib made for her special occasion feasts. Unfortunately, like every kitchen in New York City, mine is too small to fit a wheelchair in, so I had to direct my daughter and my friend from the dining room.

Emily looked up. The kitchen in Sarah's apartment, just blocks from Sunrise Squat, could accommodate a wheelchair basketball team. The next bit was what she had copied, rewritten slightly, and slipped into another essay about pasta, in order to give the first memoir the title Lucy chose, years ago.

Sarah, always an impatient child, stared at the pot of water, willing it to boil. Emily teased, "What is it they say about a watched pot?"

"It's going to boil eventually," Sarah said. I was struck by this wisdom. I mean, it's just thermodynamics.

In fact, a watched pot is fascinating. The water swirls in perpetual motion, as warmer water rises from the bottom and cooler water sinks from the top. If you've added oil (as you need not), you can watch it bead and bubble through the water; if you've added salt (as you always should), you can watch the grains dissolve. (While you're at it, add more salt.) You'll see tiny bubbles crowd one another on the bottom of the pot, like people waiting to get into the hot new dance club. Sometimes a thin stream of such bubbles will shake loose from the floor and travel to the surface in a silvery column. Soon, you'll see steam rise from the pot. It's been doing it all along, evaporating, but only now is it becoming visible. The bubbles will grow, jostle, eat one another up, and then they will free themselves and rise to the surface to pop in small, joyous explosions. And there you have it: you just watched a pot boil. It's no different than watching your child grow, or your friends change, as they make their way through the world. Think of all the other things you don't see on this earth, just because your eyes were somewhere else!

Emily poured a little salt in her hand and tossed it into the *tahdig*. Couldn't hurt. She read farther down the page:

The *tahdig* my daughter and my friend made was a delicious mess, as it should be. The only thing missing was all the salads and sides and rich, buttery sauces that should accompany it. The only thing missing was all the other people who should have been eating it with me, Grandma Habib and my parents and my sister and a lifetime's worth of friends. The only thing missing was me not dying, but at least I'm finally writing about that. My friend says that will sell some books. I'm sorry I won't know if she's right. (Unless she's wrong, in which case I don't want to know anyway. In the great beyond, all books are *New York Times* bestsellers.)

I knew that day that I would have to send Sarah away. A child who would not avert her eyes from a pot of water is one who would watch me to the ugly end. Put enough heat under me, and eventually I'll boil. No way do I want her there for that.

I would not say that I am dying well. I'm doing the best I can, but there are so many indignities, and I have never faced indignities with much grace. The best I can do is to keep my eyes and mind open and alert. I'm doing my best to honor the world, a world that seems in such a hurry to be rid of me, by paying attention. I'm noticing every stream of silvery bubbles, every burn from a splash of hot oil, every time a friend gives me the gift of laughing at a bad joke. My sister and I are spending time together we should have spent before, under better circumstances, but I'm determined to be here with her every day I can be. The love she's showing me, in caring for my body, deserves that, at least.

Every one of us is done when we're done, as I told my friend. You flip us over at the end and see what life did to us. Every watched pot boils eventually. Every sauce would benefit from a little more butter. And every recipe serves four—but you can always stretch it to six or seven.

Dinner was, if she did say so herself, delicious. They had salads and sides and sauces for the *tahdig*, and she'd plopped an extra pat of butter in each one. Lisa made mac and cheese and collards and oyster dressing, "straight from southern Maryland," which Emily had assumed would be awful but was remarkable. Emily brought two pies from a bakery by her apartment. Jane, that slacker, contributed nothing.

Around the table, the conversation turned to her work situation. "So they just cleared him?" Emily said, outraged.

"They said there was no proof of sexual harassment," she said. "He does have to go to sensitivity training."

"There's that, at least," said Alan.

"For him, that'll be like waterboarding."

"That guy," Sarah said. "He didn't *not* hit on me, let's say."

"When will he be back in the office?"

"He's already back," she said. "His assistant is icing me out."

"What can they do to you? You've got a *New York Times* bestseller!" *It's Done* had bounced on and off the bottom half of the list all summer and fall, and *Can't Complain* even made the extended fiction list one week.

"Well, he has no control over marketing or publicity, so my books are doing fine on those fronts. But it's hard for me to push things I want to acquire through the edit group without his support." She had gone over Peter's head to get okayed to spend on a memoir last week, and that hadn't helped things. "Mostly it just sucks that everyone is taking a side, and you can't do anything in the office without figuring out what side the person you're dealing with is on."

"You should just quit," said Emily, who kept a list of fourteen different jobs she had quit in her life.

"I'm not going to just quit."

"Fuck those—" Emily, to her credit, halted herself and looked guiltily at Jane. "Screw those jerks."

"Those jerks are why I have health insurance," she said. Emily made a wanking gesture. "Come on, be real."

"I am real! You have spent two decades of your life—"

"How old do you think I am?"

"Okay, *nearly* two decades of your life bringing other people's books into the world. Enough bridesmaiding!"

"You want me to write a book," she said. "I don't have any ideas for books I want to write. I don't even particularly want to write a book!"

"Are you really satisfied with this life here?" Emily asked. "Just a husband and a baby and other people's books?"

"Emily!" Sarah said.

"Uh, the husband is right here," Lisa said, her arm around her brother. "Watch it."

"Of course I'm satisfied!" she said, realizing it even as she said it. "It's my life. I love my husband, and I love my baby." Jane, with exquisite comic timing, belched. It defused the tension around the table long enough to change the subject.

As Alan and Sarah did the dishes, she sat, still seething, looking out the window. Down the avenue the signs were all unfamiliar; the restaurants and stores and clubs she had once patronized were long gone.

"Will you come on a walk with me?" Emily asked. She was already wearing her coat.

"Sure," she said.

They walked side by side up Avenue B. Emily lit a cigarette and offered it to her. She declined, then changed her mind and took it. It was her first cigarette in years, since Bloomberg's smoking ban. "Jesus, that's good," she said.

"Real downside to addiction," Emily said. "It's never that good anymore."

They walked past two boarded-up storefronts, which would both become blow-dry bars. "Hey, I'm sorry," Emily said. "That was out of line."

"Thank you for apologizing." They crossed the street together. She noticed, for the first time, that Emily no longer charged forward on the sidewalk as if shot from a cannon. "I've been thinking," she continued, "about what I need to apologize to *you* for."

Emily glanced at her. Her voice betrayed surprise. "What did you come up with?"

"I've spent years," she said, "thinking about how you let me down. But I let you down, too." They were passing Tompkins Square, where young mothers walked around with their babies like it was nothing. "I didn't see you. I only saw what you couldn't be for me."

"I was a huge pain in the ass," Emily said. "You weren't the only one I drove away."

"Well, I should have tried harder. You were trying to get away from Rob. I shouldn't have left you with him. I'm sorry."

"Ugh, Rob," Emily said. "The problem was, by then you were done with me. Not that I can blame you."

"But I could've—"

"I mean," Emily interrupted, "I wish you had tried harder, too. It would mean something now. But if you had stuck it out, there's no way we'd be friends again. If you'd seen me . . ." Emily wiped her eyes on her sleeve as they turned down Twelfth Street.

"No, no," she said, but she knew it was true, knew how quickly she'd cut bait when things were getting hard, knew how unprepared she'd been for them to get harder. "I don't know. But I can say that if things get bad—I know you won't use again, but if something happens—I won't bail this time."

They were standing in front of Sunrise Squat. "I still can't believe I wasn't there that day," Emily said. "Jesus, I'm so sorry about that. I'm sorry about losing the squat. I even lost the fucking *Angels in America* tickets."

She hugged her friend. "I'm sorry, too," she said.

"I'm sorry I got lost."

"I'm sorry I lost you!" They wept together. A woman in exquisite shoes walked out of the building that once was Sunrise Squat, looked alarmed at the two sobbing women clutching each other, veered away, accidentally kicked a garbage bag, and shrieked when a rat scampered across her foot. So then they stopped crying, anyway.

"You know you didn't lose the tickets, right?" she asked on their way back. "That was me who fucked that up."

"No, I lost them. Didn't I?" Emily said.

"No! I wrote down the wrong time for the show."

"Oh, Christ. Thank you."

"I'm not gonna stay at St. Martin's, you know. I've already got emails out. Someone will hire me. I've got a *New York Times* bestseller."

"Another editing job."

"Well, yeah."

There was the briefest of pauses, a microsecond at most, and then Emily said, "But—sorry, I can't let it go—didn't you feel something different, doing our show? Like, there, you were actually *making* something. And you were so fucking good at it!"

"I'm always making something," she said. "That's what you never get. That's what editing is for me."

"Come on, it's not the same."

"Of course not. But that's fine. What I'm good at is helping artists make their art better than it ever could have been. I wasn't the play-wright. I wasn't the director. I was your *eyes*."

"My eyes."

"I watched. I noticed. I had ideas. I exerted my taste. I *edited*. Why do you think it was so good?"

"It was really good," Emily admitted. "*Your Eyes* is a good title for your novel."

"Oh my God, put this conversation behind glass in the Emily Me-morial Library," she said.

"Are you two all right?" Alan asked when they walked back into Sarah's apartment. *Trust* was playing on the TV, a DVD that Emily had swiped from Kim's years and years ago.

"Well, we still have some things to talk about," she said. "But we finished this particular argument on our walk."

They all sat and watched *Trust* and ate pie. In the movie, Adrienne Shelly was wearing her smart-girl glasses. "I'll marry you," her char-acter said to Martin Donovan, "if you admit that respect, admiration, and trust equal love."

"Okay," Martin Donovan said, with his perfect lips. "They equal love."

When *Trust* was over, Emily said, "What a movie! I'm so glad I stole this."

"You hated this movie the first time we saw it."

"I think that's unlikely."

"We saw it at the Village East, and you said it was an arch exercise in stylelessness."

"That does sound like something I would say," Emily said. "I guess"—she raised both hands in the air as if calling the orchestra to attention—"I was wrong."

They helped Sarah finish cleaning up, then they carried Jane and the stroller and the bags full of leftovers downstairs. Lisa hugged everyone and caught a cab to Brooklyn. Emily had to walk south, to the F, and they had to walk west, to Union Square. While Alan debated Jane about who would buckle her straps, she faced her friend.

"Goodbye," Emily said.

— • —

"Do you see her?"

"I see her," Alan said. "She's still splashing in the tide pool."

"Okay."

Emily turned the page. *Tartuffe* was a funny play, but this translation was not exactly beach reading. She had to really pay attention to make her way through the thickets of language, and reading slowly was not her usual mode. *EMILY T./DRAMATURG* was printed at the top of every page. In the margins, she made notes for the production Emily had been hired to direct by an actual theater, a first for her. "It's a little bit square," Emily had said when she gave her the script, "but I do love money." She thought they could do some interesting stuff with Tartuffe and male entitlement.

"Do you see her?"

"Still in the tide pool."

"Okay."

They were spending Christmas in Florida with her dad and Kathy. Her father had been generous with the gifts—too generous, really, to the point that on Christmas morning Jane sort of fell into a fugue state unwrapping the fifteenth present, and Emily didn't know how they would get everything back to New York. But in terms of actual grandparenting, he seemed to view the purchasing of presents as fulfilling his essential duties. Having raised his own kids, he wasn't actually all that interested in interacting with new ones. Maybe she would feel the same way when she was his age, who knew. She thought he might do better when Jane got old enough to play golf.

Here on the beach, her father and Kathy were both fast asleep. As

they'd learned in Annapolis this summer, a beach vacation with a little kid was not actually a vacation in the sense of being able to relax.
Jane wanted to build *so many* sandcastles, an activity Emily found
stultifying. (She loved her, she loved her, she loved her.) Even in the
rare moments when she would play on her own, someone had to have
eyes on her at every moment, because otherwise she might be swept
into the gulf or eaten by a walrus.

They split their beach time into roughly thirty-minute shifts. Right
now Emily was supposed to be reading while Alan was supervising,
but Emily was having trouble relinquishing focus.

"Do you see her?" she asked again.

"You know, I'm just gonna go down there with her."

"Sooorrrry." But even this didn't help, because they were so adorable dancing together in the surf she had to put down her script and
take some photos. She'd gotten used to taking most pictures with
her phone, but this moment deserved the actual camera. Through
the viewfinder she watched her husband and her daughter prance
through the water, hands on their hips.

When they came back up to the chairs, Kathy was awake and un-
packing the picnic lunch she'd prepared: cold spaghetti with pesto
sauce. Emily and Alan affixed each other with a mordant stare; Kathy
meant well, but the meal—in its difficulty to eat with a fork, its potential for stains, and its objectionable greenness—was so terrible a
choice for a three-year-old they could have been on a prank show.

They'd packed PB&J, obviously.

Kathy had also brought a bottle of rosé, and Emily filled her plastic
cup just a quarter full, which she hoped might forestall questions. She
was pregnant again, the unsurprising-in-retrospect result of all their
careless humping this fall. When she'd first found out, she'd panicked;
they were so overwhelmed already, and she was interviewing for jobs,
and where would they put a baby in their tiny apartment? She thought
about her mom, and her pregnancy scare, and the relief she read on

her mom's face in that snapshot of her and Lucy. She and Alan had a tearful discussion of whether it would be better to just have an abortion, the seriousness of the talk only undercut by the fact that they had just watched *Knocked Up* and kept calling it a "shmushmortion."

But she had already started having dreams about the baby, good dreams, dreams of Jane and a little brother waving to her in Isham Park. She had an interview at HarperCollins next week. So she guessed she was going through with this whole thing. She would tell her dad and Kathy soon, but she wanted to tell Anne-Marie first—Anne-Marie, whose own attempts to conceive were so difficult, whose own sister didn't understand what she was going through, who even years after that ordeal had responded to the news of Emily's first pregnancy with tears. Happy tears, but not only happy tears.

After Jane finished her sandwich, she asked Emily to go back to the tide pool with her. Emily left the camera in her bag—this would be full-contact parenting, she suspected. They splashed together in the warm water. Jane liked it when Emily rubbed wet sand on her fat little tummy. Jane explained that she'd named all the minnows, and all their names were Archbar.

"Archbar?"

"Archbar."

A crab scuttled across the sand. Jane chased it away, saying, "Shoo! Mommy wants to eat you!" She came back, pointed to her Little Mermaid swimsuit, and asked, "Does Ariel want to eat Sebastian the crab?"

"No, they're friends," she said. "We don't eat our friends."

Emily looked out at the water. She looked at the sky, the clouds scudding across. She looked up the beach toward her husband, who was talking to her father, possibly a continuation of their previous conversation about why black people didn't play baseball anymore. Bless Alan.

She looked at her daughter. Jane had started an indoor gymnastics class once the weather got bad in New York and believed herself able to do cartwheels. More accurately, they were bad roundoffs, but out here in the wide open of Florida she had been spending a lot of time working on them. Now she stuck out her lower lip, placed one foot forward, and raised her arms in the air. "Watch me, Mommy!" she said.

"I'm always watching," Emily said.

for Erica and Julia and Allison

for Heather and Claire and Alia

Notes

Latecomers by Anita Brookner; *Bop* by Maxine Chernoff; *I Look Divine* by Christopher Coe; *Happy All the Time* by Laurie Colwin; *The Colorist* by Susan Daitch; *Bad Behavior* by Mary Gaitskill; *Elbowing the Seducer* by T. Gertler; *Dancing in the Dark* by Janet Hobhouse; *Fiskadoro* by Denis Johnson; *Asa, As I Knew Him* by Susanna Kaysen; *A Handbook for Visitors from Outer Space* by Kathryn Kramer; *The Garden State* by Gary Krist; *It Was Gonna Be Like Paris* by Emily Listfield; *Bright Lights, Big City* by Jay McInerney; *Family Resemblances* by Lowry Pei; *Clea and Zeus Divorce* by Emily Prager; *All It Takes* by Patricia Volk; *Taking Care* by Joy Williams.

The Vanity Fair Diaries by Tina Brown; *Cool Town: How Athens, Georgia, Launched Alternative Music and Changed American Culture* by Grace Elizabeth Hale; *Salt Fat Acid Heat* by Samin Nosrat; *Shopping Manhattan*, 1992 edition, by Corky Pollan; *Girl to City* by Amy Rigby; *Ours to Lose: When Squatters Became Homeowners in New York City* by Amy Starecheski; *Kill City: Lower East Side Squatters 1992–2000* by Ash Thayer.

"Create to Destroy," a 2014 interview of Bill Cashman in *Maximum Rock 'n' Roll*; "Polly Platt: The Invisible Woman" on Karina Longworth's You Must Remember This podcast; "Vintage Contemporaries" by Sean Manning on the blog *Talking Covers*.

Thanks to Daniel Pelavin for sharing his memories of Lorraine Louie.

About the Author

DAN KOIS is the author of three nonfiction books: *How to Be a Family*, a memoir; *The World Only Spins Forward*, an oral history of Tony Kushner's *Angels in America* (with Isaac Butler); and *Facing Future*, part of the 33 1/3 series of music criticism. He's a longtime writer, editor, and podcaster at *Slate*. He lives in Arlington, Virginia, with his family.